MR. DARCY PRESENTS
HIS BRIDE

MR. DARCY PRESENTS HIS BRIDE

A SEQUEL TO
JANE AUSTEN'S
PRIDE & PREJUDICE

Helen Halstead

Ulysses Press

Published in the United States by
Ulysses Press
P.O. Box 3440
Berkeley, CA 94703
www.ulyssespress.com

First published as *A Private Performance: A Sequel to Jane Austen's Pride and Prejudice* in 2005 in Australia by Random House Australia Pty Ltd.

Library of Congress Catalog Number 2006938952
ISBN10: 1-56975-588-4
ISBN13: 978-1-56975-588-4

Front cover design: DiAnna Van Eycke
Back cover design: what!design @ whatweb.com
Cover illustration: Fine Art Photographic, Gettyimages.com
U.S. Proofreader: Ruth Marcus
U.S. Production: Lisa Kester, Matt Orendorff

Printed in Canada by Transcontinental Printing

10 9 8 7 6 5 4 3 2 1

For my mother

ACKNOWLEDGMENTS

I gratefully acknowledge the invaluable help and encouragement I have received from many friends and colleagues.

For their assistance and support, I particularly thank Beverley Rainsford, Irina Lemaire, Madge Mitton, Jeanne Sayers, Victoria Brown, Dawn Lace, Erinna Gooley, Diana Carter, James Ogilvy and Peter Angrave.

To Jeanne Ryckmans, my publisher at Random House, my warm thanks for being marvellous.

For her loving faith in me, I thank my sister, Barbara Golden.

Lastly, I thank the members of the Jane Austen Society of Adelaide for their enthusiastic support. In pleasing these wonderful, exacting and knowledgeable ladies, my book passed a major test!

CHAPTER 1

Autumn, 1813

WHAT A JOY IT IS to have a worthy topic of conversation, to hold the power to amaze! Mrs. Bennet found herself to be in possession of a piece of news granting her this very power. It was for her to impart or withhold information that would provoke wonder among her neighbors. In the privacy of her home, at Longbourn, she had shrieked and exclaimed; she had come well-nigh to fainting with joy. Yet, delicacy forbade her sharing her knowledge for some days, certainly not before the marriage articles had been signed.

In the breakfast room, Mrs. Bennet's gaze rested upon her four daughters in turn; she looked with unwonted fondness upon her second daughter, Elizabeth.

"Do you know, my dears, the whole district is talking of nothing but Lizzy's engagement."

"Mama! I would prefer that you not speak of it yet," said Elizabeth.

"Oh, stuff! What did I say? The merest slip! Do you know, girls, our neighbors are saying that Mr. Darcy was all but engaged to his cousin. That he has given up an enormous fortune to marry Lizzy!"

"He was not engaged to her!"

"Oh, I daresay not." Mrs. Bennet dismissed the details with a wave of her handkerchief. "Yet Lizzy, can you not see that such a tale does add to your triumph? My sister reports that everyone is saying you have enraptured Mr. Darcy with nought but your charm. Is that not pleasing?"

"I would rather they did not speak of it at all, until I am out of the district."

Mrs. Bennet was all amazement.

"Until you are out of the district, child! What else are people to speak of when they hear you are to marry a man so rich, so highly placed in society, so . . . rich?"

"I am sorry if our neighbors care so little for my happiness and care only for my material advantages."

"You are a silly girl. Of course they care for your happiness." Even while she chuckled, an unpleasant feeling blew across the little pool of her joy. Her daughters saw her frown and glanced at each other. Their father looked up at the sudden quiet and grimaced. Mrs. Bennet's sister, who had called at the unseemly hour of nine o'clock, rarely had undiluted pleasantries to impart. In fact, that lady had also reported hearing a certain curate's widow express a hope that "sweet Elizabeth's advantages might not be bought too dear." She had suggested that Mr. Darcy was a "difficult man" who "considers himself quite above us all."

Mrs. Bennet felt a rush of irritation. For a moment, she thought she might need her smelling salts. She became aware of the silence at the table and brightened, as she recalled how dowdy were the widow's nieces.

"I confess I never even liked the shabby creature and I know not how she'll ever find husbands for those girls."

"Which girls, Mama?" asked the most juvenile of the young ladies. Her mother ploughed on.

"Mr. Darcy would scarcely notice an ugly girl whose family does not even keep their own carriage!" Her listeners, not privy to her chain of thought, merely looked puzzled, until Elizabeth said, "I thought it was my charm that enraptured Mr. Darcy—now I discover the bait to be my father's carriage."

Mrs. Bennet laughed heartily. "How many carriages does Mr. Darcy keep, Lizzy? You shall have your own, my love. Mr. Darcy will order you a new carriage and you shall choose the color—I know, for I asked him!"

Elizabeth blushed and her sisters responded in their several ways. Jane looked sympathetic, while one sister turned up her nose and the other gave vent to an excess of merriment.

Mr. Bennet raised his grizzled eyebrows and cleared his throat.

"Elizabeth is to abandon us for the delights of Mr. Darcy's establishment, and her sister Jane for that of Mr. Bingley. In my diminished household, I shall have the opportunity to enjoy more the company offered by my two remaining daughters."

"Indeed," replied Mrs. Bennet. "We shall be very cosy."

"I, at least, shall be driven to the coziness of my library with even greater frequency, as all the sense to be found in my daughters leaves the house at once."

"Mr. Bennet, how can you be so cruel?" cried his wife.

"If speaking the truth is cruelty, Mrs. Bennet, then I cannot acquit myself of the charge."

He continued eating. Mrs. Bennet sniffed and looked away, fiddling with her lace.

A loud knock echoed from the front hall.

"'Tis a messenger, for sure," cried Mrs. Bennet. "It is my brother, I know it! He is dead!" She put her handkerchief to her eyes.

"Are you certain, Mrs. Bennet?" asked her husband. "I had not heard he was so close to death as to cause this apprehension." He turned to Elizabeth, his mouth turned down in mock grief. She dearly wanted to laugh.

Her sister, Jane, stretched out a comforting hand to her mother and said, "Do not alarm yourself, Mama. Only last week, our uncle was reported to be in excellent health."

The footman entered and brought the letter tray to Elizabeth. She picked up the letter. It was of the finest quality paper. She studied the direction, in a woman's hand, unusually firm and plain.

"Who has sent it, Lizzy?" said Mrs. Bennet.

"I know not," said Elizabeth, slipping the letter into her pocket. "Some friend of Mr. Darcy's, I imagine, has written to me with her congratulations."

"Before the marriage articles have been signed? That is highly unlikely. Read it to me!"

"Mama, pray let me read it first."

"Nonsense, girl. I shall see it at once."

Elizabeth turned to her father.

"I think our daughter might be trusted to keep respectable correspondence, Mrs. Bennet," he said.

"Oh, very well then, Miss Have-it-your-way."

Elizabeth walked out across the lawn into the small wood which skirted Longbourn's eastern boundary. The early promise of a beautiful day had proved illusory, as grey clouds had moved in to cover the sun. She studied the letter for a moment before she opened it.

Lady Catherine de Bourgh to Miss Elizabeth Bennet
Miss Bennet,
I send you no courtesies, for you deserve none. I have learned that you are perversely continuing with your plan to advance yourself, while ruining forever the name of Darcy. Last April, I condescended to invite you into my home. You abused my kindness to entice my nephew into a misalliance that he will rue the moment his infatuation wears off. Then he will bitterly regret that he has been robbed of his rightful bride, my daughter, Miss Anne de Bourgh.

None of Mr. Darcy's relations will ever consent to speak to you. Due to you, my nephew will be cast off from all his family.

Furthermore, you will be received by no one of note, for such is the respect and esteem in which the name of de Bourgh is held.

May God forgive your crime, for I shall not.

Lady Catherine de Bourgh

Elizabeth was, for a moment, breathless with shock. She walked about, hardly aware of her direction.

"Arrogant woman! Held in respect and esteem, is she? Not by me!"

The themes expressed in the letter came as no surprise, for Lady Catherine had already made these accusations to her face some weeks past, but the injustice seemed even more bitter in writing.

The allegation of entrapping Darcy she found highly offensive. From the beginning of their acquaintance, she had disliked him intensely until she learned to know him. He had fought for, and won, first her respect and then her affection.

"Nevertheless," she mused, "it is inevitable that many will believe my motives to be mercenary."

It was the meanest spite for Lady Catherine to take her revenge by trying to destroy them in society. As if she could! Lady Catherine relished wielding her power over those dependent upon her goodwill. However, Darcy's friends had no such need of her influence, so why should they turn their backs upon them both at the behest of his aunt? No, they could not be so silly. Surely?

She left the wood through the back gate, and walked to the dairy, and fed the letter to the goats.

The sun was shimmering around the edge of a cloud, as Elizabeth retraced her steps into the wood. She turned a corner and saw, dark against a ray of sunshine, a tall figure, clad in grey, waiting at the spot where the paths diverged. He had his back to her, looking in the direction of the woods. She uttered a little laugh of surprise; he turned and in the shadows, his eyes were obscured. He bowed and came to her side.

She nodded and said, "You have come early."

"Not so early as I would have liked."

He raised her hand to his lips; then turning it, kissed the tiny space between her sleeve and her glove.

"I have written my instructions to my solicitor, whom I expect to see, at his earliest convenience, with the marriage contract."

She smiled, and took his arm. They escaped further into the wood, the wind blowing away the dead leaves before their feet.

They walked in silence for a moment, before he said, "Mrs. Bennet told me just now that you received a letter, which you thought to be from a connection of mine."

"I believe I used the word 'friend,' although 'connection' is perhaps a more apt expression."

His countenance froze. "Lady Catherine has dared to write to you?"

"One does not usually think of your respected aunt as daring to do; she simply does."

"Will you let me see it?"

"No, I could not show it even if I wished to do so, although I could point out its general whereabouts. Suffice it to say that Lady

Catherine has been so kind as to give me the benefit of her opinion. She gently warns me of the chilly reception I shall receive from everyone in the world, should ever I poke my head from my door again."

In spite of himself, he laughed. "I wish I could take these insults as lightly as you do."

"I was angry enough an hour ago, but you know my character."

"I certainly do. Your spirits rise at every attempt to intimidate you."

"Indeed they do."

He winced at the thought of a letter from a certain earl, his uncle, who wrote of the folly of courting a young woman, "less than a nobody," a girl he "could have had without marrying her." He would insure she never discovered the contents of that letter.

He touched a curl escaped from her bonnet.

"When I first knew I loved you, I felt a wistful . . . almost a happiness. Yet, after I parted from you, my feelings changed until I ached with longing to gaze upon your countenance, though it be only once more."

Elizabeth's mouth moved, seemingly in the beginning of laughter, and her eye was caught by the twirling fall of a leaf. How significant that fall seemed, in the fading sounds of the woods.

She thought to look at him but, somehow, did not.

He continued, "I learned what it means to yearn. I'd had no conception of the pain."

The woods were filled with silence. She felt his arm around her waist and felt him drawing her against him, felt the prickly texture of his coat against her cheek. So very near they were! A sudden scudding of the wind sent the leaves dancing around them. His lips touched her forehead.

"Elizabeth, my avowed one, you cannot know how I love you."

She raised her head and, for an instant, he thought he read in her eyes something never yet spoken, words hidden behind her other meanings. Her lips, slightly parted as she seemed about to speak, were now very close.

"Pray, tell me your feelings."

She turned her head aside, then looked back up at him with that sweet mockery, which had intrigued him from the first.

He released her and drew her hand into his arm. The wild careering of his heart began to steady. They walked on, in the sparkling crispness of the air.

CHAPTER 2

WHILE LADY CATHERINE'S LETTER MAY have given Elizabeth a momentary qualm, and her neighbors alarmed themselves with thoughts of the difficulties in the bride's path, Mrs. Bennet was joyfully oblivious to danger. She had two serious sources of pre-occupation: the terms of Elizabeth's marriage contract and the preparation of wedding clothes for not one, but two daughters.

There would be the excitement of a double wedding in November. Jane Bennet, the eldest of her daughters, was also engaged and would marry Darcy's friend, Charles Bingley, in the same ceremony that would unite Elizabeth and Darcy.

In the matter of the clothes, Mrs. Bennet was sparing neither trouble nor expense in this, the most important preparation for the girls' married lives. She ordered all manner of items from city ware-houses and horrified her spouse by sending for a London dressmaker.

In regard to the marriage contract, Mrs. Bennet hardly knew which aspect to delight in the most: Elizabeth's dress allowance, her carriage, or her jewels. Her husband disobliged her by devoting considerable energy to a lengthy perusal of the articles and none at all to entering into her transports of joy. He was more concerned with Elizabeth's provision should she be widowed without produc-ing an heir to Pemberley. What nonsense! If Mr. Darcy were so inconsiderate as to die early, Elizabeth would, in the meantime, have had a son. At last, Mr. Bennet announced himself well satisfied with the document.

Elizabeth was called into the room. Darcy stood at the window, gazing out into the grey afternoon. He turned as she entered. His very stance, like the impeccability of his dress, seemed an outward statement of his inner certainties. She was just beginning to know him.

Her uncle, an attorney, smiled expansively and gestured to Darcy's attorney to speak.

"Mr. Darcy, Miss Bennet," the other said, "I am obliged to insure that you both understand the solemn promise given in the signing of these articles of marriage."

The sun had struggled through the greyness; a shaft of pale light lit the room. Darcy crossed to the desk, took up the pen and signed, neatly, firmly. He held it out to Elizabeth. Her fingers fluttered on the quill. She found that she was holding her breath. She watched her own hand sign her name. She watched as the pen formed the scratching twirls of her mother's signature, the old-fashioned loops of her father's and the practiced smoothness of the two lawyers' names.

It was done.

The following morning, Mrs. Bennet could return to the delights of watching her daughters try on gowns and bonnets, cloaks and pelisses. She busied herself by getting in the way of the dressmaker and bothering the seamstresses with her criticisms.

Mr. Bennet rolled his eyes. "I had best take those two young men shooting again this morning, I suppose."

"Yes, you must take them away for I cannot have them constantly underfoot," replied his lady.

"Well, Lizzy," said her father, his grey eyes twinkling, "did you ever think to hear your mother speak those words about two bachelors under the age of seventy?"

"Indeed not, Papa," said Elizabeth, walking over to the window. "Yet we will shortly find out if Mama has quite hardened her heart to the species. Here come Mr. Bingley and Mr. Darcy now, with three, nay, four other young gentlemen."

"What!" cried her mother. "Where are they?" She hurried to the window. "What nonsense you speak, girl. They are alone." She flapped her lace handkerchief in irritation as her daughters giggled.

"What a pity, Mrs. Bennet," chuckled Mr. Bennet. "We might have got rid of all four girls in November."

"Oh, well. Time enough for that later," said Mrs. Bennet, with a complacent smile. She settled herself in her armchair, adjusting her lace. "With Lizzy and Jane so well settled, I have no more fears for the future. They will be able to provide for their younger sisters when their parents are no more. I look to them to supply their sisters with bridegrooms too, for I have exhausted my resources."

Mr. Bennet rose. "You were subtle, Mrs. Bennet, in your pursuit of Mr. Darcy for a son-in-law . . ." He paused at the door and added, ". . . but then, he is a subtle man."

"Certainly, he is," said his wife.

The door had barely closed on Mr. Bennet when the future bridegrooms were announced.

Charles Bingley was not so tall, so handsome nor so wealthy as Fitzwilliam Darcy, but some considered him more desirable as a companion.

"My dear Mrs. Bennet!" he said, happily. Crossing the room to her, he bowed. "I hope you are in good health."

"I am, Mr. Bingley, and it is very kind of you to inquire, given that your thoughts are occupied with another person altogether!" She wagged her finger under his nose. Bingley laughed but Elizabeth blushed when she noticed how Darcy flinched at this want of refinement.

Mrs. Bennet turned to him, and said, "Mr. Darcy, good morning." She received a stiff bow.

"Good morning, Mrs. Bennet. I am pleased to hear you are well."

"I thank you, sir."

She could not think of another word to say and Darcy was equally lacking in inspiration. Fortunately, Bingley knew how to go on. He complimented Mrs. Bennet on her new gown; Darcy wondered that he had noticed. He commented on the change that the wind had made in the landscape in the past few days: so many leaves fallen. Darcy had not thought Mrs. Bennet would be interested in such a thing and was amazed to hear her comment on the bareness of the park. Bingley's eyes kept turning towards Jane, who beamed at him from her mother's right. Darcy acutely felt Elizabeth's presence behind him, but kept his eyes upon his hostess until she said, "Here are my daughters, sirs, waiting to greet you. I suppose they may be bothered to say good morning to you." She laughed merrily at her own jest, never suspecting herself of vulgarity. Bingley laughed too, and Jane joined him.

Darcy turned to Elizabeth. She was pale and tense. He greeted her gravely, bowed to her sisters, who curtsied with equal gravity; then he sat down.

Only minutes later, Mrs. Bennet called upon the young people to go for a walk, before Mr. Bennet took the gentlemen shooting.

Once out of doors, they separated quickly into pairs. The younger Miss Bennets, instructed to call upon their aunt, set off down the drive. Bingley and Jane dawdled behind their companions. In no time, Elizabeth and Darcy were alone among the trees.

They were silent for a while. Gradually, Elizabeth felt her irritation and embarrassment at her mother's indecorous behavior fall away. Their conversation turned to future plans, and Elizabeth's longing grew for the elegance and calm of her future life.

CHAPTER 3

THE WEDDING WAS BUT THREE days away when Darcy alarmed Mrs. Bennet by announcing the arrival of his sister, Miss Georgiana Darcy. Although the girl was but sixteen, Mrs. Bennet was nervous of this meeting, having heard a report of the young lady's pride. She was mollified when Darcy presented not only Georgiana, but his cousin, Colonel Henry Fitzwilliam, of the noble Fitzwilliam family, in whose honor Darcy had been christened.

Mrs. Bennet was always delighted to meet a new young bachelor. After they left, the scent of her lace wafted through the air, as she cried, "What a charming man! Such easy manners, a perfect conversationalist! Not good looking, it is true, but who cares for that?"

"I believe there are those who do, Mama," said Elizabeth, perhaps recalling her mother's transports of joy over the handsomeness of her future sons-in-law.

"Lizzy, you are a sly thing, never to say a word about him when you came home from your visit to Kent!"

"Did I forget, Mama?"

"Forget, indeed! You are quite sure, Lizzy, that he has no regular income other than his army pay?"

"Quite sure, Mama. Colonel Fitzwilliam must marry money."

"Such a pity it is that younger sons so often have all the personal charm and heirs have none."

Elizabeth chose not to construe this as a criticism of her betrothed. "The colonel has a very pleasing manner, Mama."

"And Miss Darcy!" Mrs. Bennet raised her hands in her excitement. "So graceful and charming! She is not so handsome as her brother, but such a figure, such elegant deportment!"

She took a few steps across the room with exaggerated grace, twirling her handkerchief, to the great amusement of her daughters; then sank into her favorite armchair.

She continued, "I feared Miss Darcy was proud, for she spoke barely above two sentences. Do you know, Lizzy, I think she may be a little shy? Bear that in mind when you introduce her to society. When is she coming out?"

"Never, I should think, if she has her way."

Indeed, after her brother's stiff introduction, Georgiana Darcy had returned Mrs. Bennet's gush of words with barely a syllable. Darcy, never at ease with Mrs. Bennet himself, allowed the colonel to carry the flag for the family.

Colonel Fitzwilliam seated himself by Mrs. Bennet. He turned to Elizabeth, and said, "Miss Bennet, I cannot tell you how delighted I am to see you again, and in circumstances such as these! Pray accept my congratulations. I do wish you both joy." Elizabeth responded with grace.

He continued, "When we parted in Kent, I thought it unlikely we should meet again. Yet we shall be cousins and, I hope, the best of friends."

Mrs. Bennet was delighted with the introduction of her favorite theme. "Lizzy has been very sly, Colonel. One moment they barely knew each other; the next they were engaged to be married."

"Barely knew each other, ma'am? Why, Darcy and I stayed with our aunt, in Kent, above three weeks last April, and I had heard high praise of Miss Elizabeth Bennet long before that." Mrs. Bennet laughed heartily.

"Mama, please," urged Elizabeth softly. She rose and moved to the table where her abandoned embroidery lay.

"Enough of your reminiscences, Cousin," said Darcy.

The door opened to admit Mr. Bennet. He looked around the room with a humorous air. He saw his spouse mopping her eyes, Elizabeth pale with anger, Mr. Darcy on his high horse by all appearances, and two strangers, who seemed not to know how to look.

"Ah, Mr. Bennet! There you are!" cried his lady, wiping her eyes. "Come and join in the fun."

Henry Fitzwilliam had risen, giving his hand to Georgiana. Mr. Bennet bowed and crossed the room to be introduced.

Elizabeth was relieved when her father's arrival caused a change of subject. To Mrs. Bennet's annoyance, her husband introduced the perennial topic of the pamphlet he planned to write some day.

"I am exploring every species of folly in the works of all the prominent writers on manners of the last century. I constantly come across these delights in my reading and have spent some time on expanding and ordering my thoughts."

"How fascinating, Mr. Bennet," said the colonel. "I await the appearance of your work with interest."

"I should not hold my breath while I waited, sir," snorted Mrs. Bennet.

There was a pained silence.

Mr. Bennet flushed somewhat while Elizabeth turned her head aside, and Georgiana looked as though the sky had fallen in.

"Madam," said the colonel, "I well understand your impatience to see your husband's worth recognized. However, it takes long years of effort to present such an original work in polished form."

"Oh, yes," thought Elizabeth, "and what long years of kindly study of others have produced manners so polished as yours?"

"I hold in the most serious disapprobation," Darcy said, "the carelessness, bordering on immorality, of those who stumble through every task as though the quality of their performance were immaterial."

Mr. Bennet nodded, in the manner of the wise old scholar. "I thank you, sir, for your sympathy with my tardiness." He smirked at Elizabeth, who felt the need to bite her lip.

Mr. Darcy bowed. "One has only to refer to the recent case, which I shall not name, of a carelessly written newspaper report leading to the . . . death of its subject."

"Oh, you mean Mr. Lound," cried Mrs. Bennet. "He took his own life, you know."

"I should be cast down indeed, if my endeavors led to such a tragedy," replied Mr. Bennet.

Georgiana glanced at Henry as, momentarily abstracted, he let his eyes linger with tenderness on Elizabeth's face. Sudden knowledge pierced Georgiana through, so that she almost missed Mrs. Bennet's next words.

"Lizzy never tells anyone her secrets, Miss Darcy. I hope you will be able to winkle something out of her, for of what other use is a sister?"

"I have ever longed for a sister; and there is no one in all the world I would rather have for the part, Mrs. Bennet," said Georgiana.

"Why, thank you," said Mrs. Bennet, taking the compliment upon herself. "Did you hear that, Lizzy? Did you ever encounter such kindness?"

The door opened again. Henry and Georgiana gazed in open admiration at the lovely young woman who entered, evidently returning from a walk. The air had brought a wonderful color to her flawless skin and deepened the blue of her eyes.

"This," said Mrs. Bennet, with a decidedly self-satisfied air, "is Jane, my eldest." Then, as a young man followed the lovely Jane, she added, "Perhaps you know Mr. Bingley, Miss Darcy."

"Mr. Bingley! How are you?" said Georgiana, and received a little nod of approval from her brother for producing another sentence.

"I daresay you know, Miss Darcy, that your brother and Lizzy must share the honors on the wedding day. Mr. Bingley and Jane are to be united in the same ceremony."

"Yes," ventured Georgiana.

"How foolish of me! Your family's acquaintance with Mr. Bingley precedes our own," she cried. "I fear you will be a little cross with Lizzy, Miss Darcy. She would send her two younger sisters on a message to the village, so that you have missed meeting them today. I told her this would happen!"

"One scarcely hopes that our daughter will equal her mother in wisdom one day," said Mr. Bennet.

Under the cover of the conversation that followed, Elizabeth said to Darcy, "Does Georgiana intend to travel with us to Pemberley?"

"She and her companion will be escorted home by Colonel Fitzwilliam, who will go directly from Pemberley to rejoin his regiment."

"He will not await our arrival?"

Darcy glanced at her moodily.

"Duty demands his occasional visits at camp," he said. "Lady Catherine orders his attendance upon her in London after Christmas." He looked out of the window.

"Her ladyship's displeasure does not embrace your cousin?"

"No, indeed, and I encouraged him to go. He is a favorite with her," and he glanced at her darkly, before adding, "as he is with so many of your sex."

A smile teased at the corners of Elizabeth's mouth.

"Indeed he is."

On the return to Bingley's house, Georgiana sank back against the cushions of her carriage, feeling a sense of achievement. Knowing not how, she had pleased her future relations at Longbourn.

She had been overwhelmed by the garrulousness of the mother, the beauty of the sister and the caustic edge to the wit of the father. Only in Elizabeth was there compensation. Of course, her brother was incapable of choosing a bride who was less than perfect.

Above the creaking of the harness and the thudding of the horses' hooves on the road, she could not hear what her brother and cousin were saying as they rode alongside the carriage.

Henry was recalling the occasion of his first meeting with Elizabeth the previous April. He had lost himself happily in her charm, while Darcy smoldered resentfully in its prison. Darcy knew that Henry was in no position to marry her, while Henry was confident that Darcy would consider her utterly ineligible. Thus it was that the slight sense of competition between them had not posed a threat. In truth it had been forgotten, at least by one of them. Henry laughed.

"What is it?" asked his cousin.

"I laugh at the memory of our time in Kent, when I so often

sought your company to ride, and found you gone. None knew where, but I."

Darcy looked at him sharply. He said, "I hope I was not thoughtless in asking you to be my groomsman."

"Good Lord, Darcy. I've always assumed we would undertake the part for each other."

"Mrs. Bennet is going to such lengths to celebrate the marriage," said Darcy. "It appeared shameful to produce only a sister."

"Miss Bennet's family do not blame you for the poor showing, I'm sure. I rather imagine they feel relief that they will not be inundated with fashionable folk, particularly in the form of angry relations."

"Relief on both sides, I dare say," said Darcy.

Henry laughed. "You might try to unbend a little, Darcy. It cannot be a good thing to be on so stiff a footing with your future mother-in-law."

"I do not know how to converse with her, Cousin. She has all the dignity of a barn fowl."

He stopped, appalled at himself.

"I take that back. It was wrong of me to speak so of Elizabeth's mother. You will never hear me do so again."

Henry nodded. "Bingley seems unperturbed by his new connections."

"Bingley has a wonderful capacity for forbearance. His sisters are not happy with the match, however, nor his brother-in-law."

"Remember that there were tradesmen too recently in their family for them to be complacent," urged the colonel. "Nothing can touch your position in society."

"You think not?"

"I am sure of it," he said. "When will Bingley's relations arrive?"

"They are coming tomorrow. Mrs. Bennet had it in mind to ask Bingley's sisters to act as bridesmaids for Jane. She was brought to see how absurd such a surfeit of attendants would look alongside Elizabeth's."

The colonel laughed.

Darcy went on, "You have come and I am grateful. However,

I placed you in an awkward relation with our aunt. What had Lady Catherine to say of your coming?"

"She was most displeased, but I told her that I cannot choose between you; that I leave it to you both to abandon me if you choose, for I shall abandon neither of you."

Darcy mumbled his thanks.

His cousin added, "She must content herself with the rest of the family casting you off."

Darcy shrugged. "Don't be a fool about this, Henry. Lady Catherine gets up in years and yet it is likely she will outlive her daughter. Her fortune must go somewhere."

"I do not believe our aunt intends to do anything for me, and I will not marry without affection."

"Our family extended that luxury to neither our cousin, Anne, nor to me," said Darcy, with some bitterness. "I grew up never questioning that I would marry her. After I met Elizabeth, I knew I could not stand before God and vow to love another woman while I yet loved her."

"Poor little Anne."

Darcy turned abruptly away. "I did not jilt her! We were never engaged; there was never any talk of such matters between us. Indeed, she has no more feeling for me than I for her."

"Yet all our relations expected it, and I fear Lady Catherine will never forgive you."

"I neither desire, nor would I accept, her forgiveness. She wrote to me applying such insulting epithets to Elizabeth as can never be forgiven."

"Time heals these wounds, Darcy."

"What wounds? She has made herself my enemy, so that she cannot wound me."

"Oh, dear."

The colonel smiled ruefully to himself. How like his aunt it was to turn so implacably against her favorite nephew; and how like him to turn as implacably against her.

CHAPTER 4

THE LITTLE CHURCH AT LONGBOURN was crowded with guests and spectators. The congregation felt properly satisfied with the solemnity of the two bridegrooms. Patches of colored light shone on them from a stained-glass window above. The demeanor of the groomsmen varied somewhat. Bingley's brother-in-law, Mr. Hurst, displayed his usual tired blandness, while Colonel Fitzwilliam's feelings appeared more complex.

"Of course, his feelings must be mixed," murmured a widow to her friend. "This is not a good marriage for his family." She nodded discreetly in the direction of Miss Georgiana Darcy.

"There is Miss Darcy, an heiress, the young lady in velvet, seated by Miss Bingley." Georgiana was modestly, though fashionably, attired in a pink coat with a matching bonnet that screened much of her face.

"Poor thing. For all her wealth and connections, what is she but an orphan, with no mother to take her side?"

"She has her pride to sustain her," the widow replied, for Georgiana bore the scrutiny of these strangers by pretending they did not exist.

Mrs. Bennet was joyfully fluttering in her pew. She cast her mind back over the breakfast preparations. Nothing was short of perfection there. What could go wrong now, ever?

The sound of footsteps at the door caused a hush. Dark against the stream of light from outside, Mr. Bennet entered with a daughter on each arm. Jane, in a pelisse of the palest green, fairly floated on her father's arm. Her eyes were modestly cast down. Sunlight ignited Elizabeth's yellow coat in a haze. As she moved into the gloom of the church, all could see her dark gaze was straight ahead and quite impossible to interpret.

Followed by the younger sisters, they moved up the aisle to join the group before the altar. A golden light from the window lit up the lovely Jane, while Elizabeth was obscured by motley splodges of color.

There was a jostling for space as the gentry poured from the church and met with the crowd of villagers and farmers' families who had been unable to find room inside As they passed under the yew arch, Mr. Darcy caught his hat, and the crowd laughed. Elizabeth glanced up at him as a flash of pained hauteur stole his smiles. She pressed his arm and looked teasingly up at him, and he laughed ruefully. The groomsmen handed bags to the bridegrooms, who sent handfuls of coins raining down among the spectators.

Mr. and Mrs. Bennet led the guests into the house for the wedding breakfast.

After the celebrations, Jane and Elizabeth retired upstairs to ready themselves for their journeys. Elizabeth and Darcy would be on the road for some days, while Jane was to travel but four miles.

Elizabeth was very fashionable in an emerald green velvet coat and bonnet, with pale satin lining that matched the green of her gloves.

"My darling girl, just look at you! You do my heart proud!" shrieked her mother. She kissed Elizabeth on both her cheeks.

"Oh, Mama!"

"Yes, oh, yes, you do."

Mrs. Bennet's eldest daughter came into the room.

"There you are, Jane! See how well your sister looks! Not so well as you, of course; there has never been so lovely a bride as you, in the whole county. What a good girl you are."

Elizabeth laughed as Jane demurred.

Their mother interrupted, "Lizzy, Mr. Darcy will be impatient to be gone, I dare say. Both of you wait upstairs for a moment. I want to go down and watch you appear."

"Oh, Jane," said Elizabeth. "We will be very far from each other."

"Lizzy, you will make me weep. We will meet very soon in London."

At the bottom of the stairs, they turned to each other. As the footman moved to open the doors of the drawing room, Jane gestured to Elizabeth to precede her.

"No, Jane."

"Dearest Lizzy, you have precedence now, and I begrudge it not at all."

Elizabeth hesitated. All her life she had paid due courtesy to her elder sister and to upset this pattern seemed disrespectful. She would accustom herself to precedence, due to her because of her husband's greater consequence. Yet it seemed too soon. She linked arms with Jane; the doorway was wide enough for them both.

Elizabeth took her father's arm as they all went out onto the drive.

"How can you leave me, Lizzy?" said Mr. Bennet. "Your conversation is my sole source of comfort."

"You must come to us very often, Papa. You know you will always be welcome."

"I hope I shall be welcome as often as I will desire to come."

They had reached the carriage. Elizabeth kissed her father and her sisters.

"Goodbye, Kitty."

"Goodbye, Mary." She turned to her mother. Mrs. Bennet was surprised by a pang of desperate maternal feeling and seized her daughter in her arms.

"Goodbye, my dearest girl. How I shall miss you! I know not how I shall get through the days!"

"Much as you always have, I daresay," Mr. Bennet suggested, helpfully.

Heedless of her worthy spouse, her awe overcome by anxiety, she turned to Darcy and said, "You will take good care of my girl, Mr. Darcy?"

"Madam, there can be no charge that gives me greater joy," he replied and kissed her hand. Was it this gallantry that brought tears to Elizabeth's eyes?

She entered the carriage and her husband got in beside her. She looked at her father, so very dear, at her suddenly concerned mother, at all their friends.

"You are ready?" Darcy said softly. She laughed and waved.

"Drive on," he called.

They were away.

That evening, Mr. Bennet knocked at the door of his wife's dressing room, where she sat in her armchair gazing into the fire. Mrs. Bennet was unused to seeing this visitor in her sanctum. She looked at him. "Gracious!" she thought. "What a number of wrinkles he has to his face."

"Mrs. Bennet," he said, "I declare you appear pensive. What has brought about this extraordinary state, at the end of such a day of incident and triumph?"

"Oh, Mr. Bennet. Lizzy is gone so far off and her husband so taciturn. Will he be severe with her? Lizzy does so love a joke. What will they find to talk about? Will she be happy?"

"'O! Call back yesterday, bid time return,' saith the bard. Mrs. Bennet, is it not late to be considering such problems? I had thought you were delighted with the match."

"So I am, of course. It was a triumph to see her drive away in such a splendid carriage with such livery! They did look so fine. Mr. Darcy is a handsome man, to be sure, and Lizzy was quite the fashionable lady in her new velvet." She adjusted the ribbons on her nightcap. "What congratulations and compliments we have been receiving. I know our guests were most impressed."

Unconcerned by her husband's silence, Mrs. Bennet fiddled with the ruffles of her wrap, and smiled complacently to herself, as she added, "All our neighbors must be envious, especially those with daughters. The mothers will be glad Jane and Lizzy will be out of the way. They always were the handsomest girls in the district, though I do say it myself."

"Quite comforted, are you, Mrs. Bennet? Our daughter cannot but be happy with such carriages, livery, velvets and envy as you describe."

"Oh, Mr. Bennet, that was not my meaning at all. Lizzy, indeed, has married better than one could dream. Mr. Darcy must love her very dearly or this match could never have taken place. What a clever girl she is! Yet, think you that she will be happy?"

"I dare say she has as fair a chance as anyone, my dear."

Mrs. Bennet was comforted by this optimistic view.

"Of course, Derbyshire is not so very far off, is it, Mr. Bennet? They will visit often."

"Perhaps, my dear, perhaps. Goodnight, Mrs. Bennet. Tomorrow begins a quiet life, indeed."

He stood at his bedroom window for a time, recalling his own youthful hopes of matrimony, and it seemed that his daughters were still driving far into the moonless night.

It was no night for travel. Half a day's drive to the north, profound quiet had settled over the inn. Only the watchman was awake. The landlord had long ago made his final round, his good lady already sunk in sleep. From the kitchen floor to the attics, the house was full of slumbering bodies.

Elizabeth awoke. She stretched and turned. He felt for her face in blackness and encountered the tumble of her curls, and touched her cheek. She opened her lips, but words did not come. He felt her eyelids close.

"I have disturbed you. Goodnight."

By the third day, not ten miles from Pemberley, the rain clouds were blown away by a stiff breeze. Elizabeth drank in the stark beauty of the Derbyshire uplands as the road skirted around the base of a craggy hill.

"Beautiful!"

"There is a splendid prospect from that next rise," Darcy said.

The carriage creaked up around the base of a peak and stopped. They alighted and walked over to the edge. The ground dropped away before their feet, and the wind gusted furiously up from below. Elizabeth's gaze roamed over the swell of the hills and sweep of the

23

vales. Her cheeks were flushed in the wind, and her eyes lustrous with joy.

"Oh, this is magnificent."

The horses snorted; their breath was blown away in great clouds of steam.

The coachman gave his opinion that this was a mistress such as Pemberley had not seen before.

His young assistant smirked. "Nor such as maister has seen, neither."

"Thee hold tha tongue, young'un. 'Tis a fine way to speak for a jumped-up blacksmith's son." Clink held his tongue.

The wind tore at the hem of his mistress's coat and blew her curls around her face, while she only laughed. She let go of Darcy's arm as she skipped up onto a boulder; then took his proffered hand to jump lightly down. She could have done it alone with ease. She picked her way surely among the rocks in her boots, wondrous dainty they seemed.

"Maybe she'll gi' boots to Annie, for they be too small for her maid."

"Much good it'll do thee, Albee Clink, for Annie will ne'er look on thee more, now she is riz to chambermaid."

The boy stared off into the distance, blinking hard.

The footmen were fixing in place the white wedding rosettes and ribbons, removed after the carriage had passed through the district where Elizabeth was known. Once she was safely back in the carriage, Elizabeth's maid bustled over from the vehicle behind to adjust her lady's curls once more.

"Will I pass my examination, Wilkins?" she said.

"Indeed, you will, ma'am," replied Wilkins, with utmost seriousness.

The horses kept to a slow trot through the little town of Lambton, while children ran ahead, shouting, drawing the lower orders to their doors and the upper to their windows.

Only one did not stop to gaze, for he leapt on the horse that stood waiting and galloped off at speed with the news. The carriage horses picked up pace on the road to Pemberley. The great wrought iron gates stood open, and they turned in. The gatekeeper's wife and children stood by the lodge and the gatekeeper himself stood in the doorway, holding a stick in one hand and the doorframe with the other. He nodded.

"I have not seen the poor fellow on his feet these eight months," said Darcy. "What effort has this taken him? I shall come and thank him for it tomorrow."

"I shall come with you," Elizabeth said.

They journeyed through a wood, then turned a corner on the drive. The old yellow stone of the mansion glowed in the light of the waning sun. By the front door, the house staff was ranged in lines, according to seniority.

"Oh dear," laughed Elizabeth. "Some of them look terrified!"

"I daresay those who do not are dissembling. It will do them no harm."

He alighted from the carriage and turned to hand Elizabeth down.

Georgiana came forward from the hall onto the steps and stopped in dismay. She watched her elegant new sister move up the steps.

"How could Elizabeth have changed so in four days? My sister is become so cold," she thought.

Elizabeth came up the steps to Georgiana and kissed her.

"Dear Georgiana."

Her husband introduced the upper servants. With cool graciousness, Elizabeth acknowledged the housekeeper, Mrs. Reynolds, the butler and the cook. In a slow sweep of her head, Elizabeth then acknowledged the nervous bows and curtsies of the other servants. The housekeeper said, "This is Annie, your chambermaid, madam. Step forward, gel."

Annie, scarlet-faced, stepped forward and curtsied, mumbling, "Good day to you, ma'am."

There the briefest nervous giggle from a footman, extinguished by the butler's glare. Elizabeth nodded to the chambermaid, not unkindly.

The family passed into the house and entered the drawing room. Mrs. Reynolds bustled off to supervise tea preparations in honor of the day.

At the door of the kitchen, Annie caught up with her.

"What ails you, Annie? You are creasing your apron." Annie pulled her hands from her pockets.

"Mrs. Reynolds, ma'am. I canna' do it."

"Do what, you silly girl? Why are you not in your mistress's chamber? Her maid, Mrs. Wilkins, will be looking for you."

"I am afeard."

"What nonsense. Mrs. Darcy will not eat you, though I may. Now go."

Elizabeth may have been a little shocked had she known how effective her appearance of sang-froid had been.

"Were you impressed with my performance?" she asked Darcy, rolling her eyes.

"Congratulations, Duchess," replied Darcy. "The servants will not immediately forget your arrival."

"By the time they do, I should have some idea of what I am about."

She sat on a settee next to Georgiana.

"Dear Georgiana, did I frighten you? I confess I quite frightened myself." Georgiana laughed uncertainly. "Can you forgive me?" said Elizabeth.

"Oh, yes. That is, there is nothing to forgive."

"Georgiana, I have much to learn in the direction of this house."

"I have never done a thing since I came home from school. Mrs. Reynolds does all."

"The more reason for me to impose my authority from the beginning. In no time, the servants will have got over their fear, and we shall all get along beautifully."

CHAPTER 5

PRIOR TO ELIZABETH'S ENGAGEMENT, the merest mention of Darcy's beautiful home in Derbyshire would have sent Mrs. Bennet into a diatribe. How she detested the man! She could not bear to be reminded of his undeserved advantages! Curiously, her dislike of him melted in the warmth of her joy in her daughter's obtaining a share of said advantages.

She even developed an interest in Pemberley's whereabouts, especially when her two unmarried daughters were invited to spend Christmas there.

Miss Catherine Bennet, known always by her sobriquet of Kitty, was eighteen years of age. Not greatly given to books and contemplation, she had come close to expiring from tedium since her family circle had been reduced by the marriages of three of her sisters. The invitation to Pemberley threw her into ecstasies.

"Gracious, child!" cried her mother. "Not for worlds would I deny you this adventure. Where is Mary? We must go through your clothes."

However, Miss Bennet, rendered capable of self-sacrifice by her greater maturity at nineteen, shocked them all by declining the kind invitation. Had pride itself not been sinful, Mary may have been able to congratulate herself on being the most selfless of the five Miss Bennets. She declared that she could not consider leaving her parents for the festive season, with only Bingley and Jane to keep them company. As it was, they would miss the company, not of only Elizabeth, but also of Mrs. Bennet's brother, Mr. Gardiner, and his family. They had always spent Christmas together, but the Gardiners were to go to Pemberley too.

Mr. Bennet, when applied to, felt he could face even many a Christmas without Mary, but the young lady could not be swayed from the path of duty.

Kitty had never travelled further than her uncle's house in

London. Her father said he would not trust her to behave herself for three hours without supervision. He insisted upon accompanying her as far as the city, where she stayed a night with her aunt and uncle, before departing with their whole family for the north.

So it came about that, mere weeks after the wedding, Kitty found herself writing on stationery marked with the magical name of "Pemberley."

From Miss Catherine Bennet to Mrs. Bennet

Pemberley

Dearest Mama,

I hope this letter finds you in good health.

We stayed two nights on the road into Derbyshire, as planned. I can scarce believe I was so brave as to tell Mr. Darcy that I wanted to see Pemberley. Now I am here but two months later.

The very gates are the most enormous I've ever seen. My aunt laughed at me, Mama, for the way my eyes widened when I saw Lizzy's house. I did not think ever to see my own sister mistress of so grand a place.

Lizzy looked so fine, in a beautiful silk gown, that I nearly called her 'Mrs. Darcy.' You can imagine how she teased me and said she hoped her aunt and uncle would not also be rendered too much in awe of her.

Just think! Miss Darcy's old nurse has been here for years with nothing to do. Now she has my four little cousins to care for, and a nursery maid brought in to help her.

Would you not love to hear of all the splendors of my room? What fun it is, writing to you on this elegant paper. I send my dearest love to you and to Papa.

Your affectionate daughter,
Kitty

P.S. Pray tell Mary what a fool she was not to come.

While the novelties of gracious living had not yet worn off, by the fourth day Kitty had begun to lament the lack of young gentlemen at Pemberley. So she was well pleased to hear that two single gentlemen were expected to dine with them that evening. When they entered the drawing room, Kitty was utterly cast down, for one was fearfully old, the other dreadfully plain, and both were clergymen. Elizabeth had promised absolutely that she liked them very much.

"How could my own sister deceive me so?" she whispered to Georgiana. "One is old, the other ugly."

Georgiana's hand flew to her mouth. "Hush, Kitty," she said.

They went into dinner. The girls were seated opposite one another, at the center of the table. Kitty caught Georgiana's eye and pulled a little face, but Georgiana looked perplexed, then frightened, turning back to listen attentively to the elderly vicar of Lambton. Kitty looked at her aunt. Mr. and Mrs. Gardiner were deep in conversation with Mr. Darcy, a circumstance she found impossible to understand. Sensing her gaze, Mrs. Gardiner looked up and nodded subtly towards Kitty's dinner partner, the ugly one. "What is his name? Oh, yes, Mr. Turner," thought Kitty. She turned to find that Elizabeth had finished her conversation with him and was speaking to Georgiana and the old vicar. Kitty took a deep breath.

"Mr. Turner," she said, prettily, "what can you tell me about Kympton?"

"Not a great deal. It is a pleasant little place."

"Is it as big as Lambton?"

"No, it is a small village. Why do you not tell me something about your home?"

Kitty livened at this interesting change of topic from another to herself.

"Longbourn? The village is the smallest ever seen, and my father's house is as dull as the grave since all my sisters went away."

Mr. Turner laughed. "And how numerous are your sisters?"

"There are five of us. Jane is the eldest. She is very beautiful, and very good, and very kind."

"A paragon?"

"Oh, yes, everyone says so. She married in the same ceremony as

29

Lizzy. Jane is married to Bingley, who is nearly as beautiful and kind and good as she is."

"Are you recounting a fairy tale, Miss Bennet?"

"It is the absolute truth."

"So they are perfectly matched? Who is next in the list?"

"Lizzy, who married Mr. Darcy, as you know."

"Two sisters well matched."

"Well matched, you say? You cannot mean it." She looked into his grey eyes. She lowered her voice to say, "Unless you mean that Mr. Darcy is so rich."

He laughed again, and Kitty blushed at her blunder.

He said, "I meant that they seem suited in temperament."

"Lizzy? Mr. Darcy?" she whispered. "You do say the strangest things."

"Do I? Who is next in the tale of the princesses of Longbourn?"

"I am, Miss Catherine Bennet," she said, with an unconsciously flirtatious air. "I shall not tell you anything of myself, lest I shock you with my immodesty."

He laughed again, and Kitty could not help laughing too, at her own success, although she tried not to.

"Then, there is the youngest of my sisters, Lydia. She was married in August to a lieutenant in the militia, Mr. Wickham. He has now joined the regulars, and they are living very far from home in the north." She took a sip of watered wine.

"And that is the end of the tale," she said.

"I think not."

"Indeed, it is."

"You told me of Princess Jane, Mrs. Bingley? Then, Princess Elizabeth, now Mrs. Darcy, and Princess Lydia, Mrs. Wickham, and the Fairy Princess Catherine. That is four. What of the mysterious fifth?"

"Oh, I quite forgot Mary," said Kitty, and added with mock gravity, "Miss Bennet, who is not with us because she feared that Mama and Papa could not survive for three weeks without her care."

"She sounds thoughtful."

"Thoughtful? You know her already! Mary never stops thinking, even for a moment."

The young vicar thought he picked up a flash of mischief in her blue eyes. She seemed about to speak, but changed her mind. Kitty said nothing more on the subject of the missing sister.

Later, Kitty came out on the steps with Elizabeth and Darcy. They watched Mr. Turner's carriage carry their guests away in the moonlight. Elizabeth put her arm around Kitty's waist as they went back indoors.

"You seemed to enjoy talking to Mr. Turner, Kitty."

"Lord, no, Lizzy. I never met so hideous a man in my life. However, I rather fancy he enjoyed my society."

"Kitty!"

"Lizzy, why are there no handsome young officers in your circle? This seems a poor sort of district, I must say."

"I thought our family had its fill of officers, Kitty. Have you learned nothing from Lydia's experience?"

"What can you mean, Lizzy? And why do you hush me every time I mention our sister's name?"

"I will come to your room, where we can speak in private."

In front of the mirror Kitty sat gazing at herself. She picked up a glass, imagining it a wine glass, put it to her lips and looked over the rim, surveying the effect. Hearing a knock at her door, she put it down hastily. Elizabeth came in and pulled up a chair to sit with her.

"Kitty, dear," she began, "I wish you to understand why it is so inappropriate for you to speak of Lydia. The whole matter of her marriage is so . . . awkward. As for Mr. Wickham, he is persona non grata in this house."

"Person who, Lizzy?"

"His is a name not mentioned at Pemberley."

"Wickham is our brother-in-law!"

"He has made his own choices in life, Kitty. Mr. Darcy will never receive him at Pemberley and it pains his family to hear that name spoken."

"Well, I never heard of such pride in all my life."

Elizabeth looked earnestly at her sister.

"Kitty, do you not understand that when Wickham eloped with Lydia, he never intended to marry her?"

"What can it matter now? It was all hushed up. How well you have married in spite of it."

Elizabeth paled.

"It pains me to hear you speak so carelessly, Kitty. It is my belief that I should never have married at all, had not Wickham been bribed and coerced into marrying Lydia. No respectable man, with a marriageable sister of his own, will tarnish his family's reputation with such a connection."

Kitty flounced aside, with the familiar jutting of her little chin and hardening of her mouth. Elizabeth sighed at the work ahead of her to correct the results of her mother's indulgence of her sister.

"When Wickham did not take Lydia to Scotland, she ought to have left him at once and gone to her relations." She waited a moment but Kitty did not turn back to her. "Kitty, know you not the fate of a woman abandoned by her seducer? She is cut off from all respectable society. If she has no income of her own, she comes to know degradation such as we cannot imagine."

Kitty spun around, defiant to the last.

"Mama kept saying we were all ruined when they eloped, but Lydia came back to Longbourn in fine form and took precedence over Jane."

"Oh, yes. After their marriage, they returned unrepentant and unashamed. You know that to demand precedence, even if it is your right, is most impolite. In their circumstances, it was outrageous." Elizabeth took Kitty's chin and turned her face back to her own.

"Look at me, Kitty!" Kitty raised her big blue eyes to the dark anger of Elizabeth's. "Wickham had to be bribed to marry her and Lydia is too stupid to feel the insult."

The deepest blush spread over Kitty's face. Elizabeth continued, "While I regard Wickham's actions with abhorrence, think you: what was there in Lydia's behavior to put such a thought in his evil head? Her loud pursuit of the officers filled me with shame; and you, Kitty, at times, were not much better."

Kitty's eyes swam with tears.

"I would not have run away, Lizzy. I never would!"

She burst into loud sobs, and buried her head in her sister's lap.

"Kitty, dearest, do you see that I had to do this? If I seem a hard substitute for Mama, I am sorry. I hope you will not hate me for it."

"It is you who hates me."

"Hate you? What nonsense is this? Now dry your eyes. Drink this water. I wish you to enjoy your stay here. There are ways of amusing yourself with grace and discretion. I shall be your teacher."

Kitty made a wondrous recovery from her gloom to write again to her mother.

> *From Miss Catherine Bennet to Mrs. Bennet*
>
> *Pemberley*
>
> *Dearest Mama,*
> *We have been at Pemberley for five days and I am just beginning to know my way about the main part of the house. The east wing, which has fifteen bedrooms, is closed off for the winter, and still they burn half a ton of coal every day.*
>
> *I have tried to do something for Lydia and Wickham, but the merest mention of their names makes everyone cross. Wickham will have to find his own way to increase his income.*
>
> *I have met a frightfully ugly clergyman who would do well for Mary. She ought come to Pemberley in the summer and see if she can get him. I daresay no one else will have him. His name is Mr. Turner. Lizzy says he has an excellent living in a place called Kympton.*
>
> *I shan't have to look at him on Christmas Day, for we shall go as usual to Lambton church. The vicar is so ancient that he hangs on to the edge of the pulpit for dear life and I amuse myself wondering if he will fall out.*

*All the carriages have been dragged out of the coach-house in readiness
for the tenants' Christmas party. I declare that the farmers' families will
have more laughs than I, for we will be a solemn party on Christmas
Day: Mr. Darcy and Lizzy, Miss Georgiana and me, my aunt and uncle
Gardiner and two old clergymen's widows (I know not why Lizzy asked
them). The vicar will come if he has strength left after his sermon. Only my
little Gardiner cousins will afford me some amusement. Think of
poor Kitty!*

*We are going out to pick holly now, so I must put my letter in the
tray. I do hope you will have a joyous Christmas. I send my duty to you
and to Papa,*

Your affectionate daughter,
Kitty

P.S. My love to my sister Mary.

They came in from holly gathering, glowing with cold and exhilaration. Mrs. Reynolds uttered a soft "ouch" as she took the holly from Elizabeth, who stepped first over the threshold.

"Prickly, was it, Reynolds?" asked Darcy.

"Yes, sir."

When they were seated and awaiting tea, Darcy said, "There's a belief in this part of England that the first holly brought into the house determines who rules for the coming year. If it is smooth, the mistress; if prickly, the master."

"I've never heard of this before," said Elizabeth, smiling. "I do believe you just invented it." Her dark eyes sparkled with challenge. His eyes smoldered back darkly, but there was a smile in their depths.

"Oh, no," said Georgiana, "Fitzwilliam would not tell a lie. It really is true . . . well, people do believe it . . . the uneducated, that is."

"Knowing of your formidable education, I imagine you mean to imply that you don't believe it," replied Elizabeth.

Georgiana fell silent.

"It is my belief," Elizabeth went on, "that these superstitions only affect those who believe them. What think you, truly, Georgiana?"

"It is not for me to determine," she replied, close to tears. She worried for the next hour that she may have implied the unthinkable: that Fitzwilliam might not rule. She missed the spark that passed between her brother and his wife.

Elizabeth had a measure of Darcy's power, but fancied her own strength against his. This was a moment of mere play, however. Had they been alone, he would have taken her in his arms, she knew. What fun it would be to slip out of them and dance across the floor ahead of his pursuit!

The door opened, and the tea tray was brought in. Elizabeth's aunt and uncle followed.

"Such a lot of holly you have gathered!" cried Mrs. Gardiner.

After tea, Elizabeth followed Georgiana into the music room to play a duet on the pianoforte.

"How I love to hide behind your talent, Georgiana. You are so clever."

"Not very clever. I wish I could be half so clever as you in conversation."

"By clever, I am sure you mean impudent."

"No! Yet no one makes fun of Fitzwilliam the way you do. He is not accustomed to it."

Elizabeth laughed. "I believe he very soon will be."

"I fear—I fear that you will make him cross."

"I daresay he will be cross at times." Georgiana's hand flew to her mouth, and her eyes widened. Elizabeth smiled and kissed her cheek.

"Married people always have quarrels, Georgiana dear. I believe I can face a row and survive. The sermons tell us to bow our heads meekly under injustice, but women did not have the writing of them. A woman had best assert herself a little, if she does not desire her husband's contempt."

Georgiana looked earnestly at Elizabeth, wondering if she feared Darcy's contempt, and puzzling over whether such a change in his feelings was possible. Elizabeth laughed and touched the frown creasing Georgiana's forehead.

"Dear Georgiana, I do not make fun of Fitzwilliam from policy but because I cannot help it." Her dark eyes were dancing, and her expression hovering between sweetness and irony. "Think you that he is so miserable on it?"

"No, indeed. I have seen him laughing more in these weeks than I ever saw in my life." Georgiana sat mesmerized. She felt half in love with Elizabeth herself. She was excited and in awe and happy, all at once. Yet beneath the happiness was a tiny sensation of unease.

"How foolish am I?" she thought. "There is nothing to fear."

In Kitty's head there was, as usual, nothing akin to anxiety, indeed, not a great deal of anything at all. She wrote her last letter from Pemberley to her mama.

From Miss Catherine Bennet to Mrs. Bennet

Pemberley

Dearest Mama,

My time at Pemberley is all but gone and I have so much to tell you.

Just as I thought, the tenants were vastly amused at their party. We donned our warmest cloaks to cross the yard in our evening finery. Two footmen lighted our way. The rafters were hung with holly and every lamp in the place had been hung upon the walls. The old people were still at table, but the young were gathered about waiting for the dance to begin. How well I understand their impatience.

Elizabeth danced with Mr. Darcy's steward, and Mr. Darcy with his good wife. A young man came forward, pushed along by his friends, and asked me to dance. A great cheering went up when I accepted. Mama, he was as handsome a lad as would grace a red coat but, Lord, how he stank of the stables! We were all applauded as though we had graced a London stage. Lizzy, Miss Darcy and I gave presents to the children. Then it was all over, for us, I mean.

I am to come back, with your permission, to Pemberley in the summer. There is to be a large party of guests staying here for Miss Darcy's coming out. Lizzy has plans for a wonderful ball. What times

I shall have then! Mary may come too and sit out all the dances at Pemberley instead of at Hertfordshire.

Pray give my thanks to Papa for his permission to stay in London with Jane and Bingley. I shall love it above all things.

Aunt Gardiner said that I must not expect to spend much time with Lizzy in London, for she will be much occupied in her introduction to the high society of her husband's circle. My aunt believes that Mr. Darcy's friends will think he has made a great mistake in marrying her, when he could have married so very well, and that Lizzy will have to work hard to correct this view. Lord, what nonsense she speaks! I envy Lizzy the grand times she will have.

Just think! The famous Twelfth Night Ball, which we read about in the newspaper every year, is to be attended by your own daughter! A wonderful engraved invitation arrived from Countess Reerdon for Lizzy and her husband. A dressmaker's assistant is come from London to take Lizzy's measurements and show her some designs. She has chosen a yellow silk and gold beads and tassels that I would die for! The packing is begun for our removal to London. We must arrive in time for Lizzy's fittings. She is to wear emeralds. I was desperate to hold the jewels against the silk but, alas, they are kept at the banker's in London.

I hope that you and Papa continue in good health. I can scarce remember my life at Longbourn. I know not when I shall see you again. Not for ever so long, I suppose.

Your affectionate daughter,
Kitty

CHAPTER 6

IT WAS THEIR SECOND DAY in London. Darcy had spent the morning sitting in his carriage, while the footman delivered their cards to his acquaintances. In previous seasons, he sent the carriage on its rounds without him, but his attendance was obligatory for the first excursion into the world of the cards engraved with the name "Mrs. Darcy."

At each of the selected houses, the footman jumped down, climbed the steps and knocked. His offering was received with appropriate formality. If the recipient was in town, courtesy demanded a return of cards the next morning, followed by a wedding visit at the house.

Darcy sat in the carriage, brooding, "The number of recipients who respond promptly remains to be seen." His dark eyes turned darker still. "Anyone who insults my wife is not worthy of my notice."

On his return, passing the door to the music room, he heard Elizabeth and Georgiana singing and went in. Pale wintry light fell across the room from the tall windows. Georgiana was playing the pianoforte, and softly singing with Elizabeth. Her eyes flew wide open at the interruption, and she stopped singing, though her fingers played on.

Elizabeth did not miss a note. The music continued. Darcy sat down, facing her. She sang with such ease. Since she was a child, people had delighted in listening to her lovely voice but it was the charm of her manner that gave her hearers much of their pleasure. She loved her music, and unaffectedly shared that love with others.

She sang now for him, and he left off brooding, losing himself in her music.

After lunch, they were perusing the theater offerings, when the footman announced Mrs. Foxwell. The lady followed the servant into the room, the brown silk of her gown billowing out with the briskness of her step.

Darcy crossed the room and greeted her warmly.

"You will excuse me, I hope, Mr. Darcy, for not having the patience to wait until tomorrow to see you."

She was not a pretty woman, somewhat mannish in feature, but she smiled up at him warmly and Elizabeth noted a hint of sardonic humor in her small brown eyes.

After being introduced and getting the usual compliments and congratulations out of the way, Mrs. Foxwell sat down. Her keen eyes soon sparkled with amusement.

"Gracious, Mrs. Darcy!" she cried, after fifteen minutes. "You will have me outstaying my welcome with all this laughter. I am forgetting the other purpose of my visit. Mr. Foxwell and I have invited a group of friends to dine this evening. I hope you are not already engaged? My husband is out for the day and I believe he does not know of your arrival in town. What a surprise for him!"

"A pleasant one, I hope," said Elizabeth.

"I doubt not. He is always overjoyed to be reunited with your husband, and I cannot see what he might object to in you." She rose, said her farewells and was gone.

"I like her very much," said Elizabeth. "I shall look forward to knowing her better. There is a certain intelligent humor in her manner, which is very promising."

She turned to Georgiana, who was looking as happy and excited as if she were included in the invitation.

"Georgiana, dear, we must postpone our visit to the theater."

"I do not mind, Elizabeth. I wish you to enjoy yourself. I will not be alone." Indeed, Georgiana felt undismayed by the thought of the many evenings she would spend with her widowed companion, while her brother and sister-in-law went out. Only too soon she would be launched upon society; that was where her terrors lay.

As Mrs. Foxwell entered her house, her husband emerged from the library.

"My dear, you are returned at last! Come in here for a moment. I have news for you."

"Have you, indeed, Foxwell?"

"My brother must be prevailed upon to take orders as soon as may be."

"This is no news; it has been our constant lament these three years."

"This I know, however, I have it on the best authority that the living promised him may fall vacant soon."

"Ah! That is news indeed. Might we postpone our exploration of the matter until after our guests leave?" She moved to the door. "I barely have time to dress. First, I must arrange for more places to be set at table."

"Only one, my dear Mrs. Foxwell. How is it that I can never surprise you?"

Mrs. Foxwell turned.

"What can you mean?"

"Lady Catherine comes alone."

"Lady Catherine?"

"Lady Catherine de Bourgh, of course. From whom, think you, had I my news? She called out to me from her carriage and I trotted over as obediently as any dog. What a lucky chance it was to invite her to dine before the Darcys come to London. It will be monstrous tricky at times, while they are all in town."

"It will be monstrous tricky tonight!" she exclaimed in exasperation. Her freckles stood out in contrast to her pallor. "Why do you persist in interfering with my arrangements?"

"Ah." He flushed. "Mr. and Mrs. Darcy are in London and are dining with us tonight?"

"Yes." She turned angrily to the door.

He jumped up.

"All will be well, my dear. I shall write Darcy a note, putting them off. Better still, I will hurry to Brougham Place myself."

"It is too late, don't you see? We cannot put off Mrs. Darcy from her first invitation of the season and it is equally impossible to deny Lady Catherine on their account. We must make the best of it."

Ever fearless in society, Elizabeth felt a pleasurable anticipation as she and Darcy followed the footman up the wide oak stairs. She squeezed her husband's arm, where her hand lay inside his elbow and he gave her the slightest nod of reassurance. The door was opened and the footman's voice rang out, "Mr. and Mrs. Darcy."

Twenty-four pairs of eyes had but one object and that was Elizabeth Darcy. Everyone in the drawing room turned towards the door and conversation all but ceased. Their hostess swept towards them, followed by a gentleman. Darcy introduced his friend, Mr. Foxwell.

"Mrs. Darcy," he cried. "I am overjoyed to make your acquaintance. I most earnestly wish you both joy, if you have not enough of the commodity without my assistance."

In all his features Elizabeth was reminded of someone: a cynical humor in the warm brown eyes, an unfortunate complexion and mousy brown hair. Of course, he was like his wife!

Darcy glanced about the room and encountered the wintry face of his aunt, Lady Catherine de Bourgh. With frigid correctness, he made his bow. She did not deign to return it.

Foxwell said, "Ah, here is my father approaching." As they turned towards the older gentleman crossing the room, Darcy said quietly to Elizabeth, "Lady Catherine is here, by the fire."

"Surely not!"

"I'm afraid so. She has just cut me."

"Oh, my dear!" She touched his arm. He covered her hand with his.

"Do not present her with further opportunities to cause you pain, and embarrassment for Mrs. Foxwell."

Elizabeth turned from the shock of this, to meet the elder Mr. Foxwell, while the son said quietly, "Darcy, my dear friend. I cannot apologize enough."

Darcy shrugged. "Do not trouble yourself, Foxwell. This undesirable convergence was inevitable."

"I regret that it should take place in my father's house."

Darcy shrugged moodily and both men joined in Elizabeth's conversation with their hosts. Foxwell said, "Mrs. Darcy, I had it in mind to come into Hertfordshire to make your acquaintance, but Darcy told me to attend to my own affairs."

"Just as well," interrupted his father. "What use would you be to Mr. Darcy before his new relations, with your rattle and prattle?"

"I must protest, sir!" cried the son. "'Prattle' is perhaps justifiable, but I am not happy with 'rattle'." He turned to Elizabeth. "I shall have opportunity to convince you of my discretion as I have the honor of taking you in to dinner."

At a sign from his daughter-in-law, the older man moved off to escort Lady Catherine to the dining room. Offering Elizabeth his arm, the son said, "I so value these opportunities to sacrifice these honors to my noble parent."

At this, Elizabeth was too clever to laugh.

The dining room was long and well-lit. Its heavy ornateness, which the old man could not be prevailed upon to relinquish, was lightened by the sparkle of the table settings. Against the background of the clinking of cutlery and the murmur of many conversations, Elizabeth steered Mr. Foxwell from the direction of Darcy's courtship to talk about his family.

With the removal of the covers after the first course came the usual shift of conversation. Mr. Foxwell said, "Reluctantly, I bow to the curiosity of our neighbors. May I introduce them to you?"

After a while, Foxwell reverted again to the subject of their courtship, this time with a wider audience.

"Matters matrimonial ought not to be arranged deep in the countryside, away from the kindly gaze of friends."

"Hertfordshire is not so very deep in the countryside, Mr. Foxwell."

"Do not let us quarrel over geography, my dear Mrs. Darcy. I just want a little taste of your secrets. You can trust me."

"Trust you indeed! I doubt not that my little taste would later be served as a full dinner."

The laughter that this sally produced confirmed her suspicions.

"Darcy," her victim cried, silencing the whole table, "is your lady always so merciless?"

"When called for, Foxwell, I am afraid she is."

"You cannot call her merciless, Mr. Foxwell," another wit called out. "She married Darcy. Now there's an act of mercy, if you like."

"Indubitably," said Darcy, with a smile.

More laughter and a shout of, "Prettily spoke, sir!" almost smothered a decided "Humph!" from Lady Catherine's end of the table.

When Mrs. Foxwell rose, signalling the time for the ladies to withdraw, Darcy glanced at Elizabeth. His aunt would be harder to avoid in the smaller group of ladies in the drawing room. She gave him one of her quick whimsical smiles. He had never felt so reluctant to sit over port.

Immediately upon entering the drawing room, Lady Catherine commandeered her armchair by the fire. Elizabeth wandered over to the pianoforte, intent on looking at the music. She was approached by a diminutive lady who had been seated near her at dinner.

"Mrs. Darcy, I so enjoyed your conversation earlier. Pray, let us take coffee together and talk some more."

"With great pleasure, Mrs. Courtney," she replied and they took their coffee to a small settee. Their conversation skipped from topic to topic. Elizabeth had never met anyone quite like this: funny and analytical, with an elfin charm that took the sting from her words. Other ladies joined them, attracted as much by curiosity to know Mrs. Darcy as by the wit of both young women. Only a few older women with, perhaps, something to gain, continued their attendance upon Lady Catherine.

When he came into the drawing room, Darcy found Elizabeth in animated conversation, having quite forgotten the presence of his aunt. Instead, she was able to introduce him to a new acquaintance, Mrs. Courtney.

For her own part, Lady Catherine was relieved that another nephew, staying with her in London, had been unable to accept tonight's invitation. She doubted her power to keep Colonel Fitzwilliam away from his cousin's bride. She bent her cold glare upon Elizabeth.

"Mrs. Darcy seems to get along famously with Mrs. Courtney," said one of her companions. "Mrs. Courtney is a very charming lady! How different she is in manner from her aunt, the marchioness."

Slowly, her ladyship turned her magnificent head to the speaker, who fell into a nervous silence.

The elder Mr. Foxwell escorted Lady Catherine down to the hall. Her ladyship stopped on the landing, and turned to him.

"I was speaking to your elder son today, sir. I told him that the living I may see fit to bestow upon your younger son, Mr. Reginald Foxwell, may fall vacant at any time now."

"Indeed, he told me of this, Your Ladyship. We are, of course, extraordinarily grateful for the very great kindness you have shown my boy."

"I have not shown it yet, Mr. Foxwell. I said the living that I may see fit to bestow."

Carefully, he replied, "With respect, Lady Catherine, we have long understood this to be a definite arrangement. My son is almost four and twenty and is well advanced in his studies. It is late for him to seek another profession."

"It is nothing to me, if a more grateful candidate should appear."

"Reginald never stops speaking of Your Ladyship with praise and gratitude."

Lady Catherine banged the floor with her stick. "But what of his family, sir? I do not like to see, in the houses I condescend to visit, a nephew who has disgraced the house of Maddersfield. Do not imagine that my brother, Lord Maddersfield, will have ought to do with him."

"I am so sorry, madam, that I did not bring up this subject myself. I did not wish to pain you. The invitation of the people to whom you refer was entirely a misunderstanding. I humbly beg your forgiveness. It will never occur again."

Lady Catherine drew herself up to her impressive height and said, "It will not occur again, because your son will never acknowledge that . . . gentleman . . . again."

Mr. Foxwell paled. "They have been friends from childhood. It is a bond as strong as any brothers feel. Can we not come to a compromise?"

"Mr. Foxwell! Do you not know who I am? I do not compromise. Give me some proof of your decision this se'enight. Goodnight to you, sir."

The Darcys left not long afterwards. In the dark carriage, Darcy gave a sigh of satisfaction.

"You were very successful this evening, Elizabeth."

"I enjoyed myself very much. Tell me, are Mr. and Mrs. Foxwell related other than by marriage?"

"Indeed, they are much alike. They are first cousins, predestined for each other from birth."

"You had that in common with him?"

"I did. Among my intimate friends, only Bingley married where he chose."

"Are the Foxwells happy, do you think?"

"After their own fashion, yes, I think so. You liked Foxwell?"

"Yes, although I am somewhat mystified."

"By what?" The darkness gave his voice a teasing quality.

"Mr. Foxwell appears a little . . . unorthodox. How came you to have such a close friendship with him?"

"I have known him since my first day at school, a few weeks after my mother's death. He was the only person that made that first term bearable."

He took her hand and continued, "Foxwell may seem somewhat 'eccentric,' if he would excuse the word. However, I am so accutomed to his style of address that I believe I respond to his intention rather than his words. Even as a child, he was capable of the greatest kindness."

Her hands were warming in his. In the darkness, she heard him say, "Elizabeth, you are the only person I have ever known, since childhood, to whom my heart has gone out, unsought and unbidden, in love or friendship."

What could she say in reply? There was nothing to say.

After the last of the guests had left, the Foxwells sat for a few minutes in the drawing room.

"Mrs. Darcy is very charming, clever and pretty, too," said Foxwell.

"They generally are in such cases, Foxwell. You did not expect her to be a fright, I daresay."

"I rather thought you liked her, my dear."

"I liked her very much. She will be an interesting addition to our circle."

Foxwell smirked in his wife's direction.

"I remember when you were charming to me," he said.

"Such nonsense you speak, Foxwell. I was never charming."

Surprised that her father-in-law did not throw in his own caustic comment, she looked at him. He was pale, and his brow creased with worry.

"Are you well, Father?"

"My dears, something has occurred that has troubled me greatly." He told them of his conversation with Lady Catherine.

"I never heard of such an outrage!" cried his son. "She cannot do this. All the world knows she has promised that living to Reginald."

His father nodded. "I should have thought that this action would seem too dishonorable for her ladyship to contemplate it."

"Are there no legal means of opposing her in this, Father?" said Mrs. Foxwell.

He shook his head. "I shall look through my correspondence tomorrow, but I am almost certain she has never put her name to the offer in writing."

"Her ladyship's impertinence beggars belief, Father!" burst out his son. "How can she imagine I am to look away as I pass my friend on stairs; to see him in the street and return his friendly greetings with coldness?"

"How else is your brother to find his way in the world, without

46

patronage in the church? What is left to him but the army? He is such a fool that he will chase after heiresses for three months, before running off with a governess."

"He is not such a fool as that, Father."

The old man stared back at him.

"Well," said the son, "he is a little impetuous, certainly."

His father snorted. "I will send for him tomorrow and see if anything can be done. He may yet have some sway with his patroness."

There was a silence.

He looked long and sadly at his son.

The young man flushed. "I hope you do not ask me to deny Darcy, sir."

CHAPTER 7

"DEAR DARCY," murmured Lady Reerdon, as the Darcys moved away towards the ballroom, "such a romantic gesture."

Lord Reerdon's pallid eyes followed the pair, his expression one of dreamy indulgence.

"How happy he must be, Mother."

"You will not follow his example, Frederick," she said quietly, and turned towards the next guests. He grimaced. What chance was there of his marrying a penniless girl, for love, with his affairs in such a muddle and his dear Mama so extravagant?

Darcy and Elizabeth paused at the top of the steps that swept down into the ballroom. He gave her a half-smile of reassurance, which she met with a flash of mischief. She turned her head to survey the room. There was the buzz of many conversations, bursts of laughter, and the background lilt of music.

How happy she was to look so well, when she saw the finery of the women. In the past, her annual dress allowance would scarce have paid for her gown. Emeralds sparkled on her neck, wrists, and in her hair. They descended into the glittering light and noise of the ballroom.

Two men standing at the foot of the stairs briefly caught Elizabeth's eye, and she could hardly forbear to laugh. An aging Bacchus addressed himself to an Apollo (both in brocade waistcoats).

"So this is the lady whose name is on everyone's lips, Whittaker?" His sneer was a wonderful source of amusement to the younger man, who said, "I rather like the look of her, Sir Graham."

"Pretty enough, I daresay, but hardly a beauty."

"Saw you that look she gave him? She will be laughing at us all tomorrow."

"Weeping, more like, when she has learned that Darcy's money ain't enough to buy her friends in this company."

Whittaker shrugged elegantly.

"Lord, if that ain't Foxwell!" cried the baronet. "He has aged in looks by twice the number of years since I last saw him."

"We have not all had the benefit of the American climate," said Whittaker, with a laugh not quite pleasing to the other man.

"We meet again, Mr. Foxwell. Good evening to you, sir," drawled Sir Graham.

"You are returned to England, Sir Graham." Foxwell's coldness caused a lift of an elegant eyebrow from Whittaker and a lowering of that of the baronet. Almost snarling, he said, "Of all men, Darcy is the last I would have expected to be such a fool, Foxwell. Hmm?"

"I am vastly pleased with him, Sir Graham. Mr. Darcy has provided me with possibly the only avenue to meet a very charming lady."

"Come now, Foxwell. You know him as well as any. Did you anticipate such a caper from Darcy, of all men?"

"You lacerate me, dear sir," interrupted Whittaker, with a yawn. "Have you no poetry in your soul?"

Sir Graham snorted. "The Italians manage these things better. The arrangement of marrying is often best left to one's relations." He allowed a pause, more uncomfortable for Foxwell than he could have known, before continuing: "I hear a whisper that one of Darcy's relations is somewhat public in her displeasure."

Foxwell winced. "At this moment, Reginald has probably arrived home," he thought. "Even now, he may be in conference with our father."

Whittaker cut in on his thoughts. "You have met Mrs. Darcy, Mr. Foxwell? Won't you be so kind as to introduce me?" Foxwell bowed and even Sir Graham gave an agreeing shrug.

The three men crossed the upper end of the room towards the small group to whom Darcy was introducing Elizabeth. She turned with pleasure to greet Mr. Foxwell, who then gestured behind him.

"Mrs. Darcy, may I present Sir Graham Eston?" he said, but Eston had walked past them. Elizabeth's color heightened slightly.

Foxwell added hastily, "This is Mr. Whittaker. Whittaker, Mrs. Darcy."

She turned a charming smile upon her new acquaintance. Sir Graham Eston seemed forgotten with the flow of Foxwell's humor, as irrepressible as at their first meeting. Even Whittaker's foppishness was totally forgiven. Her wit sparkled, and as she laughed the gems in her hair sparkled with the bobbing of her curls. All the while she felt Darcy's presence as keenly as if they were touching. The baronet's rudeness she could laugh off for herself, but not for her Darcy. Had she looked at him, she would have seen he was white with anger.

The orchestra's change of melody signalled the beginning of the dance. She glanced up and Darcy bowed and put his hand out to her, just as Mr. Whittaker bowed and requested the same honor.

"Thank you, sir, but I am already engaged for this dance."

"Then, madam, will you do me the honor of dancing the next with me?"

"With pleasure."

Elizabeth stood opposite Darcy in the set. As he straightened from his bow, he caught the flash of a question in her eyes before she smiled. As they circled each other, he said, "You have encountered a man whom I despise. He is beneath your notice and thus lacks the capability to offend with his insults."

"Of whom do you speak?"

"Exactly so," he replied.

They drew more than one curious pair of eyes. In the autumn, rumors of Darcy's engagement to a girl of insignificant connections and no fortune had astounded his acquaintances. His fastidiousness was well-known and oft-lamented; yet how susceptible he had proved at last.

She smiled at the sight of a cluster of people hovering near a lady of middle years. Their facial expressions were calculated to express infinite boredom, but somehow the anxious hope of being noticed betrayed them.

"Who is that lady, Fitzwilliam?" He followed her glance.

"The Marchioness of Englebury, my love."

"Truly? That is Lady Englebury?" One of England's most celebrated characters, a woman of immense intellect and incalculable influence at court, was embodied in a dumpy little form, indifferently adorned.

"A woman of such reputation! She looks so . . . commonplace."

"Indeed, yet you picked her out from this crowd."

"So I did! I shall tell Papa I saw her. He reads out her bon mots from the newspaper."

They danced on. When they spoke, she felt, in the slight lean of his body, a shift of his whole being towards her in total attentiveness. She felt a lifting sensation in her spine, a sudden pride in this man, in his person, and in the exclusiveness of his accessibility. She was learning, too, that her very manner when passing behind him in the dance, in looking away and looking back at him he found immeasurably erotic.

When the dance ended, a young woman came to the marchioness's side.

"Dear Aunt, there is someone here I would wish you to know. I encountered her at the Foxwells on Tuesday. Will you meet her? She is wondrous witty."

"Amelia, I am here for nought but to give countenance to your tedious cousin, Cecile. Mere mention of your Foxwells and those other dull friends of Mr. Courtney adds to my torments." Amelia took her aunt's arm and pressed close to her side. Her green eyes looked laughingly into her aunt's face.

"Don't give me such looks, pray! Amelia, I would that you abandon these wheedling ways."

"Will you not do me one small favor, Aunt, when I have always striven to please you?"

"Humph!"

"I will read that book you gave me. There!"

"Introduce her to me then, but be warned, I give her just two minutes of my time."

Thus, after she had been in London but three days, Elizabeth met the formidable Marchioness of Englebury. Elizabeth, while fascinated by this opportunity, had no more expectation from the exchange than the other lady. Yet something about the girl intrigued the marchioness, who saw that, despite her essential vitality, Elizabeth had a way of holding herself still that spoke of fearlessness. She liked the intelligence in the beautiful dark eyes and a promising piquancy around the mouth.

"I am to wish you joy, I believe," declared the old lady.

"That is the convention in our present circumstances," said Elizabeth.

"Then I wish you joy." Her eyes moved on at last and she nodded up at Darcy. "I hope you will both be very happy."

A change in the tempo of the music informed the crowd of the beginning of the next dance. Mr. Whittaker appeared at Elizabeth's side to claim her as his partner. With the extravagance of his bow, scent wafted out, and he said:

"My dear Marchioness,

Tho' to see you is my heart's delight,

I now whisk this lady from your sight."

Lady Englebury snorted.

"Mrs. Darcy," she said, "Mrs. Courtney may bring you to see me, one morning, when you find yourself at liberty from your wedding visits."

"I thank you, ma'am."

The news of Lady Englebury's invitation whirled around the room much faster than Mrs. Darcy whirled into the dance with her new partner. Elizabeth knew nothing of this. She was caught up by the music, her delight in the dance, and by the entertainment of analyzing a new and beguiling acquaintance.

At five and twenty, Mr. Whittaker was a man of virtue. The virtues he possessed consisted of blond good looks and a pleasing financial competency. He provided Elizabeth with some interesting, if not altogether credible, information about their fellow dancers.

At one stage in the dance, a young lady floated past, the epitome of fashionable lethargy. Elizabeth thought she caught the glimmer of a smile flashed to Mr. Whittaker, but it vanished, like a ripple on a still pond, leaving her lovely face as impassive as before.

"Who on earth was that?" asked Whittaker. "Most people wake up in the morning. She merely opens her eyes."

Elizabeth laughed, irresistibly drawn in by his venom, and said, "There is a line with the fineness of a razor's edge between the states of elegance and unconsciousness. I have not yet dared to tread it."

She felt his laughing gaze stroke her face. "No," he said. "I believe that is one fine line you never tread."

At the end of the dance, he said, "May I have the honor of introducing my sister to you?"

He led her to the very same young lady whom he had affected not to know. Elizabeth gave him an accusatory look, in the face of which he smiled the smile of an innocent. Looking at them standing together, Elizabeth wondered that she had not spotted their relationship. They were both tall, with the same fair complexions and Grecian features. Even in their grey eyes, she detected a similarity of expression.

The evening was crowded with incident. Elizabeth despaired of remembering all the people she met. She danced every dance, and spent little time with her husband apart from a few minutes between dances, when he could find her. As she danced, Elizabeth caught glimpses of Darcy walking about, engaged in conversation, then standing alone. Finally he exerted himself to dance. This was just the behavior she had found so supercilious in the early days of their acquaintance, and she smiled.

How easy she found it! Every person introduced to her seemed to have another friend longing for her acquaintance. Yet her Aunt Gardiner had warned her not to take it to heart if she found herself snubbed somewhat, at first, by the London Ton.

Lord Reerdon escorted her in to supper, having been her partner for that dance. They sat at the bottom of the second table, Darcy almost opposite her. Fortunately, the aromas of pheasant and partridge soon competed with the odor of Lord Reerdon's perspiration and Elizabeth found herself to be hungry.

As supper ended, the Twelfth Night entertainments began. To the sound of flute and drum the "attendants" of the court ran in and assembled on the platform at the end of the room. The "Twelfth Cake" was carried in. The sides of this massive concoction were sculptured like desert dunes, and on the top rode a miniature procession of figures representing the three Magi and their camels. A drumming brought silence and a boy unrolled a scroll and read aloud:

"Now the revelry comes.
For in this cake of plums
Is the coin for the King.
For his Queen the ring.
They'll reign over us here,
Both commoner and peer."

The cake was carried around in procession, before returning to the dais to be cut.

"Have you ever been King?" Elizabeth asked Darcy.

"Fortunately not. Rumor has it that aspiring kings bribe Lord Misrule for a chance at the coin."

"Who plays his part?"

"Except for the King and Queen, they are all actors."

The herald went on:

"So that justice may be,
Let Lord Misrule oversee!"

Through the door by the dais, leapt Lord Misrule. From his noisy welcome, it was clear that not much was expected in the way of justice. A team of footmen served cake first to the ladies, then replenished their trays to serve the gentlemen. Elizabeth noted how many eyes at the table watched the gentlemen pick through their sweet, in hope, or fear, of finding the coin.

Lord Misrule paced fiercely about the room until a shout of "The King!" alerted everyone to the whereabouts of the coin. Three hundred heads turned in the direction of the shout. There was a long drum roll. Nobody claimed the throne, although smothered giggles were heard from the center table. The drums continued to rattle, rattle, rattle. Elizabeth found she was caught between laughter and a pitch of excitement.

Then, taking his time, Mr. Whittaker raised his hand and clicked his fingers to summon a footman, who pulled back his chair and dusted his lap. He rose, to loud applause.

"Whittaker will give us the best theater of them all," said Darcy.

Lord Misrule ran about the room, banging the floor with his staff, drawing attention back to himself. By some trick, he transformed his staff into a banner, and Elizabeth found she was one of many who gasped. Only then did he lead Mr. Whittaker to the dais. Elizabeth laughed at the solemnity with which the "king" allowed the cloak to fall about his shoulders. He seemed almost to groan with the weight of the cardboard crown and braced his arm to receive the orb, made of gilded paste. Elizabeth could not but admire Whittaker's imperial transformation, as he responded to the salutes of his fellow guests with a flourish of pure arrogance.

"I must say," said Lord Reerdon, "he is very good."

Lord Misrule bellowed, "Behold your king!" and the whole assembly rose to bow low.

The King seated himself on the throne, and there was a scraping of chairs as the guests all sat down. The pipers piped up and a little page boy entered. On a massive cushion he carried a ring, the diamonds of which would have been worth a king's ransom were they real.

Then Lord Misrule spoke again:

"Here is the ring,
The page boy doth bring.
Let the King choose his bride
To rule by his side."

The king was only expected to name the queen, but Mr. Whittaker had a reputation to keep up. Leaning back in his throne, he produced expectant laughter with a slight gesture of his hand. Then he drawled:

"Too fair to find fit compliment,
Shines a new star in our firmament."

Several young ladies newly launched upon society were the object of speculative looks, in particular, a young lady with whom Mr. Whittaker had danced twice. He raised one limp hand to his forehead in grief:

"Tho' first beheld this eventide,
Alas, another's took her for his bride."

Elizabeth looked at Darcy, her dark eyes alight with laughter, but she felt that the smile Darcy gave her at that moment was somehow forced, and he was not the only person who looked her way.

"As the color of her gems, you see,
So glows my heart with jealousy."

With a true actor's gift, Mr. Whittaker paused again. Those lacking wit enough to solve the riddle needed only follow his eyes.

"Now I exert my kingly power
And take her from him for an hour."

Lord Misrule paced across and bowed deeply before Elizabeth.

Before she had a chance to react, an objection was raised from another table. "Unfair! It is too long a parting for newlyweds."

There were shouts of laughter, buried in coughs as Lady Reerdon frowned, always disapproving of jokes which threatened embarrassment to her guests.

With a shout, Lord Misrule declared:

"Choose again, O Lord my King.
This lady does not want your ring.
Have mercy; they were wed this day,
Another year I think she may."

Over the top of hoots of laughter, another "courtier" called out, from the dais:

"'Tis a man in haste, or sure of his sway,
Would wed on Topsy-Turvy Day."

Lady Reerdon moved to rise, and the room fell silent. Elizabeth's wit rose too quickly to check and she replied:

"It was on Twelfth Day not at all.
For we were wed when leaves did fall."

This was rewarded with a standing ovation as she rose and followed Lord Misrule to the dais, and accepted her crown, cloak and ring. She turned, took the King's offered hand and they stepped to the front of the dais; and, in answer to the shout "Behold your Queen!," she accepted the deep obeisance of her court.

"Oh, Lizzy!" Kitty exclaimed. "Were you not dreadfully embarrassed?" She had come at two o'clock in the afternoon, finding her sister still at breakfast with her husband.

"Why should she be?" asked her brother-in-law. "She looked the part."

"I own to feeling somewhat prominent, but it is remarkable to what one can accustom oneself."

"How many people were there?"

"Three hundred or so. They next performed the play."

"Was it very amusing?" asked Kitty eagerly.

"The usual Twelfth Night nonsense," replied Darcy.

"Were there no more dances? Did you not dance, Lizzy, after they made you queen?"

"There were two more dances. The first I must dance with the king."

"Did you like him?" Kitty looked guiltily at her brother-in-law, hoping he would not object to this.

"Mr. Whittaker?" said Elizabeth. "I cannot say. He is amusing certainly, but not, I think, altogether sincere. He is of a cynical turn and, I should imagine, very vain. I know not why he chose me. I fancy he would hate to attribute his choice to gallantry."

Kitty found her eyes again wandering irresistibly to Darcy. His expression was impenetrable. Elizabeth continued: "We walked all the way up the set to the top, with all the other dancers bowing their deepest bows. Some of the ladies are very accomplished, sinking almost to the floor. Were I not so modest, I may have found the experience intoxicating."

"With whom did you dance the last?" Kitty needs must have every detail.

On the way to the ball Elizabeth and Darcy had arranged to have the final dance together. Elizabeth's promotion to queen interfered with this. Mr. Whittaker had gallantly chosen the hostess, as indeed the king always did.

Then Lord Misrule proclaimed:

"From o'er one hundred gentlemen fine,
Now choose, O Queen, which shall be thine."

Certain gentlemen felt that their rank and talents qualified them to be the queen's partner. Elizabeth named her partner to Lord Misrule, who called:

"She's looked at one then at the rest;
And since she's queen, she'll take the best."

He looked around:

"From the way I see them preen,
More than one man thinks it's him she's seen."

Elizabeth caught Darcy's impassive look. He gave her a rueful little smile. Then Lord Misrule called:

"It matters not if she speaks not his name;
One courtier or another it's all the same.
She believes he hails from the north, do you see,
He's tall and he's dark, his initials F.D."

"Off with his head!" called Mr. Whittaker.

However, the queen had spoken; and they had the happiness of enjoying the last dance together after all.

It was after four in the morning when the guests were finally on their way home.

In the darkness of their carriage, Amelia Courtney said: "Do you know, Teddy, Lady Englebury told me that Mrs. Darcy puts her in mind of someone. I imagine she means Lady Jeanette. My poor aunt, to have lost her only child."

"Who would have been but the second marchioness in her own right in the family. Her death was a great misfortune for one of her ladyship's views."

"That is very ungenerous of you! I wish you to try to like her more."

"I beg your pardon, my love. I will try, though your aunt seems loath to return the compliment," said Courtney. Then, musingly, he added, "Still, her ladyship's loss was a gain for Lord Bradford, who has but a tottering uncle in his way to become marquess. The tragedy of Jeanette's death may also prove invaluable to your new friend."

In the Darcy carriage, Elizabeth sank back in weariness. Her husband found her hand in the darkness.

"Queen of the Fair, I was so proud of you. You carried that off with wit as well as grace."

"I thank you, sir,"

"I thank you," he said.

"For what?"

"For choosing me. Again."

"I feared it may be a dreadful blunder. Instead, everyone seemed to think I was rather sweet, which is a terrible blunder."

"I thought you would make a more politic selection—Lord Reerdon, for example. I was feeling a little jealous in advance."

"Of Lord Reerdon? Ugh! I thought you might rather not have the attention."

"No, I did not object to that particular moment of prominence." He paused. "Did you converse long with Mr. and Mrs. Foxwell?"

"I saw the lady but briefly. I danced with Mr. Foxwell."

"How did you find him?"

"Very pleasant. My acquaintance with him is very short, so it must be difficult for me to judge. Why do you ask?"

"I felt him to be somewhat constrained in manner. I asked his lady if he were in good health. She replied most vehemently that he will always be as he ever was."

"How strange."

"Strange, indeed."

CHAPTER 8

Mrs. Courtney watched Elizabeth's face for her reaction to Lady Englebury's home and indeed Elizabeth was impressed. Light seemingly poured from two enormous sun-drenched seascapes in the hall. At the top of the stairs was an extraordinary forest, which seemed curiously real, with its deep purple shadows. The drawing room was characterized by an elegant plainness; the furnishings were the very best, but they were a mere backdrop for her ladyship's collection of contemporary art.

"You are interested in my paintings, Mrs. Darcy? You have made a study of the subject?"

"Unfortunately, I have but little talent for painting and, spending my life almost exclusively in Hertfordshire, I had few opportunities to look at exhibitions."

"Excellent!" barked the older woman. "The senseless daubs of the modern young woman are but poor imitations of art that died years ago, or ought to have died."

"I am sorry to hear that so many young ladies are expending their energies fruitlessly, your Ladyship."

Despite the marchioness's penetrating stare, Elizabeth's dark eyes looked serenely back.

"Ha! Ha! Come with me," ordered the marchioness.

On the boudoir wall, a creature created almost of light itself emerged from a cave.

"The birth of a soul," murmured Amelia.

"A pity the light generally goes out," said her aunt. "Certain artists of today are seeing beyond the mere shapes of the objects before them. Some have the gift to share that insight with us."

Elizabeth said little. While she was fascinated to see paintings of a style of which she had only read, she felt unqualified to take a critical approach to them.

She was struck by two landscapes hanging side by side, alike and yet so different. The sight of the very Derbyshire peak she had climbed with her husband took her breath for a moment.

"These paintings are of a place in Derbyshire," she said. "The different light and weather make them almost seem different places. One is all gloomy desolation, and the other raptures of wildness."

The older woman looked at her sharply, suspecting a hidden significance in her remarks. She said, dryly, "Of course the viewers also have their private interpretation."

"Think you so, madam?" questioned Elizabeth, in mock doubt. "I daresay such a phenomenon is possible . . . in some cases." Something essentially playful in Elizabeth's riposte made this not quite saucy, and Lady Englebury gave a bark of laughter. A blush or simper would have demolished the girl in her good opinion.

"I hope you will keep next Tuesday evening free, Mrs. Darcy. That is when I hold my little gatherings. I shall send you a note to remind you."

When Elizabeth came home she sought Darcy in the library. She lightly told him of the invitation and discovered that she had just gained admittance to one of the most exclusive salons in London.

"It cannot be!" she said. "Her ladyship's famous salon is peopled by bluestockings and writers."

"The main criterion for inclusion, I believe, is a decided facility in conversation."

"How very daunting that sounds," said Elizabeth. "However, we will enjoy it, I daresay."

"I doubt very much that the marchioness has even considered inviting me, my love." His calm shocked her.

"If this is so, I shall refuse," she said. "It would be most ungracious of Lady Englebury to invite only one of us to an evening party."

"No insult has been intended, Elizabeth. Lady Englebury is known for her disregard of the marital state of those whom she admits to her circle."

Elizabeth sank into an armchair opposite his.

"I would rather stay at home with you and Georgiana."

"I am most gratified that you should express this sentiment, Elizabeth. However, we will receive separate invitations at times; and some that cannot be refused. I feel that concern for my feelings is inadequate reason to deny yourself this pleasure."

He paused. He rose from his chair and walked over to her. From her expression, he saw that Elizabeth could readily be persuaded. She wanted to go, with or without him. He continued, "The marchioness could be an invaluable connection for you, dearest."

Elizabeth jumped up. They faced each other across the leaping light of the fire. She said, "I am the last person to be influenced by such an argument as this! Why do you not know this of me?"

"Do you deny her ladyship's influence in society?"

"I'll not flatter her!"

"Elizabeth, you know I cannot abide sycophants. There is a difference between fawning on someone on account of her rank, and acknowledging the indisputable fact that your connection with that person gives you consequence."

"Spare me your indisputable facts. I do not desire consequence purchased in this way. I will not think of my friendships in such terms. I am your wife; that is enough for me."

"It is because you are my wife that I do not accept your spurning of this honor."

His words seemed to echo Lady Catherine's angry prediction of their marriage, "You are determined to make him the contempt of the world." Elizabeth had refused to believe those words, though she was shaken when Sir Graham so rudely slighted her. Still, she refused to be cowed by the notion that her value was gauged in society's scales against the weight of her connections.

"I do not recognize you at this moment, Mr. Darcy." (In fact she did, but she had thought this pride was buried in the past.) "I had not thought you so eager to raise me in the opinion of the world."

The sparks of her anger ignited his. "You inform me of my feelings, and I am to justify them, I presume." He was meeting her fire with ice.

He winced inwardly at the expressiveness of her lips, in her anger. She said, "Then you deny that you believe the marchioness's patronage may counterbalance my social deficiencies a little? A very little, I cannot help fearing."

"There is no point in denying it. Lady Englebury is one of the most sought-after women in London, not merely on account of her rank. To be distinguished by her is seen as a great honor. Elizabeth, I wish only to protect you."

"From what, sir?" Her voice was mild, but scorn flashed in the lovely eyes. He was reining in his anger, and she knew it, yet put the spur to it.

"From the insults of unmannerly baronets?" she cried, giving away that her feelings on this point were stronger than she had pretended at the time, but he was too angry to pick this up.

He said coldly, "I'll warrant Sir Graham Eston was regretting his rash action before the night was out. He is desperate to regain the footing he once held in society."

She stared at him, puzzled, silent, as he said, "It was the talk of the ballroom that you had been distinguished by the marchioness. People were all but congratulating me openly, and he had insulted you."

"What do you mean?"

"Did you expect to experience such a degree of success at the ball? If so, you do not know the secret cruelty exerted by the Ton, in protection of the citadel of position."

"Then they are all fools." She was looking for a way to climb down from the peak of her anger.

"Certainly, yet this is the world in which we find ourselves." ("Why is she so confoundedly proud?" he thought. Yet he loved her the more for it.)

"Elizabeth, there is nothing I would not sacrifice for you." His exasperation was at its limit.

Her words burst out, "You have sacrificed the good opinion and notice of your relations. I cannot bear the thought that you might feel you sacrifice your honor, too."

"Not my honor, Elizabeth." He strode over to the window and stared out at the steely cold of the street. He turned back to her. Her color was high, and the light of the fire leapt about her. He had still so much to learn about her. His anger was crumbling.

"I knew I would anger my family by marrying you, although I underestimated their severity," he said. "However, dearest, you have taught me to esteem and value you above everything. I discard, without regret, the friendship of any of my circle who do not respect and honor you. When I see you distinguished by such new friends as you have made, I know their friendship protects you, by silencing critics."

Sudden suspicion led her to say, "Is Lady Reerdon's kindness influenced by the marchioness's interest in me?"

"Lady Reerdon's?" he said. "No, indeed not. I never doubted her friendship. I see I have upset you needlessly. Forgive me my ungovernable temper."

"Never mind. It is just that I have been so cross. No, there is more. I could not bear to think the countess had been insincere to me when she called yesterday."

"What did she say, Elizabeth?"

Elizabeth found she had to take a breath to settle the emotion that rose in her.

"That she had known your mother better than anyone in the world; and that there was no doubt in her mind that Lady Anne Darcy, had she lived, would have quickly learned to esteem and love me."

He said, "What else could she have done, had she known you?"

"Lady Reerdon's kindness to me is offered in memory of your mother. I do not claim it for myself, but her words meant more to me that I can express."

Her hands were trembling. He held them.

"We have quarreled, my dearest," she said.

"Have we slain that dragon?" he asked.

"I think we were fighting its ghost." She looked away, then slowly, slowly back to him. She smiled and tilted up her chin as she said, "I will bear in mind, if Lady Englebury pursues this strange friendship, that she is a useful connection. I may be prepared to make allowances."

"I think you are wise," he said, looking very wise himself.

"Very small allowances," she added.

"Indeed, there is no call for excessive compromise of your dignity."

She continued, "I shall make these very small allowances . . . so long as she amuses me."

He laughed, replying, "She does amuse you? Are you not curious to partake of conversation of a brilliance you may never find elsewhere?"

"I am intrigued, in spite of myself." There was a little flare of excitement in her eyes, and, preoccupied, she did not notice the oddness of his smile. He was reaching out, needing to hold her, when a footman entered.

"Mr. and Mrs. Hurst are here, madam, and Miss Bingley. I have shown them into the drawing room," he said.

"Thank you. Please tell them I shall be with them presently."

The footman withdrew.

"Well," she said, "this is an exciting conclusion to our morning."

The two ladies awaiting them in the drawing room were the elder of Charles Bingley's sisters. Miss Caroline Bingley was a tall, handsome young woman, whose bearing left one in no doubt of her high estimation of her own worth.

Caroline was accompanied by her sister, Louisa, along with Louisa's husband, Mr. Hurst. The three represented the epitome of fashion, in dress and in manner.

"What an age it seems since your wedding!" declared Miss Caroline. "How the weeks have flown!"

"Indeed, they have," replied Elizabeth.

"Such a happy time that was. I have never felt such joy as on the day when our two families were united by matrimony, and I was able to call your sister Jane my very own sister."

"I am most gratified to hear it," said Elizabeth, although "surprised" might have been closer to the mark. "Have you seen Jane and Charles since you arrived in town?"

"We shall wait upon them after we leave you, dear Mrs. Darcy."

Mr. and Mrs. Hurst added their compliments and congratulations. Then Miss Bingley turned to Darcy.

"Mr. Darcy, where is dear Georgiana? I long to see her again."

"My sister is, at this moment, receiving her music instruction. I am sure she would not object to your waiting upon her in the music room for a few moments." He began to rise, but Caroline's longing had not reached a pitch intense enough to propel her from the drawing room.

"I see you have made some pleasant little changes to the arrangements already, Mrs. Darcy," said Mrs. Hurst. "I do not recollect seeing that delightful little cabinet last season."

Her husband levered himself out of his seat and went over to the ornament stand in question. He put his glass up to his eye to examine the inlay work on the top shelf.

"A dainty little piece, indeed," he declared.

"We greatly treasure this item," said Darcy. "It was presented to Elizabeth by Lady Reerdon."

Mr. Hurst gave a grunt to indicate his appreciation of this fact. Caroline looked at the little cabinet, her expression betraying a certain sourness. In truth, she had not yet become accustomed to the idea that Darcy was a married man.

"This should have been mine," she thought. "What is more, I would have placed it better." Aloud, she said, "A charming piece, Mrs. Darcy. An elegant gift, from a very gracious lady."

"Indeed," said Elizabeth, "Lady Reerdon has been very kind to me."

"Naturally, she has," said Mr. Hurst, startling Elizabeth with a burst of chivalry. "Who could be less? Mmm?"

She had not opportunity to frame a response, as Mr. and Miss Whittaker were announced. Elizabeth glanced at Darcy in surprise, as he had not spoken of them as friends. He shrugged.

Miss Bingley felt a flash of alarm, as Miss Whittaker's beauty, wealth and connections were the talk of London and could be a threat to her. She then recollected that Darcy was already married.

Arabella Whittaker knew how to enter a room; one could not but admire. She greeted her hosts elegantly, then turned to greet each of the other visitors in turn, having made their acquaintance the previous winter.

Caroline noted the graceful lines of Arabella's jacket, the tassels of which hung in a particularly attractive manner. She shifted her attention to the brother. She thought how pleasing were his looks also, and elegant his dress.

Mr. Whittaker regaled the other visitors with an entertaining account of the ball, while the sister, a raconteur's perfect partner, inserted some amusing asides and adjustments.

"Mrs. Darcy recited a sonnet composed on the spot, putting right certain errors made by the dastardly M.C.," he said.

Elizabeth interjected, "Mr. Whittaker, two lines of doggerel scarcely constitute a sonnet."

"Madam, the reception your offering received guarantees that it will go down in the history of the Twelfth Night frolic as a sonnet worthy of the bard." Elizabeth looked laughingly at Darcy, but he had got into one of his humorless moods.

"I do hope you enjoyed the ball, Mrs. Darcy," said Mr. Whittaker.

"I thank you, Mr. Whittaker, I enjoyed myself very much."

Caroline Bingley turned to Darcy.

"I hardly dare hope that you enjoyed yourself, Mr. Darcy. I so sympathize with your views on the tediousness of balls," she said.

After a moment's thought, he said, "I thank you, Miss Bingley. I might say that this year's Twelfth Night Ball was the first I truly enjoyed."

Miss Whittaker's voice floated dreamily on the air.

"We will dine with Lady Englebury this evening, Mrs. Darcy," she said. "Dear Mrs. Courtney will be there. I understand that you were to see the marchioness this morning."

"Her ladyship was kind enough to receive me."

"She is full of kindness . . . when she likes someone. She felt constrained to attend the ball to launch the marquess's niece upon society," Arabella continued. "Her ladyship suffered dreadfully there, for she cannot bear to talk to dull people, let alone watch them hop about in the dance."

"Then she has something in common with Miss Bingley. She cannot abide the stupidity of balls," said Elizabeth.

"I don't believe I said that!" cried Miss Bingley. "Dancing is perfectly acceptable when the company and conversation are superior."

"I believe our aunt was never fond of dancing, even in her youth," said Whittaker.

"What is your connection with Lady Englebury?" Elizabeth asked.

"Our late lamented father was her ladyship's brother; and your friend, Mrs. Courtney, our cousin, by her sister."

Elizabeth said, "I am sorry to hear of your father's passing."

"You are most kind." Miss Whittaker raised one eyebrow, and her brother did the same. For a moment they looked absurdly alike. Then, realizing they were in danger of staying too long, the elegant pair rose, made their farewells and departed.

"The Marchioness of Englebury, eh?" said Mr. Hurst, in another burst of articulateness.

Miss Bingley had heard enough, and a glance at her sister was sufficient to move their party off too.

Caroline felt quite put out for a day or so, and complained to Louisa.

"I have so longed to attend Lady Reerdon's Twelfth Night Ball. We'll never be invited to it now, I suppose." She paced about the room, and Louisa smiled sympathetically.

"What did Mr. Darcy ever really do for us in society, Louisa? Nothing that put him out in the slightest, when one looks back upon it."

"My darling Caroline, he could hardly ask us to his friends' parties. We did meet Lady Reerdon at his house on two occasions last winter. As I recollect, we were pleased with the honor."

"I wonder if we are to be included in any more such entertainments, now that Mrs. Darcy will be drawing up the guest lists."

Louisa sighed. "If only we'd been more pleasant towards her, Caroline."

"How could I be more attentive to her than I am?"

"I mean from the beginning of our acquaintance with her, in Hertfordshire. Great heavens, if I'd known Mr. Darcy would marry her!"

"Indeed, and I suffered needless anxiety last winter thinking Miss Whittaker would make a set at him. His affections were already engaged elsewhere."

"You see, sweet Caroline, you have gained peace of mind from Darcy's marriage." She rose gracefully and went to sit beside her sister on the settee. "What think you of Mr. Whittaker? He has come into an excellent fortune, and he appears an intelligent man. You do like intelligence in a man, do you not?"

Miss Bingley patted her sister's hand. She went over to the fireplace and studied her reflection in the mirror above.

"I like intelligence well enough, in combination with a good fortune. If there is one without the other, I may find I must make a sacrifice." She turned to Louisa with an air of mock sanctity. "The intelligence must be my burnt offering."

They enjoyed a comfortable sisterly laugh together.

CHAPTER 9

MR. BENNET HAD DETERMINED NOT to visit Elizabeth in town until she was settled there at least six weeks, but, missing her, he took the post for London, arriving at Brougham Place on Tuesday afternoon. Finding daughter and son-in-law out, he said he would wait and settled down by the library fire with a drink and a book.

He looked about him with satisfaction. While the room was not comfortably worn in like his library at home, it was decorated with masculine good taste. He rang for another glass of wine.

A little later, the door opened. "Papa!" Slowly putting down his drink, he turned.

"Ah, it's you, my dear."

Elizabeth ran over and kissed him.

"You have certainly taken your time in coming home, Elizabeth."

She sat on the arm of his chair. "Why did you not let me know you were coming?"

"We were not always on such a formal standing."

"We were living in the same house, Papa."

"So we were, my dear. So we were."

"How are Mama and Mary?"

"Your mother suffers yet with her nerves and finds the quiet less beneficial than she hoped. Your sister, Mary, however, is become positively giddy, unaccustomed as she is to sustained converse with her mother. Why, she has only read, I think, one or two sermons in the past week."

"So few? I am shocked."

"She was very disturbed by the gowns you sent her. They were much too décolleté and had hardly been worn. I make no comment on the first complaint, but, as to the second, you are not wasting your husband's money, I hope?"

"I spend it as fast as I can, Papa, but not fast enough to satisfy him. Those gowns are quite useless to me now because the fashions have altered since autumn."

She laughed and added, "Pray tell Mary to let me know if she does not want me to send more, because my maid regards anything I send away as property stolen from her."

"I doubt that Mary's disapproval extends quite so far as that. She got herself up rather nicely for the last assembly, filling in the neck of the gown to save the morals of Meryton from corruption. She even had a few dances, to your mother's great satisfaction; and her own, if she'd but admit it."

Elizabeth laughed.

"Papa, the picture of Mary hopping about in the dance, giving her partner a little sermon in between times, is so wonderful I would almost wish to be there to see it."

"Almost, but not quite," said Mr. Bennet. "That tells me what I most want to know. You are happy, my Lizzy."

"Papa, how can I tell you how happy I am?"

"Well, well, enough of these effusions," he said, with an irritable little wave of his hand.

"Papa, come to the drawing room, where my little family awaits you. I shall send a note to Kitty. She may come to dinner if she is better."

"What's the matter with the foolish girl?"

"Her old cough is back again. Should she be still unwell tomorrow, we can go to see her, if you like."

"Very well, Lizzy, if you think I must have my dose of folly, even when I am on holiday."

Elizabeth resisted the temptation to defend Kitty, well knowing how fond her father was of his prejudices. To intervene may have brought more scorn upon Kitty than less.

"Come and take refreshment, Papa."

The butler was followed by the footmen into the drawing room.

"You are returned, Setchly," said Elizabeth. "Did you have a pleasant day out?"

"Indeed, I did. I thank you, madam. I visited my sister, as I usually do when in London." He paused to watch the footmen move to the side of the room, before continuing. "On the way, I happened to see the elder Mr. Foxwell with young Mr. Reginald."

"Mr. Reginald Foxwell is in town?" said Darcy. He frowned, thinking it odd considering that the young man had only gone back up to Cambridge a few days before, with the avowed intention of studying with his tutor before the term began.

"Indeed, sir." The servant continued, "Seeing them brought to mind that I had not yet paid my friend Grey the courtesy of a call. He is Mr. Foxwell's butler, madam." Elizabeth smiled on hearing this convenient information. "Therefore, after I left my sister, I thought I might as well call upon him before returning."

"Setchly!" said Mr. Bennet, "You set an example to us all in the nicety of your manners."

"Thank you, sir. I am happy to report that the old gentleman has recovered his good health."

"Mr. Foxwell has been ill, Setchly?" said Darcy.

"Did you not know, sir? Mr. Foxwell was taken ill on the evening you dined there. He stood some time on the landing with Lady Catherine and, when her ladyship departed, he had to be helped up the stairs. My friend says that he looked a dreadful color, but he insisted on going back into the drawing room."

"I am very sorry to hear it. I wonder he did not go to bed," said Elizabeth. Setchly leaned forward and said quietly, "My friend at Mr. Foxwell's house informs me that her ladyship quite shouted at their master in the course of their exchange. It appears that Mr. Reginald's name was mentioned." He straightened and stood solemnly in his place.

"You know something more, Setchly," said Elizabeth.

"You had best continue, now you have started your tale," said Darcy.

"Mr. Reginald returned to London on Saturday night, sir. Yesterday, he went with his father to see Lady Catherine. The coachman says that old Mr. Foxwell got back in the carriage in a very dark mood, but you know Mr. Reginald yourself, sir. He was in as blithe a spirit as ever." He paused, before delivering his climax. "It seems that her ladyship has denied Mr. Reginald the living she has promised him these ten years."

"Good God!" said Darcy, forgetting his manners in expressing his astonishment and shock. "You are quite certain of this, Setchly?"

"Of course, sir, I give no weight to the gossip of lower servants, but I am confident that my friend Mr. Grey would never exaggerate, especially in a matter appertaining to his master."

"Indeed not," said Darcy. "Thank you."

Setchly withdrew.

Darcy said, "It seems incredible that Reginald Foxwell, with no money of his own, should behave in such a manner as to lose so eligible a living, and given freely, too."

"Is he likely to find another such, Mr. Darcy?" asked Mr. Bennet.

"I have no knowledge of one. At this late stage, his father will have to purchase a living for him, as like as not."

"That could set him back by fifteen hundred pounds or more and, even then, he will have to wait for the incumbent to die."

"It was never Reginald Foxwell's inclination to take Holy Orders," said Darcy, thoughtfully. "I clearly recall him begging his father to allow him to go to sea instead of to school."

"Every lad rages for a life of adventure at that age," retorted his father-in-law. "At four and twenty he ought to have the sense to secure an eligible situation, if he can get it."

"It seems that this young man has not," said Elizabeth. "I wonder what could have caused their quarrel, Fitzwilliam. It seems it began on the stairs at Foxwells."

"I have a theory on that subject, but I will ask Foxwell, man to man, for the truth before I share it, even with you, my dear."

Elizabeth went upstairs to change for dinner. As she submitted to Wilkins's ministrations, she could not help but speculate. Could there be a link between her ladyship's disgust at her nephew's marriage and her betrayal of the hopes of Reginald Foxwell's family? Was this a sample of the revenge Lady Catherine had threatened?

Mr. Bennet was dazzled by his daughter's fashionable appearance.

"Do you always get yourself up in such finery for a family dinner, Lizzy?"

"As near as I can, Papa. Tonight I am especially fine in honor of the marchioness. I told you this was the very night of her salon."

"Well, it is a fine way to honor your father, going off by yourself as soon as you have had your dinner."

"Papa, if you want to find us at home, you must make an appointment. Did you order the carriage, Fitzwilliam?"

"Certainly. I shall accompany you, Elizabeth."

"Two footmen, armed to the teeth, cannot be enough protection."

"In a fog such as we see tonight, perhaps not. Certainly, I shall accompany you, and call for you too." He turned to his sister. "Georgiana, will you feel deserted if we leave you for a few hours?"

"I shan't be alone, Fitzwilliam, for Mrs. Annesley is here."

He turned to his father-in-law. "Mr. Bennet, do you wish to come to my club, sir, if you are not too wearied by your journey?"

"I am happy to try this experiment. I hope it may produce as many examples of human folly as I enjoy in Hertfordshire, on those occasions on which I am drawn from my fireside."

Darcy looked taken aback.

"Indeed," his father-in-law added, "more sport should be had on account of the freshness of the subjects."

"Papa!" remonstrated Elizabeth, though the corners of her mouth would twitch.

"Fear not, Elizabeth," he replied. "I shall be as well-behaved a father-in-law as your husband has ever had." Rising, he straightened his waistcoat, bowed to the ladies and declared himself ready for adventure.

At the club, one of the first acquaintances that Darcy encountered was Foxwell. Once Mr. Bennet was safely entertained in a group of older men by the fire, Darcy took Foxwell aside. They sat in one of the many corners, where armchairs were placed conveniently for private conversation.

His friend was to confirm Darcy's suspicions. He would have shielded Darcy from the truth, that his mother's sister now hated him enough to attempt the destruction of his oldest friendship.

"My father spent long hours in preparing his speeches, and Reginald's too, but Reginald demolished all his plans in five minutes. My brother actually told her ladyship that he was disgusted at seeing me placed in so difficult a position. Further, he told her that he would not accept his future comfort 'purchased with my brother's honor,' as he put it. This speech caused Lady Catherine the most grave displeasure, as you may imagine. Such words were spoken as must lead to a permanent breach between them."

"I am sorry, Foxwell, that my relative has brought about this difficulty in your family."

"Reginald is much to blame, for his nature is flawed by this impetuousness." He clapped his hand on Darcy's shoulder. "Do not trouble yourself. Reginald would not have made a good clergyman and he has his way at last. My father has purchased him a commission in the army."

"Where will that lead him? If he hopes to marry money, he will find competition among his brother officers."

"He is full of ambition and confidence." Foxwell laughed. "Reginald had a great part to play, and played it to the full. He was genuinely outraged, Darcy. However, I must say that he has used the situation much to his own advantage."

Darcy nodded. There was silence until Foxwell added, "I should never have denied our friendship, Darcy. I hope that you know that."

Some hours later, coffee was being served in Lady Englebury's drawing room.

"Mr. Darcy, how very punctual you are! The hour is one precisely."

Darcy bowed. "Good evening, your Ladyship." The marchioness looked questioningly at his companion.

"May I present my father-in-law, Mr. Bennet?"

"Indeed you may. Mr. Bennet, I am most interested to make your acquaintance. Please sit down." Dismissed, another visitor had no choice but to vacate the chair next to her ladyship.

Darcy stood beside their chairs and scanned the room for Elizabeth. She was bright and sweet in her favorite yellow, her dark eyes dancing with laughter. Peregrine Whittaker looked up from where he lounged beside her on the sofa and caught Darcy's eye. "She is delicious," his look seemed to say. Darcy bowed stiffly and looked at the gentleman standing before Elizabeth. He was of middling height and thin, gesticulating almost in a foreign way. Dark hair flopped on his brow; dark eyes brooded, even when he laughed. The caricaturists had caught his essence to perfection; at once, Darcy recognized the playwright, Simon Glover. Elizabeth looked up and saw her husband.

Following her gaze, Mr. Whittaker said, "Perhaps you will sing for this gentleman just arrived, since you will not sing for me."

"I think not, Mr. Whittaker, for Mr. Darcy is come to take me home."

Whittaker watched as they made their farewell speeches to the marchioness.

"Back in the cage, little bird," he murmured. Then, to Glover, "I believe she stipulated in the marriage contract that she has four hours of freedom each week. What think you? He undertakes to pay the milliners' bills, and she, by way of exchange, agrees to be the beloved object."

"You know nothing of their lives, Whittaker, although I have not noticed your ignorance of a subject stemming your eloquence." Whittaker smiled and yawned.

"Ah! The merest jest, Glover, and you fly off the handle. For my own part, I have not noticed the triviality of an offense stemming your fury."

The drawing room door closed.

Elizabeth said, "Look at these paintings, Fitzwilliam."

Then to her father, "This place is in Derbyshire, Papa."

The three of them stood before the pictures. Darcy turned towards her and for an instant they were alone in all the world, on the brink of that precipice, as the wind gusted up furiously around them, and he felt assured of her unspoken love. His sulkiness melted away.

A burst of sound from the room behind them broke the spell. She took her father's arm and they left the house.

The next morning, Elizabeth's hope to have her father's company for two weeks at least was dashed. On calling at Bingley's house, they found that Kitty had suffered dreadfully in the night. Mr. Bennet put a rein on his sarcastic humor for once, when he saw how pale and exhausted she looked. At the unwonted kindness of his kiss, Kitty's eyes filled with tears.

"You need your mother, my dear. I shall take you home."

"No, Papa," Kitty whispered hoarsely. "I want to stay in London."

The physician felt differently, however, and recommended the young lady's immediate removal. Kitty made a cry of protest that was at once swallowed up by a coughing fit.

Elizabeth remonstrated with her.

"Dear Kitty, we must act upon the best advice we can obtain. The air in London is too damp for you at this time of year."

"The air is not merely damp, madam, but filthy," replied the physician. "Winter is the worst time, it is true, but we may well find that Miss Bennet is unable to tolerate the air of London in any season."

"No!" croaked the hapless girl.

They journeyed to Hertfordshire as gently as possible, in Darcy's barouche. On their arrival Mrs. Bennet flew into hysterics, feeling sure that Kitty, suddenly the precious pearl among her children, was not long for this world. However, as a few days' rest restored her jewel to health, other feelings appeared.

"I love to have Kitty at home," she confided to her friend Lady Lucas. "I missed her dreadfully." She smiled complacently. "As, indeed, I miss all my girls that are gone away." (She loved to remind other mothers of her success in getting rid of daughters.)

Lady Lucas murmured her sympathy.

"Why did they send Kitty home so hastily? She is very nearly recovered, and now Mr. Bennet will not think of her going back to London. How am I to find a husband for her here? There isn't an eligible bachelor in the county, I'm sure."

Mrs. Bennet's standards of eligibility had risen somewhat since her eldest daughters had married so very well. Of course she could not expect Mary or Kitty to do so well as Elizabeth had done. That sort of good fortune was rare. However, she liked to have Kitty in the home of her wealthy son-in-law, where she pictured her meeting an army of his rich bachelor friends.

Mercifully for Lady Lucas, they were interrupted by her husband, Sir William, who hurried in with the newspaper.

"Mrs. Bennet," he exclaimed, "did you know Mrs. Darcy has conversed with the Regent!"

"I daresay, Sir William," she replied, with an airy nonchalance impossible a year before. "Countess Reerdon presented her at St. James weeks ago."

"This is altogether different!" he said triumphantly, putting the newspaper before her. He pointed out the lines he had circled in the court news, informing the world that, "Accompanied by the Marchioness of Englebury to a musical evening, the fascinating Mrs. Darcy had conversed with the Prince of Wales."

Mrs. Bennet hurried home to tell her consort. He never troubled to read this important section of the newspaper that men of Sir William's sense turned to first.

"Mr. Bennet, Mr. Bennet, listen my dear, such news!" she said, as she burst into the sanctum of his library. Mr. Bennet was his usual vexatious self, refusing to become excited, then capping off with the casual words, "I thought her ladyship seemed too intelligent a woman to waste her time with such nonsense. Lizzy despises the Regent."

"Mr. Bennet! You have met the marchioness? Why did you not tell me all about her?"

Mr. Bennet silently mused. How proud he had felt of his daughter, as she sat calmly accepting the admiration of the extraordinary people gathered about Lady Englebury. She had appeared unperturbed by the analytical gaze of one of the most powerful women in London. She had appreciated the older woman's cleverness, and had happily topped her sharp comments with her own, equally clever, while spoken with a charm no one in that room could have matched. Yet she was barely one-and-twenty!

"Lizzy!" he had cried, when they were in the carriage on the way home from the marchioness's house. "There is none like you, and I feel I must take some of the credit for your mind, as for your splendid spirit."

Mr. Bennet chuckled privately at the memory.

"Now he laughs!" exclaimed his wife. "Mr. Bennet, you provoke me at every turn!"

CHAPTER 10

DARCY'S HOPE THAT HIS COUSIN Henry might benefit from his own falling out of favor with their aunt was seemingly based on an imperfect understanding of the nature of her ladyship's Christian Charity. Lady Catherine expressed her benevolence chiefly by busying herself in the affairs of others. It was inconceivable that she might throw away Anne's fortune on a man who had nothing more than his character to recommend him.

When Darcy married to disoblige her, she had been all but immobilized by rage. Indeed, Elizabeth and her husband both had relatives sunk in gloom. By an interesting coincidence, these relatives lived on properties separated only by a lane. On one side of the lane stood the pleasant little vicarage of Hunsford. On the other lay the extensive estate of Lady Catherine de Bourgh. The living at Hunsford was one of many favors in her gift. On the demise of the old vicar, some eighteen months earlier, chance had drawn her attention to Mr. Collins, and, to his profound gratitude, she had bestowed the position upon him. Mr. Collins was Mr. Bennet's cousin.

On Darcy's marriage, her ladyship's rage had encompassed Mr. Collins and his wife, Charlotte. Collins had committed unpardonable offenses. He had, in the first place, a cousin Elizabeth, whom he invited to stay at the vicarage when Mr. Darcy was visiting his aunt. Then, most seriously, he had made no perceivable attempt to prevent the artful minx from getting her hooks into him. In vain did Mr. Collins protest that he had never imagined such a sacrilege. In vain did Charlotte Collins avow her dismay at the match.

So unpleasant had their life become under her ladyship's displeasure that they had escaped to Hertfordshire to stay with Charlotte's family, hoping that her ladyship's wrath would abate in time.

At last, time had procured an apparent pardon. In December, Lady Catherine had exercised the Christian tolerance for which she was famed, and sent for Mr. Collins to return. His father-in-law lent the couple his carriage that they might lose no speed. They arrived home at dinner time and the vicar prepared himself to pay his respects to his august benefactress.

"My dear Mr. Collins," said Charlotte, "pray take a few moments to rest and eat your dinner. You are much fatigued."

Mr. Collins gulped for breath, even before he began his walk.

"My dear Charlotte, Lady Catherine will take it amiss if I do not attend upon her directly. As for dinner, I could not eat a mouthful!"

Off he had duly trotted. The footman who opened the door to him would not admit him, however. He disdainfully promised to convey Mr. Collins's message to her ladyship, before closing the door in his face.

The loss of her ladyship's favor was grievous indeed, but Mr. Collins could not give up hope. Whenever her carriage went by, he rushed out, as he had always done, and bowed low. On Sundays, he ushered her respectfully out from the church, but instead of bestowing a condescending word, she merely said, "Do not imagine, Mr. Collins, that you can worm your way back into my good graces with such attentions as these. My character is renowned for its firmness. I am impervious to flattery."

"Your Ladyship," he replied, "I am quite aware of my unworthiness. I am humbly grateful to be in your Ladyship's vicinity for a few moments."

She sailed by, followed by her daughter, who was supported in her trials by her waiting woman. Perhaps Miss de Bourgh's face had become rather pinched by a lifetime of whining, and her little body wasted with lack of exercise and peculiar diets. Of course, a happy and friendly expression can make up for such deficiencies. Unfortunately, her face rarely displayed such a look. However, Collins was able to see beyond the mere exterior and his expression indicated that the inner beauty and glory of Miss de Bourgh overwhelmed him with admiration.

He could not understand Darcy's preference for Elizabeth over such a one. Certainly Elizabeth was pretty, vivacious and witty. She had a certain quality that may appeal to some men's baser instincts, but Miss de Bourgh . . . ah! Sublime! She saw his expression and sniffed contemptuously.

Mr. Collins was blessed with a wife of intelligence and good nature, but Charlotte was great with child and somewhat less with patience. It was not to her taste, just then, to toil down the long path to Rosings. She had tired of leaving tinctures to lift the spirits or soothe the throat, calm the mind or vitalize the liver of Miss de Bourgh. Leaving such offerings, day after day, with a supercilious servant, then having the door closed to her was an effort beyond what she felt was worthwhile in obsequiousness.

After they had been home three weeks, she said one evening, "My dear Mr. Collins, I fear there is little to gain from my making a lavender bag for Miss de Bourgh. I am sure she must have plenty such."

"Do you think so, Charlotte? What might you make instead?"

"Nothing at all, my dear."

"My dear Charlotte!" said Mr. Collins, in a voice heavy with moral remonstrance. Suddenly a suspicion crossed his mind, and he said playfully, through his next mouthful of mutton, "I believe you are having a little mood, due to your condition."

Charlotte flinched. "Mr. Collins, pray do not speak with your mouth full."

"I do beg your pardon. I shall endeavor to remember this rule."

"I thank you. I should like to put an idea to you regarding our little difficulty with Lady Catherine."

"Ah!" he said, with a wave of his finger. "Having a man's intelligence and great deal more education than yourself, I am undoubtedly better suited to guide, than be guided by, you."

If Charlotte had any doubts of the value of this man's intelligence, she did not say so. Instead, she said, "I have been meditating upon an idea originally suggested by you, as I tend to do in my spare moments."

"Charlotte, my little love! I see it now. Pray remind me."

"You were saying the other day that our current line of conduct towards Lady Catherine seems to avail us nothing."

"Did I?"

"Yes. How can you have forgotten? You went on to say that her ladyship will very likely come around sooner if we neglect her a little. Bow as her carriage passes, but only if you happen to be out of doors. Usher her from the church, but not to the very gate. I recognized it at once as one of your flashes of inspiration." In her first days of matrimony, Charlotte would not have laid the flattery on with a trowel, but she knew him well by now.

"We shall put my plan into operation at once. Charlotte, I forbid you to visit Rosings again, unless you are expressly invited thither."

"Certainly, Mr. Collins."

Habit dies hard, and Charlotte had to bodily prevent her husband from rushing out at the sound of the de Bourgh equipage. In church a little fainting fit had been necessary to distract him from kissing the hem of Miss de Bourgh's garment, as it were. Within five days, her ladyship actually lowered herself to ask the servants if there had been any message from Mrs. Collins. In a week came an invitation from Rosings, to take tea.

Matters had proceeded very nicely from there, with a tacit agreement never to mention the disgraceful hussy and scapegrace nephew.

In late December Charlotte gave birth to a son. Mr. Collins's elation was clouded when he learned that Charlotte had made up her mind to nurse the child herself. He believed that it was a husband's sacred duty to regularly express his affection in a certain way. He also knew that a suspension of marital favors was called for during the period of feeding at the mother's bosom. It was an indisputable fact that indulgence in such pleasures spoilt the milk. He sought the assistance of the midwife to change his wife's mind.

"Mrs. Biggins, my good lady tells me she has cancelled her arrangements with the wet-nurse."

"A good notion, sir. That Tilly Perkins is nought but a nasty slut."

"Mrs. Biggins, the Good Lord commands one to love one's neighbor as oneself."

"He didna mean loving no slut. When I see them two Jones children, side by side of her own two youngest, well, if they're not of the same father, I ain't got eyes in me head."

"Oh, dear! There are other wet-nurses about, though?"

"There be, sir, but your lady is very set on nursing the babe herself."

"Indeed. Do you not feel that Mrs. Collins is too delicate for this task? I fear greatly that her strength will be undermined."

"Lord, sir, no. Your lady is very sound in her health."

"Mrs. Biggins, a husband sees signs of weakness, and they fill him with fear."

Husbands' fears were not unfamiliar to Mrs. Biggins; among the cottagers, she had been known to give husbands the sharp side of her tongue. This, however, was the vicar.

"My experience tells me you need have no fears for Mrs. Collins, sir."

"You can set my mind at rest?" he asked mournfully.

"I can, sir. What is more, there be no kinder, tolerating lady in all the parish. The babe will take in her goodness with the milk. As for Tilly Perkins—"

"Yes, yes. That will be all."

He thought he might look upon these next months as a succession of Lents. Charlotte did feel it had been his idea not to put the baby out to nurse. He was gratified that she treasured up his little remarks and wished he could recall them. The happiness of the married state had quite muddled his memory.

Things may not have taken this turn had the child been a girl. Mr. Collins had the advantage of being the closest male relation of Mr. Bennet, whose estate at Longbourn was entailed on the male line. Charlotte relied upon having a boy to insure their family inheritance of Longbourn, once Mr. Bennet was sadly out of the way. Now, in the melancholy event of Mr. Collins also passing, she would have a son with whom to live in that comfortable house.

Mr. Collins felt bound, in his position as clergyman, to remonstrate with Tilly Perkins in regard to her reputation. Fortunately, he thought to share this view with his wife first. Charlotte pointed out the oddness of accusing Mrs. Perkins of no more than having two children who looked a little like those of the local attorney. Of course, should the rumor be true, their son had been saved from the contamination of spending his first twelve months at the bosom of a fallen woman.

They named the child William, for his father. They would have added Lewis, in honor of Lady Catherine's late spouse, but the icy stare that this presumption produced caused a hasty change to Richard, for no one in particular.

In the New Year, Lady Catherine had gone up to town to survey the available bachelors. She dispensed invitations to certain suitable persons to visit Rosings in the spring. By the end of the season, she would make her choice. Anne, along with a handsome sum of money, must be engaged to be married, well and soon, to show Darcy how little thought they gave to him.

Her ladyship's encounter with her enemies, on her very first dinner engagement in town, had done nothing to improve her temper. Then came Mr. Reginald Foxwell's base ingratitude in rejecting her patronage and his unspeakable impertinence in implying there could be any dishonor in her ladyship's conduct. This encounter had stirred up a fury that swept aside all her triumph in the coming entertainment of no less than three eligible peers of the realm.

Fortunately, a letter from Elizabeth warned Mrs. Collins of Lady Catherine's misfortunes in London, giving Charlotte and her spouse time to ready themselves. From being determined to use all the scorn in her considerable store of fire to wither the vicar to ash, her ladyship found herself so buoyed up by Mr. Collins's adroit use of the Scriptures, and so soothed by Mrs. Collins's sympathy, that they began to seem her most valued supporters. Before she knew what she was about, Lady Catherine de Bourgh, who frowned upon duality, had offered the vacant living to her favorite. Mr. Collins, of course, totally agreed with her ladyship's general rule on dual livings, but he also totally agreed that there were times when the Lord did place an extra burden upon his most hard-working servants. Of course, he would pay the usual slender salary to a curate for the other parish and continue to reside in the slightly smaller Hunsford vicarage, in order to have the close vicinity and time required to be of service to his benefactress.

If Charlotte sighed a little at this decision, she was comforted by the threefold increase in their income, and the excellent employment prospects for a second son, if one such should make his appearance.

CHAPTER 11

OF ALL GEORGIANA'S RELATIONS, Henry Fitzwilliam was the only one of whom she had never been in awe. From childhood, her heart had nestled in the warm safety of his affection. She believed she loved her brother more than she loved Henry, yet always felt the need to strive for Fitzwilliam's approval. Not so with Henry, dear Henry, whose affection never altered, whose face never froze with even a moment's disapproval.

In the last year or so, however, something had changed between them. He cared for her still, she knew, but, in some sense she could not define, he had withdrawn himself a little.

He had come to Brougham Square only once since they arrived in London, and that was merely a brief wedding visit. Now he had come again at last, and they sat together in the coziness of her own sitting room. The firelight danced on the deep pink of the curtains and upholstery, reflecting warmth around them.

"You have neglected us most sorrowfully, Henry," she said. "It is almost three weeks since you last called."

"I have thought of you all constantly, of course. I trust you received my notes."

"Yes, and I thank you for them."

His eyes fixed on a framed drawing upon her table.

"Is this picture of your execution, Georgiana? Let me see it." He picked up the crayon sketch of Elizabeth.

"It is not very good, but I love my sister too well to discard it."

"Discard it! You shall do no such thing! What think you, Mrs. Annesley?" He turned to his cousin's companion, seated quietly by the window.

"I think it very like its subject, sir."

Henry looked once more at the picture.

"Your skill improves constantly, Cousin."

She looked as though she took no pleasure in the praise.

She reached out and took back the portrait, and returned it to its place.

"You must excuse my absence, Georgiana," he said. "My position, at present, is exceedingly awkward."

"You are staying with Lady Catherine, still?"

"Yes. My father has ordered me to attend upon her most assiduously. He fell short of forbidding me from calling here, but bids me pay every attention to her ladyship's desires."

"Is the earl very angry with us, Henry?'

"Not with you, dear girl! Even Lady Catherine falls short of blaming you for her woes. She has expressed a desire to rescue you from contamination and bring you to live with her."

Georgiana paled. "Henry, please do not try to make me go."

He laughed and took her hands in his. "You are perfectly safe. Can you imagine your brother giving you up to her?"

"Of course, he would never betray me," she declared.

"How does your brother fare in the matrimonial state? Does all go well?"

"Fitzwilliam is so very happy, Henry. Elizabeth is worth more than he has sacrificed."

"Certainly, she is," he said, quietly.

The sound of the fire crackling filled the silence.

Though Georgiana tried, she could feel but little compassion for him. He was jealous now, as he had been ever since he heard of the betrothal. She felt a hot spurt of anger. She sat gazing into her lap, and felt the slow trickle of a tear slide down her cheek and fall onto her hand.

"Sweet little cousin, do not weep for me. I shall recover. People always do, you know."

"Do they, Henry?"

"Great heavens, yes! Younger sons are especially immune to despair—unless the lady concerned is very well endowed with government bonds. They feel keen regret then, I assure you."

She laughed, then jumped up, when the door opened.

"Oh, Elizabeth, Fitzwilliam, see who is come!"

They brought the breath of the outdoors with them.

"Welcome, Cousin," said Darcy, crossing the room to the colonel. "We do not see enough of you."

"You have all been in my thoughts, but I've been kept as busy as a bee. Tomorrow I must return to my regiment. I come to take my leave of you."

"You are to be gone no sooner than you arrive, Colonel," said Elizabeth. "Will you not stay and dine with us? You will be very welcome."

"I should dearly love to do so, but I fear my aunt would not be happy."

"Would she deny you the opportunity to meet Lady Englebury?"

"I fear that your power to extend such a favor to me would rub salt in Lady Catherine's wounds. Only yesterday she was declaring that she is comforted by the knowledge that the marchioness will never honor you with a visit. Recent events have heightened her sensitivity to insult."

"Do you mean her sensitivity to others doing as they please, which she perceives as insult?" said Darcy.

Colonel Fitzwilliam smiled ruefully.

"My father has commanded me to give her ladyship what assistance I can to ameliorate her present suffering."

"In what manner does the earl anticipate this attention will be rewarded?" said Darcy.

The colonel laughed. "I have reminded my father that the purpose of her ladyship's visit to London is to arrange a match for our cousin, Anne. He, however, follows his own counsel."

"How is his lordship?" asked Elizabeth.

"He is very well, I thank you. I am charged with a message for you, Darcy, and I hope you will be pleased. The earl says that he regrets the hasty wording of the letter he sent you before your marriage, and hopes it did not offend." Henry's smile faded as his cousin tersely replied, "The earl exhibits an excessive misjudgment of my character, if he expresses any doubts on that score," said

Darcy. "Indeed, his letter did offend. Had he made his views public, I should have called him out, despite his age."

"Fitzwilliam, please! You are speaking to his son and your own good friend," said Elizabeth.

"Forgive me, Cousin," mumbled Darcy.

Henry chose not to take offense. "You know my father's choleric nature, by now. He says he is sorry and that is, in itself, highly unusual."

Elizabeth laughed to herself. She could not help wondering how widespread this family failing might be.

"What has brought about this surprising state of remorse, Colonel?" she said.

The colonel smiled. "My father manifests a strong curiosity to see Mrs. Darcy, now that she has been taken up by Lady Englebury."

"'Taken up by Lady Englebury!' That makes me sound like a lap dog," Elizabeth exclaimed. "Perhaps I am a little like one. I feel an urge at times to suppress a saucy remark, like a naughty dog that will not do its tricks for the visitors." Her hearers laughed.

Henry added, "My father waits only upon his sister's pleasure, before desiring to make your acquaintance."

"I shall languish away from his recognition for a very long time indeed, if your father waits for Lady Catherine to forgive me," said Elizabeth.

"The earl does not wait for that miracle," replied Henry. "He waits to see how Lady Catherine ties up her fortune when a certain event takes place."

"I see!" cried Elizabeth. "Your neglect of us is quite forgiven, for it was all in a good cause."

Henry bowed, his manner as light-hearted as her own.

Elizabeth continued, "Lady Catherine does not share your father's faith in the marchioness's judgment?"

"She has faith, alas, only in her own."

"Which is as well," put in Darcy, "for I never intend communicating with her again."

"Oh, my dear." Elizabeth put her hand on his arm.

"I shall not vary in my determination, Elizabeth. Her ladyship's behavior was unpardonable." He turned to his sister.

"I have not been besieged by your complaints, Georgiana. Do you not miss your aunt's tender solicitude?"

"I'm sure it is ungrateful of me, Fitzwilliam, that I do not miss her. I was always a little frightened of her, you see."

"Why only a little frightened?" asked the colonel.

Darcy said, "When Elizabeth first came face to face with Lady Catherine, she did not tremble; but in our defense, I must point out that she was permitted to reach the safety of adulthood before the first awful confrontation took place."

"Fitzwilliam, I fear you will say something you may later regret," she said.

"I can assure you that I have, and will have, no regrets whatsoever in regard to my conduct towards Lady Catherine."

Lord Maddersfield had been disgusted to see his nephew throw himself away on a penniless young woman with such appalling connections. Now her friendship with a marchioness of vast influence at court promised future benefits to the family.

Over dinner the evening before, the earl had said to Henry, "My boy, you shall see that Mrs. Darcy has barely begun to harvest the rewards of the marchioness's regard. I doubt not that, if she plays her cards well, she will live to see her husband with a title."

"I think the lady would scorn to employ such cunning, sir, and Darcy, too, would scruple to accept honors purchased with his wife's flattery," Henry had replied.

"Highty-tighty!" retorted his father. "Every man has his price. People soon forget whence came a title once you have it."

Henry knew well the futility of continuing the argument. He was gratified that his father was softening in his view of Darcy's marriage. He felt that his aunt may soon find herself alone in her condemnation. Poor Lady Catherine! He did feel sorry for her. His aunt had questioned him closely in regard to his visit to Brougham

Place, and he made as much as he could of Georgiana's supervision and attainments.

"You have found no sign of contamination then from that woman?"

This stung him but he simply replied, "I believe we may always have confidence in Georgiana's propriety."

Her ladyship grunted. "That creature, who is in my daughter's rightful place, may have been received in Park Lane, but the marchioness will never honor such a nobody by condescending to visit her in return."

Of course, that very evening was the first occasion on which Elizabeth was to receive her influential new friend at dinner, although Henry forbore to mention this event to Lady Catherine.

Elizabeth and Darcy stood by the drawing room door, receiving the last of their guests. At one end of a settee Lady Reerdon sat, consummate grace and refinement. At the other was the marchioness.

The countess laid her hand on the space between them.

"I find Mrs. Darcy most charming, very sweet. I grow quite fond of her," she said.

"Sweet? You find her sweet!" barked the marchioness.

"Certainly. She will be wonderfully good for Darcy."

"I don't care a fig for Darcy. One only hopes he improves upon acquaintance."

"I imagine you do not speak thus to his wife," said the countess.

"Ha! Ha! I would soon be sent packing. That is her sweetness for you. I hear she cut Sir Graham Eston in Bond Street the other day. I wish I had seen it, for I loathe the man."

"Mrs. Darcy cut him? How so?"

"It seems he had the effrontery to approach her as she walked to the bookshop."

"Sir Graham accosted her in a public street, without her addressing him first? That was ungentlemanlike of him! What motive could he have had?"

"My nephew Whittaker tells me that Eston refused, to her face, to be introduced to her at your ball. She had only just entered the room. Perry was most annoyed with him."

Lady Reerdon smiled inwardly at the incongruity of annoyance, indeed, any emotion, in the languid Peregrine Whittaker. Aloud, she said, "Sir Graham must feel very sorry for his neglect of Mrs. Darcy, now that she is making so many friends."

"That can be the only motive for him seeking her acquaintance now." The marchioness chuckled and continued, "I hear that he called her name, and when she did not look at him, he hurried after her and began some explanation of himself. She said, 'Sir, I have not the honor of your acquaintance.' Half of Bond Street heard her, and there was a deal of laughter, I understand."

"Then I feel sorry for him, although he deserved his punishment," said the countess.

"I daresay his standards of decorum have suffered dreadfully in the ten years he has spent in the wilds of the Americas. How came he to be at your hop?"

"I feel Sir Graham ought to be given some chance in society, Marchioness," said Lady Reerdon. "That scandal was long ago and he has cooled his heels abroad for such a long time. He shot poor Houghton, but what else could he do? Houghton all but accused him of drowning Lady Eston."

The marchioness frowned. "The girl was Houghton's sister, and drowned herself after three weeks of marriage; she was but sixteen."

"I am sure Lady Eston's death was an accident, as he says. Nevertheless, I'd not have asked him, had not Frederick done so before I had a chance to warn him. Frederick was a schoolboy at the time of the duel and any details he learned then he has since forgotten. Darcy was cross to see Sir Graham at the ball."

"Oh?"

"Darcy was Houghton's second, you know. Poor boy, he saw his friend shot dead before his eyes. The unfortunate Mrs. Houghton lost two children in such violent ways. Houghton's brother succeeded to the estate. So long ago, but time will procure no pardon for his lordship in the eyes of all the Houghtons' intimates."

"Long ago enough for scores of fond parents to be eager to throw their daughters in his path," said Lady Englebury.

"He is highly eligible, a baronet with an excellent estate."

"What comfort are riches for a woman married to a bully?"

"What, indeed?" agreed Lady Reerdon. "But we know not that he is so."

"How long must we wait until women have the protection of the law and the compassion of society when they must live separately from their husbands?" said the marchioness.

Lady Reerdon looked startled. "Forever, I should think."

Her companion looked around the room.

"Ah, there is my niece, just arrived."

Lady Reerdon's mild gaze followed her friend's across the room to the door. Amelia's little gloved hands held both of Elizabeth's, while she leaned forward confidentially. They both laughed, although Mrs. Courtney had but offered an apology for their tardiness, which she attempted to blame upon her husband, who stood, gravely correct, at her side.

The role of host brought out a quality of kindness not always seen in Darcy. He was welcoming, almost genial, and responded to Amelia's intimate smile with courtly kindness. "He enjoys looking after people," thought the marchioness. "Amelia's little tricks are quite wasted." Aloud, she said to the countess, "I daresay Mr. Darcy could not flirt if his life depended upon it."

"I am sure you are correct. How very charming Mrs. Courtney is."

The marchioness went into dinner on Darcy's arm and, for the duration of the first course, had the longest conversation she had ever had with him. She conceded to herself that his intelligence equalled his wife's. He had obviously taken the fullest advantage of his much superior education. He even showed a certain dry wit. Given the worldly advantages he had bestowed upon Elizabeth, she felt that he was perhaps worthy of his bride, but not, alas, of a great deal of interest to herself.

Her ladyship looked up the long table to where Elizabeth sat.

She was deep in conversation with Lord Reerdon. She laughed, and her eyes sparkled in the candlelight. "How has the girl managed to draw wit from Reerdon?" she thought.

His lordship had just recounted a joke told by a new acquaintance of his, one Colonel Fitzwilliam.

"I was most impressed with the colonel," he said. "A very interesting and gentlemanlike man."

"He is indeed!" said Elizabeth.

"You are acquainted with him?" cried his lordship. He winced at a sudden memory.

"Are you quite well, my lord?" said Elizabeth.

"Yes, indeed, I am. Thank you." He had merely recalled his mother's instruction that he not mention his meeting with the colonel, but it was too late. He went on, "Of course you have made the colonel's acquaintance. We even talked about you."

"Now you are frightening me, sir."

Lord Reerdon laughed. "There is no need for fear. Our conversation was highly flattering to yourself. You met the colonel in Kent, I believe."

"Yes, I did. The colonel was staying with his aunt, Lady Catherine de Bourgh, at her ladyship's estate, Rosings Park. I was staying with my cousin Mr. Collins, who is the vicar of that parish."

"Did you happen to visit Rosings, by any chance?" he asked.

"Many times."

"What is it like?" he asked, with forced casualness.

"I liked the grounds very much. There are some beautiful walks to be had."

"And the house? How would you describe it?"

"The house at Rosings is modern and very pleasing, my lord." Elizabeth would make him specify.

"Is it very . . . large?"

"Suffice it to say that Mr. Collins pointed out to me how very numerous are the windows."

He laughed. "That is exactly what her ladyship said. She is very proud of her windows."

She looked all puzzlement. "Can you mean Lady Catherine de Bourgh?"

"Yes," he said. "I met her when I went to see Mr. Darcy's cousin. At least, he was there, at her ladyship's house." He involuntarily glanced down the table towards his mother. "If I know you too long, you will learn all my secrets."

She leaned forward. He thought her utterly enchanting as she said softly, "I never tell." He laughed again, and she laughed with him.

After dinner Elizabeth was prevailed upon to sing. The continued popularity of her singing, among the accomplished ladies in her new circle, surprised her. Certainly her performance was improving under the tutelage of an expert master, but it was still essentially the loveliness of her voice and the artlessness of her manner that charmed her audience.

The marchioness asked her to come one morning to sing for her nephew. Whittaker fancied himself a composer and would much like to hear her. Darcy looked quickly at Elizabeth, who smiled an unfathomable smile.

"Do say you will go, Mrs. Darcy," said Mrs. Courtney. "I shall accompany you, if you like."

Elizabeth continued to feel a disinclination for the society of the Whittakers, despite the brittle wit of their conversation. She had returned their visit with a brief call. She could not avoid them, as they were received almost everywhere and were firm favorites with their aunt. It seemed churlish to refuse.

For all Elizabeth's proud rejection of the notion of Lady Englebury's usefulness, she was gratified that it might lead to a healing of the breach with so important a relation as the Earl of Maddersfield.

As she slipped into bed that night, she said, "How right you were in your assessment of the power of Lady Englebury's notice. I give you warning, however, that being so often right is unpardonable in a husband."

He cupped her face in his palms and let his fingers wander in her hair, as he said, "Almost from the very beginning of our acquaintance, I informed you of how studiously I form my opinions. Did you not take warning from that?"

"Indeed, I did not."

She slid down beneath the covers. "Now I am in your power."

"Are you?" he said. In the wavering light of the candle, he watched the movement of her mouth as she said, "That is for you to discover."

"How did you do it?" Darcy asked her. "I rode into the battlefield, sword drawn ready to defend you, and you slew the archenemy with a word and enslaved her followers with a look."

"I hope you do not call the marchioness the archenemy. I cannot imagine you mean that I have conquered your aunt."

"Mine is a metaphorical archenemy, the illiberality and cruelty of the Ton."

"Did you truly feel that you may have to defend me?"

"When we were first in London, very much so." He raised a long curl to his lips.

"Pray do not imagine that I doubted your reception among those I count as friends. However, I was aware of the prejudices of some among my acquaintances and prepared to cast off any who offended."

"Really? At first, I felt a little nervousness, but not fear. Since childhood, I cannot recollect feeling real fear of another person."

"Your courage was one of the first things I admired in you."

She turned her face from the light of the candle.

"Although I never felt afraid . . ." she began.

He wrapped her in his arms. "Well?"

"Well, what?" she laughed.

"Although you never felt afraid—what follows?"

"It is well for you that my papa has enjoyed such good health."

"This is a change of subject."

"Is it? If my father had died before any of his daughters had married, we should never have met. I would be living in a pinched way in a cottage with Mama and all my sisters. Bingley's sisters might have heard of our plight and sent us some of their old gowns."

"They would have enjoyed that, I should think," he laughed.

"So they ought." She raised herself onto one elbow. "Virtue should have earthly as well as heavenly rewards." She blew out the candle.

"Is it your design to bestow upon me an earthly reward, madam?"

She laughed softly in the darkness.

CHAPTER 12

LADY CATHERINE MADE ARRANGEMENTS TO receive various guests in the spring, and went home to Kent. Colonel Fitzwilliam returned to his regiment. Kitty Bennet languished in Hertfordshire, vainly importuning her papa, at every turn, for permission to return to London.

Their absence did nothing to dampen Elizabeth's pleasure in her first London season.

She took great delight in her opportunities to be with her sister Jane, now Mrs. Bingley. Bingley's friendship with Darcy insured that there was pleasure for all in their frequent meetings. She also enjoyed the society of the Foxwells and their circle, albeit that it was diminished by the loss of Lady Catherine's notice.

By March, it became clear to all of fashionable London that Mrs. Fitzwilliam Darcy was firmly established in the esteem of the Marchioness of Englebury. If one or two of Darcy's former acquaintances had been somewhat cold when first introduced to Elizabeth, she knew nothing of it. Darcy suspected his aunt's influence and dismissed them from his thoughts. Elizabeth's success coincided with a change of attitude in some of those bigots. Their overtures were met with Darcy's well-known frigid politeness.

Elizabeth had learned long ago to employ her wits to distance herself from the powerless position life thrust on her at birth. Ladies who had been prepared to be kind to the provincial girl to whom Darcy had so inexplicably lost his heart (and sense), found their condescension not required. She was sought after—not seeking others—initially for her success with the marchioness, but later equally for her charm and wit. Yet one could not say whether others would have valued these assets had she not been so fortunate as to gain the esteem of Lady Englebury.

Her ladyship's circle inevitably became a part of their lives. However, Elizabeth knew how little Darcy liked his house filled with strangers, and entertained them there only as frequently as politeness required. Thus those friendships took on a degree of separateness.

Elizabeth went with Mrs. Courtney to visit Miss Whittaker, with the express purpose of singing to both brother and sister. Mr. Whittaker declared himself inspired by the experience of hearing her. His eyelids barely open, he gestured elegantly towards his sister.

"Beloved Bella, my spirits require support! I am overpowered by sensation."

Arabella rang for tea.

Elizabeth said, with that sweetness that softened the edges of her barbs, "I shall, on future occasions, be more careful of the sensibilities of my audience," she said.

Miss Whittaker smiled her slow, knowing smile and carried the conversation forward, without reference to her afflicted relative.

"I found your performance delightful, Mrs. Darcy. I do hope I shall have further opportunities to hear you."

"You are very kind, Miss Whittaker. I do not deserve the kindness of my hearers, as I have so rarely taken the trouble of practicing."

"Pray do not become too perfect. The charm of your performance lies in your naturalness."

They continued to talk of music, while the gentleman maintained an artistic silence. Elizabeth asked Miss Whittaker to play for her.

"No, Arabella!" cried her brother, falling back on the settee. "I hear a plaintive cry; my muse calls. You must not interrupt my suffering with the pleasure produced by your tinkling fingers."

"You really are ghastly, Peregrine," said his sister.

"Am I, Sister?" he asked, unperturbed. He turned to Elizabeth. "You shall be my muse. You recollect that poor Glover has written the words for two songs for his next comedy?"

"Why poor Glover? There can be few playwrights who enjoy such popularity as his, and at a young age."

"I acknowledge that he can write a tolerable play, in the comic line, but he is totally devoid of musical talent. From you, madam, I have received the inspiration for a line of melody, enabling him to turn his latest poems into song. I shall have to rework his lines a little to make them fit."

"Mrs. Darcy can have no interest in your inspirations, Peregrine," said Amelia.

"Amelia, dearest, you cut me to the quick," he said, stifling a yawn. He leaned back, eyes closed, one hand beating a slow rhythm in the air. Elizabeth could not but smile, and stored up her impressions for when she next wrote to her father.

In Elizabeth's mail, at breakfast one morning, came the result of Whittaker's inspiration: two songs, dedicated to her, and called "Songs of the Birds."

"His impertinence is beyond belief," she murmured. In glancing at the lyrics, her eyes fell on the phrase, "My wings are broke against these bars," among others tending along the theme of the caged bird, and she whitened in anger.

"What is wrong, Elizabeth?" asked Darcy.

"Mr. Whittaker has sent me some songs, composed with help from Mr. Glover, and he is impertinent enough to dedicate them to me."

"Is it your desire that I attend to this matter, my dear?"

She scarcely hesitated to say, "Pray do." As she handed them to the footman to give to him, she added, "They really are not worth a glance, Fitzwilliam."

"I shall rely upon your taste and not waste my time."

She dismissed the matter from her mind.

That afternoon, Mr. Whittaker picked up the packet as he came into his house. He went to show it to his sister, who was lying on a settee in her sitting room.

"Look at this note, Bella, written in an ominously masculine hand. How horridly neatly the man writes. I don't believe he has a soul."

"Perry, dear, not everyone can boast your poetical scrawl. The ability to produce a legible hand does not of necessity place one on the level of the beasts."

"Hear it, Arabella, then speak," replied her brother.

"Sir,

I enclose your songs. I am sorry for your wasted effort, as Mrs. Darcy declines to receive them.

F. Darcy"

"What a charming little epistle. I believe he rather likes me."

"I would differ from you on this occasion, Peregrine."

Whittaker draped himself elegantly across the back of her settee. "Think you that she even saw my songs?" he asked.

"I imagine she did. This is one campaign I feel you must abandon, dear Brother."

"I can hardly bear to give up such a challenge."

She reached up and touched his face, and said, "She is much too clever to flirt with you, dearest."

"Come, Bella! I need her cleverness. It is only clever women who appreciate me!"

"Perhaps she is in love with her husband."

"With Darcy?" Perfume wafted in the air as he waved his handkerchief. "What a disgusting notion!"

Arabella gave her brother a long cool look.

"Take care you do not fall in love with her, Perry."

"If I but could, dear Bella, the endless tedium of existence would be in hiatus for a time."

"Content yourself with gazing with longing upon her portrait, for which the lady is sitting, perhaps even as we speak. Our aunt has plans to see the likeness exhibited at the Academy and all London agog."

"Arabella, you would not have your brother stand amongst all the world and his wife! Imagine my suffering. I must confine my adoring glances to the original."

The portrait was, in fact, completed. The marchioness visited her favorite with the express purpose of viewing the painting. Her attention was arrested the moment she entered the hall at Brougham Place.

"This is just such a success as I predicted," she said.

"Indeed, it is," said Darcy. "I am very grateful to your Ladyship for your recommendation of an artist I had not considered. The painter has captured my wife's spirit."

"Exactly. There is playful intelligence in the manner in which she looks over the edge of the book, with that smile."

"I shall remember those words, Lady Englebury," said Elizabeth. "How often should I look over the top of my book, think you? Is every five minutes excessive?"

"Ha! Ha! Once will serve for always, for this picture will make a decided impression at the Portrait Exhibition."

Darcy was taken aback. "I had not thought to enter Mrs. Darcy's portrait in the exhibition," he said. "It will leave London with us, and hang in the gallery at Pemberley."

"Your lady will not be on display in person!" she replied. "It is my wish to promote both sitter and painter."

"Madam," he said, "I am most reluctant to deny you, after your kindness to Mrs. Darcy, but I feel an abhorrence of the very notion."

"Mrs. Darcy, pray add your opinion," said the marchioness.

"That yellow silk is my favorite, Lady Englebury. How shall I ever wear it again, if half of London gazes upon it?" she said, with a laugh.

When the Darcys attended the exhibition, Elizabeth felt her husband was vindicated. The walls of the long gallery were plastered from top to bottom with the latest portraits and the floor equally crammed with visitors. Small children and even a dog or two darted about beneath the elbows of the spectators, many of whom aimed their eyeglasses upon the crowd, seemingly more intent upon locating their friends than on looking at the pictures. Were it not for her urgent desire to see Jane's portrait hanging there, Elizabeth would have found the crowd too insufferable to be endured.

At last, greeting some acquaintances and avoiding others, they managed to move through the press of people to the far wall, where they stood looking at the portrait of Jane, whose loveliness was a work of art in itself. Jane, pictured in an elegant white gown with green ornaments, radiated virtue as well as beauty. Elizabeth could have wept with pride in being her sister.

Then she caught a whispered comment on the sitter's figure, an appreciative comment, but spoken in such a tone that Jane may have been nothing more than a horse. She turned her head towards Darcy, but did not raise her eyes. He squeezed the hand lying on his arm, and they went away.

How glad she was the marchioness had not persuaded her husband to enter her portrait. Already she was finding that the marchioness's view of the world did not always quite coincide with her own. Despite her enjoyment of Lady Englebury's society and the value of her influence, Elizabeth was determined to employ her own judgment on matters concerning herself and her family.

CHAPTER 13

As the season progressed, Elizabeth could not warm to the Whittakers. However, their cousin, Amelia Courtney, was quite another case. Elizabeth had been for some time disillusioned with the notion of intimate friendships. Her dearest friend in Hertfordshire, Charlotte, had disappointed her by marrying Mr. Collins, whom Elizabeth deemed "one of the stupidest men in England." Having thought she knew her friend well, she had been shocked by Charlotte's pragmatic view that marriage was solely a means to insure one's comfort. Elizabeth had sworn to herself that she would not be drawn into so close a friendship again.

Mrs. Courtney was wooing her away from her reticence. She was witty, charming and playful. Elizabeth sensed Darcy's dislike of this friendship. He may have liked to condemn Amelia for flippancy, but she was like Elizabeth in reserving her witticisms for ridiculing folly.

"She flirts!" he said. "Even in her husband's presence."

"Not with universal success," said Elizabeth, looking at him pointedly. Indeed, there had been a change in Amelia's manner towards Darcy.

"I cannot imagine you wish me to behave towards other women in a manner that suggests I am susceptible to their charms."

"No, indeed." In fact, Elizabeth was not sure that he knew how to convey this susceptibility. "Nevertheless, Fitzwilliam, there was a time when you thought I was playing the coquette with you, and I understand you found that enticing."

"That was a different circumstance altogether. The repugnant aspect of flirtation is its essential dishonesty, in the implication of false promises. I believed that the manner in which you addressed me, in Kent, promised a favorable response; and yes, it was, indeed, enticing."

"Do you fear Mrs. Courtney will teach me to flirt, dearest?" Her lips were pursed, almost to a kiss.

"What? I should not permit it."

"Really? Should you not?" The free playfulness of her eyes danced against the stoniness of his.

"I hope you do not wish to try me, Elizabeth."

She did and she did not.

"It is not in my nature to flirt," she said, "but if you understood what it is to be a woman, you might see Mrs. Courtney's behavior as nothing more than seeking the approval of men."

"She should pay more attention to seeking her husband's approval," said Darcy.

"He dotes upon her. Had you not noticed?"

"It seems to me that we have a sufficiency of friends precluding the necessity for you to seek more."

"I do not seek Mrs. Courtney's friendship, she offers it. I like her. As for our friends, they were not of my choosing. They are your friends." Then hastily, at the sight of his expression, "I do not mean that I do not like them, for I do. Yet I have never met with anyone like Mrs. Courtney before."

Elizabeth's eyes lost all their seriousness and came alive with laughter at some elusive absurdity. She was not with him, in spirit, at that moment. She added, "To converse with her is . . . a frolic in words."

He was silent.

"Do you not yearn to frolic, on occasion, Fitzwilliam?"

"I am sorry, indeed, that my character is found to be so deficient in conversational worth," he said.

She laughed. "Mrs. Courtney is not so blessed with good qualities that I desire to have her for my husband!"

He winced. How she caught him out, before he even knew his own feelings!

By the middle of March, Elizabeth was making out her invitations for entertainment at Pemberley in the summer. She brought her list into the library to discuss the contents with her husband. He rose, half bowing, from his seat at the desk, indicated the chair opposite and quickly perused the list. Seeing him frown, she said, "I hope

I have not forgotten anyone you would particularly like to have with us."

"You think to invite Mr. and Mrs. Courtney to Pemberley?"

"Certainly. They are acquainted with many of our other friends."

"I do not wish it."

"Why not, pray?" He walked across to the window, and stood there, looking out.

"I do not feel bound to explain myself." He turned and looked at her, eyes coolly veiled. She drew breath sharply and, pale with anger, said, "Are you saying that you forbid it?"

"I am saying I do not wish it." In his tone, the words were indistinguishable in meaning.

"For no reason but to thwart me, and to deny me pleasure."

She turned to the door.

"Elizabeth, wait."

She turned back and looked at him, her face white marble, dark eyes unfathomable. The set of her mouth almost seemed to border on scorn. He shrugged. She left the room.

He walked up and down. He was an expert in rational thought, in reason unpolluted by emotion. Yet, try as he might, he could not form a satisfactory intellectual appraisal of this situation, in which reason could be reconciled with his feelings.

They were to dine that evening with Lady Reerdon and some of her friends, before going on to the theater. Mr. Glover's new comedy was to open.

Wilkins so enjoyed turning her lady out well. Tonight, though, she found her mistress a little hard to bear with. She was angrily preoccupied and would not take any interest in her dress. She had come from her bath, and stood, eyes smoldering, as Wilkins adjusted her petticoat.

She was rehearsing a little speech, but could not feel satisfied with it. The foundation of her esteem for her husband was his sense of honor, and she believed he had transgressed that now. Wilkins slipped the new gown over her mistress's head. Of the palest silvery silk, it was so cunningly trimmed that Elizabeth was distracted by her own reflection. She sat and watched as Wilkins drew up her thick hair into a smooth roll, then artfully teased out curls around her ears and onto the back of her neck. The maid picked up her mistress's hair ornament, a recent gift from Darcy.

"Not that one, Wilkins."

"Have you changed your mind, madam? I recall you chose the color of the gown for its match with this light-colored silver."

"I did, indeed. Go ahead."

Elizabeth indicated her velvet wrap, and Wilkins held it while she slipped it on.

Wilkins watched as her mistress descended the stairs. Darcy emerged from the drawing room and bowed. She inclined her head.

"You look . . . enchanting," he said, his mood very formal.

"I thank you, sir."

He offered his arm. She took it. They turned and went down to the hall, acknowledged the footmen but slightly, and went out to the carriage.

Wilkins turned as Darcy's valet appeared on the landing, at her side.

"Dear, dear, Mrs. Wilkins, a black humor tonight!" he chuckled.

"I do not understand your meaning, Mr. Benson."

"Do you not? You have not been with your lady long. I have been with my gentleman since he first went up to Cambridge."

Wilkins bridled up. "I know my mistress every bit as well as you know your master, Mr. Benson, even if you have been with him since the days of Cromwell."

"You fear your lady will get the worst of it? Let's put a sixpence on it."

"Mr. Benson! Gamble on our employers' quarrels? Sixpence, indeed! You must have sixpences aplenty." She stalked off upstairs.

"Thruppence?" he called up after her.

The atmosphere in the carriage was thick with silence, but the ride was short. Lady Reerdon's peerless grace smoothed their entrance wonderfully. Elizabeth had not imagined how easy it could be to put anger aside for an evening. The moment his mother turned to her next guests, Lord Reerdon carried Elizabeth off to introduce her to a cousin who was eager to meet her.

At dinner, Elizabeth and Darcy were seated in reasonable proximity, but both were caught up in conversation with others. When the ladies withdrew, Lady Reerdon insisted on Elizabeth sitting by her, and the countess's discreet warmth of manner was very soothing to her young guest's feelings. The gentlemen did not tarry over their port, as the play was to start at ten o'clock, the last presentation of the evening.

The theater was full and noisy with the chatter and movement of so many people. In the pit, the lower orders scanned the gentry in the boxes and gallery, nudging their friends and pointing out the sights to each other. From those lofty seats, opera glasses and glances were discreetly employed for much the same purpose. Every seat in Lady Reerdon's box was taken. They had an excellent vantage point, both to see and be seen.

Opposite, the marchioness was seated in the front of her box. She bowed to Lady Reerdon, then, quite pointedly, to Elizabeth, an honor noted by many. Elizabeth turned to Darcy, with a smile, but she could not tease much of a smile in return. Darcy would be saturnine, but Elizabeth could not quell her excitement for the play to begin.

"This is the first public performance I have seen of a work by one of the marchioness's protégés," she said to the countess.

"Has Mr. Glover discussed the play in your presence?" Lady Reerdon replied, entering into her pleasure.

"Indeed he has. We have heard much about it, and the playwright has read extracts of it at Lady Englebury's Tuesdays."

Several of the countess's friends looked at Elizabeth with wonder. Neither the fortunes nor connections of any of this group had secured for them the privilege Mrs. Darcy had gained without effort. She was unaware, watching for the play to begin. Then thunderous applause broke out as a woman strolled onto the stage, a great bunch of dark curls piled on her head. Mr. Glover would have been highly gratified to obtain Mrs. Jordan for the leading role in his play.

At interval they received a note from the marchioness, desiring Elizabeth and her husband to join her in her box.

"You must go. I insist," said Lady Reerdon. "I shall not be quite bereft of company." After a polite exchange, the Darcys left her.

Frederick leaned forward to whisper, "Mother, Mrs. Darcy would be an ornament to a coronet."

Behind her fan, his mother said, "I like her exceedingly well, Frederick, as you know, but I would not have you marry one such, though she came with a million pounds."

"Why ever not?"

"Hush, my dear. You are dazzled by her wit and charm. Behind them, she possesses an intelligence so keen it would cut you."

"What of Darcy, then? Will it not cut him?"

The countess looked at her son. All the maternal fondness in the world could not blind her to the disparity between Frederick's intelligence and Darcy's.

"If he is cut, it will not be by her wits," she replied. "However, he has met his match, I believe."

His lordship's reply was buried in the applause that met Mrs. Jordan's return to the stage.

The marchioness had seated Elizabeth near her, and Darcy took a seat behind her, where he had a view of his wife's profile. The rest of the play was very humorous; even Darcy was heard to laugh. At the end, Mr. Glover came onto the stage, to the great appreciation of the audience. He had an announcement to make.

"Mrs. Jordan is to pay me the great compliment, and us all the delight, of singing a new song." Enthusiastic applause broke out. "While the words are my own . . ." he bowed in response to another noisy accolade, "I am indebted to an anonymous composer for the music. I have called it 'The Captured Bird.' Together, we dedicate it to 'The Lady with the Dark, Dark Eyes.'"

Elizabeth paled. She felt her husband's scrutiny and glanced over her shoulder, but did not meet his eyes.

Mr. Glover bowed deeply in the direction of the marchioness's box, and her ladyship nodded.

"Wot lady wiv dark eyes, Mr. Glover?" came a call from the pit.

"What lady, sir? That I cannot say." Dark hair flopped in his eyes as he looked down to the crowd.

"The one wot 'e sees in the looking glass," cried another. Guffaws broke out from below, while titters could be heard from the gallery. Glover stood motionless, dismayed. A missile landed by his feet.

"Come off, Mr. Glover," hissed the manager. He stumbled into the darkness of the wings as Mrs. Jordan swept past him.

"She's plump li'l bird," laughed someone. "She'd not be 'ard to catch."

"Hush!"

In no time the little round actress on the stage had two thousand souls mesmerized and weeping for her, as she sang:

"My wings are broke against these bars.

Release me, from my prison,

Set me free."

In the crush of people leaving the theater, Elizabeth and Darcy were forced to spend long minutes standing, together, her hand on his arm, while they waited for an opportunity to descend the stairs. The touch between her hand and his arm seemed almost irksome, as acquaintances pressed around them; the silence between them heavier for the constant necessity of conversation with others. At last they went down.

Darcy got in beside her and sat as motionless as the carriage, which could not move in the crowd of vehicles. All her anger over his refusal to receive her friends at Pemberley came rushing back. It was doubled, nay tripled, by the reaction she sensed in him, to Mr. Glover seemingly dedicating his stupid song to her, though no one else in all of London could have known to whom the buffoon referred. She stifled a yawn. These last several evenings seemed very long.

He glanced at her, barely visible in the dark of the carriage. It occurred to him that he knew as little of her manner at Lady Englebury's as he could see of her now. How did she look, in that salon? What did she say? Did she look open and happy, as she seemed when talking with Lady Englebury in the theater? Or was she brittle, and teasing? What need had she of those people?

"What do these people mean to you, Elizabeth?" he asked. His question was abrupt, even to his own ears.

"Of whom do you speak? Lady Reerdon? Mrs. Foxwell?"

"You are perfectly aware of whom I speak. I refer to the marchioness and all her cronies."

Her answer came, not like a slap, but a cold touch. "Given that you all but ordered me to seek Lady Englebury's regard, I would have thought she meant a good deal to you, at least."

There was certain justice to the facts of her reply, but no justice at all to his feelings.

"I desired you to accept her friendship, certainly. I acknowledge that the marchioness has been of use to you, Elizabeth, to us both."

"Fitzwilliam, perhaps the favor is to be reciprocated. It seems the marchioness wants me to be of use to her, although I cannot imagine in what capacity."

"Be of use to her, by all means. It is for the satellites who dance attendance upon her that I feel the deepest suspicion and disapprobation."

"How am I to have one without the others? The marchioness is very fond of her protégés, although she does not train them to lick her shoes as other titled ladies have been known to do."

"Since I have forfeited my aunt's regard on your account, I see no justification in this attack upon her," he said stiffly.

"I did not name her, although I own that my remark could be construed as a reference. She is a distraction just now." She turned to him in the darkness.

"Who or what is at the core of your disapproval?" Her words knifed through the heaviness.

He thought for a moment.

"I wish to know what it is in your deportment towards Mr. Glover and Mr. Whittaker that gives them license to take the liberties that they have."

"Their liberties have been very minor. Are you accusing me?"

"No. That would be absurd."

"Then what?"

The carriage gave a little jolt forward, then stopped.

Every reply he thought of seemed too preposterous to voice. How could he say that he felt the marchioness sought to take Elizabeth from him?

"I find Glover's behavior abhorrent. Firstly, he sought to link your name with the theater and I am sure Whittaker is his ally in that regard. Secondly, he was so undignified about it in answering that insolence from the pit. He appeared no gentleman and a complete fool."

"'Buffoon' was the word that came to my mind," she said.

"Elizabeth!" He felt for her hands and raised them to his lips. She was perplexed.

"Is this all?" she thought. Aloud, she said, "We can agree that Mr. Glover is a buffoon and Mr. Whittaker is laughable in his own way. I long to see Papa again for I cannot convey the whole impression of Peregrine and Arabella Whittaker by letter."

He laughed, in relief. "If ever a woman was her father's daughter, it is you."

She did not laugh with him. He fell silent, waiting.

"And what of Mrs. Courtney, Fitzwilliam? What is her crime?"

"I have no particular objection to her. I had wanted, assumed, that we would spend the summer free of all those new friends."

"Free of my particular friends, you mean."

"That is one conjectural position, I suppose. Elizabeth, I am withdrawing from my opposition to including Mr. and Mrs. Courtney in our party at Pemberley." She felt too weary to respond. He continued, "I am now assured that my house will not, in future, be filled with Glovers and Whittakers."

The carriage jerked into motion again, and this time, continued a gentle roll into the street.

She yawned.

"I am sorry to have been so tedious."

"I am merely tired, Fitzwilliam, tired to death."

He was silent for a moment, too shocked to speak.

"Elizabeth, are you not well?"

"I long to walk in the fresh air, and to run among the trees."

"Have you tired of London so soon, when the season has yet to reach its zenith?"

"I have enjoyed all this dissipation immensely, but it is enough for now."

Hope leapt up in him. "You would find the air of Derbyshire fresh indeed at this time of year."

"I am not afraid of it. Fitzwilliam, shall we go home to Pemberley?"

"There is nothing that would give me more pleasure. Here we dine alone barely once in ten days."

"We shall experience solitude aplenty in Derbyshire."

"Bingley and his party will be with us in June. Can you pass the time that intervenes, with only Georgiana and your dull husband for company, until then?"

"Yes, indeed!"

If he found this reply a little lacking in flattery, he soon forgot it. She leaned towards him and kissed him, a tiny kiss that pulled at his lip.

In the morning, he said, "We ought take in Hertfordshire and visit your parents before returning home."

He was surprised by her look of dismay. For all her love of her father, her natural affection for her mother was much tempered with embarrassment for her indelicate behavior.

"If neglected, your mother will conclude that I do not permit you to visit her," he said.

"I do see that, of course." She thought for a moment. "If we delay our departure for two weeks, Jane and Bingley will be returning to

115

Netherfield. I am sure we will be welcome to stay with them. I shall call upon Mama every day that we are in the district. She will be content with that."

"If you prefer then, we will stay in London, until the beginning of April."

CHAPTER 14

ELIZABETH CAME DOWN THE STAIRS at Netherfield, and stood in the doorway of the library.

Darcy looked up.

"Should you be out of bed, Elizabeth? You still do not look well."

"I cannot lie down all day—I wish to walk. Will you come with me?"

It was weather that could get Elizabeth skipping, the air cool and soft on her face, leaf buds unfolding on the trees. Yet she walked quite slowly, her arm through his. He thought back and realized it must be a fortnight since she had seemed really well. Was it his imagination that her cheeks had lost fullness? She seemed to suffer an unfamiliar debility. This, with the duskiness beneath her eyes, led him to a sudden thought, so painful that fear was reflected in his expression. He stopped and looked down at her.

"You are not fearful for me?" she asked.

"For a moment, yes, I was."

She dropped his arm and turned towards him.

"Fitzwilliam, dear, I am not ill. Just a little tired. Can you not guess?" Unconsciously she was smoothing the faultless lie of his sleeve, touching the cuff of his shirt. "I am increasing, my dear."

A momentary confusion clouded his countenance. She looked down at her slender figure and said, laughing, "I do not display a great talent for it just yet, but I think you might see some improvement, by and by."

"We are to have a child?"

She looked up at last. His delighted smile, which so became him, suited her more, meant more to her than whoops of joy could have from any other man.

When Elizabeth had not arrived at Longbourn by midday the next day, Mrs. Bennet set off at once for Netherfield, accompanied by

Kitty and Mary. Not for the first time, she looked out of the window with great satisfaction as the carriage entered the drive.

"It is an excellent prospect, and no mistake, girls. One day I hope to see each of you with an establishment equal to this."

"What fun that would be, Mama," cried Kitty and her mother laughed with her. Mary sniffed.

After greeting the gentlemen, they went upstairs with Jane. Mrs. Bennet sailed into Elizabeth's room, Kitty and Mary in her wake.

"Mama," sighed Elizabeth. "How are you? Mary, Kitty."

"Never mind our health! What is this?" said Mrs. Bennet. "You used not to lie abed all morning." Indeed, Elizabeth, who boasted the most robust health of all five daughters, presented a sight unusual to her mother's keen eyes. She was pale, and her slenderness seemed to be wearing to thinness about her face.

"I am very tired, Mama, as I am sure anyone ought to be if they spent the last weeks in such relentless pursuit of pleasure as I have."

"Mr. Darcy seems his normal self." She smiled broadly. "What a delightful dressing gown! Later you must show us all your London fashions."

"Oh, do, Lizzy," begged Kitty.

"I care nothing for such frippery," said Mary. She could not approve of Elizabeth's appearance, in a wrap that was near transparent, all muslin and lace. There almost appeared to be nothing beneath, if one looked closely. Her luxuriant dark curls, instead of being covered, were decorated by a tiny cap. "One scarcely knows where to look!" Mary thought. "How can a gentleman of Mr. Darcy's dignity tolerate seeing his wife in this state?"

"What is this?" Mrs. Bennet's train of thought returned to the business of her visit. She picked up the tea cup from the tray on the bed, and examined the dregs suspiciously.

Elizabeth moved to take it from her.

"It is some concoction of Wilkins's making. She delights in having me prostrate. I tell her she should have been much happier as a nursery maid." Mrs. Bennet determined on a little private conversation with her daughter's maid, and bustled into the dressing room in search of her.

"O, Lizzy, how I should adore to wear something like this," said Kitty, stroking her sister's sleeve.

"That would hardly be appropriate in your situation, Kitty," replied Elizabeth, drawing her arm away.

"I am determined to have such things when I am married."

"I certainly should not," put in Mary. "A wife has a sacred duty to always encourage her husband's thoughts to adhere to a lofty sphere."

"Get the husband first, then tell Lizzy how it's done!" said Kitty. Miss Bennet did not dignify this impudence with an answer.

Meanwhile, Mrs. Bennet had hedged Wilkins about with questions, and by her evasive answers had satisfied herself. Returning, she flapped her handkerchief at her maiden daughters.

"Out! Out you go!" she cried, shooing them out like two puppies, then sat on the bed.

"Lizzy!" she cried. "You are a good, clever girl!" She kissed her soundly. "Married five months and breeding before either of your married sisters!" Elizabeth was all but stifled in a warm embrace. She pulled away.

"Mama, please allow me to breathe."

"Mr. Darcy will be very pleased with you, Lizzy, as I am myself. Ha! 'Breeding,' I cannot hear enough of the word."

"I am very happy to be the cause of this delight, Mama, but I would fain not have my success broadcast, at this early time."

"There is no point in all this secrecy, Lizzy," she declared. "You have no idea of how changed you appear. Many ladies will suspect at once."

"Pray, Mama, do not embarrass me before my husband and Miss Darcy."

Mrs. Bennet turned a high color. "Embarrass you, Lizzy? Why should I embarrass my own child? You always were excessively delicate!"

"I beg pardon, madam, if I have caused you pain."

"You always did disappoint me, Lizzy. I am proud enough of the match you have made, and proud, too, that you are doing your duty in trying to provide your husband with an heir. You might enter my pleasure a little, and not constantly tear my poor nerves to shreds with your superiority."

Elizabeth sighed and set about the invalid's duty of comforting the visitor.

While Mrs. Bennet had received a shock at Elizabeth's words, the nonsense of them was sufficient to buoy up her spirits. She returned to Longbourn in fine form.

Her husband was established in the quiet of his library.

"Mr. Bennet! Mr. Bennet! Such news!" she cried, bursting in at the door. "She is expecting. I knew it as soon as I received that note this morning."

"Who is expecting, Mrs. Bennet, and what does she expect? In your excitement, you do not complete your news."

"Why, Lizzy, of course. She is breeding. Fancy her being the first of the three; I never would have guessed it. Of course, it is very important for her, much more so than for her sisters."

"How so, Mrs. Bennet?"

"You are tiresome, Mr. Bennet. Mr. Darcy must have an heir, so the sooner Lizzy has a son the better. This first must be a son, followed by one or two more, to insure against the loss of the first. Then I shall have no worries on her account."

"Madam," replied her husband, "for how many years did we hope for a son? How many lamentations have I heard on the subject these twenty years? I will hear no talk of grandsons. I will not have my daughter worried on this subject."

"Lizzy worried? It is she who worries me. She was mighty high with me, her own mother! I scarce had opportunity to speak."

"How fortunate for her. Now, if you please, I will have my library to myself."

CHAPTER 15

TWO DAY'S REST, some fresh air and exercise saw Elizabeth much recovered. Their two weeks in Hertfordshire passed with compensations to outweigh the disadvantages.

Anyone who assumed that Darcy's pleasure in his expected parenthood lay solely in the hope of an heir mistook the case. In his, at times, overbearing care of his friends, he had been practicing for fatherhood for years. Elizabeth felt an unfamiliar fragility of spirit as well as body, which Darcy did his best to ameliorate with every kindness. Mrs. Bennet was able, with the authority of her experience, to assure her daughter that her sensibility would not last long. This was a pleasing comfort to Elizabeth, who did not relish the thought of being added permanently to her husband's list of "children."

The early hours in country society were welcome to her. She could not keep her news from Jane, especially as her mother knew, and then, of course, Georgiana could not be left out. Bingley must know, to spare him anxiety. Dear Charles could hardly be more happy if it were he becoming a father.

Elizabeth delighted in the time she could spend with her father. How they laughed over the follies of the world of the Ton. Even poor Lord Reerdon came in for some harmless mockery, but Mr. Whittaker's affected ennui and the foolery of Mr. Glover upon the stage afforded him the most amusement.

"Papa," she bent to whisper close to his ear, "I believe Mr. Darcy was a little jealous of my success with those fine gentlemen." He chuckled.

"Ha! Jealous of a popinjay and a buffoon! What fools love makes of us all! I hope you put his mind at rest, Lizzy."

"I would not have him suffer for a moment."

Mrs. Bennet did not need to spend much time actually with Elizabeth to take pleasure in her visit. She had the satisfaction of seeing her daughter given precedence, at dinners and parties everywhere in the district. She delighted in hearing mention of the names of some of her daughter's new friends, although she had not the patience to hear of the Foxwells and others such. "Tell me about the lords and their ladies, Lizzy!" she cried.

To her mother's disappointment, Elizabeth and Darcy passed up the opportunity to attend the Assembly at Meryton, although the Bingleys happily went along. The local populace whispered sympathetically that poor Mrs. Darcy, always so fond of dancing, must often miss out now, having married such a husband.

On their last evening in Hertfordshire, the Bennets and their friends the Lucases were all invited to dine at Netherfield. Sir William Lucas had been elevated to a knighthood for oratory services to the Crown. He had given up his business and established himself as a gentleman. Lady Lucas was Mrs. Bennet's particular friend.

During the first course, Darcy had the task of entertaining Lady Lucas, and given that lady's self-effacing reticence and his own reserve, not much jollity could be anticipated between them.

Elizabeth had the privilege of Sir William as her dinner partner. He pestered her with questions about her London experiences, eager for information about her friend, the marchioness. (The word "marchioness" was like honey on his tongue.) He was bewildered to find that she had never once been to the Assembly at St. James Court.

"After being presented at His Highness's drawing room by a countess, you would need no further assistance, you know, or I might have come to London myself to introduce you at the Assembly."

Elizabeth smiled. "Thank you for your kindness, Sir William. However, it was not timidity that kept me from the Assembly."

"Ah, Mr. Darcy is not fond of dancing, I recollect. Perhaps you felt disinclined to press him on the subject."

"Sir, I believe I should not have found the necessity to press Mr. Darcy if I earnestly desired to go there. I did not go because we have been so occupied with other dissipations that I welcomed any rare chance to stay at home."

"Indeed, I have heard of some of these entertainments, Mrs. Darcy, not the least, your meeting with the Regent. It was at a private party?"

The word "Regent" caught the attention of the other diners.

"Yes, we are close friends already. We had a long conversation, three or four sentences at least."

"It is a good beginning. Perhaps other opportunities will arise." Little phrases flitted in his mind, such as, "my friend, Mrs. Darcy, a favorite with His Highness, you know . . ."

Elizabeth interrupted his pleasant musings.

"Pray do not wish such trials upon me, Sir William. I had not understood the royal ears to be so delicately attuned. Conversation is not enjoyable when one's every word must be carefully weighed."

Bingley laughed and turned to Darcy and said, "The topic is Elizabeth and the Prince of Wales."

Darcy explained, "Mrs. Darcy made a little joke with His Highness and felt that this was regarded with excessive amazement by the company."

"Lizzy!" expostulated Mrs. Bennet.

"Ha! Ha!" cried Mr. Bennet.

Their fellow diners waited, in various emotional states ranging from the utmost tension in Sir William to obliviousness in the elderly vicar of Meryton, who had nodded off.

Elizabeth said, "I made a comment about a comic song we had heard; the Regent seemed to appreciate it. He said I was to come to the Assembly, and he would give orders to insure I have plenty of partners. He waved his hand vaguely behind him at his waiting lords, one of whom actually got out a notebook. I thanked him for his very great kindness and said, 'However, if I cannot find any for myself, perhaps I don't deserve them.' There was the most horrible silence, for about ten minutes."

"Fifteen seconds perhaps," said Darcy.

"It seemed longer."

"They passed slowly."

"We are led to believe that the royal wits are prodigious, but it took him a good time to begin to laugh. At once sixty people felt it was the funniest remark they had ever heard. I cannot tell you how relieved I felt. I feared they would stand me in the corner." She looked at her husband. "Should you have disowned me if they did?"

"I should have stood there with you," he replied, with his little bow.

"I believe you would."

Sir William's daughter, Maria, spoke up, "Should they have stood you in the corner, Lizzy, I mean Mrs. Darcy? How dreadful!"

On that note, the ladies rose to retire to the drawing room and Elizabeth faltered, and caught hold of the back of her chair.

"Elizabeth?" Darcy was at her side at once. She smiled.

"Might I be permitted to trip?"

Once out of the room, she whispered, "Jane, dear, help me." Jane put her arm around her sister's waist and helped her into the drawing room.

"Lizzy, what is the matter?" said Mrs. Bennet.

"I feel a little faint, Mama."

Cushions were piled onto the end of the sofa, and Mrs. Bennet fussed Elizabeth onto them.

"Kitty! Bring my smelling salts!"

"Here they are, Mama," cried Kitty, putting them beneath her mother's nose.

"Stupid girl!" said her mother. "They are for Lizzy!"

Elizabeth pushed away her sister's hand, and Kitty flounced off to the other side of the room.

"Mama, please do not fuss so," cried Elizabeth. "I am a little tired, that is all. I will go up to my room."

It came again: that pain, a dull ache pushing into her back. Her mother's face filled her view, the eyes searching. Elizabeth turned her face aside.

Across the room, Georgiana sat with Mary. She longed to go to Elizabeth, but she was unsure of her place there.

"You must not move, darling girl," cried Mrs. Bennet. "We have sent for your maid. Is there any pain?"

Elizabeth closed her eyes.

"There is! I know it!"

"Mama, pray do not fuss so. Where is Wilkins?"

"I am here, madam." Wilkins had not been able to get around Mrs. Bennet, as she bent over the sofa.

"What are you standing there for, woman? Do something!" shrieked Mrs. Bennet. Jane put her hand gently on her mother's arm.

"Dearest Mama, please come and sit down. You are agitating your nerves."

"My nerves! What care I for them at this time!" said Mrs. Bennet, quite out of character in her fears.

"Help me upstairs please, Wilkins," said Elizabeth.

"Madam, you must not attempt to walk."

"Wilkins, send for Mr. Darcy." The maid moved towards the door.

"What nonsense is this? What use can he be, dearest child?" said Mrs. Bennet.

"Jane." Elizabeth reached out her hand to her sister. "I want Fitzwilliam."

"Wilkins has sent a footman for him."

"Dear heart, what is the matter?" His presence, his nearness, one hand on hers, the other caressing her hair, all gave her comfort. He gave no sign of the shock he received at her skin nearly as white as her gown.

Her voice was a whisper, "I am afraid."

His mother-in-law leapt from her chair and cried, "Mr. Darcy, there is still hope, but she must not get up." Waving her handkerchief, she attempted to shoo him from the sofa, but he was long impervious to such control.

"Madam, pray sit down, calm yourself. You are causing Elizabeth further alarm."

Mrs. Bennet turned huffily away, flapping her lace.

He bent over the sofa. Elizabeth put her arms around his neck; and he carried her up to her room.

125

He laid her on the bed. Wilkins was close behind him, and followed by the chambermaid. Superfluous, he went out and waited in the corridor.

There Jane found him five minutes later.

She said, "I have persuaded my mother to rest in the drawing room, but she says she will not leave without seeing Elizabeth settled."

"Then you had best prepare a bedroom for her, Jane. Elizabeth will never be settled while her mother has hysterics at her side."

"Mama means well. It is the excess of her affection for her children that makes her so readily excited over us."

He bowed. She looked into his eyes, and saw there a complexity of emotion that she could not entirely fathom. However, she recognized a certain warmth towards herself, saw the utter futility of trying to influence his decision. She touched his arm.

"I hope you will not be too disappointed if . . ."

He shrugged. The door opened and Wilkins held it open for Darcy to come in.

He gestured for Jane to precede him.

"I will come in a moment," she said.

He sat by the bed and held Elizabeth's hand.

"Think only of your own recovery." Her eyes pricked with tears. He kissed them, first one then the other.

There was a knock so soft it must be Jane. Wilkins spoke to her at the door, quite bold enough to keep her out, and Jane quite unassuming enough to let her.

"Is that my sister? Let me see her."

"Lizzy, dearest, our guests are leaving. They all charge me with their kindest wishes. Mama desires to see you."

"I cannot bear it."

"I will tell her then." She hesitated. "What shall I say?"

Darcy stood up. "No task for you, Jane. Allow me to speak to her."

"Mr. Darcy, you could tell her that Elizabeth is . . . almost asleep."

"It would not be the truth."

They watched him out of the room. The sisters looked at each other.

"He will not injure her feelings, Lizzy, do you think?"

"He is almost certain to. He does not do so intentionally. He feels so awkward with her."

He exercised such diplomacy as he possessed, but Mrs. Bennet's insistence upon seeing her child brought forth a flat refusal on his part to allow her to see Elizabeth until the morning. Mrs. Bennet left in high dudgeon, and Mr. Bennet had to bear with her all the way home.

The night wore away and, with it, Elizabeth's hopes. All the care of those dearest to her could not save the tiny scrap of a Darcy.

Even as she awoke, she felt aching pressure against her heart, before she remembered the cause. Darcy was with her as she drank her tea.

"Try not to be too disappointed, my love," he said, in an unconscious echo of Jane. "You are but one and twenty and we have been married less than half a year."

Perhaps this logic ought to have stopped her tears, but they slid out, hotly. He took out his handkerchief and dried them, and those that followed. She sniffed the faint masculine cologne that was part of the smell of him. She put her hand against his cheek. She vaguely thought of what luxury this was, to give way. She thought that even the utmost grief might be bearable with his devotion. She blinked away her tears, unable to voice her feelings. She wiped her eyes, and smiled at her own foolishness.

Knowing how her mother would be fretting, Jane sent a note very early to Longbourn, advising her mother of Elizabeth's disappointment. Mrs. Bennet set off again for Netherfield, with feelings very different from those with which she had come two weeks before.

Miss Bennet accompanied her mother on a visit to Elizabeth. She had arisen early to mark out some passages in the Bible and in two or three volumes of sermons, which she brought along for her sister's comfort and edification.

Mrs. Bennet stayed with Elizabeth long enough to assure her that she would be breeding again in no time and that these common events cannot be helped. It was fortunate, indeed, that Elizabeth had long learned not to take her mother's pronouncements too much to heart; her devoted parent added that it was very likely all Elizabeth's own fault for running about so much. Having dispensed that comfort, she left the room to give Wilkins the benefit of her wisdom. Then Mary began to give her sister the benefit of hers.

Jane was in her sitting room, giving the morning's instructions to her housekeeper, when Wilkins begged leave to interrupt.

"Madam, I wish you would come. My mistress is most upset between the two of them."

"Of whom are you speaking, Wilkins?"

"Begging your pardon, madam, Miss Bennet has upset my mistress ever so, and Mrs. Bennet is very angry with her, Miss Bennet, that is, and is shouting. I know not what to do."

Jane hurried to Elizabeth's room. In the enormous bed, Elizabeth lay back, white as the pillows. Her mother stood at the bedside, hands on hips and very red about the face, as she berated Mary. Jane took her hands and said, "Hush, Mama. All will be well. Mary, please leave the room."

"Why should I, the only member of my family to seek a spiritual interpretation of this event?"

Jane was splendid. "Mary, I insist that you leave the room immediately." Mary closed the door with elaborate care as she left.

Mrs. Bennet collapsed into an armchair, fanning herself.

Jane went to her sister. Elizabeth's eyes were wide and dark with pain. Jane took her hands.

"What has happened now, dearest sister? Let me share your trouble."

Elizabeth's eyes filled with tears.

"Jane!" shrieked their mother. "My nerves are in shreds! Bring my smelling salts. Jane, what can you be thinking of?"

"Here, Mama," she said, fishing out the salts from her mother's reticule.

"Ah!" cried the afflicted lady. "That girl will be the death of me. Of course, no one cares for my feelings."

Jane went to her sister and whispered her promise to be with her very soon. She calmed her mother in the way only she could, and persuaded her to rest in another room.

In the library, the gentlemen were immune to the disturbance. Mr. Bennet was enjoying a quiet hour's conversation with Bingley. Darcy left the window and crossed to the bookshelves, pulled out a book, looked vaguely at the cover and put it back.

"I'm such a pitiful fellow when it comes to getting a library together," Bingley said. "Darcy has quite given up on me."

"Mmm? What was that?" Not waiting for an answer, Darcy shrugged his shoulders and walked back to the window. Outside, the heavy greyness was broken only by a relentless drizzling of rain. He turned and left the room, wandering into the adjoining parlor. Mary had been studiously perusing a volume, but jumped up. Her cheeks had spots of high color and her expression was strange. Bowing without speaking, he left the room, going straight upstairs, giving the girl no more thought.

He found Jane holding a cup to her sister's lips, while Wilkins stood by with lavender water. Jane smiled up at Darcy, yet feared the consequences of his talking to Elizabeth before Mary were got out of the house. Darcy saw the ambivalence in her look. Then he saw some books on the bed and picked one up and opened it at the marker.

"What is the significance of this?"

"Her intentions are good," said Jane.

"Mary?" Jane nodded helplessly.

Jane kissed her sister and relinquished her place to Darcy. Wilkins put down the lavender water and they left the room, softly shutting the door. Darcy picked up the cloth and bathed Elizabeth's face with a gentleness she had never had from her mother's hands.

"Am I a good wife to you, Fitzwilliam?"

"Dearest love, can you doubt it? Has a day gone by in which I have not told you how happy you have made me?"

"I know you are happy, but why is our baby gone? Why did God take it away?"

"Dearest, who can know? These mishaps often occur, do they not?"

"Mary says it is a punishment."

"What? She dares to speak so!"

"She said I am wrong in everything. The way I address you, my whole manner towards you, that I dress to . . . to arouse; even that I use Lady Englebury for ends of my own."

Anger burst up from his gut. That Elizabeth could even listen to such cant showed how laid open she was by her loss. He walked across to the window. He calmed himself, and came back to the bedside.

"Dearest Elizabeth, of all those traits for which I love you, the depth of your integrity and your pride are the keystones. You could not satisfy Mary's ideal unless your spirit were broken, and the woman I love destroyed."

"Indeed, I cannot be other than I am."

"Now this is a better spirit. Do you not remember your claim that your courage rises with every attempt to intimidate you? When you said that at Rosings, I was vain enough to think you were flirting with me. If you had married me then, we would have had some wonderful battles while you taught me that you had spoken the absolute truth."

"It is ironic that Mary is so dissatisfied with me, given that I have more respect for you than for any man alive."

"I shall endeavor to deserve it."

She closed her eyes and sank against the pillows.

"Can you try . . ." she said.

"Yes, Elizabeth. What do you wish of me?"

She was too tired to think.

"I will do everything in my power for you, as you know."

The soporific scent of lavender and the mild narcotic her maid had administered were taking their effect. He said no more, but stayed by her side until she was deeply asleep.

When Mrs. Bennet had recovered sufficiently to come downstairs, she scarcely noticed that Georgiana was in the parlor. She shut the door firmly and glared at her daughter.

"I am not going to mention your foolish and impertinent behavior, Mary, until we are at home," she said. "I have told Jane I will say nothing, and I shall be as good as my word. I am very angry indeed."

Georgiana made an unconscious little backwards movement, but Mary gave a huffy little shrug.

"How dare you shrug at me, miss? Shrug at me again and I shall slap your face. You will drive me to my death with your nonsense. What could you know, girl, of matters between husband and wife?"

"Mama," whispered Jane.

"What is it, Jane? Oh, I have nothing to say on the subject, but what Elizabeth's husband will say I know not what to think."

She was spared the necessity for thought, for Darcy strode in. Georgiana started up quickly. Darcy turned to Jane and spoke with obvious self-constraint.

"Jane, will you kindly take care of my sister for a few minutes?" Jane inclined her head and the two went out.

He turned to Mrs. Bennet. "Madam," he said, "I wish to speak to Mary about an action of hers that has greatly displeased me."

"Say what you like, sir. Mary cannot hear any words harsher than she will have at home, I assure you."

Darcy turned back to Mary. Her hands shook as she looked up at him, and she put them behind her.

"You committed a grave error, Miss Bennet, when you dared to speak to my wife as you have this morning."

Mary pressed her lips together, tilted up her chin, and answered, "She is my sister and it was done for her own good."

"For her own good? Are you sure you had even a sole thought for her good? You waited until she was alone, knowing her to be defenseless with disappointment and exhaustion, before you prosecuted her with this mean and ignorant attack."

She quailed, but her mouth was stubbornly set. "It was not ignorant! It is based on Holy Writ."

"You call this Holy Writ?" He snatched up a pamphlet, and Mary flinched at his sudden movement. "Even the evangelicals would call this cant!" In frustration, he tossed it onto the floor. Mary made a move towards retrieving it, and then fell back.

He picked up the Bible. "Show me where in this book anyone, let alone you, is authorized to speak in the name of God, and to tell another that their suffering is His punishment?" In his anger, Darcy almost consigned the Holy Book after the first. He held it for a few confused seconds, then put it down, and turned again to Mary.

"Do not again interfere between me and mine," he said.

He left the room.

He was in the hall, putting on his greatcoat, when Bingley came after him.

"Darcy, don't leave us like this."

"If I remain in that room another moment with Mary, I shall shake her."

"Oh, dear, I know not exactly what has occurred but come and talk with me. You need not see Mary again." He smiled hopefully.

"Bingley, Elizabeth is asleep. Will you ask Jane to keep that wretched tribe out of her room? I must have solitude."

"What of your sister? Perhaps she would like to see Elizabeth."

"Georgiana? What can she do? She will be sick with worry if she sees Elizabeth."

"She is no longer a child, Darcy."

"What?" He did not wait for Bingley to elucidate that strange remark. Moments later he was on his horse and galloping away into the park, in the rain.

Atop a small hill he reined in and turned to look back, brooding, at the house. Inside, Elizabeth was sleeping, in the care of her maid and Jane. He heartily wished the rest of her relations to the other side of the world. He was learning to appreciate the caustic edges of Mr. Bennet's humor, but why had this highly intelligent man never exerted himself? He might have taught his wife and younger daughters how to conduct themselves with dignity, instead of standing by and laughing at them. While Kitty's manners were improving, so that her society was tolerable, he could not abide Mary Bennet's arrogant display of false piety. Her mother was simply intolerable in her vulgarity. How obviously she gloated over Elizabeth's new wealth and consequence! Truly, it appeared that Mrs. Bennet had never valued Elizabeth, the best of her children, until she so raised herself in society.

The horse stood still, but for the occasional toss of his head, and Darcy sat unmoving, seeing nothing of the view spread before him. He thought of the heavy price he had paid to have Elizabeth for his wife. He had forfeited his cousin, Anne's, great fortune, nearly equal to his own. Almost all of his relations had discarded him. Lady Catherine's revenge spread even to his friends, so that Reginald Foxwell had been denied his living, though he felt no regret.

Darcy raised his eyes to the distant hills. If only Elizabeth had carried the babe to its term. He allowed himself now the luxury of feeling that loss. What a compensation it would have been to carry a small son around the estate, showing him all that would be his. That would be some revenge upon his cousin, and heir, in Scotland, who had snubbed him altogether on his marriage.

"Good God!" he thought, starting out of his reverie. "What a great tragedy I am constructing of this inconsequential setback. We will leave this place as soon as Elizabeth is well, and return to our proper abode." He shrugged slightly, and looked out towards the road. He pictured Elizabeth, her laughing dark eyes, the movement of her lips as she wove her spells with words, the flame of her anger when wronged. He thought with pleasure of the little threesome they would form again with Georgiana at Pemberley, where, for a time, all the world would be excluded.

CHAPTER 16

WITH HER SHAWL CLOSE ABOUT her, Mrs. Edgeley sat in the sun and watched as her three eldest daughters strolled beside the lake with Mrs. Darcy. All four were dressed in simple muslin gowns. The Misses Edgeley wore shawls, while Mrs. Darcy was set apart by the elegant cut of her jacket. The curate's wife sighed. Had her girls ever had that bounce in their step? Mrs. Darcy must be about the same age as Emily, twenty-one. Yet how differently life had molded them. Had this young woman, married less than a year, always had such assurance? Somehow she felt that Elizabeth Darcy had always known her own worth.

Anna was but twenty-three, yet her looks, plain enough, seemed already to have lost the bloom of youth. A teacher at Greystead School now these past four years, she no longer spoke as if she envisioned any other future.

Emily, however, could bear "imprisonment" in those walls no more. She was prettier than her sister. Her mother knew that her spark, rather than extinguished, was contained. Margaret was just sixteen. Time enough to think about her later.

She looked out across the lake, shimmering in the sun, and let her eyes wander the shades of the woods beyond. What a pleasure, a luxury, it was to have her girls at home with her on their first vacation in four years.

Emily and Margaret walked behind, whispering about Mrs. Darcy's clothes, her rings and her hair.

Anna, moving ahead with her hostess, had other matters on her mind.

"Mrs. Darcy, Emily has been doing the school accounts now this past year."

"In addition to teaching?"

"Her position of assistant teacher places a small demand on her many abilities, and the accounts occupy but a few hours each week."

"I see," said Elizabeth, wondering how few shillings account-keeping paid.

"My father always believed my name and Emily's were put forward for scholarships at Greystead, as the competition is fierce. Examining the books, Emily discovered that our 'scholarships,' so called, were funded by Mr. Darcy, who arranged that they appear to be awarded by the school on merit."

Elizabeth smiled. How like him to assist a struggling curate in this anonymous way, to spare his feelings.

Anna continued, "I would not wish my father to know this. For all his reputation for humility, he has his pride. Will you thank Mr. Darcy for us?"

"Certainly, I will."

"I thank him from the bottom of my heart, for how else could my dear Mama manage?" She turned and looked back at her mother, and held back the tears so that her grey eyes stung.

Mrs. Edgeley looked older than her forty-three years, and how could it be otherwise? She dearly loved her children, but they were too numerous. She was worn out, both with child-bearing and the struggle to provide for her family respectably. Year by year, Mr. Edgeley's chances of being made vicar seemed to recede, as the incumbent stubbornly lived on. She woke from her reverie and waved.

"What sad thoughts I have been having in such a beautiful place," she thought. "God will care for us, as dear Mr. Edgeley says. Our situation is improving all the time. Next term Sarah will be at school, John at University, and Samuel away with his brother Egbert at sea. Dear little Samuel, everyone's darling, but he is eight years old, and must begin to be a man. Yes, in the autumn there will be but seven children still at home and Mr. Edgeley can take in boarding scholars."

Elizabeth and Anna wandered ahead of the other two, and their conversation turned to music. The faintest glow lit Anna's pale face.

"We practice on the church organ every day and Emily has her lute, so we do not languish for want of instruments at home, although I miss the harp."

"Then will you come and play for us? I am sure Miss Darcy would like to hear you, as would I."

"I would be honored, Mrs. Darcy." Anna hesitated. "I have heard of your lovely voice, madam. You look surprised. Mr. Turner spoke of the pleasure he had in hearing you sing."

Elizabeth laughed, and said, archly, "Perhaps Mr. Turner wishes to gratify my husband, who has some excuse, I suppose, for overestimating my talents."

Anna flushed. "Mr. Turner would never speak with insincerity."

"Well, well," thought Elizabeth, "am I bruising tender feelings?"

"Miss Edgeley, I was speaking lightly and did not intend my comment as a reflection upon Mr. Turner. Does your sister Emily play instruments other than the lute?"

"Yes, indeed. She plays the pianoforte very well, and the harp. She teaches singing, although she does not like to sing before company."

"She is very talented then."

"Certainly. She speaks French and Italian very well and knows some Latin, which my father taught us before we left home."

Elizabeth smiled wryly, recalling her own haphazard education.

"I envy your sister, and, no doubt, you as well, though you do not boast of your own accomplishments." She stopped and turned to face Anna.

"What will you think of me, Miss Edgeley, should I tell you of how I came by my small stock of French phrases?" she asked, her head to one side, and a mischievous smile playing about her little mouth.

"We had a master who was appointed to teach French to the three eldest girls. However, there existed two very small sisters, who would come into the room and chase each other about, snatch up his papers and scribble upon his books." Anna stared at Elizabeth in horror. She had not the benefit of teachers other than her father until she went to school and could not imagine a life in which masters should not be revered.

Elizabeth laughed ruefully. "I have shocked you, I see. I shall never forget his face: he had the most tremendous black eyebrows. One day, my little sisters were running about, squealing, and he, trying to ignore them, was shouting, 'Je suis heureuse! Tu es heureuse!'. I am afraid I was naughty enough to laugh. My mama came in at that moment and he was dismissed on the spot. How dared he shout at her precious children? It was several years before I learned that the French do not go about furiously bellowing, 'I am happy! You are happy!'"

Anna laughed.

"The music master managed to get the attention of us older girls by dint of the clever trick of convincing our mama that we were vastly talented, and that nothing must disturb our instruction."

"I am sure it was no trick, Mrs. Darcy."

"I think it was, and fooled my mother to this day, and she is never content without poor Mary and me displaying our gift to her amazed guests. I wish her conviction of my genius had led to her insisting upon my practicing more. Your sister, however, has made excellent use of her opportunities."

"She knew that she must." Anna stopped, half turned to Elizabeth and said, "Emily hopes to obtain a position as governess. Do you think she will have difficulty in finding a suitable position?"

"Not with such qualifications as hers. I may be able to assist her, if she so wishes."

"We would be most grateful for your help, madam."

"Truly, it would be a pleasure. What of you, Miss Edgeley? Do you find your work rewarding?"

Anna looked calmly out across the water. It was impossible to read her feelings.

"Greystead School lacks the variety that an interesting household may provide, but I am reconciled to spending many years there. I infinitely prefer it to the uncertainties of a governess's post."

"I understand you perfectly."

Before they parted, Elizabeth arranged for the two eldest Miss Edgeleys to visit Pemberley again.

Three days later, Mr. Turner climbed the stairs at Pemberley and went along the picture gallery. From the closed door of the music room, the sounds of Mozart rippled out. The young man's eyes were riveted by the portrait. When one came upon it suddenly, something of Mrs. Darcy's essence seemed to leap out at one. He traced the lines of the face, searching for the likeness.

"You consider the portrait faithful to the original, Mr. Turner?" He jumped.

"Mr. Darcy, good morning. Yes, it is very like."

"I am very pleased with it. I trust you have not been waiting long."

"A few minutes only, pleasantly spent listening to Miss Darcy play."

"I believe that it is not my sister playing." Georgiana was an accomplished pianist, but did not produce such volume from the instrument. "Have you time to delay our business? Mrs. Darcy is entertaining some callers this morning. Would you like to hear them?"

"In truth, I should be delighted."

As they entered, Emily finished playing. Turner had met the Edgeley girls several times. Elizabeth watched the greeting between him and Anna, his normal gentlemanlike manner, and her usual calm.

Anna seated herself at the harp. Her eyes half closed, she seemed to lean into the music itself. Her usually pallid complexion was glowing. Her music resonated, sank to a murmur, and ceased.

Her audience seemed to hold its breath before applauding. Elizabeth ran over to her.

"Miss Edgeley, that was quite the loveliest thing I have ever heard."

"Thank you," said Anna. Already her face was losing its color. In spite of herself, her eyes sought Edward Turner's and she smiled briefly at his compliments. He turned to reply to a question from Darcy. Elizabeth noted the color of Anna's eyes, which had seemed to deepen as she played, fading again to cool grey.

"She is retreating again," thought Elizabeth. She said, "Will you come and play for us again? We are expecting guests next week, among them are two ladies whose performance upon the pianoforte is formidable."

"More so than that of the present company? This I cannot believe," said Mr. Turner.

"Believe it you must, sir. Miss Bingley and Mrs. Hurst draw forth all the dash that the instrument affords."

"What of your sister, Miss Catherine Bennet? Does she play?"

"Kitty was somewhat delicate as a child. My mother felt the exertion of sitting at the instrument would tax her strength," said Elizabeth, inwardly smiling at her mother's oft-repeated excuse.

During refreshments, Edward Turner talked with Miss Edgeley. Elizabeth watched them from time to time. She laughed at her own thoughts. She would have suspected nothing if not for Anna's small flare of anger, when she suspected Elizabeth of doubting Turner's sincerity, as they walked by the lake. He was a lover of music, and Anna a performer of music worth loving. What a wonderful ending it might be. He was earnestly desiring Anna to play again. Emily looked at them furtively from time to time. Anna was all stillness; she had an evenness as smooth and unadorned as her simple stone-colored gown.

"Yes, I enjoyed the visit," she was to say to Emily, in the privacy in their shared bed. "Pemberley is all superlatives. The house is splendid. Mr. Darcy is the epitome of the handsome gentleman, perfectly polite and good. Miss Darcy is the epitome of modesty, accomplishment and sweetness. They had everything but someone to make them laugh. So God sent them Mrs. Darcy."

"Anna, he must adore her, do you not think so?"

"Why did you not ask him, if you feel you must know?"

"Oh, Anna, why do you not long to get away from Greystead?" The only sound in the darkness was of Margaret or Janet turning in sleep. "I cannot bear the thought of another term there. Mrs. Darcy mentioned that she has written to a lady she knows who has a very wide acquaintance and may know of a situation for me. Her name is Lady Reerdon."

"Lady Reerdon? She sounds very grand."

"I hope . . ."

"Emily, for what do you hope? Take care, my love. Guard your heart and govern your thoughts. If we can but find a family who will treat you with respect and pupils who will obey you, I will be content."

"Surely life has more for me than Greystead can offer. I must get away!"

"I know."

"Anna, Mr. Turner is attentive to you."

"He has taken the trouble to speak to me of music; that is all. I do not wish to speak of him, dear. Good night."

"Good night, Anna."

CHAPTER 17

THE CARRIAGE REACHED THE TOP of the hill and stopped for a moment. Jane gasped. Across the little valley stood Pemberley House, bathed in the late morning sunshine. The lake and the park had all the natural beauty Elizabeth had described.

"Oh, Lizzy," she breathed, and Charles nodded in understanding.

"Jane, my sweet," said Caroline, "when you see the north front and inside the house—so delightful!"

Jane recalled asking Elizabeth, when she became engaged to Darcy, how long she had been in love with him. Elizabeth had laughingly replied that it was since first seeing the beautiful grounds at Pemberley. Now Jane was ready to accept that these words were spoken only half in jest. The carriage crossed the bridge and pulled up at the steps, where their hosts waited to receive them. As they alighted, Mr. Hurst's carriage pulled up behind them.

There was time for a short rest in their rooms and for the ladies to perform the second toilette of the day before coming down, freshly gowned and coiffed, for luncheon.

Mr. Hurst beamed towards the top of the table, then turned to his host.

"Darcy, pray allow me to say how splendid it is to see Pemberley with a mistress."

"I thank you, Hurst. It is indeed."

Having exhausted his fund of flattery, Hurst added, "Might there be time for some fishing after luncheon?"

Mrs. Hurst did not even show a flicker of irritation. She was too tired nowadays, although she looked forward eagerly to the birth of her first child, after which she might regain her figure and her pleasure in the society of the wide circle of their acquaintances.

Leaving Bingley's sisters to exclaim over Georgiana's latest artistic efforts, Elizabeth disappeared out of doors with Jane and

Kitty. Arms around each other's waists, they strolled along the edge of the lake.

"Lizzy," said Jane, "words could not have prepared me for the beauty of Pemberley, or for its peacefulness."

"Indeed, yes. Once one is in the valley, the world is excluded. Even the estate workers' cottages are behind the hill."

"You have lost your seclusion now."

"Dear, dear Jane. Dear Kitty, too. I delight in having you here. I think there is room enough for you."

They all giggled and, as one, turned to look back at the house.

"It is a palace, or near enough to it," said Jane.

"It is, and I am the queen."

"In Lambton, she could not be more a queen if she were a duchess," said Kitty. "Why are you laughing at me?"

They turned and walked on.

"I think Mary was mad not to come," declared Kitty. "Lizzy, can you believe that she says she will not visit Pemberley until Mr. Darcy apologizes. Mr. Darcy! Papa had such a good laugh. He says you will languish for her presence forever if that is the case."

"What a grim sentence," said Elizabeth. "She wrote that she could not leave Mama in her uncertain health. Is our mother really suffering so from want of spirits?"

"Not in the least!" cried Kitty. "Mama was desperate for Mary to come after I told her there was a frightfully ugly bachelor vicar in the district."

"Kitty!" Elizabeth remonstrated. "I trust you are not referring to Mr. Turner. He is not handsome, perhaps, but I will hear nothing against him."

"La! The only distinction I make is between handsome and hideous."

"Kitty, dearest," said Jane gently, "a gentleman's appearance is the least important aspect to be considered."

"Really?" said Kitty. "What a pity it is that your husbands are not ugly, or you might have proven your point. In any case, Mary has other fish to fry." She smirked at Elizabeth's expression of curiosity.

"Mrs. Long had the most dreadful nephew staying with her. He's preparing to take Holy Orders and he is utterly horrid. He has the most awful opinions on female dress and decorum and . . . his name is Mr. Brown."

"Mr. Brown? That really is unpardonable," said Elizabeth.

Kitty let go of her sister's arm and pranced ahead of them. Turning, she tilted her little nose in the air, put her hands behind her back and adopted an expression of pained disapproval.

"Miss Catherine," she mimicked, "is it fitting for a young lady, such as yourself, to push forward her opinion in this company?"

They all giggled.

"On what weighty matter did you dare to contribute your views, Kitty? Was it a question of doctrinal importance or your impassioned views on taxes?"

"Lord, no, Lizzy! I said I thought it might rain."

"Kitty, you are become very bold!"

Jane added, "Mary has put aside the gowns you sent her, and is back to her high necks."

"She gets into corners with Mr. Brown and they read sermons to each other. I suppose she thinks Mr. Brown will marry her."

"He departed with no mention of ever returning to Hertfordshire, but Mary appeared undismayed," said Jane.

"You may be sure I shall never marry a clergyman," said Kitty, and both her sisters laughed merrily at the thought.

They had reached the point where the stream flowed into the lake. A short distance away, the gentlemen could be seen at their sport.

"Look, Mr. Hurst has caught a fish!" cried Kitty.

"That will put him in a good mood at dinner," said Jane.

Mr. Hurst was wrestling manfully with a sizeable trout and brushed aside the attendance of the servant. As he reeled in his catch, he jerked the line too hard and the fish flopped against his coat, and slid down his trousers to his boots, where it hung for a moment. The sportsman could then be heard berating the poor attendant for his slowness.

"Ugh!" said Kitty, wrinkling her nose. "How he shall smell!"

"We shall not speak to him again until he has bathed," said Elizabeth. "Have you seen enough of the men at their sport? I shall send their refreshments out into the garden."

They turned back to the house.

"I imagine you have been much occupied, Lizzy, preparing for Miss Darcy's coming out," said Jane.

"Indeed, yes. There has been more beating of carpets and airing of beds than I could have imagined, though I did order it myself. We have decorated anew the entire east wing, which has been in disuse these seventeen years, ever since the death of Lady Anne Darcy. I found the choosing of papers and curtains in London highly diverting, but the presence of the workmen and the constant questions of their foreman have disrupted my leisure sorrowfully."

"You do not look so very sad, Lizzy!" said Jane, giving her a kiss. "I imagine the greenhouse beds are filled to bursting."

"Indeed, they are. Tomorrow I shall take you on a tour of the produce beds in the kitchen garden and the greenhouses. We shall be prepared to feed all of Derbyshire, if need be."

Miss Bingley joined in the tour to view the new arrangements in the east wing. She knew not over which aspect to agonize more: the fact that ownership of these rooms had slipped through her fingers, or the fact that the improvements to them were so very successful.

"Another Chinese room!" she trilled. "So light and interesting! How clever you are, Mrs. Darcy, to have known the patterns could look well with such delightfully old-fashioned beds."

"Most of the furniture in this part of the house has been at Pemberley since the first section was completed," said Elizabeth. "Mr. Darcy and I could not bring ourselves to discard it."

"I declare I quite envy the people who will sleep here," averred Caroline.

"Choose whichever room you like best, Miss Bingley, and I will give orders for your things to be moved at once."

"You are so kind, Mrs. Darcy, but I would not dream of permitting such trouble on my account."

"I assure you, it is no trouble at all."

However, Miss Bingley felt that a certain prestige attached to the main guest rooms, and went on to explain that her envy was not so pressing as perhaps it had sounded.

"Which is to be Lady Reerdon's room, Lizzy?" asked Kitty.

"Her ladyship will be in the main wing." They returned to the landing above the main stairs and Elizabeth opened a door. The room glowed with a soft yellow light from the silk curtains, to the bed covers, to the roses.

"Lizzy, those yellow roses are perfect, and to think I said it would look too plain."

"It is beautiful. I confess to a certain feeling of satisfaction."

"I can assure you that Lady Reerdon will be utterly delighted," said Caroline, sounding for all the world like the lady's closest friend.

"Do you think so? I do so want her to be happy here. She has been very good to me."

"You have so many new friends, Lizzy," sighed Kitty.

"Most of them are my husband's friends, Kitty, and that is not altogether the same thing."

"I heard Mr. Darcy tell Papa that half of his friends are in love with you."

"I am quite sure he said no such thing, Kitty. I wish you would amend your habit of exaggerating."

"It was something very like," muttered Kitty.

"In any case, although success with the gentlemen might seem of paramount importance to you, Kitty, believe me, pleasing the ladies is far more crucial in society."

"What of Lady Englebury, Lizzy? When will she pay a visit to Pemberley?"

"Never, I should think. This party would not suit her taste in the least," said Elizabeth. She smiled wryly, thinking that her ladyship's presence at Pemberley would be equally unpalatable to Darcy's taste.

"Besides," she added, aloud, "The marchioness seldom leaves her country house in the summer."

"Deepdene," breathed Caroline. "What a noble seat that is! One scarcely wonders that the marquess rarely stirs from his hearth."

"Indeed, one cannot wonder at him. You must be weary after your journey. Do you desire to rest before dinner?" asked Elizabeth. The ladies readily assented to this, with Miss Bingley exclaiming over her neglect of her sister, who had been lying down, all alone, for an hour.

Elizabeth went to spend a few minutes in her sitting room. She curled up with a book on the wide window ledge. The sky was clouding over and, looking down to the lawns by the lake, she could see the gentlemen returning to the house. A servant was carrying a laden basket around to the kitchen. There would be fish for dinner and, no doubt, some of cook's specialty, fish pie, tomorrow, when Lord and Lady Reerdon were expected and Colonel Fitzwilliam was to come, bringing a friend from his regiment, Captain Westcombe.

Darcy looked up, unconsciously scanning the upper windows. She waved and the three men raised their hats.

"Lord, Louisa," Hurst was to say to his wife, "there she sat, in a window, for all the world like a child of twelve."

"I wish that I could contemplate accommodating myself upon a window sill," she replied, stroking her bulging stomach. "Why did you bring me here, Mr. Hurst, when I am too weary to enjoy myself?"

"'Twas because you wanted to come, as I recollect."

"I did not wish to remain all alone at your mother's house."

"Am I to give up my summer's fishing at Pemberley?" he asked, in honest outrage.

CHAPTER 18

KITTY'S FEELINGS WERE ALL THAT they should be on driving in a carriage with a coronet upon the door. She sat very straight, next to a real earl, the very first of the species that she had encountered. Lord Reerdon, it must be said, was not made of such stuff as to delight a maiden's heart. His looks were middling, his conversation dull, and his manners had a quality that, were he not of noble birth, she may have been tempted to call gawkish. She looked across at Lady Reerdon. The countess, for all her grace and elegance, was an old lady, more than forty years of age, although perhaps she could not help that. Catching her look, Lady Reerdon smiled kindly and Kitty felt her spirits rise. What an adventure! She looked out on the view, more steep and rocky with every moment.

At last the carriage pulled up in a little spot open to the sun and sheltered from the wind. Blankets and cushions had been spread upon the grass and a servant was lifting a chair down from the cart.

The other carriages rolled up and, after much exclaiming over the charms of the place, everyone went off, in knots of three or four, to explore. Georgiana asked Kitty to accompany her on a short climb to better see the view. Georgiana was arm in arm with her cousin, Colonel Fitzwilliam. How much less plain he looked in his regimentals! Why did he not always wear them? His friend, Captain Westcombe, offered Kitty his arm to accompany them, his sleeve that alluring red, his tassels gleaming in the sun. Kitty looked from this temptation to the path, which seemed very steep. She knew not how to say she feared the exertion of it.

"Thank you kindly, sir," she said prettily. "I would delight in such a walk, but I have set my heart upon gathering some of these flowers from amongst the rocks."

"May I help you?" he asked, gallantly.

"Indeed, you may."

After a few moments, he said, "Miss Darcy and her cousin are very great friends."

"Lord, yes. I believe there is no one higher in her estimation."

"You are in her confidence, then?"

Kitty smiled up at him, her head on one side, her smile an unconscious imitation of Elizabeth's, but with an effect of utter naivety.

"Of course I am," she said, laughing up into his earnest brown eyes.

She suffered a stab of guilt on seeing Miss Edgeley standing to one side with Mr. Turner.

"I promised my sister to be attentive to the Miss Edgeleys and I quite forgot." The captain in attendance, she tripped over to the pair and invited them to sit with her and take a glass of wine, while they waited for the more adventurous of the party to descend from their climb.

Miss Bingley lounged gracefully against a rock, softened with cushions, and looked about her. She could not imagine for what purpose Mrs. Darcy had invited the Miss Edgeleys. She could scarce keep her countenance when she first set eyes on the dowdy creatures. She looked on satirically as Miss Emily sat on the blanket at Lady Reerdon's feet.

Mr. Turner had come back from a little stroll among the rocks with Miss Edgeley. Kitty and Captain Westcombe had joined them. "One can trust Miss Kitty to fasten upon a penniless officer, the moment she sees him," she thought. Turner was fetching cushions for the two ladies.

"Now Mr. Turner is a gentlemanlike man, but a clergyman never can be really fashionable. Indeed, who could be on an income of eight hundred pounds?" (Caroline was not desperate yet.)

Below them lay the road that led back to the haven of Pemberley. Above! She shuddered as she looked at the mass of rocks rearing up behind them. Had they travelled so far for the sake of a view of rocks? Lord Reerdon manfully threw himself down alongside her, and groaned as his hip met the unforgiving surface of a hidden rock.

"Have you abandoned the ascent, my lord?"

"Scrambling about is not my sort of thing at all."

"A different matter if he'd said 'tumbling about,'" she thought. "It would be something to be a countess, even if one's consort were such a clot. Precedence over Mrs. Darcy would be pleasant. Yet what has he but a title and debts that are rumored to swallow up his income before he receives it? The oddest thing was that one cannot help almost . . . liking him."

Across the clearing, Caroline saw Jane, leaning back against her mound of cushions, her husband beside her.

"Dearest Jane, you are not tired, my love?" she called.

"No, I thank you, Caroline. Charles has made me a comfortable seat here."

"Charles, dear, you are very good," she cried, thinking, "I hope as much fuss is made of me, if ever I find myself in that condition."

"Look! There's Colonel Fitzwilliam and Miss Darcy sitting on a rock. They have climbed high," said Charles happily.

"Well, I wish they'd come down again," replied his sister. "I'm starved."

Moments later they could see the figures of Elizabeth and Darcy even higher. "They have reached the summit!" cried Bingley.

Darcy was poised, as though to catch her if she tripped, while Elizabeth skipped down from one rock to the next.

"She could allow him to assist her more," Caroline thought. "The way she scampers about is . . ."

"Extraordinary. Is not Elizabeth extraordinary?" declared Charles.

"Precisely my own thought, dear Brother."

Lord Reerdon eyed Miss Bingley's profile as he drank his wine. Handsome girl, in a regal sort of way. Of course, Anne had her good points, delicate little thing and meek, too. He couldn't stand a domineering woman. She would come with an excellent marriage portion, fifty thousand pounds. Perhaps he should have been firmer on having in writing that he would be Lady Catherine's heir should Anne die first. Heavens, it was possible; the old girl was the imperishable sort. Still, a fellow would seem a cad to appear too pushing. Surely Lady Catherine would do the right thing by him.

Elizabeth looked down on their party from on high. "What tiny guests we have," she said.

"They would do well to partake of something substantial with the wine."

She put her hand on Darcy's arm and nodded to a spot around the brow of the hill, out of view of their party. A shepherd and a farm girl were frolicking on the grass. He bowed deeply, she curtsied and, even from the distance, her gestures could be discerned as a parody of her betters behind the curve of the mount.

Darcy frowned. "That is Bentridge's shepherd," he said.

"Fitzwilliam," she laughed, "are you offended?"

The girl below picked up the lunch basket and turned away, ready to trip back to the farmhouse. The boy leapt across the grass to her, caught her by the waist and spun her around to face him. She put on a show of reluctance, and they kissed.

"Now I am shocked!" said Elizabeth.

"If we spy upon them, my love, we are no better than they," Darcy said.

She turned towards him, her head down.

"It was very wrong of me and I am most contrite." Button by button, her eyes travelled up his waistcoat; then studied his cravat, his chin and lips, until she reached his eyes.

"Elizabeth, you are laughing at me."

"Pray believe me that I would not do so if I could possibly help it."

"I should very much like to kiss you."

"Yes," she said, laughing. "You would." She darted off down to the path.

After luncheon, the plates were whisked out of sight by the footmen, and the party settled down for some music. Miss Emily had brought her lute.

"A charming instrument, Miss Emily," said Miss Bingley.

"I thank you. It was a present from my sister." She smiled fondly at Anna, knowing with what sacrifices Anna must have paid for it. Emily ran her fingers along the strings.

Elizabeth leaned back against a tree, cushions at her back and Darcy beside her.

He took her hand in his and held it for a moment. She gave him one of her more cryptic smiles. Seeing them, Georgiana blushed, and glanced at her cousin Henry. Biting his lip, he studied the ground. As the music began to ripple around them, Elizabeth's attention was caught by Georgiana's tiny movement as her hand touched Henry's for an instant. He gave her a self-deprecating smile and turned towards the musician. The girl studied him for a moment, then she turned her head aside.

Edward Turner lounged between Kitty and Anna Edgeley. He looked at Anna's profile, framed by her old straw hat. Her keen intelligence and deep study must add to her appreciation of the music. The faint tint that lit her alabaster complexion was, no doubt, fuelled equally by love for the musician and for the music itself. Just then, her plain face glowed with that beauty that comes from within.

His eyes turned to Kitty. Leaning against her cushions, she was playing with the wildflowers in her lap. For a mad moment, he imagined playing with them too, his fingers touching hers. She wore a pretty green bonnet with a matching sash that emphasized the freshness of her white muslin gown. He thought what a pity it was that she had been denied the opportunity to study music! No one could doubt her sensitivity to the melancholy essence of the melody, which caused her lower lip to protrude in that sweet fashion.

Kitty sighed, with a crossness that did not mar her expression with frowns. "Are there to be nought but these two officers at Georgiana's ball?" she thought. "They are poor and plain, and Colonel Fitzwilliam only laughed at me when I asked him if he would wear his red coat."

The young vicar looked across at Mrs. Darcy. There was a similarity in the faces of the sisters. He could see it now, especially as a melancholy not there a moment ago had robbed Elizabeth's face of its mobility. The plaintive air finished. There was clapping and sighing.

"Thank you, Miss Edgeley," said Darcy. "That was beautiful. Will you play for us again?"

"What would you like to hear?"

"Something lively, if you please."

Miss Emily inclined her head, and thought for a moment.

Darcy looked at Elizabeth, concern in his eyes. She shook herself out of her despondent mood.

As the guests prepared themselves for departure, Elizabeth strolled towards the carriages with Lord Reerdon. She became aware that her mind had wandered away from the babbling brook of the earl's discourse.

"Indeed, your Lordship?"

"Yes, Mother and I spent a month at Rosings."

"So long? You found much to entertain you then?"

"Lord, yes. Lady Catherine's a marvellous old lady."

"Was Miss de Bourgh well when you left Kent?"

"I am sorry to say that she was not in good health. Yet she is patient and uncomplaining."

"Really?" said Elizabeth.

"Such a pale and delicate creature, quite ethereal."

"Indeed, she is, my lord."

Lady Reerdon was escorted to her carriage by Darcy.

"At last I can speak to you in private," she said. He waited for her to continue.

"I wished to be the first to tell you that we are to be related. Frederick is engaged to be married to your cousin, Miss de Bourgh."

He expressed all the sentiments to be expected: his congratulations, his pleasure, his hopes for the happiness of his lordship and his bride.

She put her hand upon his arm.

"This is the very outcome to serve all our purposes. Lady Catherine, I believe, sought a title for her daughter; I sought a solution for the confusion of our family circumstances." (Thus did her ladyship delicately refer to Reerdon's mountain of debt, to which she was, herself, prone to add.) "Fortunately, the young people were not loath to agree to the notion."

"I hope we shall always be friends, Countess."

"Naturally, we shall. As I said to Lady Catherine, the love that I bore your mother does not permit of quarrels with her son."

"What had her ladyship to say to that?"

"After establishing that the love she bore her own sister could have no equal in the heart of a mere friend, she wished us to be in accord in our conduct towards you."

"Are you expressing that accord in gracing Pemberley with your presence?" he asked.

She laughed. "You know how I hate to quarrel."

Darcy bowed. (Her ladyship was famous for always getting her own way while never appearing to disagree with anyone.)

She went on. "I mentioned to Lady Catherine that her other guests had no doubt ascertained that a certain direction was to be expected in the friendship between our children. It would hardly do to disappoint them of the satisfaction of being right."

It would, of course, have been disastrous for Anne de Bourgh to be seen as twice disappointed. Lady Catherine was in no position to make bargains so late in the proceedings. Darcy smiled. He handed Lady Reerdon into her carriage.

She put the window down to add, "It often happens that a small twist of fate can be cunningly employed to end a quarrel."

He bowed and turned to watch as the footman assisted Kitty into the carriage. The earl loped up alongside him.

"Please accept my congratulation, my lord. I hope you will be very happy."

"I thank you, Darcy. I am sure I shall."

CHAPTER 19

ELIZABETH FAIRLY SKIPPED ALONG THE path, matching Darcy's pace with ease. They wound up through the woods, the leafy green canopy delicious despite the cold day. Patches of sunlight lit the path and glades.

They stopped at a turn in the path, which afforded a brief view of the house. Somewhere in its rooms or about the gardens were their guests. The distant figures of Georgiana and Kitty could be seen walking along the terrace. They stopped by the fountain and Georgiana bent gracefully at its rim.

"Georgiana so loved that fountain when she was a babe," said Darcy. "The sound of its splashing drew her like a magnet."

"Did it, indeed?"

"Very much so. She would break away from her nurse, toddle to the basin and endeavor to clamber into it, squealing in ecstasy."

"How wondrously naughty! How I love her for it!"

"These adventures came to an end. One day she succeeded and, as the nurse pulled her from the water, our father's voice cut short Georgiana's triumph. 'Nurse, what can you be thinking of? Do you seek to drown the child?' Those were his precise words."

"You were present?"

"I was. My father turned to me." Darcy repeated his father's next words with difficulty. "'As for you, sir, I did not think to find you so derelict in your duty to your sister.'"

Elizabeth put her hand on his arm.

"What harm would have come to her with her nurse and brother so close by? I think your father was a little harsh."

"Not at all, Elizabeth. He was perfectly correct." A faint blush colored his cheeks. "I am ashamed to say that I was laughing."

"That is a crime indeed. What age were you, may I ask?"

"Old enough to know better. I was thirteen."

She looked into his eyes. "You are equally hard upon yourself,

154

Fitzwilliam."

"I believe my father never looked on my sister without mourning my mother. I knew he had a morbid fear of losing his daughter."

"That is very sad. Do you know that I cannot think of a single member of my family who would not have laughed heartily at such antics?"

"What!"

"Except that my mother, perhaps, may have expressed irritation . . ."

"Naturally."

Laughing, she continued, ". . . if the child's dress were new and the basin full of weeds and dirt." She turned and looked down at the far off fountain, with Georgiana standing at its edge.

Darcy said, "I do not believe poor Georgiana understood that my father's anger was directed against the nurse and myself. She knew only his displeasure. He looked down on her, a scrap of humanity, a pool of water collecting round her feet, and he frowned."

"Poor man."

"Georgiana never again jumped into the fountain."

Elizabeth felt a cold prickling on the skin of her arms. She shivered.

"I hope we do not leave too many of these uncomfortable memories with our own children," she said.

At once she was reminded of all the unhappiness and quarrels at Netherfield following the loss of her unborn child.

"If we have any such," she thought.

He was looking at her steadily. She looked up and smiled.

He said, "Elizabeth, I hope you do not dwell overmuch on events in Hertfordshire."

"No, I assure you." She took his arm. They turned again away from the house and followed the path further up the hill. He covered her hand with his.

"I know how disappointed you felt, dearest, but recollect for how short a time we have been married."

"I know. I know. I am over that pain, Fitzwilliam. Yet how much easier it would have been to bear, if none but ourselves had known of my condition."

"It is my ungovernable temper that has led to this estrangement from your sister Mary."

"You were perfectly right to be angry and Papa's decree that she could not come here until she has apologized has been of great convenience to me."

She took a little skipping step. "It has freed me from Mary's embarrassing exhibitions of her self-applauded talent and her false piety. It is quite convenient for me that she is so stiff-necked."

He wondered if he should remonstrate with her on this unfeeling view of her own sister, but he could not, for laughter.

They continued up the path. Moving out of sight of the house, they wound around the side of the valley and across a little bridge. They were totally hidden here, from above by the overhanging rocks and from below by the trees. The air was redolent with the smell of damp and mosses, and with the sounds of running water.

"Avert your eyes, sir!" Elizabeth said. She hitched up her skirt a little into her sash, and they picked their way along a mossy path that branched off among the rocks.

The water gushed out of a fissure in the rock and fed a deep pool in the side of the hill. Darcy spread his coat over a rock and they sat together. Ripples spread out through the green reflections of the trees. She leaned her head against him and they sat in silent companionship.

At last, Elizabeth raised her head from his shoulder and her eyes from the pool.

She looked at her watch.

"Gracious, Fitzwilliam! It is past eleven, and we have an hour's walk back to the house." He rose, reluctance in all his movements. He put out his hand to her and she rose. All her contemplative peacefulness was gone. She was alive with excitement.

"I would not have my friends arrive at Pemberley and find me absent."

"Indeed not. Mr. and Mrs. Courtney must not find us negligent."

They began to trace the little track to the path. Elizabeth turned to bid the pool farewell.

"How Mrs. Courtney would love this spot."

Darcy recoiled inwardly.

"Never mind," said Elizabeth. "She shall not know of its existence. I doubt if she has ever walked so far or climbed so high a hill in her life."

Darcy felt a rush of relief, somewhat tempered by a lack of satisfaction in her reasons for keeping her friend from this spot.

"We shall, in all probability, lack the opportunity to repeat this excursion ourselves these next three weeks, dearest. By tomorrow we shall have fifty guests in the house, and I shall treasure each moment I spend alone with you."

She raised her eyebrows. They set off briskly to return to the house.

Kitty was fascinated by Mrs. Courtney. She was quite the smallest person at table for luncheon, but by no means the least significant. She sparkled away on her host's right hand, listening to him, then making him laugh. Kitty could scarcely attend to her neighbors for wondering what Mrs. Courtney might be saying.

Darcy had gravely questioned his guest regarding her family's health. She told him that Mr. Courtney, as could plainly be seen, was "disgracefully stout in his constitution." Her aunt, the marchioness, was likewise, although she showed her usual end-of-the-season dissatisfaction with her protégés.

"I am sorry to hear it," said Darcy. She laughed.

"Mr. Glover was invited to pay an extended visit to the estate of an admirer, who offers him patronage he cannot afford to scorn. When he carefully broke the news, Lady Englebury's response was to wave him off with an injunction to partake of some fresh air and return exhibiting some color. Her ladyship looked about her drawing room and commented on how surrounded she was with (here Amelia mimicked her aunt's expression of scorn and distaste) 'pasty-complexioned men.' She well-nigh broke his heart."

Darcy laughed.

Mrs. Courtney watched him, as she added, "The marchioness said, 'If I cannot have Mrs. Darcy, I want no one.'" Darcy merely inclined his head.

Mrs. Courtney looked archly at her host. "You have won such a prize in your lady, Mr. Darcy."

He smiled. "Indeed, I know this."

"Lady Englebury has gone to Deepdene without her disciples. Of course, I do not mean that she abandoned my cousins. Miss Whittaker and her brother will spend three weeks with her, after visiting their friends in Somerset. Her ladyship says that she cannot survive five months on wholesome country fare, without a generous seasoning of Peregrine's spite." Amelia noted the pleasure with which Mr. Darcy received that remark.

Any hopes Kitty might have cherished of conversation with Amelia Courtney after the meal were dashed. Elizabeth carried her friend off to drive around the estate in her new phaeton. Kitty watched from her window as the groom fussed over the placement of the blanket on their knees. She saw Elizabeth turn and speak to him, as he leapt up onto the narrow step on the back of the vehicle. The coachman half turned his head, seemingly in surprise. The groom had jumped down and stood in a woebegone posture. Elizabeth could be seen to laugh. He jumped up again, and the coachman turned back, with squared shoulders and handed up the reins to his mistress. They were off, all as it should be, with the mistress of Pemberley properly escorted when away from her house.

Kitty sighed. How was she to pass the afternoon? Miss Bingley and Miss Darcy were at their music. Jane was driving out with Bingley. Oh, for the morrow, when there would be any number of young people about the house. She sat at her little desk to compose a letter to her sister Lydia.

Pemberley

Dearest Lydia,

I thank you for your kind invitation. How I long to be with you again. What fun we should have at the balls and parties you speak of. It must be ecstasy to be so surrounded by officers. Our father, alas, writes that I may not go to you.

I think the dressmaker is horrid to give you no more credit. I cannot lend you any money, for I shall need all my allowance, even the extra ten pounds Papa gave to me! The people here play so high! I lost two pounds at Lotteries and Lizzy read me such a sermon. I patiently listened to it, all for nought, for she refused to give me so much as a shilling.

It is but two days to Miss Georgiana's ball. Mr. Darcy has given me earrings and a necklace of sapphires. Mary would have received as good, if she had come. Since she is in such a pet, she is saving my brother-in-law some money. Lizzy had an exquisite gown made for me. It is of white silk, with beading on the sleeves and neck . . .

Kitty looked out across the park, to a little summer house, where the sun streamed in. How picturesque she would look sitting there, with the light shining through her muslin gown. It was a little cold out, to be sure, but she might wear her velvet pelisse. Kitty gathered up her paper and implements and set off for the summer house. She seated herself prettily by the window and unpacked her little basket. Just as she imagined, the sun came in and illuminated her nicely. The pink frills of velvet glowed around her neck and wrists, while the light fabric of her skirt shone almost transparent. And there was no one to see her! She picked up her pen.

. . . Oh, Lydia! Tomorrow, at last, there are to be some young men in the house. Naturally there will be young ladies too, but I have no fear of them. Yet, woe is me! I cannot find that there are to be above two officers at the ball. They are Mr. Darcy's cousin, Colonel Fitzwilliam, and the

159

colonel's friend, Captain Westcombe, both poor and plain. Miss Darcy spends hours at a time sitting between them. I teased her a little about the way Captain Westcombe hangs upon her words, few as they are. She turned the brightest pink and declared, "I am sure you are mistaken, Kitty. Captain Westcombe is a younger son!" She might just as well have said he were a stable-boy, or even a dog! She dares not even attribute an atom of feeling to this species, the penniless cadet, for I daresay she will marry where she is directed and that will be to a man of property.

Jane and Bingley intend to give up Netherfield and are looking to purchase an estate in Derbyshire or possibly Yorkshire. They are out today, looking at a place near Derby. Mama will have an attack of the vapors when she knows of their plans . . .

From the safety of distance, Kitty smiled at the thought of her mother's hysterics. For the first time, she noticed the buzzing of insects in the flowers that sprawled over the roof of the summer house. She moistened her little red mouth with the tip of her tongue. As she dipped the pen in the ink, a sound intruded upon her. It was a footstep. She looked up and gasped. She jumped up and the pen rolled from the little table to the floor. The intruder stepped forward and bent to retrieve it. Gold tassels swung forward from his epaulettes; gold buttons adorned the front of his red coat. He held out the pen to her. Kitty gazed into his handsome face. He bowed. Brown eyes sparkled with warmth and humor. Under his teasing smile, a strong chin jutted out over his gold-braided collar.

"Madam, may I present myself for your protection?"

"Oh, no!" she said. "I do not know you, sir."

Snatching up her letter, she stepped out of the revealing ray of sunlight and passed him on the steps, her eyes averted. She tripped back across the grass, never once looking back. He laughed to himself and picked up the little basket she seemed to have forgotten. At a distance, he followed her back to the house.

. . . Past midnight

*Dear, dear Lydia, would that you were here! I have passed such an
evening as you cannot imagine! I was seated at table with the
handsomest officer I have ever seen. Wickham is nothing to him. We had
ever such a romantic encounter in the summer house. He is Lieutenant
Foxwell, the young brother of Mr. Darcy's friend. He is but newly
become an officer and he is to be at Pemberley for three weeks. I intend
that he shall monopolize me entirely. Lizzy says I am not to encourage
his compliments, for he must look for a fortune if he wishes to marry.
Why are all the best young men poor?*

*As soon as the weather is warmer, he promises to row me on the
lake.*

I shall wear my pink bonnet to remind him of our first encounter.

*I shall write again soon and tell you all about Georgiana's ball.
You must write to me and not such a short note as your last, if you
please.*

Give my best to Wickham,

Your loving sister,
Kitty

Kitty may have had no fears of the charms of the other young ladies
invited to Pemberley. However, she had not taken into account their
virtues. Miss Robson had arrived, along with her fortune of twenty-
five thousand pounds, a virtue which quite outbalanced her plainness, making her appear very pretty indeed. The young lady was
accompanied by her aunt, a wealthy widow, who was rumored to
have willed all of her own estate, too, upon the fortunate girl.

With all the luck of a novice, Reginald Foxwell, with the help of
his uniform, captivated both the girl and her aunt.

Kitty wrote to Lydia of her justified outrage.

*P.S. All my joy is turned to ashes!! Miss Darcy's friend from school is
come. She is the most hideous creature you ever saw and blushes and
stammers when my beau is about! He is all gallantry to her, for her
fortune, but she would be in a green fit of jealousy if she could hear how*

he compliments me when she is not about. Her horrid old aunt simply dotes upon him. Everyone must share my feelings of disgust at seeing such an ugly old woman tapping his wrist with her fan and laughing at his jokes. I daresay she means to marry him herself! I will get him away from Miss Tedious, rich aunt and all, and dance half the night with him at the ball. Of course I must be on the watch for Lizzy. You would laugh to see me so demure and obedient to my sister, but Papa has said that at the first whisper of a complaint from Lizzy, I come home at once. Hertfordshire! How did I ever tolerate its dullness!

After tossing and turning, in agonies of the heart, for at least a quarter of an hour, Kitty fell asleep and did not awaken until eleven. It was the day of the ball! She nearly sprang out of bed, but stopped herself in time. She reached up and rang for her maid.

Elizabeth had treated herself to a peaceful breakfast in her room, on what promised to be a busy day. She supervised the floral decorations in the ballroom, then called into the still room, where she was almost overpowered by the delicious scent of thirty rose bouquets, set out in a rainbow of colors, each chosen to match a lady's gown.

She stepped out into the sunlight and wandered along the terrace. It was a beautiful day. She would go to the summer saloon and see if some of the ladies desired to walk around the lake.

As she turned the corner, she saw a horse at the steps. Captain Westcombe was just coming out of the house with the colonel.

"Mrs. Darcy, I have been looking for you."

"You are not leaving us, Captain?"

"Indeed I must. I have received an urgent message from my mother. My brother, the earl, is very ill with scarlet fever."

"I am very sorry to lose your society and for such a cause as this. Will you not take a carriage?"

"My mother sends a carriage to meet me. I thank you for your kindness."

"I will not delay you. Our thoughts will be with you and all your family."

He hesitated.

"Will you say goodbye to Miss Darcy for me? I have so enjoyed our conversations."

"Of course."

They said hasty farewells and Elizabeth watched as he rode away up the drive.

She turned to Henry.

"How serious is Lord Bradford's condition, Colonel?"

"Serious enough. It seems he has been nursed through a fit and has not recovered his senses."

Elizabeth's thoughts returned frequently to the captain's family. They would be feeling the keenest anxiety over the third of four brothers to face premature death. His aunt by marriage, Lady Englebury, and the marquess would feel an additional concern because Lord Bradford, now lying dangerously ill, was heir to the marquess. Of course, Captain Westcombe was next in line. A wild thought entered her head. She laughed ruefully; the poor earl was not even dead, and the captain was rumored to have long loved his cousin Arabella, who would not so much as look at a younger son.

The main dining hall was filled to capacity. The long table sparkled with silver and glass settings complemented by the silver ribbons and glass ornaments set on fine wires among the hothouse flowers.

In view of the special night, the hostess had waived precedence considerations for the young unmarried people. The center of the table was the scene of gaiety with a concentration of girls and young men. Lord Reerdon was among them, feeling rather dashing on his last chance to play at being available.

Poor Kitty was stationed between a stodgy young man, somebody else's younger son, and the Reverend Edward Turner! She noticed Lieutenant Foxwell glancing in her direction on occasion. She revenged herself by devoting her time to chattering prettily to Mr. Turner. She had never spoken to him for so long together, and found him quite nice, the poor thing.

Georgiana was not enjoying herself. She had accepted Captain Westcombe's request for the honor of the first dance. As he was called to his brother's sickbed, she lacked a partner. Now, capping her dread of being the first to step onto the dance floor, she had to endure everyone's attention as three gentlemen all desired her hand for the opening dance. One young Lothario suggested they fight for the honor since she would not name the lucky man.

"Gentlemen!" Elizabeth remonstrated, with a hint of laughter. Darcy began to rise, with no such hint on his countenance, when Henry Fitzwilliam forestalled him.

"You are too late, sirs. My cousin has already made her choice. I am the fortunate man!" Amongst the cries of disappointment, Georgiana gave him a look of loving gratitude.

As the orchestra introduced the opening dance, Georgiana Darcy was led onto the floor by the man most qualified to give her confidence. She was all grace and womanliness. The bodice of her white silk gown was embroidered with pink roses and pearl beading, her rose bouquet pinned beneath her full bosom. Kitty would have liked to see the colonel in his red coat, but to Georgiana, he looked perfect as he was.

Lord Reerdon bowed, took his hostess's hand and they followed Henry and Georgiana. Darcy led out Lady Reerdon, and the set formed below them.

CHAPTER 20

THREE DAYS OF BALMY WEATHER followed the ball, and the weather was a perfect excuse for laziness. Some of the guests were relaxing in the saloon, where the windows yawned open onto the lawn. Others sat on chairs or lounged on cushions near the lake. Two young ladies made desultory efforts at painting, while three young men reclined on the grass nearby, admiring their work, or their persons. Tea was being set up under the spread of the chestnut trees.

Henry rested from his rowing for a moment and the boat drifted into a patch of afternoon shade. Elizabeth sighed.

"What a beautiful day this is. This weather is extraordinary." She put her hand on Georgiana's. "Tell me, what are your feelings having been launched upon society?"

"Everyone expects me to talk to them. I was so relieved to come in the boat with you."

"They thought you were silent before because you were not 'out.' Now they hope for a flood of words. They must accept you as they find you."

"Which is perfect," said Henry.

"It is very kind of you to say so, Cousin, but I fear I will be found wanting."

"I dare anyone to find you wanting," said Elizabeth. "Did you enjoy your ball?"

"I did. It is thanks to you, Elizabeth, that it was so splendid. I enjoyed the dancing, but people would keep looking at me so."

"What could they do but look at you when you were so lovely?" Henry's question floated away on the still air. At this instant, he felt no longing, no aloneness.

Elizabeth said, "I cherish the privacy here with my dear sister and my—I nearly called you brother." She smiled and looked away over the water, missing the touch of bitterness in his smile.

165

He said, "Darcy has been as a brother to me, more so than my own."

He took up the oars again. He felt how unreasonable was his envy of his cousin. Most of his life this feeling had pecked away at his affection for Darcy, who had never stood in his way and who had been unstintingly generous towards him. His feeling for Elizabeth, now a married woman, was not honorable; he would struggle against it.

Elizabeth glanced at Georgiana. There was a sadness that had not been there before. Henry brought the boat against the little pier.

Darcy came over to them and handed the ladies out. Elizabeth tucked her hand in his arm and they turned away to join the guests under the trees.

Elizabeth nodded to the butler to serve refreshments. She sat by her friend Mrs. Courtney who, on impulse, reached out to touch her hand.

"I continue to marvel over the success of your ball, Elizabeth."

"I confess to feeling a good deal of self-satisfaction. Too much of this experience will make me intolerable."

"I doubt that very much. You have chosen your guests perfectly. No one is left 'on a limb.'" She leaned over to whisper, "Especially Mr. Reginald Foxwell. How well he looks in a scarlet coat, and how the ladies admire him in it."

Elizabeth laughed. "He is really abominably handsome. How the ladies of his congregation would have adored him in the pulpit."

"I imagine he will receive adoration enough in the comfort of his own establishment, with an aunt as well as a wife to worship him," whispered Amelia.

"It is very good of him to provide me with a successful romance from my little party," Elizabeth answered and they both laughed. Mrs. Darcy caught the eye of Mrs. Foxwell, whose nod to her hostess conveyed a certain satisfaction.

It seemed an understanding was inevitable between Reginald Foxwell and Miss Robson. He had danced half the night with her at the ball. Ever since, he had sat by her side, plying her with attentions, which she accepted in a daze of happiness.

Kitty was taking it very well, sitting amongst a group of young men and women, talking, smiling and never looking his way. Elizabeth took a mental note to praise her sister for this decorum later. Meanwhile, she enjoyed a gracious repose at her beautiful home, surrounded by guests among whom she could count several dear to her. What need had she of marchionesses and the self-serving attentions of the London Ton?

Her fruit sat untouched. Breezes rippled the patterns of light and shade and wafted the scent of flowers about her. There was a splashing of the ducks on the water, the faint hum of bees and the soft cry of birds from the woods. She felt the intensity of his gaze, and knew her husband looked at her. Their eyes met. Henry saw Darcy's warm, approving smile. She smiled, too, as enigmatically as ever, but Henry fancied her brief glance to say something like, "How dear your face is become to me."

"I have been impertinent," Henry thought. He rose and walked back to the lake.

He felt her presence at his side even before he turned—dear Georgiana. She put her arm through his. They walked in silence for several minutes. Then she replied to his unspoken thought.

"She does love him. It is not true what some people say."

"What do they say, little one?"

"Why, that she married him for his fortune. How I hate them!"

"They are not worthy of your hatred. They mean no real criticism of her, you know. Our society is so fine that those who marry into a higher sphere are to be congratulated, even if they wed solely for worldly gain. Whereas those who marry beneath them are seen as fools, regardless of how passionately they love, or indeed of the happiness they find."

She squeezed his arm and they walked on, Henry looking bleakly over the lake.

"Will your little friend marry Lieutenant Foxwell?"

"I think so, Henry, if he asks her."

"Of course he'll ask her and sooner rather than later."

"I think she is making a terrible mistake. Did you notice how he pursued Miss Bennet before the arrival of an heiress changed his course?"

"Indeed I did."

"Miss Robson came to my room last night, full of talk of him. She told me that her aunt more than approves; she thinks the world of him. They have known him but four days. What can I do?"

"Nothing whatever."

"Will he make her happy?"

He did not answer, perhaps feeling a little tired of other people's happiness. They walked along in silence, until he said, "Darcy will be pleased."

"Why?"

"This marriage will remove the last trace of the guilt he felt when Lady Catherine deprived young Foxwell of his living. I doubt he would have made a conquest like this from his vicarage."

"She is but his prey! As I may be, courted for nought but my fortune."

"Your friends will take better care of you than Miss Robson's have of her, never fear."

"I wish you would not go, Henry," whispered Georgiana.

"My father bids me home; I know not what he wants of me." She was cut through, unaccustomed to this cynical tone. Unaware, he continued, "Then I must attend upon Lady Catherine, until it is time to return to my regiment."

A tear slid down her cheek. "Do you weep for me still, Georgiana? Do you not know I have just begun my cure?"

"I am happy to hear it."

"Then I am happy too."

"Next winter, I will be out, and I must accompany Fitzwilliam and Elizabeth, when they are invited into society. Last winter, I would sometimes sit in Elizabeth's dressing room and watch her dress to go out—do not laugh at me."

"When have I laughed at you?"

"I would pretend to myself that I were a little girl and she my mother."

His heart yawned open. Such tiny figures they seemed, Georgiana and he, standing on the rim of the world.

"Dear Georgiana, your brother and I did our best for you. Yet we could not manage the part of mother." She smiled and looked away.

"Let us take a little tour around the lake, for I must away after luncheon."

She took his arm again and tucked herself in at his side.

"Dear Georgiana," he said, "you are the only being, in all the world for whom I am not superfluous."

The colonel left, duty-bound, but three more weeks of summer pleasures went by at Pemberley. By day, there were walks and drives for the ladies and fishing for the men. In the evening, there was music, dancing and cards. The last entertainment was a concert.

Mr. and Mrs. Edgeley did not accompany their daughters to the musical evening. The curate's health was the given reason, but, in truth, it was so long since his wife had a new evening gown that she lacked the courage to face such a fashionable crowd. The lure of the music was too great for Anna, and the adventure for Emily.

Elizabeth was pleased to see Mr. Turner make a point of speaking to the Misses Edgeley, staying with them in the drawing room until dinner.

When the ladies withdrew, Elizabeth ran up to the music room to insure that all was in readiness. As she re-entered the drawing room, the first ladies she encountered were Anna and Emily with Miss Bingley. Caroline was saying, "I adore nothing so much as a simple meal followed by an impromptu little concert among friends." Perhaps Caroline did not know that the sumptuous array of dishes served at dinner was not seen by everyone as a simple repast. She turned to Miss Edgeley. "Your performance upon the harp last month was exquisite. I do hope you will honor us again this evening."

The faintest of flushes heightened Anna's marble cheeks at the implication she was a hired musician.

"I think not, Miss Bingley."

"Oh?"

"Why have they come then?" Caroline thought. She saw her hostess.

"My dear Mrs. Darcy, I declare I am heartbroken, for Miss Edgeley says she will not play for us this evening."

"I have hired musicians, Miss Bingley, so my guests will hardly play."

"What a foolish mistake. I do beg your pardon." She curtsied deeply to Anna and swept away.

Elizabeth followed her with her eyes for a moment. "Insolent girl. What motive could she possibly have for insulting young women so inoffensive and unprotected as these?" she thought.

When the gentlemen joined the ladies, Edward Turner looked around the room. He saw Kitty with a lively group of elegant young people. He hesitated, before rejoining the Misses Edgeley.

Quite lacking in talent for small talk, Anna was a stimulating conversationalist for a cultivated man such as this. Her musical knowledge was formidable and she was as well read as any other lady in the room, doubtless much better read than most. Emily was happy to stay in the background, watching the faint spark that lit the cool grey of her sister's eyes.

Miss Robson slipped out of the room for a few moments and, immediately, Lieutenant Foxwell approached Kitty. With an innocent smile to the officer, she walked straight past him and went to the nearest available young man.

"Mr. Turner," she cooed sweetly, "I had not seen you. How do you do, sir?" Whence came the color in her cheeks? Turner feared it was matched by his own.

Kitty turned, and said, "Miss Edgeley, Miss Emily, I am so happy to see you again. I hope your parents are in good health?"

"They are tolerably well, thank you," Miss Edgeley replied. "I understand you have not been in good health yourself, Miss Bennet."

"I took a cold, from dancing on the terrace at the ball, and you must take the blame, Mr. Turner, for you would make me do it." He laughed at the injustice of this claim, while Kitty turned back to the ladies and continued, "It was such a splendid evening. All the doors were open, and the terrace lit up with torches. It looked so gothic, so thrilling. Some of us ran outside and formed our own set on the terrace." In spite of herself, Emily's imagination was fired, but Anna felt a chill. "I was dancing with Mr. Turner and he made me go out too, although I knew I must not, for I always catch cold. Lizzy was ever so cross with me, but I got better after a day or two, so she was wrong, after all."

His voice was warm. "I am much relieved that you have recovered, Miss Bennet. I should never have allowed it, had I known of this delicacy."

"How should you have prevented me?"

He looked into her upturned face. "I know not." She looked up at him with the suggestion of a pout.

"Mr. Turner, I shall leave you now, for I have interrupted a very learned conversation, I am sure."

"Perhaps you have, but the interruption was not unwelcome."

"I think it must have been. I daresay you were talking of music. I cannot talk about music, for I am fearfully ignorant of it." Mr. Turner looked as though he thought this an admirable trait.

She put her hand on his arm and said, "I shall tell you why sometime, if you promise your secrecy." Leaning towards him, she was seemingly unaware that her bodice gaped ever so slightly.

Miss Edgeley became suddenly very interested in the painting on the wall behind them, and turned away. Emily gazed at her in helpless sympathy.

"Do not, Emily, pray." Emily turned to the picture.

Edward spoke softly. "Tell me, now, Miss Bennet, I beg you."

She looked down demurely. "A very horrible man would come to our house. He was a . . . music master." On his quiet little laugh, she looked up. "He said to Mama that it was 'quite hopeless' to try to teach me. Do you not think that very cruel?" Where was the articulateness with which Edward had so impressed Mr. Darcy? He could scarcely answer her.

"Yes."

"Will the weather continue fine, do you think, Mr. Turner?"

"The weather? Not for very much longer, I should think. It has been unusually warm for this part of the country."

"I do so hope it does, for I go to Scarborough next week and I am determined to go sea bathing."

"You go to Scarborough? When will you return?"

"I know not if I shall ever return," she said carelessly. "Perhaps I shall go with my sister Mrs. Bingley to Hertfordshire."

Turning to the Miss Edgeleys, she said, "The music is about to begin. Shall we go up together?"

She seated the curate's daughters one each side of her. Wonderfully dainty she looked between them.

"You shall sit there, Mr. Turner," she said, indicating the seat next to Anna. "And the two of you can say clever things to each other."

Elizabeth sent Kitty an approving smile, and Kitty's demure look seemed to say, "Am I not good to be so kind to these poor things?"

She thought she would sit with them for the first part of the program, after which she would surely have done her duty by them.

Indeed, when they moved into the reception room for refreshments, Kitty stayed only a moment or two at their side, before flitting off in the direction of the same happy group she had found so entertaining earlier. Turner occupied himself with helping Anna and Emily to cake and champagne. Darcy came to speak to them. If he had hoped for a lively discussion of the first part of the program, he was disappointed. The atmosphere was constrained. In someone else's house, he would have wandered off again. As host, he made an effort to animate them. After a few minutes, Darcy asked Turner if he had spoken to the bishop, who, with his wife, was spending a few days at Pemberley on their way north. As he had not, he took the young vicar from the ladies.

Anna and Emily watched their retreating backs. Emily whispered, "I believe Mr. Turner is attentive to Miss Bennet out of respect for her brother-in-law."

"I judge differently, Emily."

"Anna—"

"I will speak of him no more."

Meanwhile, it was arranged that the bishop and his wife, with the Darcys, would come to church at Kympton on Sunday. Mr. Turner felt emboldened to invite them to breakfast at the vicarage.

Kitty did not quite know how it happened that she sat next to Mr. Turner for the second half of the concert. Perhaps it was his hopeful look. She looked straight ahead at the flautist, fascinated by the rapt look in his eyes and the way his lips pursed against the instrument. The sound of the music must have affected her strangely, for she felt disturbed. She never turned her head, but did not forget, for a moment, the man beside her. Never before had maleness made quite this impression upon her. He looked at her flushed face, her dark hair curled neatly against her head. How slight was her figure, how tiny her bosom. He turned back to the flautist. Sitting on the other side of him, Anna called on the discipline of years and attuned her mind solely to the music. There was nothing else for her here.

CHAPTER 21

OVER THE NEXT DAY OR SO, the carriages rolled away from the steps and up the hill.

Amelia leaned out of her carriage window.

"Dear, dear Elizabeth, until London then, I bid you farewell. I have so enjoyed myself. However, too much of a good thing spoils one. Tomorrow, I make my obeisance to Mother."

"Goodbye," laughed Elizabeth.

Amelia sank back in her seat.

"Do not look so cross, Teddy. It was but a jest."

Bingley was anxious on leaving. Before getting into the carriage, he said, "Darcy, I do wish you had viewed Rushly Manor before we quite settled upon it."

"You would rush into the decision, Bingley. You still have the opportunity to withdraw. Have you retained my notes regarding the points we discussed?"

"Yes, absolutely." He added hopefully, "We did so like the house, Darcy."

"Your enthusiasm will wane in winter, especially if you are tardy in bringing down the trees on the south side of the house. Be sure to insist upon all salient points with the agent, before you sign."

"Of course, I wouldn't consider buying the place if any practical matters were left unsatisfactory."

"Unless the price is adjusted accordingly."

"Yes, indeed. That would make it all right."

From the carriage steps, Miss Bingley turned.

"I will insure that my brother follows your excellent advice, Mr. Darcy."

Elizabeth added, "If you are still uncertain, you can turn to Kitty for her views."

"Yes, Kitty!" cried Bingley. "You must give us your opinion on everything."

"In that case I am relieved of all uneasiness," muttered Darcy.

Elizabeth took Jane's hands in hers. "Dear Jane, I hope your heart is not too set upon making Rushly Manor your home, for my husband may yet forbid Charles buying it."

"Lizzy!" The gentle reproof dissolved in laughter.

"Jane, Jane. When I think that in four months we will be but three hours' journey from each other, I am delirious with joy."

"And I, Lizzy. My happiness will be complete."

"In more ways than one," whispered her sister, with a subtle glance towards Jane's stomach, its small swell hidden by the folds of her coat.

"Away you all go! Buy Rushly Manor this very night, then fly to Scarborough. Get yourselves very wet by day and dazzle the local populace by night."

They watched the carriage drive away. Darcy said, "He is capable of purchasing the place without making the slightest claim for the cost of repairs. He took Netherfield on a ten-year lease without even going upstairs."

Elizabeth put her arm through his.

"Bingley is fortunate to have such a very sensible friend as you to keep him from harm."

"There can be no argument against that."

She smiled. "Of course, you are fortunate, too, in having a friend who so appreciates your guidance."

He looked at her coolly. "A compensation, I suppose, for lacking a wife who does?"

"I appreciate your guidance exceedingly. I do not, perhaps, prostrate myself every time you part your lips, but should you like it if I did?"

"I have not been given the opportunity to assess the happiness of such a circumstance."

"You may enjoy the performance the first time, but within two months of the day that you conquered me so completely, you would cease to notice me altogether."

"Perhaps." He laughed.

"Walk with me, Fitzwilliam? We have a week to ourselves, before the Gardiners come. Let us begin to enjoy it now."

She took one arm and Georgiana the other, and they walked towards the bridge across the stream.

"The Hursts and Miss Bingley were disappointed that you did not join their adventure to Scarborough, Georgiana Kitty was thrilled to take your place."

"I should much rather stay here with you and Fitzwilliam. I hope Kitty will enjoy her stay there. She . . ."

"Go on."

"It is nothing worth mentioning."

"I am sure it is," laughed Elizabeth.

"I thought that Kitty was in two minds about going to Scarborough just at the end."

"That would have been the effect of the letter from my papa. I showed a passage in it to Mrs. Hurst, who promised faithfully not to let Kitty within twenty feet of a red coat."

"I suppose it must be that."

"You can be quite sure of it."

They stopped on the bridge, looking out over the stream to the lake. Reflections of billowing clouds rippled across the water. Georgiana drew her coat about her. They crossed the bridge and entered the wood, their usually brisk pace adjusted to Georgiana's slower step. The wind was freshening as they wound around the paths. Elizabeth skipped ahead and turned to face them.

"How wonderful it is to be alone together," she said. "I love to be with my friends, and I love to be without them, too."

"Daily my disinclination for society grows," said Darcy. "Can you not imagine us living happily here, always?"

Elizabeth danced away from them, laughing.

"For a time."

"We are not enough for you?" he asked, smiling slightly.

"Not nearly enough. I am like my papa. At whom can I laugh, if I lack fresh subjects for my study?"

He smiled, but not with his eyes.

She said, "You would not separate me from my sisters."

"You have a sister here," he said, "who loves you with all the devotion of a lifetime's acquaintance, I believe."

"I cannot bear comparison to the sisters whom Elizabeth has loved all her life," protested Georgiana.

"Indeed you can and do!" declared Elizabeth. "Yet I do not stop caring for Jane because I care for you."

"Naturally, our relations are included in our family party," said Darcy.

She smiled and turned to walk up the path ahead of them. After a moment's silence, she said, over her shoulder, "I believe you mean to keep me from London, sir!"

"No, indeed. My pleasure in this opportunity to monopolize your society has bred a momentary fancy to be ever thus."

"Good Lord!" she cried, and faced them again. "If you are to begin having momentary fancies, I shan't know who you are, Fitzwilliam."

He laughed and put out his hand to her. She came back to them, and took his arm. They walked on.

The wind began to creak in the trees and pull at the ladies' coats. Georgiana shivered and they turned back to the house. By the time they recrossed the little bridge, dark clouds had massed. As the footman took Elizabeth's coat, he said, "A letter is just come for you from Deepdene, madam."

The envelope lay on the tray, its black border announcing its contents before it was opened. The marchioness wrote that her nephew, Lord Bradford, had died, without recovering consciousness. Their immediate concern was to calm Lady Bradford, whose display of hysterical grief threatened the safety of her unborn babe. Until the babe was delivered, the identity of the next earl, indeed the next marquess, too, remained unknown.

Georgiana flushed. How he would change, the kind and thoughtful lieutenant, should he succeed his brother to the title. He would be too full of his own importance to ever trouble himself again about anyone else's feelings but his own.

At Scarborough, the sad news of the death did not unduly disturb the party. Caroline had barely noticed the colonel's quiet friend, and now wished she had. Her sister, Mrs. Hurst, was engrossed in her responsibilities. Caroline needed no watching, but under Louisa's chaperonage, Kitty would be protected indeed. At more than one assembly and party, requests were made by officers of the regiment, encamped near Scarborough, to be introduced to Miss Bennet. These were met by Mrs. Hurst's gracious refusals on the grounds of the young lady's excessive shyness. Her little nod let the M.C. at the assembly know that Miss Bennet's timidity may be overcome by a certain minimum income.

Mr. Hurst was, on occasion, prevailed upon to accompany the ladies on their promenades. He snuffed up the air as he strolled along the sea front, his wife on his arm. Mrs. Hurst looked as elegant as ever, despite a certain plumpness that lingered after her confinement. She planned to deal with this setback by long walks and sea bathing. At times, they called to mind their tiny offspring, safely fostered in a village.

"We could look in on the dear little fellow on our way to London in November, Mr. Hurst," said Louisa.

"I see no call for that until he is walking and able to say something for himself. Then, perhaps, we might bring him home with us."

"Certainly, there is no call to bring him home for a year or so. However, I should like to see how he goes on in a month or so."

"You won't need to do that, Louisa. Mrs. Thingum, that curate's wife, visits him, don't she?"

"Indeed she does, my dear. I would not have her say she takes more interest in my child than does its mother."

"For what purpose am I paying the foster fee, Louisa?"

"I know Lady Reerdon does not approve of children being left unvisited for long periods."

"Oh, Lady Reerdon, you say. Well, well, we had best take a look at 'im, though I must say it is out of our way."

Mrs. Hurst smiled and turned to look over her shoulder to where Caroline was walking arm in arm with Kitty.

"Caroline, dearest, is that not Miss Whittaker?"

"I declare it is. Look, Kitty, over yonder, did you ever see a bonnet more cunning?"

"Is that Miss Arabella Whittaker, the niece of the marchioness? How beautiful she is!" cried Kitty.

"That is she," said Caroline. "Her looks are fashionable certainly, and her features tolerable, but I cannot see her celebrated beauty."

"Lizzy says she is like a Greek goddess."

"I will own her brother to be very handsome. Will you speak to her, Louisa, or shall I?"

Before Louisa could reply, Miss Whittaker saw them and bowed most cordially. Kitty was deeply impressed by every detail of Miss Whittaker's brother: his looks, his air, his dress. She was delighted when the reunion was followed by an invitation to take tea with the pair.

Mr. Whittaker did not improve upon acquaintance. She knew not what to make of manners such as the Whittakers'. They were elegant, they were indolent, they were witty, but she did not understand above one word in five of their conversation. She felt that they were teasing her, though so subtly she did not know what to think. She wrote to Elizabeth that she had never met such stupid people, though they were so handsome and so rich. Both had particularly asked to be remembered to the "bewitching" Mrs. Darcy. Mr. Whittaker, indeed, referred to Elizabeth's especial qualities, with an insinuating air that almost frightened Kitty. She was very glad when they said they were not to stay long in Scarborough, as they were "persecuted by so many invitations."

Otherwise Kitty passed her time pleasantly enough, finding time for only one letter to her sister Lydia.

Scarborough

Dearest Lydia,
We have been at Scarborough these two weeks and I like it very well.

179

We attended the assembly on Tuesday evening and I wore my white silk. We were a very grand party. I danced every dance, but imagine my disappointment! That horrible Mrs. Hurst would not permit the M.C. to introduce a single officer to me! This is Lizzy's doing!

Just imagine, a terribly old, dreadfully repulsive man asked to be introduced to Miss Bingley. His name is Mr. Houlter. Can you picture my amazement when she stood up with him? It seems he is a widower with a great fortune. Mrs. Hurst said he is not at all old, but in the prime of life, which seems to mean much the same thing. If I am an old maid at twenty-four, I hope I shall not be so desperate as Miss Bingley.

I danced one dance with Mr. Houlter and he makes the most horrid snorting noise when he laughs.

Jane has consulted a physician who orders the most terrible regime for me. I must go sea bathing every day, regardless of the weather. I walk constantly, accompanied by Mrs. Hurst and Miss Bingley. Mr. Houlter is always to be found dawdling about in hopes of seeing Caroline. He bows low over her hand and looks at her adoringly over his big red nose. How can she bear it? Everyone supposes he will soon make her an offer of marriage.

I cannot understand him being so cold-hearted in marrying for the second time. I should expect my husband to mourn me forever!

I quite forgot to tell you that Miss Robson is to marry my admirer, Lieutenant Foxwell. Lizzy said that he is a man who will be unlikely to stop flirting after the honeymoon. Can you imagine what it would be like to be married to a man who pursues other women? I should hate it, should not you?

It was very droll listening to Mr. Turner preach after dancing with him on the terrace at the ball. He is the vicar of Kympton, a sweet village, but with not so many shops as Lambton. Perhaps Wickham knows of it.

The vicarage is not so big as Longbourn, but is a very comfortable house. Mr. Turner showed us everything, while the bishop slept in his chair. Mr. Darcy asked a score of questions, even what is his income from the glebe! I know not what makes him so inquisitive.

He showed me some chicks. Mr. Turner, I mean.

I should like to return to Pemberley when our party here breaks up, but Jane has said I am to come with them to Hertfordshire. They are to supervise the packing up of the house, for Bingley has purchased an estate in Yorkshire called Rushly Manor. Such a sweet house with mullioned windows and two little towers, each with a conical roof! Much work is needed, for the roof leaks dreadfully and the attics are ruined. The work is starting at once, as Bingley does not wish Mr. Darcy to see the place as it is. When all is made new, it will be the charmingest place in the world. See if I do not have adventures there!

Give my best to Wickham. Take very good care of yourself, now you are so near your time. Soon I shall be "Aunt Catherine." How fearsome that sounds!

Your affectionate sister,
Kitty

CHAPTER 22

AT LONGBOURN, some weeks later, Mr. Bennet quite failed to appreciate the drollery of his new title of grandpapa. He tossed the letter on the breakfast table.

"Our daughter has excelled herself, Mrs. Bennet."

"Of which of the girls do you speak, Mr. Bennet? Is it my darling Lydia?"

"Certainly. This letter is from Mr. Wickham, and very pleased with himself he sounds."

"What news, Mr. Bennet? Is it a boy then?"

"Two boys, Mrs. Bennet, and Wickham has not even the sense to be alarmed by the excess."

"My darling Lydia. Twins! What a clever little thing she is."

"If this is a variety of genius, Mrs. Bennet, perhaps it is as well she is so productive. Her husband may not be able to provide for these sons, but they are proof at last of her talent. Their names are George and John."

"George for their father and, I am sure, John to honor their grandfather."

"If they have twenty sons and name them all for me, I will give them no money."

"O, Mr. Bennet!"

"I am determined. Would you have Kitty or Mary think she may marry as foolishly and then call upon her father for assistance?"

"I believe," put in Mary, "that favoring a wayward child is not regarded with approval by the church."

"Hold your tongue, girl! Find Kitty and prepare yourselves for a visit to Netherfield. We must pass on the news!"

The Bingleys had arrived home with Kitty two weeks before and had found the courage, after several days, to announce their plans to remove to Yorkshire. The depth of Mrs. Bennet's grief was demonstrated by a fit of hysterics, and hard words were spoken to Jane, the sweetest-natured of her children.

The following morning, all was forgotten.

"My, Jane, how well you look! This is the best time for a woman's appearance, four months or so before her confinement. I have come with news about Lydia. Your father had a letter from dear Wickham this morning. Can you guess his news?"

"It can only be a boy or a girl, I suppose?"

"There you are wrong, Jane. She has two boys—twins! She has a start upon her sisters!"

"I am very happy for her."

"I shall send her a little extra money. I promised to pay for the child to be put out to nurse this next twelve-month. It will cost more now."

"Why does she not care for them herself?" asked Mary.

"Lord, no! What an idea! Lydia was not brought up to play the nursemaid."

"She may as well hire a nurse to care for them," said Kitty.

"How can you be so foolish, child?" said Mrs. Bennet. "What did you think? That Wickham's as rich as Croesus?"

"I knew not that they were so poor as this."

"How will she manage without my help when I die? Her father will give her nothing, I know. He has a heart of stone!" said Mrs. Bennet. "There will be no officer for you, my girl—unless he has a private income."

"You seemed to like the officers very well, Mama, when they were encamped in Meryton. You said you loved a red coat when you were a girl."

"Yes, I liked them well enough but when it came to marriage, I took your father, a man with a good fortune."

Mrs. Bennet became happily immersed in talk of small clothes.

Kitty sighed. The time was passing, not too slowly, for she made a certain impression in Hertfordshire nowadays. She blushed to recall how she and Lydia used to shout across the street to a group of officers, and how Aunt Phillips would call out from her drawing room window to young gentlemen of her acquaintance to come in and take refreshments with her nieces. Such behavior had been good enough for the drawing rooms and assemblies of Meryton, but time spent in Elizabeth's house had given her polish. She had an air that had not been there a year before. There was a modesty in her demeanor, attractively spiced with naive-sounding remarks and large-eyed gazes. In short, she had learned more ladylike ways to play.

She had a fondness still for a scarlet coat, but she remembered also a time when she had stood quite close to someone in a black coat, and their fingers had touched fleetingly as he put a little chick in her hands. Her nose had flinched a little at the smell of the poultry. She could still hear the clucking of the hens, and the squeaking of the chick. She felt again its fluttering warmth in her hands, and the sensation of his fingers brushing her own. She started as the door opened to admit Miss Bingley. This young lady greeted Mrs. Bennet and her daughters with all her customary warmth, and said to Kitty, "You were a great success at the assembly, Miss Kitty. I recall you always did have a way with the gentlemen of Hertfordshire." There was something in the way she pronounced "gentlemen" that may have needled Kitty's mama, were she not in such an excellent mood.

"Kitty is in great demand since she came home from Derbyshire," cried the proud mother.

"Of course Kitty meant to be kind, but it is not absolutely needful to stand up with a physician."

"Mr. Walsh never forgets his place!" snapped Mrs. Bennet. "When there is a shortage of gentlemen for the assembly, we are happy to include him."

Caroline sniggered quietly and turned to her sister.

"Dearest Jane!" she said. "Allow me to assist you. You will tire yourself excessively over that sweet little dress."

Caroline made herself very useful in this phase of Jane's life by having an opinion on everything and being ready to scold any servant whose performance was not up to her standards. She missed the position of mistress of the house and sometimes thought wistfully of Mr. Houlter's wealth.

"Did I do right in refusing his marriage proposal?" she wondered. She recalled their meetings, in the streets and drawing rooms of Scarborough. All along, she had intended accepting him but when he seized her hand she had been so filled with revulsion that she had changed her mind at once. She recalled the gracious terms in which she couched her refusal: her "deep respect," her "high esteem" and the devotion of which he was "so deserving." In a matter of weeks she would again be in London, where she would waste no opportunity to secure an eligible establishment of her own.

While she embroidered small garments, Mrs. Bennet talked of the grandchildren she now had and the little Bingley to come. She thought of Lizzy, who had proved she could do her duty in producing an heir for Mr. Darcy. If only she would get on with it! She knotted her thread with a jerk and snipped it off sharply.

She desired the young women to tell her all about Scarborough and was startled when informed it was to the east of Derbyshire. Gracious, she had quite thought it to be westerly.

Was it near Newcastle then, where dwelt her darling Lydia? Not so very near? How far off Newcastle must be!

"I suppose Mr. Darcy was not inclined to allow Lizzy to join you in Scarborough," she said. "How dull poor Lizzy will be feeling. I shall write her a nice long letter to cheer her up."

CHAPTER 23

AT PEMBERLEY, the last days of summer had passed very pleasantly, with the solitude interrupted only by visits from the Gardiners and from Mr. Bennet, who delighted Elizabeth by arriving unannounced, just as he had in London. Apart from exploring the park with his daughter and touring the farms with his son-in-law, Mr. Bennet spent many blissful hours in Darcy's library. He had asked Bingley for details of the collection and the young man had told his father-in-law everything he knew, which was that Darcy had a fearful number of books. He had returned to Longbourn with a supply to last him until he next saw them.

Every season that Elizabeth spent at Pemberley became her new favorite. She loved to walk in the groves with scarlet and gold leaves swirling about her. She kicked up the debris; she ran along the paths with the wind blowing in her face.

She had never spent so long a time with so little society. They entertained only the local clergy, for the immediate district offered no families of their standing. They did not miss society. They had each other. Of course, they had Georgiana, too. Elizabeth asked her if it were too dull for her, but, no, she did not want society.

There was but one cloud on Elizabeth's happiness. She had never read Lady Catherine's reply to Darcy's announcement of their engagement; but, be it ever so offensive, she did not like to be a cause of his quarreling with his relations. Lady Catherine had had some cause for anger with her nephew, in feeling that her daughter had been thrown over—and for a girl whom all society must see as beneath him.

Elizabeth wished him to heal the breach.

"Fitzwilliam, shall you write to Miss de Bourgh on the occasion of her marriage?"

"Certainly, I shall write this week. Have you any message to add?"

"Tell her I look forward to seeing them both at Pemberley."

"I will be most surprised if we ever receive her here. We may not even receive a reply, Elizabeth. You will take no offense, I hope."

"I would not fly into a huff. However, Lord Reerdon will surely wish her to reply, as his mother is a particular friend of yours. If she does, we will find our capacity for forgiveness untested."

"Anne is her mother's creature."

"Fitzwilliam, this might be an appropriate occasion to write also to Lady Catherine. What say you?"

"I think not, Elizabeth. Her behavior was unpardonable and I shall not pardon it. Until she apologizes, I shall never communicate with her." She rose and came across to where he sat. She stood beside him and bent her head to touch his.

"'Never' is so long a word. Her ladyship grows old and will be soon alone."

He took her hand, held it to his lips, then said, "This is something you must leave to me, dearest."

Lord Maddersfield wrote to his nephew from Rosings, where he was staying with his sister, Lady Catherine. He wrote of the excellence of the match and continued:

That fool Reerdon has signed the marriage articles without any reference to what becomes of her ladyship's fortune should Anne die before her mother. She will keep him dancing at her pleasure these twenty years, if he wants to be sure of Rosings Park.

I have told Lady C. that, from all I hear of Mrs. Darcy's sauciness, she is a prize and just the type of girl I fancy for myself. "Yes, indeed," I said, "Had I met Darcy's lady first, he'd have been calling her Aunt, not Wife." (Now that would have stuck in your throat, my boy!) There followed a tremendous row, as you can imagine. Lady C. impersonated Medusa and Reerdon came nigh to fainting. Henry soothed them all, in his way. It was all tremendous fun.

Two more days of this entertainment and they will be wed. They are to be married by a clownish parson called Collins. I never met with such an ass. Anne whispered to me that he is Mrs. D.'s cousin, but that will be just her spite.

Should you write to your cousin Anne, you need not mention this letter. I see no need to antagonize my sister unduly.

Yours etc.
Maddersfield

A few days later, this letter was followed by one from Darcy's cousin.

From Countess Reerdon to Mr. Darcy

Rosings

My dear Cousin,
I thank you for your kind letter, but then you have always been a good and generous friend to me, who had no one else so akin to a brother.

(This gush of affection may have startled Darcy less had he seen that Lady Reerdon was perched upon his lordship's pillow as she wrote.)

Please convey my gratitude and compliments to your charming wife. My Lord Reerdon and I will be delighted to visit you at Pemberley. Of course, we will be more than happy to receive you any time you can come to Cumberwell or to either of our houses in Scotland and Surrey.

You will be surprised to see our address is still at Rosings. We intend to winter in Surrey just so soon as his lordship is well enough to be moved. Lord Reerdon met with a carriage accident on the day of our marriage. Fortunately, the surgeon has not had to amputate the limb, and we expect him to be fully recovered in a few weeks, or months at most.

If you wish to communicate with us, you might do so through Mr. Collins. We have found Mrs. Darcy's cousin has been a most Christian and obliging spiritual shepherd during a somewhat difficult period.

I remain,

Your grateful and affectionate cousin,
Anne, Countess of Reerdon-on-Adswater

"I had no notion of what a sweet cousin you had been to Miss de Bourgh!" said Elizabeth.

"I feel she is rendering history more interesting. As children we hated one another with utmost vehemence. Once my probable matrimonial fate dawned upon me, I subsided into doomed silence. It has been years since she said much more to me than 'Good morning, Fitzwilliam' or 'Good night, Fitzwilliam.'"

"Of course you endeavored to draw her out."

He smiled. "Perhaps not. At all events, you are vindicated, my love. She has not only replied, but with an unexpected cordiality."

"You are more than a little curious?"

"Not at all," he said. "It is no business of mine what occurs in the privacy of another's home."

"I am curious, although you are not. Your stance is highly moral, and I shall respect it by not breathing a word to you on this subject, should I find out more."

"It is a wife's duty to confide in her husband."

"Wonderful news! Let us say, then, when we gossip, that I am being dutiful, and you are being . . . what?"

He smiled.

Events at Hunsford justified curiosity, and their effects were to be felt in the family.

With Anne advantageously engaged, and the Collinses fully reinstated as pet sycophants, life at Rosings had continued with all the pleasantness that was customary there.

As the time of Anne's marriage approached, Lady Reerdon returned to stay again at Rosings, bringing her son that he might pass a period of courtship before the wedding.

In no time at all, Lady Catherine began to feel a certain disquiet.

Firstly, a disagreement sprang up about the young couple's destination after the wedding. Lady Catherine had decided upon Bath. Lord Reerdon had the presumption to cry, "Not that dull place!"

"I beg your pardon, my lord?" said Lady Catherine.

"Ah," he replied, and thought perhaps he'd let it go, but he felt he was getting off to a poor start.

Lady Catherine also objected to the way Reerdon had taken to addressing his intended. One morning, when he came into breakfast, he chucked Anne under the chin and said, "Good morning, my little sparrow."

"Good morning, Frederick," she simpered.

"Humph!" said Lady Catherine.

Lord Maddersfield gave one of his snorts, which he knew so irritated his sister.

Lord Reerdon sat down and whispered to Anne, "When we are married, I shall dress you up in bright colors and make you my little parrot instead."

"What did you say, my lord? I will not permit conversations in which I have no part," said Lady Catherine.

"I said nothing worthy of repetition, ma'am, but I shall now say whatever you like."

"Ha! Very handsome offer," called Maddersfield. "You cannot complain about that, Sister."

Anne smiled up at Frederick. How brave he was, and how exciting to think that her clothes would soon be chosen by someone with an eye to color! Her mother had always chosen rather dull clothes for her.

Further evidence of Anne's erratic behavior was seen one evening when Reerdon asked her to show him the whereabouts of the dictionary. This was obviously a pretext to get her out of the room. As they came back in, a little smirk on the face of each aroused her ladyship's suspicions. Yet the way he tripped on the edge of the carpet, and all but sprawled on the floor, somehow put her mind at rest.

(Anne was not exactly permitting liberties. He did kiss her, on her lips, but she told him he was naughty. He answered her with the intriguing smile of a man of the world. She felt breathless and fluttery, a little faint. She wanted, but she knew not what.)

Her ladyship began to heartily look forward to getting the wedding out of the way.

The many blessings of Lady Catherine's patronage were never far from the mind of Mr. Collins. Few clergymen have the honor to officiate at such a ceremony as the marriage between Lord Reerdon and Miss Anne de Bourgh. After an excellent breakfast, all that was lacking was that the young people drive away. Anne was handed gallantly into the carriage by her husband. Through the window, she glanced once more at the austere face of her mother. Their eyes met and the bride felt a delicious sensation. Her new commander, Lord of the Ascendant, leapt for the carriage step. He missed it.

Thus on his wedding day was Frederick Lester, ninth earl of Reerdon-on-Adswater, carried back into his mother-in-law's house, whence he ought to have been carrying his prize away. He should have looked first. He had only himself to blame.

He was placed in his room and the surgeon called. The wound was certainly untimely, but the fracture of a degree that should easily mend.

"Anne," said her mother, "you will return to your old room."

"I fear not, Mother," said she. "Frederick has requested that I sleep in his room. Perhaps a small bed might be carried in for me."

"Preposterous!" cried Lady Catherine. "You shall sleep in your old room."

Anne's mouth pursed up, and she tried to hold her mother's stare. She looked down. Lady Catherine smiled.

"You are yourself again, I see. I will disregard this outburst, Anne. You will go now and lie down for an hour."

"Yes, Mama."

She crept up to her room and found it prepared for her. She lay down upon her bed, intending to think very hard, and promptly fell asleep. When she awoke, the hour had passed. She trotted along to Reerdon's room.

The very sight of her valiant lord lying back pale, his eyes dull with pain, filled her with remorse for her cowardice.

"Oh, Frederick dear, Mama will not allow me to sleep in here, and I so want to be near you."

"Never mind, little sparrow. I would be no use to you, with my leg like this."

"Frederick, I thought I could be of use to you. I thought you wanted me here."

"So I do, but what's to be done? I would soon straighten the matter out, if I were well." The firmness of his tone sent a shiver through her.

"Are you cold, poppet? Sit up next to me, then. Good gracious, you weigh no more than a will-o'-th'-wisp." She felt the movement of his muscles through his nightshirt. He pulled her close. He kissed her, quite differently from that time before. She could feel his hand pressing against the spot under her arm where her heart beat, so fast. She knew not if she wished or feared that he might reach a little further. He groaned.

"What did they give me, Anne?"

"Laudanum."

Someone knocked sharply at the door and opened it so quickly that she had only time to sit up primly on the bed. Lady Catherine strode in, followed by Lady Reerdon. Anne slipped off the bed and faced them. Reerdon squinted, his vision out of focus, and he made out a fierce old lady glaring at his poppet.

"Go to your room, Anne," said her mother.

Anne shook with a feeling of which she did not know the name. Breath came to her with such a struggle; she was suffocating. The words burst out, "I shall only leave if my husband bids me go."

It was long since her mother's eyes had looked at her like this, with a chill that scorched her. Her blood was pounding in her ears; her stomach churned. One thing could save her. She must throw herself on her knees and beg her mother's forgiveness, grovel, cry and clutch the hem of her gown.

But . . . rising through the fear was something new.

"My dear Anne—" began Lady Reerdon reasonably.

"She stays," slurred Reerdon. "You hear me."

Anne straightened. Her eyes twitched as she tried to hold her mother's stare.

Like icicles on a frosty night, the ever-dreaded words dropped from her ladyship's lips. "Anne, I am most seriously displeased."

Anne's lips trembled so that she knew her fear could be seen. She put her shaking hands behind her.

Then twenty-three years of a feeling, so deeply buried she had scarcely known it was there, surged up hotly through her. It was rage. Fury beat in her ears and in her head.

"I care not!"

Her face a mask of hatred, Lady Catherine swept from the room.

"You plucky little love," mumbled Reerdon.

"You pair of fools!" hissed his mother and hurried after her hostess.

"Give me a kiss, Anne," muttered the bridegroom, and he lost consciousness.

Later, Reerdon's valet ushered in the hired nurse. The patient was sunk in deep slumber and, her tear-stained face next to his on the pillow, lay Anne, fast asleep. As the nurse began to lift her in her meaty arms, the bride stirred, reached out and clasped a handful of Frederick's nightshirt.

"Best ring for her maid, Mr. Larton. Poor thing."

The two women changed Anne into her nightdress and tucked her in beside her husband.

"I never before sat up with a married couple on their nuptial night!" chuckled the nurse. "If his lordship wakes and gets frisky, I'll 'it him on the 'ead."

"I hardly think there will be call for that, Nurse."

The nurse snorted leeringly.

"There's not much for him to get a hold of, anyhow."

The maid frowned. "I shall sleep in here tonight, to be near should Miss de—the Countess need me," said the maid haughtily. "I shall take the settee."

"Just as you like, dearie. I have no need of it, for I shall be on duty."

Anne and Frederick slept the night away in each others' arms. With her fingers in her ears, the maid tossed on the hard settee, to the tuneful accompaniment of the snores of the nurse in her armchair.

Day followed long day at Rosings, and neither party varied in determination. Never could the dowager Lady Reerdon have predicted such a pass.

"My dear Frederick," she pleaded, "I beg you to temper your conduct with a thought to Lady Catherine's fortune."

"Mother, there are times in a man's life when he must stand up for what is right, without fear or favor."

"I do not see you standing just now. Frederick, I fear you will regret this foolishness."

"It will do the old girl good, Mother, to see she cannot have her way in all things. No permanent damage will be done, you'll see."

"What I do see is that it has taken but two days of married life for you to forget the purpose of your marriage."

"Well, I will not be ruled by Lady Catherine—and neither shall Anne."

Therein lay the crux of the difficulty. Never before had the dowager found her son unmanageable. Frederick's delight in his wife beggared belief. After meeting Anne for the first time, he had groaned that a man couldn't possibly be asked to marry such a creature, and was only brought to face the necessity by having the mortgage papers thrust under his nose. Now the girl led him around by the selfsame proboscis.

Relations between the new countess and her mother were very strained. Anne trembled in anticipation of each meeting, but, with her husband's encouragement, steeled herself to behave with cool respect.

Lord Maddersfield agreed with Lady Catherine that Anne was behaving outrageously, and promised her to do the best he could for the family. He had a private audience with his niece, telling her he liked a lass with spirit and that he'd never liked her so well as now. If she buckled under, after throwing off the yoke, her mother would dominate both her and her husband forever.

He returned to the drawing room and shrugged his shoulders.

"I endeavored to talk sense into her, Sister, but she thinks nothing of the wisdom of her elders nowadays, it seems."

Mr. Collins rushed to Rosings the morning after the wedding to inquire after the invalid. Lady Catherine was so steaming with rage that she was ready to talk about it, even to him.

"Yes," he said. "It seems rash of the earl to insist that his wife sleep there. She may have rolled on the injured limb in the night."

"What care I for his injured limb?" cried her ladyship. "I care nothing for it. My daughter and son-in-law have treated me with grave disrespect, and for that I care very much indeed."

"Perhaps there is an explanation for their neglect of their duty to Your Ladyship, to whom they owe the utmost gratitude and deference," said Collins.

"You think there may be a rational explanation for their conduct, and they will be led to make suitable apology to me?"

"When they realize they have fallen from your Ladyship's good graces, and by their own fault, they will be overcome with remorse . . . desolation, may I say?"

"You, Mr. Collins, are just the person to point out their fault to them."

"I, Your Ladyship? I am most honored by your trust in me but I cannot aspire to the belief that I might influence matters amongst those in a position so much more exalted than my own humble station." He mopped his brow.

"Your belief is immaterial, Mr. Collins. Ring the bell."

The countess submitted to a lecture on filial duty, then put some earnest questions about wifely duty, which rather distracted the parson from the correct line of his discourse. In fact, during the next few days, Mr. Collins performed so many volte-faces that he resembled a conversational spinning top.

Colonel Fitzwilliam begged Anne to have a thought for her

mother's years and for their coming separation. What harm could it do to apologize, even if her mother were in the wrong? In truth, he felt compassion for his aunt, terrible old tyrant though she was. He sensed what no others seemed to see—the pain behind her rage—and he feared for the loneliness of her old age.

"Dear Henry," said Lady Catherine. "You are the only relation who has not betrayed me. Will you desert me, too?"

"You know I will not, but, my dear Aunt, Anne has been a good and dutiful daughter to you all her life. I am convinced that she is longing for your forgiveness. One affectionate word and all will be as it was before."

"It will never be as it was before, but I am ready to forgive her when she acknowledges her fault. I have ever been renowned for Christian charity."

Lady Catherine did not get the opportunity to practice her Christian benevolence, for how can one forgive a wrong for which there has been no humble apology? Anne was brought to say she was sorry her mother felt pained, but she would not say she was sorry for the grievous crimes of sleeping in her husband's bed on their wedding night and saying she did not care what her mother thought about it. She followed the Collins Method, as she saw it; she was respectful towards her mother, but with a new under-layer of confidence. Lady Catherine saw her meekness for the performance that it now was.

Two weeks after the wedding, Lady Catherine sent for her attorneys. On her death, her daughter, Anne, was to be left with investments and property amounting to less than a third of her mother's total fortune. Future inheritance of Rosings and its estates, with all its rents from farms and cottages, was made over irrevocably to her ladyship's beloved nephew, the Honorable Henry Fitzwilliam. Her attorneys' urgent advice, that she not take so drastic and final a step, went unheard.

The injured mother of the bridegroom swept into the invalid's chamber, where her juniors looked at her in trepidation.

"I warned you, Frederick, from the beginning. Why did you sign the marriage articles without ensuring Anne's inheritance?"

"I know not, Mother. She glared at me so."

"I begged you to temper your behavior, although I never imagined a result as disastrous as this!"

"A gentleman's honor, Mother, is a . . . um, gentleman's honor."

"Your honor was bought rather high. Pray do not look so frightened, Anne. We will simply make the best of the situation."

"You are very kind, Countess."

"Kind I always endeavor to be, but you are the countess now, my dear. I have sent for the physician to ascertain the earliest possible date for our departure." She left the room.

Silence deepened around the two. Reerdon was sunk in thought, and gave a sigh. Certainly, Anne's dowry would release his houses in Surrey and London from mortgage. His income was free now for the overdue refurnishing of Cumberwell House. Yet the loss of Rosings was grievous. He sighed again. Anne's eyes stung, and hot tears spilled over. A little sob escaped her.

"There is no gain in shedding tears over money, Anne."

"They are not for the money. I only feared . . . feared that you married for it and now . . ."

"I married you for your fortune? What put that idea in your head, you odd girl? Come and give me a kiss."

Various promises were made and tears wiped away. His lordship rather enjoyed the power of making unhappiness flee, and her ladyship rather enjoyed—well—power.

CHAPTER 24

A YEAR HAD PASSED SINCE Elizabeth's marriage and the groves of Pemberley began to take on their winter aspect. The north wind came down the valley a little unkindly on the day the Bingley party descended from their carriage. Miss Bingley shuddered as she glanced over the park.

"I have previously seen Pemberley only in summer. I had quite forgotten the northern winters," she said.

"I hope you will not be too troubled, Caroline," said Charles, happily. "I daresay it is even colder at Rushly."

He handed down Jane with great care. Kitty took the footman's hand and jumped down. She clapped her hands and cried, "Oh, dear, dear Pemberley. How lovely it looks." She hid from Elizabeth's teasing look in a quite fervent embrace.

They moved into the warmth of the winter parlor. Gathering around the fire, the visitors passed on news of their journey and of their friends in Hertfordshire.

Mr. Darcy suggested they all be up a little earlier than usual on Sunday to attend the morning service at Kympton.

"Splendid," said Bingley. "What is the name of the vicar there? Do I know him?"

"Mr. Turner," Darcy replied. "You have made his acquaintance."

"What a memory I have! What does he look like?"

Darcy turned to Kitty.

"What was your accolade, Catherine, after your first meeting? 'Hideous' was your choice of expression, I believe."

"I am sure I said no such thing!" cried Kitty, with a creditable attempt to stare her brother-in-law down. "Lizzy, I did not speak so, did I?"

"I cannot lay claim to my husband's precise memory of the conversation, Kitty, but I do recall you were not impressed by Mr. Turner's charms."

"Why should I be? I scarcely knew him." Kitty hoped she looked less confused than she felt.

"Like many of us he improves upon acquaintance," said Jane. "He is a very kind and gentlemanlike man. Once one understands him, his character makes a far stronger impression than his slight tendency towards plainness."

"Certainly," said Darcy. "One day some young lady will see him as a veritable Adonis on account of this phenomenon."

Caroline trilled, "Mr. Darcy, how very amusing you are! However, we might remember that Miss Kitty has merely promoted Mr. Turner from 'hideous' to, perhaps, 'not exactly hideous.'"

"I trust I am the last man to embroider upon such flimsy evidence, Miss Bingley," he replied. "Although, speaking generally, young ladies have been known to say things such as, 'You are the last man I would ever be prevailed upon to marry.' Then within months they chastise the poor fellow for his tardiness in renewing his suit."

"Ha! Ha! Ha!" trilled Caroline again. "What abominable things you say! You know full well we ladies could never be so cruel. What say you, Mrs. Darcy?"

"I think such a lady would be exceptional," Elizabeth replied.

"She would surely be exceptional," Darcy replied, "for him to hazard further punishment."

"He would be courageous!" cried Bingley. "I should crawl under a stone, if I were so used."

Kitty laughed with the others, relieved to have the conversation diverted from Mr. Turner. If she had called him "hideous," what of it? He was very plain, but she would like to see him again. She would tease him a little, then skip out of his reach again, just as she did in the summer.

It must have been the anticipation of this fun that caused Kitty to take special care with her appearance on Sunday morning. She wore a new muslin gown prettily embroidered on the sleeves, and a new coat, fur-trimmed about the neck and cuffs.

A little stir always enlivened the Kympton congregation when the Darcy pew was occupied. On her previous attendance at the church, Kitty had enjoyed the sensation. This time, as their party entered the church, she was scarcely aware of it, occupied as she was with the strange irregularity of her heartbeat.

In the vestry, Mr. Turner knew nothing of that stir.

After the collect, the vicar turned to the kneeling congregation and said, "God spake these words . . ."

He saw her, one whom he had not seen since her last visit to Kympton, too many weeks before. The silence lasted two, three seconds. She lifted her eyes, in a wide gaze, then lowered them. Others looked up too, but he did not see them. He looked away and recited firmly, "God spake these words, and said, 'I am the Lord thy God, Thou shalt have no other gods but me.'"

The rest of the service was got through, with varying degrees of patience.

Once again, Mr. Turner invited the whole party to breakfast.

As they passed out of the dining room, Kitty found herself next to the vicar, and, looking up, she sweetly said, "How do your chicks fare, Mr. Turner?"

"They are chicks no longer, Miss Bennet. Would you like to see them?"

As it happened, she thought she might as well, and the others, feeling less urgency in regard to avian welfare, stood about in the hall.

Kitty was startled. "Why, they are grown large! In so short a time!"

"You call it a short time. It has been fifteen weeks since last you were here," he said, his voice very soft. She seemed to find his waist-coat interesting.

"I had no idea it was so long," she said.

"I have been counting the days, and the weeks, until I despaired of your return."

"You scarcely know me," she said, with a flash of wisdom.

"I would wish to remedy this."

He tried to see her down-turned face beneath her bonnet. He took her hand, put it through his arm and led her out of the fowl house. They were sheltered from view by the hedge.

"Miss Bennet."

"Yes."

"Do you know that I love you?"

"Yes," she whispered.

"Here is my hand." He held it out to her. "Will you take it? Will you be my wife?"

"Mr. Turner, I . . ." Her voice died away, and her little gloved hand was laid in his.

"Kitty. Kitty."

She looked up, and, in a childlike way, she offered her cheek to be kissed.

Mr. Turner may have wondered if Miss Bennet were the kind of girl his family had in mind for him. Did he recollect his mother's hope that he marry a young woman of fortune, good breeding and culture? Maternal hopes have only so much power against passion. When he wrote to his mother, seeking not her permission but her blessing upon a union already arranged, she knew she was forestalled. She comforted herself with the value of the connection with the Darcys.

Elizabeth was pleased with the match, but wondered whether Kitty had the maturity of understanding to make so important a decision. She talked to her about the duties of a clergyman's wife. A man such as Edward Turner, who took so active an interest in his parish, had a right to expect the support of his wife. Kitty had a fit of sulks and flew to her room. Elizabeth found her, face down upon her bed. She sat up on her sister's entrance.

"You think I am just a silly baby, when I have tried ever so hard to please you!" cried Kitty. "He could have married one such as Anna Edgeley if he were so eager to have a dull wife. She is as clever and serious as can be, and would have got him if she could."

"Kitty, that is unkind. You know nothing of Miss Edgeley's feelings, and should not speak so if you did."

"I should not, had you not made me do so with your disapproval. Why are you not happy for me?"

"Naturally, I am happy for you, Kitty. I am merely taken by surprise. You and Mr. Turner differ so in your tastes."

Kitty slipped off the bed, and stood looking at her sister. "Yes, we do." An expression came over her face that Elizabeth did not at all like. "Lizzy, you think Mr. Turner an excellent man, do you not?"

"Well . . . yes, I do."

"You wonder what can he want with Kitty? Pray do not look so shocked, Lizzy. You cannot even deny it, can you?" Kitty walked across the room. She turned to face Elizabeth, who stood unmoving. Kitty went on, "You do not know what it is to be Kitty. Do you know what my feelings have been, when every day of my life, my father says, 'Kitty is foolish, Kitty is ignorant, one of the silliest girls in England'?"

For a moment, Elizabeth could not speak for shock.

Then she said, "He does not mean it, Kitty, not in his heart."

"If he does not, how am I to know it? You can forgive him his faults for you are safely enthroned in his affections."

"I was hardly a favorite with our mother."

"No, she loved you least of all her children, Lizzy, but did you care?"

"I have never forgotten my duty to our mother."

"Your duty? Of course you did not forget that, although Mama may have wanted something warmer from you."

"Mama may have wanted something warmer from me?"

Kitty put her hands on her hips. "Never fear, I do not need to be reminded of your perfections. My mother can do that. Oh, yes, nowadays it is 'Lizzy this . . . Lizzy that . . . my daughter, Mrs. Darcy . . . ten thousand pounds . . . marchioness'."

Elizabeth's voice trembled. "Kitty, no good can come of this. Let us be friends."

Kitty crossed the room and kissed her sister.

"I shall please Edward, Lizzy. I know I can. He loves me." She danced a little dance over to the mirror and back again. "It was not at all difficult, Lizzy. In the beginning, I was not even trying. I saw how he liked to be teased."

"Kitty!"

"Don't pretend, Lizzy. Just as Mama has always said, if you want to catch a husband, you must use whatever means are at your disposal. We had little money to bait our traps with, but look how well we do!"

"Jane won Mr. Bingley's regard with her goodness and dignity."

"You forgot to mention her beauty, dear."

"She did not use it consciously!"

"She did not need to. Lydia slipped a little in being too generous with her charms but was luckily rescued."

"I do not in the least approve of using such cunning!"

"Say what you like, Lizzy. Our mother says that there must have been some moment when you realized Mr. Darcy admired you. Most girls would have picked up their skirts and run after him, and his admiration would have turned to disdain. You, no doubt, turned up your nose and laughed at him. He is so used to having whatever he wants that he made up his mind that you would not get away."

"I like to believe there was a little more than that to promote our union."

Kitty shrugged. "What does it matter? I do not see Mr. Turner as an Adonis, as Mr. Darcy predicted some young lady will, but his looks are not so very bad. Is that promising of love, do you think?"

Elizabeth laughed. "Bless you, dearest, I wish you all the happiness in the world."

In Hertfordshire there were no such reservations. Mrs. Bennet was ecstatic over her daughter's success and instructed her to come home at once to order her wedding clothes. However, Kitty was pledged to go to Rushly Manor for Christmas and, as her Edward was included in the invitation, she could hardly drag herself away just yet.

Mr. Bennet cloaked his pleasure in exclamations over Turner's folly in choosing, as wife, one of the silliest girls in England. At least, he said, she used to be so, but lately she appeared to be merely as silly as most other girls in England, and had thus lost what little distinction she had.

As for Lydia, on hearing the glad news, she wrote at once to her sister. Kitty opened her letter in Elizabeth's sitting room, where her sister was going through the month's accounts Elizabeth looked up to see Kitty's eyes filled with tears. She crossed to the sofa and sat by her.

"From whom does this letter come, Kitty?"

Kitty handed her the letter.

From Mrs. Wickham to Miss Catherine Bennet
Newcastle

My dearest Kitty,
How Wickham and I laughed to hear that you are to marry an ugly old clergyman.

What a joke! Still, he has a good income, and I suppose that must suffice for you, you sensible girl! I would not exchange my dear Wickham for all the parsonages in England, but love is everything to such as I.

Now for some wonderful news. I will see you at Rushly at the end of January for W. is taking me there on his way to London, where he has some dreary business. He would so love me to go with him, but says we cannot afford it, and I fear he is right. Wickham can travel so much more cheaply alone and he does not care where he stays. I hardly know how I shall bear to be separated from him, but you will console me.

I intend to stay with the Bingleys until they go to Hertfordshire for your wedding, so that I might travel with them.

I shall take in Pemberley on my way south. Dear W. says it would be too painful for him to go there, as the memories of old Mr. Darcy would overcome him with grief.

Pray tell Lizzy to send me some gloves and stockings; six pairs of each would nicely equip me for my travels.

Your affectionate sister,
Lydia Wickham

"Thoughtless, thoughtless Lydia," said Elizabeth. "Throw her letter into the fire, Kitty." She thought, "So Lydia plans to come here. She will miss us this time for we will be in London, but we cannot evade her forever. What an unpleasant thought!"

In a poky sitting room in Newcastle, there had been a scene when Lydia gaily told her husband about her humorous letter to Kitty.

"What possessed you to write such a thing!"

"We did laugh, George. You said it was the greatest joke you had ever heard."

"I did not write so to her. I cannot comprehend your stupidity!"

"Kitty will know it is just my way of joking."

"She writes so slightingly of me, does she?" he asked.

"I should be very angry with her if she did!" exclaimed Lydia stoutly.

"What do you imagine will be her feelings as she reads your letter? You fool, do you not understand how important your family is to us? How would we have obtained these lodgings without the money Lizzy sent you when we were given notice at the last place? Will I ever be promoted without help from your damned brother-in-law?"

Lydia had grown so accustomed to Wickham's expletives that she was no longer offended by them.

"She owes me aid, for she is rich, and must provide for me if my husband cannot."

Wickham flushed. "I could provide for you if you could bring down your expenses."

"Bring down your own, then. If you dined more at home . . . I daresay you regret marrying me."

This was tempting, but Lydia would never be among those women who had outlived their usefulness to him. Wickham could never leave her without sinking his reputation irrevocably, and he desired to keep some sway over her. So he contented himself with, "My only regret is not getting more out of Darcy. If I had known he was after your sister, I would have got another five

205

thousand settled on you. Now, get paper and pen and write an apology."

From Mrs. Wickham to Miss Catherine Bennet
Newcastle

To my darling Kitty,
My very dearest sister,
  I fear you may have misunderstood my letter of Wednesday last. Did you know I was jesting when I said that Wickham and I laughed about your engagement? We were delighted for you both. I am sure Mr. Turner is an excellent man and that you must love him very much. We are so pleased to think of you in comfortable circumstances. We will come and stay with you in your parsonage and have such jolly times together.
  Mama writes that she had a very pleasing letter from Mrs. Turner, who praised you to the skies, tho' she's not met you even once!
  I could not bear to share my Wickham with anyone, so I am glad that all his relations are dead.
  Trusting you will forgive my foolish little joke,

Your most affectionate sister,
Lydia Wickham

The Bingleys set off for Yorkshire after a short stay, leaving Kitty to follow with the Darcys. There was but a month available for courtship before Kitty must return to Hertfordshire. It was a sweet month and did not suffer from being so short.

Georgiana received another invitation and had the agony of a decision.

"Fitzwilliam, our uncle has invited me to Radwick Hall for Christmas. Perhaps I ought to go?"

"Good Lord, surely you have no desire to go there, Georgiana!" said Darcy.

"I should not mind it. I would like to see the children; they must be much grown."

"There will be, with their size, a corresponding increase in their roughness and noise. You had much better come with us to Rushly."

"My uncle writes that Lady Catherine will be there and would like to see me after all this time," she ventured.

"Your aunt desires to ascertain the damage done by association with Elizabeth, no doubt."

"Then I shan't go."

"Go, by all means," said Elizabeth. "I could send you with a note, challenging her ladyship to find the ways in which I have contaminated you."

"Pray don't, Elizabeth! I should be frightened indeed to carry such a message," cried Georgiana.

"Elizabeth is joking, Georgiana."

"Oh, I see. Henry will be there."

"Henry will keep, never fear!" reassured Darcy.

"Henry's keeping qualities may be considerably diminished by his expectations," said Elizabeth. "I should not be surprised to see him go off quite soon."

"A wonderful increase must have taken place in our cousin's popularity, Georgiana," said her brother. "Now he is heir to Rosings, a stream of young ladies will visit Lady Catherine to judge her likely longevity."

"I should think them horrid and would get him away from them, if I could!" she replied.

"We may be certain Henry will not remain a bachelor much longer. You cannot be his favorite forever."

"I only meant I like to see him."

"Fitzwilliam, if it is what she wishes, why can she not go there?"

"Certainly, she may, although she will better enjoy herself with our party. However, if it is really what you wish, Georgiana, go to Radwick Hall, by all means."

"No, I shall come to Rushly."

Darcy said, "Excellent. It pleases me to see you consider your own wishes, rather than always falling in with others' plans in order to please them."

Elizabeth laughed.

"Why do you laugh, Elizabeth?" he asked.

"I beg your pardon. Did you intend no irony in that last statement?"

She turned to her letters. On the top lay an envelope directed in the distinctive handwriting of Lady Englebury. She read through two pages of her ladyship's stimulating news, Darcy glancing at her at times. She came to a hasty postscript.

"What news!" she cried. "Fitzwilliam, Georgiana, just listen to what her ladyship has to say.

"The dowager countess has, just now, been safely delivered of her babe, for I have her here with me at Deepdene. The fearsome child came into the world, full of loud cries, a great kicking of its sturdy limbs and waving of fists. 'Tis a girl! Captain Joseph Westcombe is become Earl of Bradford and, one day, Marquess of Englebury and I'm glad of it, for he is a deserving man.'"

"I must endorse her ladyship's comment," said Darcy. "This is one occasion when I heartily agree with her." He turned to his sister. "What say you, Georgiana? Are you not delighted that Henry's good friend is so rewarded by fortune?"

"I . . . I . . . that is, of course."

Her brother and sister stared at her. Her cheeks were covered with the deepest blush and she fled from the room.

After a time Elizabeth followed her. Georgiana, with admirable calm, said, "I had begun to see Captain Westcombe as my own good friend. I am glad for him but I was selfishly upset that there is an end now to our pleasant conversations."

"Why should that be? I cannot imagine he will drop all his old friends now he is ennobled."

"He will never have the same easy way."

Elizabeth looked keenly at her sister. The corners of her mouth began to twitch. Georgiana looked aghast. Color flooded back into her cheeks.

"No, Elizabeth! I do assure you, you are quite mistaken."

Elizabeth and Fitzwilliam spent their second Christmas together in the warmth of a family party at Rushly Manor. They were a happy little group: Mr. and Mrs. Darcy, Mr. and Mrs. Bingley (with a decided bump soon to become little Bingley), Kitty with her intended, Georgiana and Caroline.

Caroline was impatient to go to London with the Darcys, where she would stay with Louisa and Mr. Hurst. She had depended upon the Twelfth Night Ball as an event compelling the Darcys to be in London by the New Year. Now she found that their departure was to be delayed until the middle of January, at the earliest!

"I am excessively delighted that we shall stay to see the babe," she cooed. "I was quite afraid you would not like to disappoint Lady Reerdon."

"Lady Reerdon?" asked Elizabeth, puzzled. "Do you mean the Twelfth Night Ball? She will not miss us in that crowd. I have long since written our excuses."

Eleven days after Christmas, Jane presented her husband with a baby girl, pronounced by all who saw her to be quite the most beautiful baby in the world. Tiny Elizabeth Angelina Bingley gurgled and slept and did a few unmentionable babylike things through Topsy-Turvy Day, and, unfortunately, Twelfth Night as well. Of the nocturnal hazards, Jane was blissfully unaware, and Nurse would not have had it otherwise.

Two more weeks passed quickly by. Edward Turner had returned to his duties. Mrs. Bennet wrote frantic notes to Kitty about wedding clothes. Mr. Bennet would meet them in London to convey Kitty home. Caroline declared she could never tear herself away from little Elizabeth Angelina, but somehow she hardened her heart, and was first in the carriage for the departure to London.

CHAPTER 25

THE INN AT MERYTON HAD distinguished guests in February. Were it thrice its size, Longbourn House would not be big enough to hold both George Wickham and Fitzwilliam Darcy. That the Darcys preferred the inn was a relief all round.

Lydia travelled to Hertfordshire in Bingley's carriage, and was welcomed back to her mother's arms with joy. Wickham was still in London, on business of dubious respectability, but he tore himself from his cares to arrive in time for dinner on the evening before Kitty's wedding. Mrs. Bennet had arranged one of her little family parties. By this, Mr. Bennet grumbled, she meant a party to show off her family.

All were assembled in the drawing room, when Lydia swaggered in on her husband's arm. Mrs. Bennet had long forgiven Wickham's attempt to ruin her daughter; a patched-together marriage is still a marriage, after all. She hardly knew of which son-in-law to be proudest: Bingley, with his charm and wealth; Darcy, with so much wealth he did not need charm; or Wickham, with his silver tongue, dashing ways and red coat.

"Mrs. Bennet," Wickham declared, "the kindest and most gracious lady ever to hold the post of mother-in-law! Your wonderful appearance gives me the inexpressible delight of knowing that you are in good health."

"His delight is not so inexpressible that he is rendered silent," Darcy muttered to Elizabeth. She squeezed his arm and laughed softly.

"Treat his performance as a comedy," she whispered. He smiled ruefully.

Wickham moved on to coo happily over his father-in-law, who replied, "I see you are the same as ever."

"I hope you will never find me changed, sir," said Wickham.

"Elizabeth, my friend of old."

"Mr. Wickham, how are you?" she replied.

"Darcy! We meet again."

Darcy bowed coldly, and Wickham dropped the hand he had begun to extend to him.

"Good evening, Mr. Wickham," said Darcy, with frigid correctness.

Wickham changed his mind and extended his hand again.

"Come, Darcy, will you not take my hand?" The whole room fell silent. Wickham looked laughingly at Elizabeth, and she turned her head away.

Darcy took the offered hand. On a being less august, his expression may have been described as sulky. Moments later, Mrs. Bennet indicated that it was time to move to the dining room. Wickham turned back to Elizabeth and said, "Come, sister, we need not stand upon ceremony. Will you take my arm?"

"You forget yourself, sir," said Darcy.

Elizabeth, in the charming manner that could soften her censure, said, "Sometimes ceremony is a useful platform on which to stand, Mr. Wickham, if it means we avoid offending our friends."

Lydia uttered a little gasp of anger and surprise, but Wickham turned to her and shrugged. Sir William Lucas stepped up to Elizabeth and bowed.

"I thank you, Sir William," said Elizabeth. She took his arm and moved away.

Mr. Bennet gave his arm to Lady Lucas. Darcy made a courtly bow to Mrs. Bennet, and she put her hand upon his arm.

"I thank you, sir," she replied, preening somewhat, and sailed ahead into her dining room, leaving any ruffled feathers to smooth themselves.

That night, Mrs. Bennet was kept busy with visitors to her dressing room.

Kitty declared that she had never said she would get married, had not meant it, and was sure that her gown did not become her.

"You will look very well, Kitty. 'Tis nothing but a fit of nerves," said her mother.

"La! You are strange!" cried Lydia. "On the eve of my wedding, I could scarcely breathe for happiness. When the glorious day dawned, I had no thoughts but of love."

Kitty burst into hysterical sobs, and locked herself in her room.

"This is no time to bring up that old story, Lydia," scolded her mother. "Your triumph is over. It is Kitty's turn."

Lydia flopped down on a footstool and, looking in the mirror, said, "I thought Mr. Darcy behaved very shabbily to poor Wickham, giving him his hand so grudgingly. As a child, Wickham was such a favorite with Mr. Darcy's father, you know."

"Men will have their quarrels, dearest girl. I never inquire into them."

"There was a time when you did, Mama! You took Wickham's side before Mr. Darcy married Lizzy!"

"Did I, Lydia? I really don't recall."

"And Lizzy is so above herself that she'll not let dear Wickham take her into dinner! She is become as proud as her husband."

"I cannot agree with you, Lydia. Sir William is a knight of the realm! It is his due to lead Lizzy into dinner. He would have been disappointed and perhaps a little angry to be denied precedence. I'm sure that Mr. Darcy would never dream of offending a lady by refusing to partner her because he has a fancy to partner someone of less consequence."

"I did not expect you to side against my husband, Mama."

"I am excessively fond of Wickham, as you know," said her mother. "None the less, we must remember what is due to Mr. Darcy."

Lydia threw down her mother's lace cap, with which she had been fidgeting.

"Come, Mama, you detest him! I know you do."

Mrs. Bennet looked at her in amazement. "What put such a thought in your head, Lydia? When I see Lizzy stepping out of her fine carriage in her beautiful clothes, and when I read her name in the newspaper, you can hardly expect me to dislike her husband."

There can be no reply to an argument such as this, so Lydia changed the subject.

"I must say Mr. Turner is as plain as a pike but I suppose he will do for Kitty."

"Your sister likes him well enough. Mr. Darcy holds him in high esteem also, which will no doubt prove very useful."

"What use will Mr. Darcy ever be, pray?" asked Lydia, somewhat forgetfully.

"He is on friendly terms with the Bishop of Derby for one thing and with the Archbishop too, I shouldn't wonder. I may live to see Kitty installed in a bishop's palace."

Lydia scowled. "What fun would a bishop's wife have in society?"

"I know not, but she would have a deal of consequence."

Lydia stared gloomily at her reflection. In the silence, Mrs. Bennet's imagination carried her into a rosy future, in which Kitty was married to a bishop, Lydia's husband promoted to general, and even Mary married well (perhaps to a baronet—stranger things have happened). At that moment Mary came in, wearing a wrap most middle-aged ladies would disdain, her mouth twisted up primly.

"Mama!" she whined. "Wickham is smoking cigars! I did not give up my room to have it polluted."

"My husband would never smoke in a lady's bedroom, you . . . ugly old maid," cried Lydia.

Mary bristled up. "Did you hear what she called me, Mama?"

"Yes, yes, and it was foolish of you, Lydia. Mary is hardly an old maid at twenty."

Mrs. Bennet picked up her cap and was straightening the ribbons, when Lydia took advantage of her inattention to poke out her tongue at her sister. Mary said piously, "I forgive you, Lydia. There were worse epithets applied to you in the district when you ran away with Wickham. However, I shall remember my Christian duty and not sully my lips by repeating them. Goodnight, dear Sister."

Lydia shrieked and leapt up.

"Goodnight, Mama," said Mary, and slipped out of the door, before Lydia could reach her.

In the morning, Kitty recalled that she had meant to marry Edward, and owned that she did look well in her gown. As she came out of the little church, even Lydia admitted to herself that the groom had a nice face, especially when he looked tenderly down at his bride.

At the wedding breakfast she suffered a stab of envy at the array of gifts.

"We might have received all this, Lydia," whispered Wickham, sourly, "if we had not run away."

"Yet how romantic it was, Wickham!" sighed his wife, putting her arm through his. He suffered it to remain there.

"Kitty," said Aunt Gardiner, "this Wedgwood dinner setting is lovely, and very like the one you admired at Pemberley."

"Yes," said Elizabeth. "Mr. Darcy first thought it might please Kitty last July."

"Last July!" said Kitty.

"Certainly," said Darcy. "That was when we breakfasted at Kympton and Mr. Turner was so very thorough in explaining his affairs to me."

The bride and groom looked at each other and blushed.

Another triumphal day ended for Mrs. Bennet. Having disposed, in matrimony, of four of her five all but portionless daughters in eighteen months, she had every reason to congratulate herself.

At noon, Kitty and Edward departed for Derbyshire.

The Darcys returned to London, where many commitments awaited them. Mr. Bennet regretted the shortness of their stay. For his good lady, however, the actual presence of Elizabeth and her husband brought little pleasure in itself: she felt uncomfortable with Darcy, and valued Elizabeth the least of all her children. Their existence, somewhere in the world, was gratification enough for her vanity.

Mrs. Turner senior was so taken with the charm of Mr. Wickham that she made room for him in her carriage, as she was going to London. Wickham said he would be back in a few days to collect his wife and return to his duties in the north.

Jane and Charles stayed with her family a week longer, before returning to the vicinity of tiny Elizabeth Angelina. After a few days, a letter from Wickham informed Lydia of his continuing "difficulties with business matters," and suggested she travel with her sister as far as Yorkshire. Thus he was able to give Bingley the trouble of conveying her northwards and of any expenses along the way.

Wickham finally returned to Newcastle, completely out of funds, to stay in the officers' quarters. He never did call at Rushly Manor for Lydia, and she did not seem surprised. They had, in fact, let their lodgings for four months, intending that Bingley would support her for that time before sending her home in his carriage. By then, Lydia's annuity was due, and they could take up their lodgings again.

The novelty of Rushly Manor wore off quickly. In no time at all, Lydia was complaining bitterly about the dullness of Yorkshire and muttering about Elizabeth's meanness in not taking her to London. The next summer she would go to Pemberley, whether Elizabeth invited her or not.

Jane was too kind to say outright that her sister's presence in her home was a trial, but some discontent slipped between the lines of her letters.

"Oh, dear," murmured Elizabeth. "Poor Jane's patience has been found to have its limits at last. She very nearly says, in this letter, that she almost wishes Lydia were gone."

CHAPTER 26

By HER SECOND SEASON IN London, Mrs. Darcy was so well-liked by certain people of impeccable connections that her own unfortunate relations were now considered irrelevant. The three or four families who, Darcy felt, had treated Elizabeth with less than due respect when they first met her, were left with only their sense of exclusiveness to comfort them. She was in demand, but they found themselves kept on bowing terms only by Darcy. Elizabeth was denied any opportunity of laughing at him for this, being unaware that these people had ever been on a friendlier footing with him.

The Darcys received more invitations than they could accept. Their circle had one very particular addition in Lord Bradford, formerly Captain Westcombe. He was often received at Brougham Place. Georgiana, to her joy, found him unchanged in his kind and unassuming manner. He confided to her of the pain he felt when some acquaintances spoke their condolences in a perfunctory tone, seeming to imply that he must rejoice in his brother's death.

"How could anyone think of the loss of a brother as other than the greatest of misfortunes?" she asked.

With Lord Bradford, she had the delight of many conversations about Henry. She sensed that Lord Bradford somewhat missed his days in the army; he often spoke of the camaraderie he had enjoyed with his fellow officers and of the joys of disinterested friendship.

"I trust your friendship, Miss Darcy, for you were my friend when I was poor," he said.

"Gracious!" she thought. "Does he not know he became my friend because he was poor?"

When whispers of an engagement between Lord Bradford and his cousin, the lovely Arabella Whittaker, were heard, Georgiana could barely wait to be alone with her sister to discuss the rumor.

"I cannot believe it, Elizabeth. You do not credit it, surely?"

"I don't know, Georgiana." Elizabeth took Georgiana's hands in hers. "He is widely believed to have carried a torch for his cousin for years. I have heard it said that she would never have considered marrying him when he was a mere officer."

"So now he is good enough for her! He was too good for her, even before he rose to earl!"

Elizabeth looked shrewdly at her sister.

"Guard yourself, dearest."

"I do not need to protect myself, Elizabeth." Georgiana had turned her head aside. "You are very good to care so for my feelings. I am merely disappointed for him. She will never make him happy. In any case, were this story true, he would have uttered some hint."

Elizabeth stood and walked across the room. She turned, "An engagement would not be made public while the family is in mourning." She skipped across to Georgiana and pulled her to her feet.

"Let us drive out in the park and amuse ourselves watching the follies of those less dear to us. We can leave my Lord Bradford to make his own mistakes in matrimony, as many another has done before him!"

The period of mourning passed with no evidence to verify the story of Bradford's engagement. Georgiana could always count on at least two dances with her friend when they met at balls. How she enjoyed those half hours, for he did not beleaguer her with clever conversation or terrify her with compliments.

Two months in London society passed, and Georgiana survived them.

One morning in April, Elizabeth received a note from Mrs. Foxwell suggesting:

"the opera and a nice little supper at Beau Harry's—just our little party. Do say you'll come. Your sister Mrs. Bingley and Mr. Bingley will be there, for I chanced upon them this morning in the park, and asked them."

"It is the very thing to most divert me!" cried Elizabeth, "With Jane to add to my delight!"

"I should enjoy such an evening," said Darcy. "When is it to be?"

"Next Tuesday . . . oh."

"You have your Englebury enclave on Tuesday, Elizabeth."

"I should infinitely prefer this. You would wish me to come with you, Fitzwilliam?"

"Naturally. However, I acknowledge the greater imperative of your arrangements with the marchioness."

"It is no fixed arrangement. My friendship with her ladyship has no greater importance than my friendship with my husband, I hope. There is no absolute expectation of my attending her gathering every week. I shall explain to her that something quite compelling draws me away. If she is truly my friend, she will understand."

"You will be missed, Elizabeth."

"Not so very much. Would you miss me?"

"More than I can say."

"I hope my motives are perfectly pure. Mr. Glover is to read a selection of his latest work at Park Lane on Tuesday. It is his sorry attempt to be tragic and I should not have known how to keep my countenance."

Their attendance at the opera was a gathering much to Darcy's taste. An evening of music, followed by conversation over supper with a group of intimate friends, was ideally suited to his temperament.

In the supper house they had an elegant alcove to themselves, though they passed through the central room to reach it. They seated themselves around the table, ordered their supper and prepared to enjoy themselves.

They discussed the opera, a new one, flawed, in Mrs. Foxwell's view, by the questionable intelligence of the hero. She observed that she liked to see "gallantry tempered by prudence."

"Which is as it should be," said Jane. "For of what use is a silly knight?"

"None," said Foxwell. "Were it not for the excellence of his singing, I should have had no patience with the fellow at all."

"One could hardly rescue a maiden by such impetuous means, were not the villain so puny in his devilry," added his wife.

Elizabeth laughed. "The villain was unworthy of his role. One would feel insulted to be his prisoner. Had I found myself so circumstanced in my maiden days, I should have demanded a more worthy oppressor."

This gave Bingley an opportunity to contribute, for even he had read Mrs. Radcliffe's works. "I daresay even the evil Signor Montoni would have little tolerance for the society of one who laughed at his foibles," he said. "He would not have kept you prisoner long enough to give Darcy the chance of rescuing you."

They all laughed.

"You would have been hurled from the top of the tower by the end of twenty pages," exclaimed Foxwell.

"No, sir!" cried Elizabeth. "My threats to laugh at him from the grave would have turned his complexion pale with fear. He would have let me loose, to ride free, with his curses ringing in my ears."

"The mountains would echo with your mocking laughter, while he paced the ramparts, gnashing his teeth," added Darcy. Elizabeth looked at him; his expression was open in his enjoyment of the moment, his manner even lively in his own way. Only certain people saw him thus. How glad she was that she had come!

They all laughed happily, comfortable in their friendship. Georgiana, though she rarely spoke, contributed a joyful countenance to the conversation. The sound of Mrs. Foxwell's somewhat masculine chortles and the sight of Jane daintily dabbing at her eyes threatened to set Elizabeth off into gales of laughter.

Foxwell was the first to see the young man standing a few feet from their table. Elizabeth looked up too, and her laughter was extinguished. She bowed her head before turning back to her friends. He stepped forward.

"Good evening, Mr. Glover," said Elizabeth with cool politeness, barely turning her head. Darcy turned sharply in his chair, and everyone looked up, laughter turning to curiosity to see the famous playwright.

"Good evening, Mrs. Darcy." He shook back a lock of black hair that had flopped across his eyes. She was turning away again, when he said, "I thought to have seen you earlier. You were much missed at Lady Englebury's."

"I believe you exaggerate, Mr. Glover." He was biting his thumb-nail and frowning moodily.

She turned pointedly away, and said to Mr. Foxwell, "You cannot imagine what an impostor I feel among Lady Englebury's literati."

"I cannot believe that you mean that!" cried Glover, with a shade of frustration in his voice.

"You will not address my wife in that manner, sir!" Darcy had risen, and Glover turned to him with a look of bewilderment. He looked back, aghast, at Elizabeth, who said mildly, "I speak as I please, Mr. Glover, and you may interpret me as you please."

He stared at her wildly for a second, and mumbled an apology. She gave the slightest of shrugs and turned away from him. He left them.

"Is this a sample of the elevated conversation to be had in Park Lane?" asked Foxwell. "He seems to be some species of gypsy."

"The marchioness would have soon nipped his ankles, had she been with us," replied Elizabeth.

"I rather like your Mr. Glover," said Foxwell. "I should be diverted to meet him at your next party."

"Yes, indeed," agreed his wife. "When seen from close at hand, he is so gaunt and tortured-looking. I quite adore him," sounding for all the world like Arabella Whittaker.

"Do you?" asked Georgiana, in surprise.

Elizabeth laughed and squeezed her hand.

"That is the great thing about owning artistic sensibilities, you know," said Foxwell. "The ruder they are, the more interesting people find you, especially the ladies. Perhaps I should cultivate a little abrasiveness."

"You are spiteful enough as it is, Foxwell," said his wife. "I will thank you to continue to deliver your venom in a gentlemanlike manner."

"And pray continue to reserve your wit for those other than ourselves," said Elizabeth.

They all laughed again. Elizabeth looked at Darcy. He glowered moodily at nothing.

The carriages were ordered. Seeing their footman had arrived, Darcy rose.

"Are you ready to go, my dear? The carriage is waiting."

They said their goodbyes. As they walked to the door, Darcy drew Elizabeth's arm through his. She leaned towards him and whispered something. He smiled and touched the hand that lay on his arm. Across the room Glover saw this and felt a despair he knew to be out of all proportion to the act. Whittaker followed his gaze and said, "Ah, there is our lovely truant with her lord, adored and adoring! What an affecting moment. Who among us will use it? I'd give it to you, Glover, except that you'd turn it into burlesque."

"I write comedies because they sell, Whittaker."

"You are touchy tonight, my friend. You should follow my lead, and treat your muse with less veneration."

"You need not make your living by your work, Whittaker. My true work is barely begun."

"We hoped to hear a small part of your new work tonight, dear sir," said another.

"I had not the inclination when the time came," Glover mumbled.

"Did the absence of our sweet lady put you off?" said Whittaker, stabbing in the dark. "Good God, it did! Do not spare her too much of your thoughts, Glover, for I daresay she never thinks of you."

"Why should I not value her opinion?" muttered the playwright. "Lady Engelbury says Mrs. Darcy is one of the most original women she has ever met, both for her wit and high principles."

"Meanwhile some of us value her sweet teasing ways and her lovely eyes."

"You can laugh, Whittaker, a man of your proclivities. I admire the way she thinks."

"She doesn't give away her thoughts, my deluded friend. No matter, for what she says is amusing enough."

Glover looked feverishly around at the table. Most of these men were decent enough to deplore this game, but the vultures of envy and spite hovered behind their shoulders. He thrust back his black hair.

"We are not all such cynics as you, praise be." He had risen, so quickly that his chair fell to the floor.

Whittaker looked up at him, an insinuating expression in his eyes, and said quietly, "If you hope to put horns on her husband, I should give up the idea. She is a deal too clever for that."

The dark eyes sparked with such abhorrence that Whittaker almost winced.

"You disgust me!" said Glover and, throwing some coins on the table, he strode off.

"Mr. Whittaker, you ought not to have used the lady's name in such a manner." Whittaker raised his eyebrows at the speaker, and then looked around at the other men, enjoying their censure.

He smiled lazily. "Hypocrites," he said.

The chamber was lit by the dying fire. She lay beside him and he pushed back the curls from her face.

"Elizabeth?"

"Yes?"

"Would you have loved me had I been poor?"

"Not the least little bit."

"Truly."

"I speak truly. If you had been poor, you would have been delighted to dance with me, when you first saw me at the Meryton Assembly. Instead, you declared that I was not handsome enough to tempt you and I was very cross. I believe crossness to be an infallible precursor to love."

"Pray be serious for a moment."

"How can I answer such a question seriously? I do not know. Your position in the world has, in part, made you what you are."

"It is as though I had everything for a rich life but life itself."

"How fortunate you are to have found me." She softly laughed, pressing herself against him, and kissed him again.

"Dearest Elizabeth, never cease to love me."

"You think too much." He felt the soft warmth of her lips on his forehead, and on his mouth.

In the morning Elizabeth was delighted with an early visitor to her dressing room.

"Amelia!" cried Elizabeth. "How very clever you are to come just as I am thinking of you."

"Dear Elizabeth, of course I am clever." She picked up a length of gold-embroidered silk. "This is lovely. Lady Northby is sick with envy at the way you find these things."

"Her ladyship is unfortunate in having no relations in trade. This is the border of an Indian court sari and quite unavailable through usual means."

"A present from your uncle, Mr. Gardiner, I suppose."

"Indeed it is. It was a gift to his agent and has passed through my uncle's hands, then mine, until it came to you."

"How can I accept it?"

"In the same happy manner in which I accepted those exquisite feathers from you. Wilkins had the impudence to tell me I cannot put them on a new turban as people will recognize them. As if I cared! In ten years' time I will tell people that I've worn them with pride in thirty different hats."

Amelia laughed.

"I do not expect you to take your gratitude so far as that," she said.

The footman entered to present a card.

"Mr. Glover, at this hour! Evans, tell the gentleman that I am engaged."

"Yes, madam."

"Wait, Evans. Take the card into Mr. Darcy."

Amelia said, "Do you continue to find Mr. Glover diverting? I own that his conversation can be very amusing."

"I begin to weigh his fascination against his eccentricity and find the balance not in his favor."

She picked up the braid and draped it over the front of Amelia's gown. "Now, are you going to wear this braid at the ball, when you go to Gladsmere Park? I want to picture you dazzling the duke and enrapturing the rakes."

Mr. Glover did not always accept life's little reverses philosophically. His barring from the lady's presence was soon followed by dismissal from the house. He strode off down the road, glaring at the ground.

Rarely were visitors admitted to Lady Englebury's dressing room, but the playwright sent so desperate a note that she made an exception. She sat enthroned in her armchair and listened, the frown deepening on her face.

"I do not see how I can help you, Mr. Glover. What madness caused you to intrude so upon Mrs. Darcy in a public place? You had best make a fitting apology."

"I made the attempt, ma'am. I have just come from Brougham Place. Her husband would not permit me to see Mrs. Darcy. I sent up my card to her, but I was ushered into the library."

"How did you get along with Mr. Darcy?"

"I have somehow offended him further. I said I had come to make my apologies to his lady. He said he would convey them to her. He claimed that Mrs. Darcy declined to see me. I did not believe him; she would not be so unkind."

There was silence. Glover looked away, towards the window, then to his feet. At last he raised his eyes. Terrible was the marchioness's look.

"You have as good as called Mr. Darcy a liar?" He bit his lip, while she watched him.

She broke the silence.

"If Mrs. Darcy comes no more to my Tuesdays, I shall be very angry with you, sir."

"What! She comes no more? Has she said so herself?"

"How could that be? Could she write and convey to me a letter in the time it has taken you to hurtle through the streets? Mr. Glover, how do you explain your behavior?"

He jumped up and began to prowl the room.

"I know not how to explain this frenzy. I cannot eat, I barely sleep. I feel that this entire world is an illusion, and the only truth to be found lies in the other world, the world of exquisite feeling, the world of my next work." He raked his hands through his hair, and then stared sullenly into the fire. The silence settled on them.

"Why do I trouble myself with this madman? He has forgotten I am here," thought her ladyship.

He looked up, stared at his benefactress, a tic working at his right eye.

"Marchioness, I should call it my first work, for up to now I have been merely playing. Yet I cannot settle to work. Only she can help me; she is my inspiration."

She flinched in irritation at his expression of acute sensitivity. The ferocity of her expression silenced even the chatter in his mind.

"Mr. Glover, are you in love with Mrs. Darcy?"

"Were it so, I should throw myself into the river."

"Kindly speak more moderately. Are you modeling your next heroine upon her?"

"I cannot pay her a higher compliment than to present the image I have of her upon the stage, your Ladyship."

"She has a husband to pay her compliments. Do you not know that Mr. Darcy would not permit his wife's portrait to be hung in the exhibition last year? Yet you wish to parade an image of her about on the stage! Have a care lest you make Mrs. Darcy wish you would drown yourself."

"Marchioness, it is to your assistance I owe my success. Without you—"

"Come, come, sir. I am gratified by your success. Thank me by behaving as a gentleman does, and do not cause embarrassment to my friends."

He nodded dumbly. "What am I to do?"

"Go home and work. Have you written anything yet?"

"I have written but two pages, in a restless night of endeavor, madam. I hoped to show them to Mrs. Darcy this morning."

The marchioness was silent. Previously, it had been to her that all his preliminary efforts came. A cold feeling engulfed her for the moment. She thrust it aside.

"I was afraid you would not like it," he muttered.

She looked back into his eyes, keenly but not unkindly.

He thrust the pages into her hands, bowed, and turned to the door.

"Mr. Glover! Do you wish me to show this to Mrs. Darcy?"

"Yes."

"Dear me, what is one to do with him?" she muttered to herself. She walked to the window and watched the young man emerge from her front door, turn abruptly and disappear down the street.

"He is capable of striding along until dark, with no notion of his whereabouts," she thought.

She sank back into her armchair, and picked the papers up again. After some thought, she enclosed them with a note, and rang for a footman.

In the afternoon, the marchioness sent for her niece.

"Amelia dear, no doubt you know this lady more intimately than I. How serious is this threat to my friendship with her?"

Amelia took the letter.

My dear Marchioness,

I thank you for your kind note and for entrusting Mr. Glover's work to me. However, that gentleman has no rational grounds for this averred dependence upon my opinion. Perhaps I ought to feel flattered, but I do not. While this fragment of work is intriguing, I am much disturbed by the suspicion that the author is painting an idealized portrait of myself.

I should so like to think that this is mere vanity, but fear it is not, given the author's eccentric attentions towards me. I need scarcely add that these attentions are most unwelcome.

Your Ladyship asks me to forgive Mr. Glover, when his greatest offense has been towards Mr. Darcy.

You have been most kind to me, and I should greatly regret losing the honor of your society and friendship. However, until he has obtained my husband's forgiveness, I feel unable to meet Mr. Glover at your house, or anywhere.

Dear Lady Englebury, I would not disappoint you for the world, but your dream of making me "one of the foremost hostesses in London" and a "patroness of the arts" is a reflection of your generous over-estimation of my talents. I have no pretensions to such prominence, which would, in any case, be anathema to the one to whom I owe my first obligation.

Believe me,

> *With sincerity and respect*
> *Ever your obliged servant,*
> *E. Darcy*

So pale did Amelia become that her aunt had her answer, even before she spoke. She saw to it that Mr. Glover wrote a suitable letter of apology, and Darcy expressed satisfaction. The marchioness felt her friendship had been little harmed. Elizabeth attended her soiree as before and dined, with her husband, in Park Lane.

However, their time remaining in London was to be brief, as they decided to leave for Derbyshire at the end of April. Lady Englebury wondered at the way they could leave London at the very height of the season to bury themselves in the country. Not even young love, had she ever experienced it, could have induced her to entomb herself with only the marquess and a silent female relation for company. She invited the Darcys to visit Deepdene in August.

Darcy anticipated little pleasure in this visit to his lordship's country seat but agreed all the same. The honor to Elizabeth could not be overlooked. Another consideration was the inclusion in the party of Lord Bradford, who seemed to admire Georgiana, seeking frequent opportunities to speak with her and dancing with her at every dance.

Bradford's reputation was spotless, he appeared very kind and he was rich, therefore likely not a fortune-hunter. He had the added commendation of the title of earl, later to be marquess. Darcy had not thought of Georgiana's marrying for two years or so, but this opportunity to exceed his stringent requirements for his sister's husband was too good to miss.

He told Elizabeth of his thoughts. "Fitzwilliam, you will not try to influence Georgiana too much in her choice of her life's partner, will you? She depends greatly upon your judgment. She may choose against her true inclination in order to please you."

"She likes him well enough."

"I feel she is a little young for this step."

"I want to see her happy, Elizabeth. That is why I planned at one time that she and Bingley marry."

"Can she not be the author of her own happiness?"

"I know the world, Elizabeth, and Georgiana does not. I knew I could rely absolutely upon Bingley's honor and generosity of spirit. Lady Catherine would not have given her sanction happily, but her views are now irrelevant to our purposes."

"The junior branches of the family do try your poor aunt to the limit." She crossed to where he sat and leaned over the back of his chair, resting her cheek against his head.

"My love, should you feel easy in your mind if Lady Catherine were to die without any attempt at reconciliation on your part?"

"She would not have written as she did if she did not desire a permanent rift. If she now regrets it, it is for her to make advances and for me to decide whether to accept them."

Elizabeth touched his mouth, and the firm set of his lips softened against her fingers as he kissed them. Quite suddenly she thought to tell him there was no one in all the world she loved a fraction as much as she loved him. Instead, she said, "Do as you think best." She smiled at his expression. "I did not imagine you would do otherwise. Yet I do not like to see your family divided on my account."

"Do you relish the prospect of again listening to Lady Catherine?"

"Perhaps I do not, but there is more to life than relishment, if there is such a word."

"There is not."

"How very sure you always are."

However, Darcy proved movable in this case, and wrote to his aunt. His letter fell like a seed among stones. Lady Catherine did not reply.

"In future, Elizabeth, I hope you will be guided by me and not attempt to push me in whatever direction your whim takes you!" he said.

She wanted to laugh at the absurdity of anyone having such an ambition, but she knew what it had cost him to make the attempt.

"I am so very proud of you," she said.

"What?"

"I am proud of you, Fitzwilliam." He turned sulkily away. Then, he gave a little shrug.

CHAPTER 27

As April came to a close, Henry Fitzwilliam returned to London. Interestingly, since the improvement in his prospects, the colonel was no longer invisible to young ladies of fortune. He called at Brougham Place, where he renewed his acquaintance with Miss Bingley. Caroline had come, with her sister, Mrs. Hurst, for a morning of music with their dear friend Georgiana.

Henry had never realized what a pleasant young woman Miss Bingley could be. He sat at her side while she played the pianoforte. Her feathers nodded elegantly when it was time for him to turn the page. As her fingers raced across the keys, she leaned slightly towards him. He looked thoughtfully at her handsome profile as she leafed through the book in search of another song. Elizabeth very nearly laughed aloud.

Henry did not forget his cousin.

"Georgiana, will you play for us, pray?"

"If you like, Henry."

Caroline declared that she would die of disappointment if her dearest friend did not play, and Georgiana took her place at the instrument. She played a plaintive little air. Miss Bingley noted Henry's fond look. She was, herself, so moved that she rose from her seat and stepped softly across to the window, where she gazed out into the cloudy skies. Her figure showed to advantage as she leaned against the rich stuff of the curtain. He was flesh and blood after all. He looked, and Mrs. Hurst noted the look.

"I am seized by such a desire to see Vauxhall Gardens again!" she cried. "Who will join me? Pray, all of you, come with me tomorrow and make a party of it."

Elizabeth and Darcy were otherwise engaged, but everyone else accepted.

How lovely the gardens looked in the crispness of the clear spring day! Georgiana would have liked to have Henry to herself, but needs must share him with Miss Bingley. They walked about, Henry with one young lady on each arm, and the Hursts strolling behind them. Then they took refreshment in the pavilion. Georgiana looked out over the grounds, seemingly crowded with half of London. She cried out, "Look! Is that gentleman in the blue coat not Lord Bradford?" Even as she spoke, she realized her mistake.

The heat rose in her cheeks as Caroline trilled with laughter.

"That gentleman has perhaps something of his Lordship's air but lamentably little resemblance to his features." She smirked at the colonel, and turned to Georgiana, whose mortification was plain.

"Have I offended you, dearest Miss Darcy? How unforgivable of me! I would not hurt you for the world. Indeed, that gentleman, though a stranger, is not unlike the earl. It was a natural mistake. I have often made similar errors myself."

Georgiana felt as though she had betrayed some secret.

"Why do you blush so, Georgiana?" asked Henry.

Caroline leaned across the colonel towards her friend, in order to take her hand.

"If you promise not to breathe a word, I will tell you a dreadful story. This happened to me at the Assembly in Bath. I was walking around the room in search of Louisa, when I came upon the gentleman to whom I had pledged the next dance, or so I thought. 'Mr. Grey!' I cried, putting out my hand, 'what lucky chance is this?'

"He bowed and said, in a horridly quizzing tone, 'Madame, this is the most fortunate chance in the world, but my name, I am afraid, is not Grey.' I had never seen him in all my life! Imagine my feelings dear, dear Miss Darcy. I thought I should die of mortification."

Georgiana looked all gratitude.

Caroline continued, "Yet I am not destroyed in society. No one knows of my mistake, but myself, the man who is not Grey, and now you, my dear friends." She looked around at them all, then at Henry, as she said, "I have placed myself in your power."

Henry lifted her hand to his lips.

"You can depend upon our secrecy, although I cannot vouch for the discretion of Not-Grey."

"I have no fears of him!" she said.

Hurst grunted. He was well-nigh asleep. "Perhaps we ought to go home now," he said.

"Mr. Hurst, you are too cruel," cried Caroline. "Miss Darcy and I had quite set our hearts upon dancing."

"Yes, indeed, Mr. Hurst," said his wife. "There is still much to entertain us."

They became interested again in their surroundings. There was an excited buzz of conversation in the crowd. Henry looked around and saw one of his men waving to him, from the press of people below the pavilion. He went to speak to him, and heard that all officers were called to headquarters at once.

He returned to the table, where his friends waited for an explanation.

"Bonaparte has escaped from Elba. I am called to duty."

"What does this mean, Colonel?" asked Louisa.

"The French are certain to rise in his support. We shall be again at war with France."

Georgiana swayed in a near faint and Henry caught her. "Come, Georgiana, you are not well. I will take you home on my way." With the briefest of farewells, they went away.

"It hardly seems proper for Georgiana to go off in a carriage with him," said Caroline, discontentedly.

"They are first cousins, my love, and she is his ward, his child almost," replied Mrs. Hurst. "You may be sure there is no harm in it."

There was no harm in it. Henry held her hands in both his own, and she sat up very straight and pressed her lips tightly together.

"This may prove a baseless rumor, Georgiana."

"No," she said miserably.

"How could you know?" His voice was very gentle.

"I know in my heart."

She felt the hot spill of her tears, she felt his arm around her and the touch of his lips on her wet eyes.

The colonel was pressed for time, but spared a few hours to go to Rosings to pay his respects to Lady Catherine.

"I am highly provoked, Henry. It was my wish that you resign your commission last November."

"Forgive me, dear Aunt. Perhaps I can win some glory for the family."

She did not notice his wry smile.

"I expect you to come back promoted. If you do not come back at all, Henry Fitzwilliam, I shall be very angry."

"I will do my best to please you, madam, so long as my return is consistent with doing my duty."

"I hope you have made your will in the way I would wish. Rosings is not to go to your booby of a brother. That would be an insult to the noble memory of Sir Lewis." She gazed up at her late husband's portrait. Henry smiled. Such invocations of his late uncle's reputation inevitably reminded him of the time when he and Darcy, on vacation from university, had stopped at a tavern in a nearby town. "Who be the young bloods, Grandad?" asked an ostler, and his hard-of-hearing ancestor loudly replied, "Why, they be nephies of Ol' Spooney o'er Hunsford way."

He looked from the portrait back to his aunt.

"Georgiana is the chief beneficiary of my will, your Ladyship."

"I hope she marries well. I daresay the girl hobnobs with all sorts of nobodies introduced by her sister-in-law."

"We believe Georgiana may have a new admirer, Aunt, in Lord Bradford. Darcy told me that he appears very struck with her."

"What has Georgiana to say about it?"

"Georgiana is too modest, I daresay, to perceive his interest for what we hope it is. She was, however, most upset at a rumor of his engagement to a cousin. He may make her an offer at the end of the period of mourning."

"Hurry him, Henry! He sounds altogether too nice to risk losing his chance for the sake of his dead brother. He is the Marquess of Englebury's heir! My niece may become marchioness; that would be an excellent match." She was silent for a moment. Her frown deepened as her thoughts took her from Georgiana, to her probable splendid marriage, and then to the possibility she would not be invited to the celebrations. By this route, she returned to her pet theme of Darcy's betrayal and his wife's dreadful connections.

"Is that disgraceful Wickham person to go to Belgium, too?"

"Lieutenant Wickham? His regiment has not been called at this stage."

"A pity. He might have been shot. I suppose he is congratulating himself on keeping out of it."

"To be fair to him, whatever accusations can be laid at Wickham's door, cowardice cannot be one of them. He has sought to transfer, without success."

"That man can always be relied upon to have some evil motive. If he does get into it, see what you can do to have him put at the front. Why do you laugh? I never jest."

Henry dined at Brougham Place on the eve of his departure. Caroline Bingley was among the guests at table.

"I declare we ought all to go to Brussels," Caroline said. "I cannot bear to be idle here when we might cheer our brave army before they do battle."

"This is war we speak of, Miss Bingley, not a summer tour," said Darcy.

"I am not afraid. I would take any risk to help our gallant heroes," she replied.

"There will be endless dancing and flirting, no doubt," continued Darcy. "Then war follows, with our forces impeded by their anxiety for the safety of a crowd of useless hangers-on, all in a state of panic."

"You are always so severe upon us, Mr. Darcy. Not all women are so cowardly as you seem to think us."

"I said nothing of women in particular, madam. It is my belief that some of the men among the civilians would be worse than any woman."

"You men claim all the superlatives for your sex; the greatest bravery and the greatest cowardice are to be attributed to you. It is most unfair," laughed Elizabeth.

"I am happy to acclaim you the bravest of mortals, my dear. However, you will not leave England at this time."

"Thank you, sir!" she cried. "I was so afraid you would make me fight."

Miss Bingley's laughter trilled merrily. Georgiana tried to laugh with the others. Henry took her hand in his and said, "I could endure a parting of any length sooner than the anxiety of having you in danger." She might not be so handsome as Miss Bingley, nor able to show off her attractive figure so well, but the look in her blue eyes was piercingly sweet. "Dear Georgiana. She may become engaged to be married while I am away," he thought. "I do not like to think of it. How selfish I am."

"I cannot contain my secret! I am going to Brussels," announced Caroline. "I leave on Tuesday with Mrs. Brompton and my dear, dear friend, Miss Jennifer Brompton."

She looked around, enjoying their astonishment, and continued, "Mrs. Brompton always follows her husband, and there are quite hundreds of people going, I believe. Colonel Brompton says there is no danger whatever, compared to some of his previous scrapes."

"What can Bingley be thinking of, allowing this?" said Darcy.

"I cannot see what Charles has to do with it."

She did not repeat Mrs. Brompton's view, "If you two girls are not engaged in a month, then I am Horatio Nelson."

Caroline looked around at them all.

"My dear friends, this may be my last meeting with you, if Mr. Darcy is correct. I hope the colonel may be able to struggle home, carrying the last message from my dying lips."

"Do prepare something poetical for us, Miss Bingley," said Elizabeth.

"I shall start work upon my composition this very night,"

Caroline said, her hand upon her heart. She turned to Henry. "Are you acquainted with Colonel Brompton, Colonel?"

"Yes, I know him quite well."

She knew he did, for she had already made sure of it.

"It will be a comfort to hear from you very regularly, Miss Bingley," Georgiana said. "We will have the earliest notice of how our army does in Belgium."

"As for that!" cried her friend. "You shall hear from me very constantly. I can pass on any messages that Colonel Fitzwilliam has for you."

Her carriage was called shortly afterwards. Leaving the colonel to make his adieux to Georgiana, Elizabeth made an excuse to take Darcy aside.

"What is it, Elizabeth?"

"I wish to give Georgiana a few moments to say good-bye to her cousin."

"I cannot see that she needs such privacy."

"Do you not? I do not in the least like this excursion of Miss Bingley's."

"She has her guns primed but he is a fighting man."

"This latest adventure throws the advantages too much in her favor."

"As her sister-in-law, it is your duty to assist her to promote herself in life."

"Let her promote herself with someone else."

"I have every confidence in my cousin's judgment in choosing a wife."

"I hope you will be vindicated."

"I shall be," he said firmly.

She touched his arm. "If Henry does not return, Georgiana will break her heart."

"It would be a great grief for us all."

"Indeed."

As they walked back to the drawing room, he said, "Are you happy to leave London, Elizabeth?"

"I love to come to London and I love to leave again."

"You were even more successful this season than last. Will you not be wearied at home with only your dull consort for company?"

"I might ask you the same question."

"Not with a great deal of sincerity." He took her hand. "You are the only person with whom I could joyfully contemplate passing six weeks in solitude. I fear it is selfish of me to take you prematurely from the scenes of your success."

"Perhaps it is, and perhaps it is not, Fitzwilliam." Elizabeth laughed, leaving him with less satisfaction than he may have liked.

CHAPTER 28

ALL THE BRISKNESS OF AN upland spring had not dampened Elizabeth's delight in being home. She was in time to see the bluebells first appear. She had followed every path of the woods. When the weather kept her indoors, she found much to employ her time, and many a wet afternoon was passed reading by the library fire with Darcy. Two months of this leisure passed, and her summer visitors arrived.

The Bennet equipage mounted the final slope of the drive and halted to allow the passengers to enjoy their first glimpse of Pemberley House.

"Ah!" shrieked Mrs. Bennet. "To think my darling Lizzy is mistress of this house. Mr. Bennet, why did you not tell me of this grand prospect?"

"I should have missed the pleasure of enjoying your surprise," he said dryly. "Mary, what think you of your sister's home?"

"It is very large, to be sure," answered that upright virgin. "Yet let us remember that 'It is harder for a camel to pass through the eye of a needle, than for a rich man—'"

"Ha!" said her father. "I was put in mind of the same animal when it came to obtaining your apology to Mr. Darcy for your impertinence last spring."

"I put aside thought of what was due to me, as I am generally wont to do, and humbled myself for the sake of my family."

"Hold your tongue, girl," snapped her mother. "I will not have you spoiling this holiday with your preaching, and I will thank you to treat Mr. Darcy with respect while you are in his house, miss."

"I trust I know my duty, Mama."

"Look at the reflection of the house in the lake. This place was made for my Lizzy," said Mr. Bennet.

"'Made for Lizzy,' indeed! This house is Jacobean, to be sure; it has stood here for years."

The carriage rolled on down the drive to the door.

Mrs. Bennet descended, determined not to feel flustered the moment she met Mr. Darcy.

"Mama! Welcome."

"Let me look at you, Daughter. How well you look!" Her mother enfolded Elizabeth in her ample embrace, then held her at arm's length. The girl's stomach seemed as flat as ever.

She turned to her son-in-law.

"Mrs. Bennet, it gives me very great pleasure to welcome you to Pemberley." He was the same man, as tall as ever, as stately in his address but, somehow, in his manner was an element of ease she had never seen in Hertfordshire.

"It gives me very great pleasure to be here, Mr. Darcy."

The party moved up the steps, Elizabeth arm in arm with her mother, Mary behind them, and the two gentlemen taking up the rear.

"Lizzy, my darling girl! What a wonderful house you have," whispered Mrs. Bennet.

"It is very nice," said Elizabeth. "Come and take some refreshment, then I will show you to your room. You must be very tired."

Mrs. Bennet was so overwhelmed by the luxury of her surroundings, the multitude of servants and by the unexpected geniality of her host that a full four and twenty hours passed before she began to be silly.

Elizabeth encouraged Darcy to entertain her father, while she passed several days in all the pleasure to be expected from hours spent in her mother's and sister's company. Mrs. Bennet found as much to marvel over as Mary found to disapprove in tours of the house, drives about the estate and explorations of Elizabeth's wardrobe.

This summer tour of the matrimonial homes of three of her daughters was highly gratifying to Mrs. Bennet's maternal pride. She had but one complaint, which she shared with Elizabeth at the earliest opportunity.

"I desire your father to take us on to Newcastle to stay with Lydia, but he is obstinate. He will not take us. You must use your influence to change his mind, Lizzy. What a chance for Mary to divert herself with so many officers."

"I shall never lower myself to visit Lydia, Mama!" cried Mary. "What is more, I hate officers."

"Nonsense, Mary. All girls like officers."

Mary jabbed the sky with her nose. "I should be content if I were never to see Lydia again."

"Unnatural child! Did you ever hear anything so unfeeling, Lizzy?"

"Madam, to speak truthfully, I think it best for Mary if she does not stay with the Wickhams. She would not enjoy the visit and . . ."

"What, pray?"

"We were all fortunate in the circumstances of Lydia's marriage being hushed up. Even so, lest the . . . irregularity become more general knowledge, it is perhaps better for Mary's reputation if she has as little to do with her sister as possible. It seems hard, but there it is."

"Lizzy, I did not think to hear you speak so. I hear your husband's words in this."

Elizabeth's eyes flashed. "Believe so if you wish, but I have mentioned Lydia's and Wickham's names but once to Mr. Darcy since we became engaged. That was to tell him that they would be at Kitty's wedding."

"Warning him, do you mean?" Mrs. Bennet's voice rose an octave.

"I told him I would understand perfectly had he stayed away."

"How dare you speak so! You tear my nerves to shreds."

Elizabeth continued. "I am very sorry that you feel so, but you do not know what Mr. Darcy has suffered at Wickham's hands. I told my husband he need not come, but he is incapable of causing that pain to Kitty."

Mrs. Bennet was somewhat mollified by this statement.

"So you did not ask your husband to use his influence to have Wickham promoted?"

"I knew not that he was promoted."

"We only heard of it the day before we left Longbourn. Lieutenant Wickham, if you please."

"So he is restored to his old rank. What made you believe that Mr. Darcy had a part in it?"

"This advance would be beyond one without powerful friends, so soon after he joined the regulars. The promotion was made conditional on his remaining longer in the north. That convinced Wickham your husband had a hand in it. Lydia was highly provoked, for Wickham cannot change regiments and go to Belgium."

"Lydia wishes to send her husband into battle?"

"Wickham would be sure to be promoted further if he goes to war." Mrs. Bennet sniffed. "I think it very hard, to have my girl so far from me."

Elizabeth smiled to herself. "He would assist my sister's husband, for my sake, and then never tell me to save me from the reminder of them."

"'Tis very strange that he did not tell you," said Mrs. Bennet.

"Not at all, Mama." Her mother could not understand that the very sound of the names of George and Lydia Wickham was distasteful to them both.

"Lydia wrote that they put on such a good spread for the other officers and their wives, in celebration," said Mrs. Bennet, with pride.

Elizabeth sighed. "That is an excellent start to paying off their debts."

She turned to her sister. "Mary, should Mama and Papa go on to Newcastle, you know you will be very welcome to stay here in their absence."

"I thank you but I shall go to Kitty's house," Mary replied. "There are some theological points I should like to discuss with Mr. Turner."

"What a treat for him," said Elizabeth, trying not to laugh. Mr. Bennet made no such effort, and laughed aloud.

"Perhaps you can begin your teasing of Mr. Turner tomorrow, Mary, when we make our visit to Kympton. I imagine he will be ready for some stimulation of the intellect after months of Kitty's company."

"Oh, Mr. Bennet!" cried his wife.

Sunday arrived. Kitty stretched and opened her eyes a little, to see Edward sitting on the edge of the bed.

"You look just like a happy little kitten," said he. She stretched her arms towards him.

"I am your happy little kitten," she said.

"I know this."

"Why are you out of bed so early, Edward?"

"It is past nine, Kitty, and time for you to ready yourself for church. Your parents will be there."

"Why did you not remind me before?" Her lower lip pushed out in a way that was very enticing to the Reverend Turner, and he kissed it.

"Kitty, I would be very happy if you could call on Mrs. Goode, before we leave for Pemberley."

"Ugh! Edward! You know how I hate to go into those dreary cottages."

"Your visits lighten her days, Kitty. The apothecary tells me there will not be many more of them. She is still talking of when you first went to see her."

"Papa was never so strict as you, Edward." She frowned. "Why do you laugh?"

"I laugh at your notion of a strict husband."

"Very well, then, I will go, but only to please you."

"I would rather you did it to please her, Kitty." She flounced aside. "Do it for my sake then, dear Kitty. Do not look at me so coldly."

She smiled and offered him her cheek for a kiss, then threw off the covers.

"How you take up my time, Edward! I must inspect the house-maid's work. Mama will be poking into everything."

After the service and an excellent breakfast, Mrs. Bennet had the pleasure of another house exploration. The vicarage had the advantage of being in need of one or two improvements, about which Mrs. Bennet felt very confident in giving her advice. This made her tour as satisfactory in its own way as her tour of Pemberley. She felt no confidence in the usefulness of her advice to Elizabeth on how to manage her home.

Edward was kept so busy in showing off his improvements to the arrangements at the parsonage that poor Mary did not have the opportunity to pose a single theological teaser. The Turners followed their party back to Pemberley, where they would stay three weeks. Edward arranged to return to Kympton for Sunday services as he was loath to neglect his parish. After returning from his first two days without Kitty, he held her close and said, "My dearest Kitty, I missed you so."

"What a big silly you are! It was but two days. How will you feel if I accompany my papa and mama to Newcastle?"

"Kitty, you are not serious? You would not leave me for so long, would you?"

"I dare say not," she said vaguely.

"In any case, I will not permit it, Kitty, not in the circumstances." He put his hand against the tiny bulge in her stomach.

"Very well, then, I shan't go."

"Would you not rather remain with me, sweet love?"

"I suppose," she said. "Even if you are such an ogre."

He kissed her pouting mouth. She returned the kiss fleetingly and he kissed her again. She pushed him away.

"It is time to dress for dinner, Edward."

"Tell me that you love me."

"I love you. Now leave me." As he closed the door, her frown vanished and she laughed happily to herself.

"I must tell the maid to put out my new night-gown," she thought. It was of the very finest lawn, and she had been saving it for one such occasion.

There were certain maternal duties the neglect of which Mrs. Bennet could never be accused. While Elizabeth was writing her letters one morning, her mother visited her sitting room.

"Do not let me interrupt you, child. I shall enjoy myself sitting quietly here watching you."

"Very well, Mama."

"What a charming room you have. Has Mr. Darcy done it up anew for you?"

"Yes."

"What a lot of letters you seem to write, Lizzy."

"Yes."

"To whom do you write just now?"

"To a lady called Mrs. McDowell, Mama."

"Who is Mrs. McDowell, my dear? I have never heard of her."

Elizabeth put down her pen, and answered a string of queries.

"She sounds most interesting, Lizzy. I think you should carry on with your letter or you'll never be done."

"Yes, Mama."

Mrs. Bennet got up and walked around the room, humming a little tune.

"Your sister Jane is expecting another child."

"Yes. I am very happy for her."

"Kitty will find herself very busy at Christmas, when she will have a babe to think of," said Mrs. Bennet.

"What? Kitty is to have a child? So soon?" Elizabeth turned earnestly to her letter.

"Lizzy?"

"Yes, Mama?"

"I wish to have a little talk with you."

"We are having a little talk, are we not?"

Mrs. Bennet coughed delicately.

"Lizzy, you are not of a discouraging disposition in regard to your husband, I hope?"

"I am of a disposition to discourage this questioning, madam."

"Have it your own way. I only wish to be of assistance to you."

"Thank you but I do not require assistance."

"Where can Mary be? I shall see if she is still in her room."

The door closed on Mrs. Bennet's form, but the nuisance of her chatter hung in the air for some minutes.

Elizabeth crossed to the window. It was a cool, clear summer day.

She looked over her shoulder as Darcy entered. He stood close to her, while she turned back to look out on the day.

"We might never have a child, Fitzwilliam, let alone a son."

"Perhaps not, although it is but fourteen months since . . ."

"He keeps count!" she thought, then said, "Fitzwilliam, if it should turn out so, will you regret it?"

"I should be disappointed. Also, I dislike extremely the thought of you being turned from your home, should I die before you. However, the word 'regret' implies I have the power to alter our fate."

"I mean, I fear you will regret . . ." The words hung between them.

"Regret what, Elizabeth?"

"Nothing. It is nothing."

"Were you contemplating the prospect that I might regret having married you?"

She turned to him, her eyes very dark. She did not speak the question, but it was there, in her hard and wary glance.

"How can you think so?" he said. "After all that has passed between us, you have so little faith in me."

"No, dearest, not that. I have every faith in you. There is no one more worthy of my trust."

"Then trust me. You are the light of my life. I did not comprehend the meaning of those words until I knew you. I scarcely knew how to laugh without you."

"Forgive me."

He shrugged. "I constantly seek to know your feelings, so I ought to hear them with gratitude."

She smiled, then turned again to the window. He held her against him.

They looked out across the lake and up to the top of the hill. The distinctive blue of the carriage was unmistakable.

"Jane is here!" she cried. "I thought she would never come!"

The increase in the family party came as a relief for Elizabeth. No longer was she closeted so much with her mother and Mary. Mrs. Bennet's delight in the society of Jane and Kitty, two more-favored daughters, returned some of Elizabeth's freedom. She spent hours in her father's company and, while he dozed by the library fire, went back to her long walks and to enjoying her music with Georgiana.

Mary secretly enjoyed herself in her own way. Elizabeth made her a present of a lovely silk evening gown, and the only fault Mary could find with it was its failure to reach her neck. Mrs. Bennet bustled in to inspect her daughter's fashionable appearance.

"Oh, good girl, Mary! That will be just the thing. The neck is perhaps a little high. What think you, Lizzy?"

"Too high, Mama! I intend wearing a lace tuck," declared Mary.

"A lace tuck, girl! What can you be thinking of? Give men the choice between a glimpse of bosom and a lecture, not one amongst them will choose the talking-to."

Mary was adamant. "I know there are gentlemen who rise above such things."

Mr. Darcy had given Mary a gift of a necklace and earrings. She could hardly bear to let the gems share space with her cross for their last evening, but was persuaded by Elizabeth's request that she consider her brother-in-law's feelings. Thus she had the advantage of looking rather nice, while retaining her moral altitude. She thanked Mr. Darcy complacently when he complimented her on her appearance. Her mother glared when she added, "Of course, a woman is never better adorned than by a simple cross."

The pleasures of that summer stay at Pemberley reconciled Mr. Bennet to sharing the holiday with the wife of his bosom. Seeing three of his daughters evidently happy in marriage, he thought, with even a little compassion, of his youngest child. He began to relent on the subject of Newcastle. Failure to visit Lydia might look like a refusal to countenance her and revive whispers that had been silenced by her sisters' success in the marriage arena. Perhaps Lydia had brought on herself the unhappiness she might suffer in marriage to such a rogue. Yet her father had never quite silenced the inner voice that said she may never have strayed had he been a more conscientious parent.

Just as Mr. Bennet was brought to agree with his spouse's proposal, Mrs. Bennet received a letter from Lydia, which, in the most affectionate terms, discouraged them from making the journey at this time. Life was, in some unspecified way, less gay in Newcastle now that war was approaching. Also Lydia did not feel well enough for visitors at present.

"I must go to her," declared Mrs. Bennet, suddenly fancying herself an excellent nurse. "Where is Kitty? Perhaps she knows the nature of her sister's illness." She bustled off.

Jane could not hide her deep concern.

"Jane, what is wrong?" asked Elizabeth.

"Lizzy, dearest, it may be nothing."

"Is Lydia seriously unwell?" Elizabeth jumped up. "You are keeping something from me, Jane. How can you?"

"I do not wish to worry you, Lizzy."

"Tell me, dear, and I promise I will not break under the burden."

"Lydia had the most horrid rash over her face when she was at Rushly. The apothecary gave her something, a tincture, I supposed, and it went away."

"Is that all?"

"No. The festering returned. I sent for a physician and although Lydia has been very secretive, I am sure she has been taking mercury."

Elizabeth sat unmoving. Jane went on, "You know how slow Charles is to anger. He called Wickham a . . . a . . . blackguard!"

"Oh!" Elizabeth walked hastily away to the window.

"I would have done anything to shield you from this, Lizzy."

"Dear Jane, why should you bear it alone? Our sister has syphilis!"

"We think this must be so. I understand that all symptoms of the disease will soon disappear, after which our poor sister may never know for certain whether she is cured. If not, she faces an end she has never deserved."

Elizabeth replied, "No, indeed. This is too much punishment for her crime." She sat without speaking for a moment, before saying, "How can we shield our parents from this knowledge? If she is fortunate, the disease will never return. If it does return with all its force, it could well be after their deaths, so that they never need learn of it."

"We must dissuade our mother from making the journey."

However, there was no dissuading Mrs. Bennet from her maternal duties, now that her husband's objection was broken down, and they left for Newcastle the next day.

Jane and Elizabeth waited anxiously for news, fearing the arrival of every messenger. They received only one short note from their mother, in which she gloated over the sturdiness of the twin boys. Lydia's luck was with her again, as she had completely recovered from her bout of illness when her parents arrived. Even better, her husband's recent good fortune at cards meant they were able to present themselves as a young family making do on a small income. Mrs. Bennet was delighted with her grandsons, and gave Lydia a gift of money to buy some new clothes and toys for them. The Bennets then returned southwards to stay at Rushly Manor.

Lydia stood with Wickham on the steps of the lodging house, waving goodbye.

"How much did the old girl give you, Lydia, my darling?" murmured Wickham.

"Never mind the 'darlings,' Wickham. You shan't have it. I mean to have a new gown for the ball next week. I shan't change my mind about the money or the other matter."

Lydia had never forgiven Wickham his last lapse and determined to optimize her chances of survival by abstinence. Wickham never could persuade her that he was a changed character and, ironically, he had changed. He never went near a prostitute again, and confined himself to seducing farm girls and the like.

Even as war brewed in Belgium, peace settled again in Derbyshire. The Bingleys took Mary to Rushly Manor, there to await the arrival of Mr. and Mrs. Bennet on their return from their errand of mercy in Newcastle.

Kitty went happily back to Kympton.

"I never want to be parted from you again, Kitty," said Edward.

"We are bound to be parted from time to time, Edward. I suppose I shall die in childbirth, and you will marry someone else and forget all about me in a year or so."

"Kitty, how can you say such dreadful things? I cannot contemplate life without you, and I would never love another."

"Promise me, Edward. Do not ever forget me. Never love anyone else."

CHAPTER 29

From Miss Caroline Bingley to Mrs. Hurst

Brussels

Dearest Louisa,

There is, in Brussels, an atmosphere of desperate enjoyment, while our gallant officers await the arrival of the French. I am all atremble, and if you think it is Bonaparte who has reduced me to this state, how sadly you are mistaken!

A certain H.F. is constantly at my side, when he is not inspecting his men's buttons. Advise me, dearest. Ought I to bring him to the point, before he goes to fight, or wait until he returns triumphant, to carry me off as spoils of war? Sending him into battle, with the promise of my devotion, may ultimately leave me with nothing more than an interesting reputation of a broken heart. I do hesitate to waste the other opportunities that abound at this time.

Pray tell our dear little G. that her cousin thinks of her and has mentioned her to me with fondness. To think that she will likely soon be my cousin!

You will remember Mr. Willis, whom we met at Mrs. Brompton's house in London. I am all amazement to see dear Miss Brompton neglect him, with all his thousands, in favor of the gentlemen in scarlet. She especially smiles upon one Major Kentley, introduced to us by our friend Colonel Fitzwilliam. This rather dashing gallant has but little income apart from his pay. Really, my dear, one cannot eat a scarlet coat.

I believe dearest Jennifer begins to regret her haste. There are signs of discontent when Mr. Willis fails to appear, yet she makes little effort to please him when he does. I have advised her to pay him subtle attentions, as I do to my gallant, but she is too proud.

Of course you will consign this note to the fire, my love. I would not, for the world, have it find its way into other hands.

Dear, dear sister, I remain always,

Your most affectionate
Caroline

While Napoleon was massing and moving his army, his enemies had indeed found time on their hands in Brussels. Caroline and Jennifer were among the young ladies who found themselves very popular. They played, sang and danced. One or two civilian gentlemen were more than eligible but in this environment even prudent young ladies could not help preferring soldiers.

Major Kentley, a rather good specimen of the species, reminded Caroline of Mr. Darcy. He was dark and tall, with a somewhat commanding presence. When she stared haughtily into his eyes, he only smiled. She turned her own brilliant smile on Henry Fitzwilliam.

"Come, Colonel Fitzwilliam, and tell me the latest news. I am agog to hear you." She led him away to a corner of the room. She glanced back as they sat down, and caught the major's eyes moving slowly up her figure.

"Impudent puppy," she murmured. Then she said aloud, "You do not say so, Colonel Fitzwilliam? You do terrify me so." Caroline's eyes strayed to her friend, Jennifer, now in conversation with Kentley, and she smiled indulgently.

While Jennifer agonized over her choice between two beaux, Caroline never wavered in her intention to be Mrs. Fitzwilliam. (What a pity Lady Catherine had not been able to confer Sir Lewis's title on her nephew, along with his estate.)

"I hear Rosings is a splendid house, Caroline," said Mrs. Brompton.

"I am led by my heart," was the arch reply.

Caroline quite hung upon every word of the colonel's. Her eyes lit up when he entered the room. She glided about, leaned and flattered only for him.

The evenings passed with cards, music and dancing. Jennifer basked in Kentley's attention, giving up her monopoly only when her mother indicated that this must be so. Mr. Willis sulked in a corner or played cards with a hangdog air. He talked of leaving Brussels; what had he to do here? However, he stayed, not knowing whom he despised the most, the major or himself.

The colonel and Mrs. Brompton held a little dance in their lodgings. The chairs had been pushed back and the doors into the hall opened. Caroline was at her best, her height shown off to advantage, as she whirled through the waltz. Her heart raced with exertion. She felt the pressure of a manly arm at her waist and fancied her partner pulled her closer. They spun through the doors and, at the end of the hall, where they ought to have turned, he stopped, and giddiness almost threw her against his chest.

"Be my wife, Caroline. Marry me."

"Really, sir!" She pulled herself away, and stared. He dropped his arm but continued to hold her hand.

"Miss Bingley, I was carried away by my feelings. Forgive me." She nodded graciously.

"You know that I love you. Will you do me the honor of consenting to be my wife?"

The next couple was almost upon them. He seized her waist once more and they spun back towards the drawing room.

"You must give me time."

"Do I truly want him?" she thought.

"We have all too little time. Pray give me your answer tonight."

"Very well, then."

"You mean you accept?"

"No. I will give you my answer tonight."

As the group of officers went into the street, one of them turned towards the light for a moment. He opened the tiny folded piece of paper and smiled as he read "Yes."

Caroline did not confide in her friends that evening. Pleading exhaustion, she escaped to her room, her mind all confusion. She wondered if she had done the right thing.

In the morning, Mrs. Brompton knocked on her door.

"My dear Caroline, there is a gentleman awaiting you downstairs."

"Pray, Mrs. Brompton, I cannot appear in dishabille. He must wait until I am dressed."

"The gentleman asserts his right to insist upon seeing you at once. Is this so, my dear? I would not press you, were you not in my care. I must be able to answer to your relations." She looked long at Caroline and continued, "I see you do not deny it."

"There is good reason for making haste this morning."

Caroline did not hurry herself unduly but, in defense, she could argue that she had no experience in rushing her toilette.

He took both her hands in his. "My dearest Caroline!" His eyes skimmed over her. She was dressed in a frilled morning gown of white muslin, and two locks of glossy brown hair still hung down her back. If her intended found Caroline less than presentable, he was an excellent actor.

"I hope you have something important to say, sir, to justify disturbing me at this early hour," she replied.

"I have just seen Mr. Willis. He has determined to leave today in order to get his sister back to England. He has room in his carriage for you, Miss Brompton, and your maids, if they will sit outside. He will ride. You must make haste as you have only two hours to prepare for the journey."

"I have no intention of running away. You greatly mistake my character if you think so."

"Caroline. It is a matter of days at most before we are at war. I must have you safely back in England. Indeed I insist upon it."

"I do not know that you are in a position to insist upon anything, sir."

"Nevertheless, I do." Caroline felt an inner tremor at his gaze. She had not imagined him so firm. She fancied she showed nothing of this, however.

"I intend to dance at the Duchess of Richmond's ball, and I defy you to prevent me."

"The duchess seems most gracious here, Caroline, but do not imagine she will recognize us in England. Do not give me the anguish of dying on the field, not knowing whether you are safe."

"Since you put it that way, very well."

"Good girl. Now give me a kiss."

"I know not that I want to."

"There may never be another chance," he said.

She felt the warmth of his hand against her cheek and the pull of his arm as he drew her to him. Her fingers brushed against his epaulettes and the braid upon his collar. Then his lips were on hers. She began to pull away just as he released her. She was struggling for breath.

He pulled a ring from his finger.

"I wished to obtain something better, but there was no time."

He put it in her hand and closed her fingers around it.

"Do you love me, Caroline?"

"I have said I will marry you. You must be content with that."

He ran his hands through the hair on her shoulders. "Pray, let me have a lock of your hair."

"My hair! Certainly not." Her hands were on her hips and her cheeks flushed, as she recalled the not disagreeable sensation of those lips on hers.

"Caroline, we may never meet again."

"No! Do not speak so!" Aghast, she felt the tears prick her eyes.

She fetched some scissors from the desk, and he cut off a long lock.

"Do you love me, Caroline?"

"Yes. Are you satisfied?"

"Inexpressibly." He folded the tress in a sheet of paper. "Fare thee well, my Betrothed. I will see Willis at once to secure your place in the carriage. I shall come to you again at my very earliest opportunity, whenever and wherever that may be."

Her discontent at the vagueness of this appointment lent a shine to her eyes. His last glimpse of her was with her chin up and his favorite haughty smile.

As he mounted his horse, he laughed aloud.

From Miss Bingley to Mrs. Hurst

Brussels,
At some unearthly hour!

My dearest Louisa,
    I write in the greatest hurry. We are packed and leave Brussels at once. Mr. Willis and his sister are below with the carriage. Do not imagine I would have flown at such a time but for the urging of my Betrothed. Yes, Louisa, I am engaged! I have scarce had time to accustom myself to the idea, for he is so forceful in sending me away. I hope he does not imagine me forever so compliant. You know how little my nature inclines me to obedience! I must fly.

Your Caroline

It was as well they left when they did. Within hours there was not a horse to be had in all Brussels, and the stranded civilians listened, with varying degrees of courage, to the distant cannon fire of Waterloo.

All London was triumphant at the news of the swift success of the military campaign. Mrs. Hurst wished more urgently to discuss the successful amatory campaign, but dared not until Caroline came home and lifted the veil of secrecy.

A letter to Pemberley was long overdue, she decided. She had not written to Georgiana in an age. Georgiana recognized her hand, and opened the letter with an odd mixture of indifference to the writer and the keenest interest in what she may write.

"We are expecting Caroline's arrival hourly, and are in the utmost anticipation. For when she comes, we will be in a position to openly acknowledge yet another link in our kinship, dear Miss Darcy."

Georgiana crumpled the letter in her hands and she looked around her numbly.

She sat for some time, unmoving.

Darcy was in the library, attending to some business, when he heard the knock.

"Come."

Georgiana stood in the doorway, her face a mask of misery. He rose.

"Geogiana, what is the matter?"

She ran across the room, threw herself into his arms and burst into tears.

"Georgiana, what is it? What on earth is wrong?"

"Henry . . ."

"Henry is safe, Georgiana. I told you of the messenger who arrived early this morning. The war is already over and Henry is unharmed. Come, I will show you the letter again."

"I know . . . but . . . Miss Bingley."

"What of her, dear?"

"They are engaged! I have just had it of Mrs. Hurst." She pulled the crumpled paper from her pocket.

He read the lines she indicated. He rang the bell and asked the servant to send for his mistress. Georgiana passed her in the hall and merely shook her head at the offer of company. Elizabeth went into the study to hear the unwelcome news.

"I cannot believe your cousin has such poor taste," Elizabeth said.

"I had too much faith in his judgment, it seems. Why, she is so false."

"Perhaps she cares for him."

"Come now! This is a woman I have tolerated as my friend's sister, and as a sister-in-law, but to see my cousin marry her is beyond bearing."

"I imagine she will suit the style of Rosings very well. I can picture her enthroned in Lady Catherine's favorite chair, giving the Collinses a hard time of it."

"I am sorry to see Georgiana react so strongly to the engagement. Think you that her feelings for him are stronger than those of a ward?" said Darcy.

"I think, perhaps, she at least fancies that they are. The visit to Deepdene will provide her with distraction."

"I had rather hoped that Lord Bradford might succeed with her."

"We must trust that he is a patient man. If the attraction he appears to feel for her proves lasting, who knows what may be, in a year or so."

Darcy stood gazing out on the park, thinking of poor Georgiana. Yet, despite his affection for his cousin, and his great concern for his sister's future happiness, he could feel little satisfaction in the thought of such a marriage. Why did the thought that his sister may have become mistress of Rosings give him so little joy? He felt only that it would have been an anticlimax.

CHAPTER 30

THE CARRIAGE SWEPT AROUND A bend in the drive and the house appeared in view. Ideally situated upon a small hill, Deepdene stood in exquisite Palladian symmetry.

"What perfection, Fitzwilliam!" cried Elizabeth.

He surveyed it moodily.

"That is Deepdene's reputation, Elizabeth," he replied. "I had not known you approved of such artifice."

"One must approve of perfection no matter how artful."

"I cannot comprehend the temerity of a woman who pulls down an historic house that has served her husband's family for generations."

She laughed. "One presumes the marquess did not vigorously object." She paused before adding, "I admit it is very like Lady Englebury to have resculpted her home with such thoroughness."

"Take care she does not resculpt you."

"You will try to enjoy yourself a little, dearest?"

"What can you mean?"

"What a bear you are when you do not have your way." She smiled teasingly, but he bent his saturnine gaze out of the window.

"He is our own and only bear, is he not, Georgiana? So we forgive him."

The Darcys found the party would be smaller than they expected. Of the marchioness's literary protégés, only the novelist Miss Bearnley, and Mr. Glover had been invited to Deepdene. It was otherwise a family party, with the marchioness's cousin, Sir Beaumont Hunt, and Lady Hunt, the ubiquitous Whittakers, the Courtneys and Georgiana's friend, formerly Captain Westcombe, now Lord Bradford and the marquess's heir.

Of course, there was the elderly marquess, too. He came to London no more and was usually to be found wandering vaguely about Deepdene. Some pitied him, imagining he was searching for the home of his youth. He was not suffering from senility, however it might appear. He had always been vague.

In the afternoon, the Darcys walked in the grounds with the Courtneys. Mr. Courtney, having little in common with the other men, was relieved to see Darcy and they dropped back in conversation, while the three ladies walked ahead, arm in arm. They all wandered down from the house towards the shrubbery.

Abruptly, Georgiana shivered, and paused. She looked around, wondering at the emptiness of the space around her and the smoothness of the grass.

"Where was the old house, Mrs. Courtney?" she asked.

"I find it quite wonderful that you should ask that question, Miss Darcy. You are standing at the bottom of the west tower, more or less."

Elizabeth marvelled. Only thirty years before, a Tudor mansion had stood in this very place. Generations of family memories were reduced to velvety grass and perfectly placed shrubs.

"Where is the famous rose garden?" she asked. "I know it to be cunningly concealed."

"We are almost upon it," said Amelia. They walked between some thickly planted shrubs and Elizabeth started as she came upon a high ancient hedge.

"The squareness of the hedge was so offensive to the landscaper that it had to be concealed lest he destroy it," said Amelia.

They followed the line of the towering green wall. At the corner of the square was a great archway. Looking back, they saw Darcy and Courtney stationary, apparently engrossed in discussing a serious point. Both were wearing the kind of dark color that ends up looking grey-brown.

"What sensible husbands we have," said Amelia, and they laughed together.

The white of their muslin gowns fluttering below the brilliant blues and greens of their short jackets, the three young women disappeared inside the arch. They stepped into a tunnel, a cascade of scent and color.

"Art and nature most ingeniously wed," said Elizabeth.

"I would have said that of Pemberley," said Amelia.

"Pemberley is art employed to make nature look perfect."

She began to run. Georgiana, arm in arm with her, had to run too. Laughing, they scampered through arches and around walls of blooms. Then the pool was before them, presided over by Erato the Lovely with her lyre. Elizabeth wanted to laugh or to weep. The patina of age and creeping mosses had disguised the hand of man, and for the past hundred years, pool and statue had looked as though they had always been there.

Georgiana sank at once onto the edge, took off a glove and dipped her hand in the water. Furtively, she raised her eyes to the sculpture. She felt inexplicably fearful and excited. Amelia jumped up on the ledge and began to trip across on the stone lily pads to the statue.

"Come, Elizabeth, and pay your respects to the muse."

Elizabeth followed her and put her hand on Erato's arm.

"Amelia, she is so time-honored, I could kiss her."

Amelia smiled wickedly, and Elizabeth added softly, "Is this what young brides feel for their venerable old consorts?"

"I doubt that very much," whispered Amelia. "Teddy says they all have young lovers."

"How came he by this knowledge?"

Amelia giggled. "Come," she said. "Let us return to the mainland."

As Elizabeth stepped onto a stone leaf, they heard a voice declaim:

"In despair, me thought my muse was cold;
But Hark! Living vision so sweet yet bold.
From her stone-hard corpse arises
Lovely ladies with flashing irises."

"Peregrine, what a horrible verse," said Amelia. "How long have you been skulking there, torturing your brain for a rhyme?"

Whittaker stepped out from a mound of greenery behind the pool and bowed with gracious ceremony. Georgiana jumped up, crushing her glove in her hand.

"How are you, Mr. Whittaker?" Elizabeth nodded with as much condescension as a lady stepping across a pool might. The embroidered hem of her gown had dipped into the water. She raised it slightly with her right hand and took his proffered hand with the other. His blue eyes had none of their usual hard edge; she had never seen his expression so unaffected. A momentary warmth of feeling caused her to look away. Then at once, the absurdity of the scene flashed upon her.

As Darcy turned the corner, he saw Elizabeth stepping down from the edge, hand in hand with this man she claimed to despise. They both turned and looked at him like laughing children confronting a sensible guardian.

"He does not like it," thought Whittaker and, oddly, felt more saddened than amused. Elizabeth felt her husband disapproved of her wet hem and dropped it with an unaccountable feeling much like guilt. Whittaker turned to his cousin and offered her his hand. He helped her down. Then he said, "With gladdened eye, I greet thee, Mr. Darcy."

The weather was too good to last. Grey clouds rolled in during the late afternoon. After dinner the ladies passed through the tall windows of the drawing room onto the terrace. They watched the changing patterns of light, as gold glistened around the edges of the looming dark masses and streams of light poured down, first on the distant hills, then over Deepdene itself. Gradually the brilliance faded. All but Elizabeth were wrapped in their shawls. The gentlemen, who had left their port, followed the ladies onto the terrace. Elizabeth shivered.

"Pray, allow me to fetch your shawl," said Whittaker and turned back towards the door. Darcy was just coming out, having picked it up on his way through the room.

"Forestalled once again," said Whittaker. Darcy shrugged.

"I knew Mrs. Darcy would feel the chill at nightfall," he said. Elizabeth felt the caress of the cashmere around her shoulders.

"Thank you, Fitzwilliam," she murmured.

They all turned back into the drawing room for coffee.

The conversation returned to a lively debate they had enjoyed at dinner. At first it was dominated by the marchioness and Whittaker. Elizabeth became more and more animated, and Darcy noticed how the others often turned to her for her response. Gradually he fell into a silence as total as Georgiana's. He was relieved when the party broke up.

He watched darkly as Elizabeth came to him and slipped into the bed.

"You excelled yourself this evening," he said. "I apologize for my dullness."

"You were very dull," she replied.

He looked away.

"Have I offended you?" She dearly wanted to laugh. He shrugged and looked back at her coolly.

"You are being ridiculous," he said.

"Shall we quarrel? Is that what you wish?" She was leaning on her elbow, looking down at him, curls falling forward. Exasperation flickered across his face.

"You do wish it!" she said, suppressing a laugh.

She bent her head and caught his upper lip between her own lips. She sank down beside him.

His hand was in her hair, his lips close to her ear.

"Elizabeth . . ."

He blew out the candle and buried his thoughts in passion.

CHAPTER 31

THE NEXT MORNING, Wilkins pulled back the curtains, and Elizabeth took in the gloom of the room.

"Oh, Wilkins, is it raining?"

"Yes, madam."

Elizabeth jumped out of bed and ran to the window. From this side of the house, there was a lovely view over the park to the woods she had wanted to explore today. Sheets of rain poured down.

"Mr. Darcy will not have his fishing, Wilkins, and her ladyship did promise it him. It was very wrong of her."

"I daresay the gentlemen will be disappointed."

From her solemnity, one would never guess that Wilkins, when in a mood to condescend, had the upper servants at Pemberley in fits of laughter with tales of their mistress's jests.

"Your bath is ready, madam."

They had a tour of the house in the morning. From Lady Englebury's perfunctory manner, it was hard to imagine her expending the massive amount of effort that it must have taken to supervise the rebuilding of Deepdene.

"Deepdene deserves its reputation," said Darcy. "These proportions are ideal."

"I thank you. No doubt they are," she replied. "I never notice the place nowadays. Englebury knew not if he were on his head or his heels for seven years, poor fellow. I wonder why I did it? Come, I wish to show you the theater."

As they went, Lady Englebury said, "Sir Beaumont is an enthusiast for theatricals." She turned to Elizabeth. "I imagine he will do his best to inveigle you into performing."

"He considers me a natural choice for a tragic heroine, I daresay."

The marchioness gave a bark of laughter.

"Mr. Glover has prepared the first act of a little drama for us."

"A drama, indeed? I thank Your Ladyship for the warning, without it I may have laughed."

The marchioness barely smiled. "Sir Beau and I shall read it to you all after luncheon."

Their hostess left them in the picture gallery. Her back to the others, Georgiana earnestly studied a landscape.

"Elizabeth, I trust you are not contemplating performing in these theatricals?" said Darcy. She turned to him and looked into the dark opaqueness of his eyes.

"I have scarce had time to decide," she said coolly.

"I might have hoped you could anticipate my disinclination for seeing you make a spectacle of yourself."

Two bright spots of pink appeared high on her cheeks. She turned and walked swiftly away.

Georgiana watched her brother furtively, as he paced furiously up to the end of the long room and back again.

"Left to herself, I imagine Elizabeth would not wish to join in the theatricals," she offered.

"Really? So my conduct as her husband ought to be one of waiting to hear her intentions, in case her designs happen to coincide with my own?"

Secretly, Georgiana thought this course may have something to recommend it; but she did not feel up to promoting the idea. Her brother walked away.

They did not meet again until luncheon. Elizabeth appeared oblivious to Darcy's altitude, high upon his dignity. Mr. Whittaker was in a mood she had never seen before; the mocking edge of his wit had softened, and she warmed to him after her husband's coolness. Miss Arabella, however, had a brittleness in her brilliance and she devoted herself to the fruitless task of stroking Darcy's vanity.

After the meal, they went into the drawing room to hear the first act of Glover's play. The day was relentlessly dark and the windows opaque with rain. Within, the flames illuminated the faces of the audience grouped about the fire. The appreciative murmurs, which punctuated the beginning of the reading, faded; even the rustling of a dress died away until the listeners scarcely breathed and barely moved their heads, but when they glanced sidelong at Mrs. Darcy. Darcy's face slowly whitened, but Elizabeth's expression remained enigmatic. The suspicions, aroused by the fragment she had read three months before, were confirmed. Mr. Glover, against her expressed wishes, had based his heroine upon her, even quoting words she had spoken in different situations and in a manner that few in the room could fail to recognize.

Darcy rose, turned his back to the room and stood gazing out of the window. The beauty of Deepdene's pleasure grounds was veiled with rain. Behind him fell a heavy cloak of silence. At last it was ripped by applause.

The marchioness put her hand out to Mr. Glover. He arose from his corner in the shadows away from the fire and came forward. He took her hand. He smiled only with his mouth, while anxiety continued to haunt his eyes.

"Good Lord, Glover, you have done it!" cried Whittaker. "Splendid work! I take back every discouraging word and beg your forgiveness for all my teasing."

Glover looked at him, all confusion, clouded dark eyes meeting the clear blue.

"I was inspired, Mr. Glover," cut in Courtney. "How does the play end? I fear our heroine will prove too exalted for a romantic denouement." Amelia looked significantly at him, and he looked back at her, puzzled. The most literal of men, he had perceived nothing amiss.

"Despair not, Courtney," said Whittaker. "For our hero to be rejected by such a goddess is as good as acceptance from ten standard females."

The marchioness looked displeased.

"I was mistaken," thought Elizabeth. He is as spiteful as ever.

"Pray do not be so light, Perry," said Arabella. "Mr. Glover has honored us with this glimpse of his first serious work before it appears in public, before it is even complete."

"I know not that it will appear in public," muttered Glover.

There was a wash of disappointed murmurs, while the marchioness smiled benignly.

Elizabeth turned to reply to a quiet remark from Amelia, next to her on the sofa. Glover flinched at her tiny movement. Whittaker followed his gaze and said, "Mrs. Darcy, we do not hear from you. We scarce know how to form an opinion without hearing yours."

"I do not imagine Mr. Glover is influenced by my views," she said. There was a chill in the room; the gathering seemed numbed. Hunt pressed onward through this.

"We ought to present these fragments as a play," he said.

"Really, Sir Beau," said Lady Hunt. "Let us not have too much of a good thing. We go next to the Blythes and life there is constant play-acting."

"Yes, my dear, but nothing so interesting as this," he said, ignoring the warning in her mild eyes. Unlike Courtney, he detected all subtleties and adored them. "What say you, Glover?"

"It is unfinished and ill-prepared," the author replied.

"Mr. Glover sought only the opinion of a few friends, for the work is quite different from anything he has attempted before," said Lady Englebury.

"I understand your feeling very well, Mr. Glover," said Miss Bearnly. "One scribbles away in private and two years can go by while one wonders whether the entire manuscript should be hurled upon the fire."

"You wonder that, Miss Bearnly?" asked Amelia, laughing. "How many manuscripts would you say you have consigned to a fiery death?"

"Mathematics were ever my weakness," replied the novelist.

"I am not so modest over my arithmetic; I hazard the answer to be nought."

There was quiet laughter, but Amelia could not divert the conversation from its course.

"The few friends liked it very well, Glover," said Sir Beau. "A little performance among those friends will give you an idea of how it looks."

All the time Elizabeth was aware of Darcy watching her from across the room. In the stillness that followed, Miss Whittaker's languid voice was heard. "I should like to hear Mrs. Darcy reading the title role."

"Thank you, but I decline," said Elizabeth.

"Will you not do us this favor, Mrs. Darcy?" persisted Arabella. Now it was she ignoring her brother's subtle gesture to desist.

Even without her anger towards Glover for having written the piece, Elizabeth would not have considered involving herself in this amusement. At the same time, her sense that Darcy was silently willing her to refuse angered her. She was not inclined to turn and look at him.

"I thank you for the compliment," Elizabeth replied. "However, I have no talent for reproducing words that are not my own with conviction."

She rose and, with a slight bow of her head to the marchioness, quitted the room.

Whittaker broke the silence. "Ah, Glover, it seems your little piece did not win universal approval! I am so sorry."

Darcy curtly said, "Excuse me," to the company as a whole and followed Elizabeth.

"Arabella! Why did you importune her in that way?" murmured her brother. She turned to him, eyebrows elegantly arched.

"What ails thee, brother? I notice you do not extend this sudden chivalry to our dear playwright."

Darcy found Elizabeth pacing along the gallery. Wordlessly, he joined her. At the end of the gallery, she stopped and looked out of one of the long windows. She longed to walk out, even in this rainstorm, she thirsted so for trees.

With studied casualness, he said, "I am surprised that Mr. Glover appears to be on such a footing with you that he feels free to parade his infatuation before all these people."

"I thought he appeared tortured with anxiety."

"That is something I cannot judge. I am not so well-acquainted with him as you are."

"How true."

"Were you privy to the nature of the work?"

"I was not expecting it." She might have told him that she had demanded the abandonment of the work, and thought she had been assured of it. She scorned to defend herself.

She turned back to the window. Bars of rain poured down the glass. Her husband stood unmoving beside her. His presence and his steady gaze upon her profile paralyzed her with fury.

At that moment Mr. Glover burst upon them. In a flash he noted the anger in their stance; his immediate thought was that Darcy was bullying her. They turned to him as his expression changed from high-pitched anxiety to outrage.

"Can I help you in some way, Mr. Glover?" asked Darcy.

Glover flinched visibly under the cold politeness of his tone. He turned to Elizabeth, who gazed back with no trace of expression.

"Pray, give me the honor of a brief interview, Mrs. Darcy."

"I am engaged at present."

"When may I speak to you?"

Without reply, she turned back to the window. Glover turned on his heel and stalked away. They waited in silence as his footsteps receded.

"Elizabeth, I must ask you—"

"This place is too public."

She turned and walked away down the gallery, and he followed. They walked two long corridors in silence until they came to her dressing room. As they went in, Wilkins, who was preparing Elizabeth's evening clothes, said, "Madam, the marchioness has sent a message that she would like to see you in her sitting room."

Elizabeth turned to Darcy. Wilkins started. She had witnessed evidence of the odd quarrel, but this moment frightened her and she scurried out. Elizabeth was reminded of Darcy's expression many months before, when they hardly knew each other and she had arrived at Netherfield Hall, with her petticoat muddied. He was judging her.

"You had something you wished to ask me?" she said coolly. In the proud carriage of her head, he read scorn.

"I believe I know all I want to know." He bowed curtly.

"Excuse me."

She went slowly along the corridor, composing herself for the interview to come.

She sat down, folded her hands in her lap and silently faced the marchioness, who began, "I see you are angry, my dear. Will you tell me the reason?"

"In April, your Ladyship assured me that Mr. Glover would not continue with his play. He has broken his word, and I know not how you can have invited me here, with my family, to have it thrust upon us without warning. You could hardly imagine I would be pleased."

"I cannot understand your objection. It is a flattering portrait, and few will know the identity of the original."

"All your friends will know and that is too many for me," said Elizabeth.

The sharp blue gaze of the marchioness's eyes softened.

"I am fond of you, my dear, as I believe you know."

"I have always been grateful for your Ladyship's kindness."

"Tush, my dear. I do not care a fig for gratitude." She paused. "My reward is in seeing the success of those whose talents I recognize and nurture."

"I should have thought that Mr. Glover has reaped reward enough to preclude all need for him to promote himself at my expense."

"I was not speaking of Glover's talent, but your own!" cried Lady Englebury. "Mr. Darcy would seek to keep you from all the world when you might, under my guidance, bring his family renown."

Elizabeth jumped up. "What if we, neither of us, desire that renown? In regard to Mr. Glover's intrusion into my life and his impertinent curiosity concerning my character, it is my own resentment you face. You will never conquer my opposition."

The old lady looked up at the younger one. How splendid she looked in all the bloom and fire of youth, and with such a proud tilt to her chin!

"The theater has been bereft of great playwrights for many years. Mr. Glover is one of few with any promise, and I believe that you will one day be celebrated as the inspiration for one of his greatest works."

"I utterly refuse Mr. Glover my permission to ever refer to me, in any public way, no matter how indirectly he makes his reference. No one can persuade me otherwise."

"No one, my dear Mrs. Darcy?

"Nobody, in all the world."

"I am mentor to some of the greatest minds in England."

"I have enjoyed enough of Your Ladyship's society to have no doubt of your abilities and influence."

The old lady looked at Elizabeth narrowly. Admiring the girl for her wits and confidence, she had not understood the depth of this pride. It was not vanity, nor pride of position. Though coming from the lowest rank of gentility, Elizabeth could scorn the assistance of a peeress equipped to advance her to its heights. She had unparalleled self-respect, and her ladyship was awed by her.

"I dread the thought of a quarrel with you, my dear," she said. "You have become indispensable to me."

"I do not seek a quarrel, madam. I do not know that we can understand one another," Elizabeth said, and she turned to the door.

Lady Englebury reached out and took her hand. "I care for you as I would a daughter. It is a feeling I have not known since being robbed of my own."

"I pity you for your loss, Lady Englebury, but I cannot take her place. I am a 'daughter' who will not suffice as she is. I feel that you have prepared a mold for me into which I do not conveniently pour." Sadness crept in at the edges of her words. "I beg to take leave of you now."

The marchioness sat quite still for several minutes.

"I shall give this matter careful thought," she declared, looking up. Mrs. Darcy had left the room.

Elizabeth gazed into the mirror absently as Wilkins finished dressing her hair. Darcy knocked and came in.

She said, "I will come down in a few minutes."

"I shall wait for you," he said, and sat down.

She felt acutely irritated by his presence. She glanced at him in the mirror; he was gazing at her steadily, an expressionless examination. She looked away.

"Are you intending to wear that gown to dinner?" he asked.

She turned gracefully on the stool and he looked at her. Her favorite yellow, the silk of the gown seemed to cling about her figure.

"I had thought you liked it."

"That was in London. I do not wish my wife to appear so here."

"Many fashionable women wear gowns more daring than this." He shrugged, with a flicker in his eyes she read as contempt. She turned back to the mirror.

"You wish me to change into something else?" He had not wished to prevail at the price of this coldness.

"I cannot comprehend that you have cause for complaint," he said.

She turned her eyes to the maid's, in the reflection of the mirror. "Wilkins, bring me something Quakerish, will you?"

"Quakerish, madam? Shall I bring the white braided silk?"

Elizabeth, without turning her head, said, "Pray, allow me five minutes." Dismissed, Darcy left the room. Georgiana was waiting by the door of her room, afraid to go down alone. They walked the length of the corridor together. Georgiana looked up at her brother furtively. He was absorbed in thought, eyes impenetrably dark.

"Fitzwilliam," she said. He looked at her in surprise, having forgotten she was there. They had walked back past Elizabeth's door.

"You will not fight him, will you?" she whispered.

"I would dearly like to thrash him, but one only fights with a gentleman. I would not duel with the son of a tradesman!" Elizabeth was standing in the doorway. Georgiana blushed as deeply as though those words had been her own. Elizabeth took Darcy's arm.

"I am so pleased you will not shoot my Uncle Gardiner, sir Shall we go down? I fear we may be late."

That evening, the ladies seemed only too happy to leave the gentlemen to their port. They played duets and sang together, even Georgiana joining in. The marchioness put some energy into entertaining and had them all laughing over her caustic wit. Elizabeth sang her ladyship's favorite song.

When the gentlemen came in, they were delighted to find the ladies so light-hearted. The marquess chuckled happily, so sick he was of politics.

Elizabeth met Darcy's moody glance and shrugged inwardly.

"Let him sulk, if he enjoys it so," she thought. Glover had been watching her, too, with his unfathomable smolder. "What a pair of blockheads they are."

"Let us have glees!" his lordship quavered. "Pray do not get up, Mrs. Darcy. You shall sing. We heard you piping away as we came from the dining room."

Sir Beau was to provide his rather thrilling baritone and Whittaker the tenor. Amelia rose. "Arabella, pray take my place. I am sure everyone wishes very much to hear you sing."

"Thank you, but I decline," she replied, with her languid smile. "I should spoil the tableau, for you all look so very well together!"

There was a general murmur of concurrence, for they did look well. Whittaker stood at Elizabeth's side, his blond good looks complementing her brunette prettiness and sparkling dark eyes, and Sir Beau's great size and leonine locks making an impressive foil for Amelia's impish charm.

"Oh, Darcy," said Courtney, with an air of tragedy. "I feel that we are become a surplus commodity."

From Darcy's expression, Elizabeth feared a sarcastic reply. It was cut off by Lady Hunt's exclamation, "Sir Beau, you look like a lion alongside a dear little elf," she said. "Beware, for I shall turn Delilah in the night if you do not call for the hairdresser soon."

"Madam, I beseech you to stay your hand. I am remaking myself as an interesting personage. You may find you admire the result."

He produced laughter, for poseurs were, in fact, the favorite butts of Sir Beau's humor. Elizabeth looked questioningly at Darcy. He met her gaze with no warmth in his expression. Elizabeth's eyes wandered on to Georgiana, who sat in a still daze. Lord Bradford, sitting at her side, leaned towards her.

"Miss Darcy?" he said softly.

She turned to him. She had only known one man as gentle as this.

"I hope I have not offended you in some way," he said.

"Oh, no, my Lord!" she said. "I do not think you could ever offend anyone." He was touched to the core by the innocence of this remark.

"Then why will you vouchsafe me no conversation tonight?"

"I am so sorry. I did not know."

"You appear troubled. You would do me the highest honor if you could let me help you."

Georgiana's eyes stung with tears repressed. "Thank you. You are very kind, but I have no troubles."

Amelia noticed them deep in conversation and gave her husband a conspiratorial glance.

At last, Lady Englebury rose to retire and many of the company seemed inclined to follow. After seeing those guests on their way upstairs, her ladyship turned back to the room.

"Nephew!"

"Yes, Aunt?"

"Come! I wish to speak with you." At the door he turned and rolled his eyes at Arabella, then followed the little round figure into the library.

As soon as he closed the door, she turned on him sharply, and said, "Peregrine, you seem determined to stir up trouble for

Mr. Glover over his present work. Do not imagine your spiteful little maneuvers are lost upon anyone."

"You know I cannot resist it at times, dear Lady Englebury. Glover, dear man, has a fit of passion over some trivial event every ten minutes. One so enjoys helping him along. Then there is the challenge of trying to get a spark of feeling out of Darcy."

"You are jealous, Peregrine."

"Jealous? My dear Aunt, you greatly mistake the case. She is very charming and so forth, but—"

"I speak of Glover, Nephew. I believe you are jealous of his success. You have always mocked him for his failure to produce a serious work. Now that he seems set to do so, you are sick with envy."

Her nephew opened his mouth to speak, and stopped. Then, "You paint an ugly picture of me, Aunt."

"If I am wrong, show me I am so by more gentlemanlike behavior. This present work of Mr. Glover's was of great importance, to the theater, as to me."

"Forgive me, madam." Then, with a wry smile he added, "Pray, do not send me away."

She took out her handkerchief and waved it, in jest. He was all but paralyzed by the sudden musky scent of her perfume. She patted him on the arm and smiled. He bent and kissed her cheek.

"Goodnight then, dear boy," she said. "Remember my words."

He stood alone in the darkened room for some time.

He heard the rustle of silk, and Arabella was beside him.

"What are you doing here, so solitary, Perry?"

"Do you know, Bella, I sometimes swear I smell still the scent of Nurse's clothing?"

"Lavender? The slightest whiff of it and she is before me."

"I mean that I smell it, when it is not there. For a mad moment, just then, I felt her iron claw plucking my fingers from our aunt's gown. Do you recall the way she would haul me into the carriage to go home?"

"The power of aromas to recall the past to mind! Four delicious years have passed since our father's death freed us, Perry, and still I cannot abide the smell of a library."

"Poor Bella."

"He was harder on you."

"Yes, but then I'd go away to school. Blessings on that wondrous institution! I used to wish I could take you with me." He put his arm around her shoulders. "I suppose you will leave me soon for some noodle with a large estate."

"I doubt I will come to such a pass. Husbands are very like fathers, so wretchedly difficult to get away from."

"Then remain with me, Lovely One. Remain with me."

He slipped his arm to her waist, and together they ascended the great staircase.

Georgiana lay in the darkness, her warm tears spilling steadily. She recalled the day her brother had first left her at school, three months after their father's death. They had toured the building with the headmistress. He had said goodbye to her in the hall, and, as he was getting in the carriage, Georgiana's little figure in black hurtled down the steps and clung to him.

"Oh, fie, Miss Darcy! Is this any way for a great girl of eleven years to behave? I hope to see more ladylike conduct in the near future."

Fitzwilliam wiped her tears and said, "I will come and see you very soon, Georgiana."

"Not before half-term, Mr. Darcy. We find that is best in a girl's first year. I am sure you will find we are correct."

She felt now precisely eleven years old. "I am but a babe, really. How am I ever to grow up?"

Why did Elizabeth not see the danger she was in? Why did she not simply ask Fitzwilliam's pardon for whatever it was? Then he would deal firmly with Mr. Glover, take them away, love Elizabeth again and they would all live happily together forever.

She thought of Lord Bradford. She guessed that Fitzwilliam

hoped she might marry him. She pictured the marchioness and trembled at the notion she might be expected one day to fill that place. Then she thought of the present marquess. Perhaps she would be more like him, and wander about lost in this vast palace with its perfect proportions and incomprehensible paintings hanging side by side with the ancestors. If he were plain Mr. Joseph Bradford, not Earl thereof, let alone his grander expectations, and if he loved her, which was most unlikely, then she might have been able to gratify her brother's wish one day. "Joseph." It was a nice name. He had almost the kindest eyes she had ever seen. He had looked so happy when she said she did not think he could offend anyone. She blushed in the darkness. What a thing to say! How Elizabeth would laugh at her! Yet he had blushed too. She recalled the way he leaned towards her. She was leaning towards him now, falling against him, her cheek resting on his shoulder, nestling there. His arms were holding her, and she felt her own arms creep up around his neck. She started awake and blushed again, hotly, in the darkness.

Darcy was lying on his back when Elizabeth came in. He watched as she took off her wrap and draped it over a chair, but he saw she remained in her secret cloak. She walked over to the bed and lay beside him.

"Good night, Fitzwilliam."

He turned on his elbow and reached across her to blow out the candle. Despite his sullen mood, he felt the stirring of desire. He wanted to talk, but he wanted this first. The smell of the wax was in her nostrils, and his face was above hers in the darkness. She felt the rage of impotence and wanted to push him away. She felt a convulsive shock at the touch of his hand in her hair and his mouth on her mouth. Then his lips on her throat, with no word of apology or endearment! She felt a crawling of repulsion through her body; he must have felt it too.

"Good night," he said and turned on his side away from her.

She stared into the darkness. Outside, the storm was raging. At last, she slept.

CHAPTER 32

THE SKY WAS CLEARING AND the sun shone weakly over Deepdene. Elizabeth eluded the others and went for a solitary walk. The ground was too wet for exploring the woods, so she passed through the arch in the high enclosing hedges and went into the rose garden. The flowers drooped their heads with the weight of the water and petals lay everywhere upon the ground. She moved towards the center and came to the pool that two days before had sparkled at the sky.

A gardener and boy were raking leaves and other debris from the water. All that remained of the muse, who had stood on her rock in the middle of the water, was the broken hem of her garment.

"What happened to the statue?" she asked.

"It is here, ma'am." The gardener indicated the wheelbarrow, filled with broken pieces of stone. She looked across the pool to the back of the rose garden. An ugly gash was torn through the hedge where the top of an old cypress had come down in the night. She had been too occupied to notice. Leaves and branches were scattered over broken rose bushes on the far side of the pool.

"Oh."

She turned back into the avenue of roses and, filling the archway darkly, was Mr. Glover. She averted her head and passed silently, but he spoke.

"Listen to me for a moment, I beg you."

She turned.

"Mrs. Darcy, pray believe that I never intended to cause you the least discomfort or annoyance."

"I cannot believe in your sincerity, Mr. Glover. In March I told the marchioness that the work she sent was unacceptable to me, and she undertook to convey that information to you."

"She did do so. Pray do not blame her. I found I could not abandon the work. I truly believed that, with your courageous disdain for the hypocrisy of our world, you would rejoice in my celebration of your spirit when you saw it finished."

"You understand nothing about me, Mr. Glover. How do you dare?"

"I beg you, madam, to grant me permission to finish the work. I will make changes, and yours will be the final decision whether or not the public will see it."

His eyes expressed some fervent feeling and she flinched in distaste. She sought to pass him, when a hand fell on Glover's arm.

"You overreach yourself, sir. You will importune this lady no longer."

"Whittaker!" Scorn spat from the dark eyes. "You will stand in the way of art for an occupation?" They were blocking her exit.

"As it happens, Glover, I need no occupation. Art is a refinement in my life."

"You are a dilettante."

"Perhaps it is best I aspire to nothing more." Whittaker paused, looking the other up and down. "There is no sight more pitiful than the clown aspiring to play Hamlet."

For a moment Elizabeth feared Glover would strike him, but he turned on his heel and rushed from the garden. They could hear the scattering of gravel as he fled along the path.

"Why do you do it, Mr. Whittaker?"

"Why indeed, Mrs. Darcy? Lady Englebury accuses me of jealousy."

Elizabeth was too startled by this unwelcome confidence to speak.

"I can understand if you doubt me," he said. "I was, myself, deeply shocked by her accusation." He looked away and, seemingly forgetful of Elizabeth's presence, continued, "Yet, I see now that I have been sick with envy, as though his success in the arts precluded me from my aunt's esteem." He started, becoming aware of her expression of surprise and faint distaste. "Why do I tell you this?"

"Indeed, sir, I know not. My question was rhetorical."

"I wish desperately for you to understand me; I know not why."

"They are all mad," she thought, and something of this was conveyed in her expression.

They were in the archway now, concealed from the shrubbery outside. She turned to go.

Blinded by emotion, Glover had brushed past Darcy unseeing. Nameless suspicion and anxiety caused Darcy to leave the path and cut across the grass to find her. She was there, with him, cheeks flushed, eyes widely dark, as Whittaker said, "I have been tortured. You are surprised. Thought you that I had no cares? I was jealous of him. Yet now, I see there is no cause." It was when he broke off that she saw Darcy.

"Come, Elizabeth." She blanched and looked a little angry at his peremptory tone.

He offered her his arm, in a manner she dared not refuse, lest she shame him before Whittaker. However, she would see he did not behave so again. They walked rapidly along the path, anger sizzling between them.

"I would thank you, sir, not to use me so again! I am not your servant."

"No, indeed, madam. You are my wife; and you will remember it," he said. She stared at him in disbelief.

"How could I forget it?" she said.

They parted without further speech and did not meet again until dinner.

Elizabeth passed the rest of the morning with the ladies. She walked out with Amelia, their gowns brushing the wet grass, scarves fluttering in the wind. They followed the gravel path up as far as the woods, where the damp ground halted them; then turned and looked back over the gardens. Amelia saw them first and touched Elizabeth's arm.

Georgiana was walking in the park with Lord Bradford.

"Miss Darcy."

The girl slowed her steps and stopped. He looked at her sweet face, her downcast eyes. Lord, how she had eclipsed the lovely Arabella in his estimation!

"Miss Darcy, since I have come to know you, you have occupied my thoughts and my heart exclusively. I scarcely dare to hope, but will you be my wife?"

She could not answer him.

"Let me care for you, love you, keep you from harm."

Georgiana spoke, so softly he had to bend his head to hear her, "It is too great an honor for me, my lord. I . . . I could not do justice to the position you offer me."

"I am a simple man, Miss Darcy. Some would say I am not fitted for my position in the world. If you would share it with me, I would not ask more than you could comfortably learn to perform."

She could not answer him for looking at his shoulder, and recalling her dream of leaning her head there. All her senses told her how his embrace would ease her pain. How could she so yearn, when she loved an unattainable other? She did, did she not?

"I feel I have spoken too soon," he said. "Do not say me nay at once, dear Miss Darcy. Allow me the chance to convince you that I can make you happy."

She nodded.

"When shall I speak again? Tell me, at the end of your stay here? Or later?"

"I know not. I feel so confused."

"You do not dismiss me?"

"Oh, no."

"Then I have your permission to hope?"

"I do not deserve your kindness," she whispered.

"You deserve more than I can offer you, and in six weeks, I shall again offer you all I have to give."

She flushed and looked away, her lips slightly parted. He looked at that mouth, which whispered so few, yet treasured, words. He would have so much liked to kiss those lips. She looked at him then and knew it, and could not draw her eyes away from his.

He sensed his chance and longed to put his question again, but wondered if it would be ungentlemanlike, after her promise to hear him again.

In that moment's pause, Georgiana slipped mutely away from him and returned to the house.

She went to her room. Something of Bradford's essence had impressed her so deeply, had made her so aware of all the love swelling her heart that she felt capable of the courage that love demanded of her. She sat at the desk and reached for the pen. She wrote the note off hastily, and rang the bell. She watched her own hand giving it to the footman and sat down, watching her clock tick away fifteen slow minutes.

She went to meet her enemy, and found him waiting. She blushed deeply, and her prepared speech burst out, "Mr. Glover, I beg you to desist from all your attentions to my sister. You do not know what unhappiness you cause her."

The left side of his face twitched. He said nothing.

She shook under his dark stare. Her throat was tight and dry. She bit her lips to quell their trembling. She said, "I tell you, sir, you must do as I say."

He stared at her. The silence, which in the past would have made her very afraid, called up a surge of emotion that shook her.

"Well?" she burst out. Her voice took her by surprise; it came out an octave lower than ever before.

"Pray, wait here for me." He rushed out. What kind of man was this? Georgiana had never met with such a one. She had told him, a man, a celebrated writer and a favorite of the marchioness, that he must obey her. What was she thinking? The previous afternoon, for all her distress and fear, she had not stilled a secret voice that whispered to her that Glover's work was the embryo of something great. A thousand deaths, including the death of their family happiness, could not halt its birth. What right had she, Georgiana, to try?

He was with her again in minutes. In his hands was a manuscript, the pages held together with a ribbon.

"Take it," he said.

She looked at him mutely. She could not reach for it.

He hurled it onto the fire. She gasped and would almost have pulled it forth. It seemed a long time that they stood there, watching as the flames licked around the edges. At last a great whoosh of destruction sucked it to oblivion.

He bowed, abrupt, yet somehow courtly in his way. He turned towards the door.

"Mr. Glover!" He turned back.

"I can only guess what this sacrifice means to you. I hope you do not think me impertinent."

"You are courageous." The fine angles of his face seemed alive with feeling. She had never known such a person existed.

"I am the most fearful person in all the world," she said.

"In the small things, perhaps. Yet in the great things, you are courageous."

"My brother and his wife are all I have in the world. I must fight for them."

"Constantly, women astound me."

"All your work. You make people so happy," she said.

"They laugh for an hour. They do not even see that they laugh at themselves. I was ambitious, but never mind. Whittaker is right; this longing to play Hamlet is every clown's tragedy."

He was halfway through the door when she said, "No! No! You must not listen to the vulgar chatter of the world. You must listen only to your own heart and to your conscience and you will do right. Then, God willing, you will succeed."

"I thought you a child," he said, and quitted the room.

By evening, the last of the storm had been chased away. Through the long windows Elizabeth looked out on to the fingers of light across the lawn. She sighed.

"You weary of us already," said a voice close behind her. She started. Whittaker stood beside her. He leaned against the window frame and gazed at her profile. He said, "I have had some dealings with Sir Graham Eston of late, and I wondered if you knew much of him. The gossip is so various."

"Really, I know him only by repute. You would do better to speak to Mr. Darcy about him," she said.

"Your husband would as soon converse with a toad as with me."

Elizabeth laughed involuntarily, a light sound that filled her with pain, and glanced across to where Darcy sat, ostensibly listening to Sir Beau but, in reality, studying his wife. Their eyes met; his gaze was impenetrable. Her laughter faded, and by habit she smiled at him with a hint of coquetry. He looked away.

She turned back to the window.

"I am sure you underestimate yourself, Mr. Whittaker. To my knowledge, Mr. Darcy never talks to toads."

He laughed out loud.

"You may have reason for complaint if he did, I think."

"Not at all. I understand that conversing with amphibians is not on that very short list of crimes about which a wife might complain."

He laughed again.

"I believe she rather enjoys Darcy's saturnine moods," he thought. "The man is sulking now because she exchanges the occasional word with a man who admires her. He must love her to distraction."

The thought of Darcy suffering distraction from any cause made him smile. "I am safe from that, at least. no one will ever hold such power over me."

Miss Whittaker called to them in her softly carrying tone, "I cannot imagine in what way my brother has deserved your attention, Mrs. Darcy. You are cruel to deprive the rest of the company of your wit."

"You are deceived by my hollow laughter, Sister," her brother replied. "Mrs. Darcy has been drawing a comparison between myself and the toad, with the latter coming out much to advantage." Elizabeth laughed in relief at his silliness.

Georgiana had bowed to pressure and was nervously taking her place at the pianoforte. Sir Beau and Arabella had been practicing a duet written by Whittaker. Elizabeth moved towards the small sofa where Darcy was sitting. He rose, with courteous alacrity, and she sat down alone.

"May I bring you something, Elizabeth—a glass of wine?"

"Thank you, no." She gave the merest flash of a polite smile.

He took up a position standing behind her. She watched as Arabella glided to the instrument to sing. She was dressed with beguiling elegance, in clinging silk of autumnal gold. "Perhaps Fitzwilliam would have married her, if he had not fallen so foolishly in love with me first," she thought. Miss Whittaker would not mourn, she imagined, when a husband's affection faded.

Whittaker approached and sat next to Elizabeth on the sofa.

"What enviable calm your sister has, Mr. Whittaker," she said. "I cannot imagine what upheaval it would take to ruffle her."

He half turned to her and said, with quiet abstraction, as though his words were involuntary, "My sister and I suffered such storms in our early life that, by contrast, any squall is nought but the most wondrously bracing breeze."

Elizabeth looked at him, astonished. His eyes were soft, open blue; she sensed in him a pain lying deep beneath his ennui, his shallow pleasures. She wanted to reply, but her lips trembled.

"A foolish remark, madam. Pray forgive me."

To her horror she felt her eyes filling with tears.

"Allow me to fetch you a glass of wine," he said, softly.

"No, thank you." Her lips moved but she could not speak aloud.

However, he gestured to a footman, who brought the wine at once. Whittaker took it from the tray and handed it to her.

She took a sip. Her tears had retreated. She knew now she would not weep. She looked down to her lap, where the glass of wine shook slightly in her hands. She must put it down. She felt fingers brush hers, as Darcy leaned down and took the glass, putting it on the little table beside her.

"Thank you," she murmured. She dared not look at him.

As she prepared for bed, Elizabeth thought of the previous night and of how her cold reception of her husband's advances must have hurt his pride. They had buried quarrels between the sheets in the past, but last night was different, for she had never previously questioned his love and esteem for her. The thought of submitting to him when his passion was only for her body was repugnant to her. She felt a chill, realizing that she had even thought in terms of submitting. Where love had been a joy, was it now to be a duty, and irksome at that?

Elizabeth looked at her image in the mirror. She thought of the qualities for which she had so loved her husband: his high sense of honor, the keenness of his mind and the passionate, tender, chivalrous love he had shown for her. Had that love been burnt up by too passionate a devotion? One read of such things—but Fitzwilliam fickle? It did not seem possible.

She owed him gratitude. She had done something, perhaps, to annoy him, although she could think of nothing that could begin to justify such coldness. Yet he had, at times, betrayed a sensitivity so keen she had been astonished.

The foolishness of their situation dawned upon her. He must love her still. They had come to misunderstand each other. Instead of standing on her pride, all she need do was apologize. She did not know for what, but he obviously did. Later she would tease him about it, which was something to anticipate.

She opened the door softly and went in. She slid in beside him.

"Thank you for rescuing my wine, Fitzwilliam," she said.

"I did not wish you to make a fool of yourself," he said.

Her exclamation of pain was so soft it sounded like a sigh.

She nearly left it there, but desired to look back on this occasion with the knowledge that she had done her duty.

"I am sorry if my behavior has caused offense, Fitzwilliam."

"You have done nothing to justify complaint."

She blew out the candle, and the cold darkness crept around them.

CHAPTER 33

FROM THE MORNING LIGHT STREAMING into the room, Elizabeth knew the weather had cleared. Her husband had likely gone fishing. She dressed with care, doing honor to herself. She breakfasted with the other ladies, then prepared for a long solitary walk. In the beautiful wood on the east side of the house she ran to lose herself far in the trees.

She gasped at the sharpness of the air, breathing deeply the delicious scent of the moist ground. Sunlight through the trees threw dappled greenish light round her. She forgot all that had come before.

She heard her name called, and turned to see a servant running up the path to her.

"We have been searching everywhere for you, ma'am. The marchioness asks if you would kindly come back to the house."

She sighed and turned back. On her way down the hill she met Darcy.

"Good morning, Fitzwilliam. What diversion is her ladyship planning now?" she said.

"Come to the house, Elizabeth. I have something to tell you."

"What is it? Pray tell me at once. It is Papa!"

"It does not concern your parents. Pray, sit on this bench." She sank down. He would have taken her hands, had he not felt this would be unwelcome.

"Elizabeth, I have just received an express letter from Mr. Turner. Your sister is gravely ill, and he begs your speedy return."

"Kitty?" She put her hand out to him and he enclosed it in his. She wanted more, wanted to feel his arms around her, but she did not wish this done in charity. She stood up and took his offered arm. As they emerged from the wood, she saw the carriage already pulled up before the steps, and footmen beginning to load the luggage. Georgiana ran across to them, put her arm around Elizabeth and walked back with her to the house. In ten minutes, their whole party was on the way to Derbyshire.

Kitty opened her eyes. "Was I sleeping?" she wondered. "Who is this man, sitting by my bed?"

"Kitty, here is Mr. Edgeley," said Edward, from the foot of the bed. "Do you remember that you asked to see him?"

"I am so sorry. I have been sleeping." Her voice was so hoarse and weak, he bent forward, straining to hear her.

"Pray, do not hurry yourself. I have all the time you need."

She looked, confused, from his kindly worn face to Edward, so sad. She remembered.

Her eyes sprang alive with fear, and she was fully present again.

At once Edward was at her side, taking her hands in his.

"My dearest, I beg you not to be afraid." His face pressed against her hands.

"Poor Edward," she said. She shuddered for breath. "Better for you if you had never seen me."

"No, no. There is still hope. I do not despair." He felt the warmth of the hand upon his shoulder.

"We pray to God that Mrs. Turner will be spared. Meanwhile, I should like to have a little conversation with her."

"I am being selfish."

"Do not be harsh upon yourself."

Edward moved away from the bed and stood near the door, where Kitty's whispers did not carry.

Kitty looked into Mr. Edgeley's eyes. Why had she wasted the opportunity to know such a man?

"If only my papa had been like you, I would have been good."

"I have many faults. You, like most of us, have done the best you could do."

"No. I have never tried to be good."

"You exposed yourself to this infection by going amongst the poor, knowing your own health to be delicate."

"I did it only to please Edward."

"Yet go there you did. Who can know what God's purpose was?"

"What will become of my baby?"

He met her wide gaze.

"If I thought this material world made sense, I should despair. One day we will understand God's will."

As they talked, the afternoon advanced, and Kitty slept.

Edward came out to see Mr. Edgeley into the carriage.

"I can never thank you enough, sir. You have settled all her fear. May I trouble you to send the carriage back in the morning? There will be no moon tonight."

"I will send it back at first light."

The Darcy carriage rumbled onto the drive.

"Mr. Turner," Elizabeth said. "How is Kitty?"

"She is sleeping. Mr. Edgeley has just been talking with her."

"Mr. Edgeley? Then Kitty's health is as bad as you feared?"

"I sent for him because Kitty asked to see him. I would not have you think I have abandoned hope." She could not hold his gaze for the bleakness she saw in his eyes.

Darcy and Georgiana alighted and they all went into the house. Mr. Turner's mother had arrived and they took refreshment with her. Shortly afterwards, having been informed that Kitty would not be able to receive them that day, Darcy and Georgiana departed for Pemberley.

Elizabeth watched as the carriage disappeared. Seemingly, her little family dwindled away from her. She went for a short walk. Returning, she saw Edward, his head lit up by the gold of the setting sun. "Kitty has awoken," he said. "Will you come in to see her?"

CHAPTER 34

Caroline swept up the aisle on her husband's arm. She paused for a moment by Georgiana.

"He's mine now," she said, in the softest whisper. "He preferred me."

"You do not love him!" cried Georgiana. There was a gasp from the assembled guests.

In the softest hiss, the bride replied, "Perhaps not, but how I shall love Rosings! What made you think you could save him, you little mouse! You cannot save him. Nobody can save him now."

Georgiana pushed past the horrid girl and rushed from the church, stumbling into the graveyard. She ran so fast that her tears flew in the wind. She ran through the abode of the dead and found herself in the avenue leading back to the gate.

She heard a voice cry out, "Georgiana!" He was coming through the gate to her, but she gestured to him to wait there. She ran along the avenue and through the gate to him. He pressed her close in a forbidden embrace. She was raising her lips to his.

"Joseph," she said.

At the sound of that name, Georgiana started awake. She stared into the velvety blackness, pressing her hands to her bosom. The sound of her heartbeat thudded in her ears.

'Oh, oh. How dreadful! Such a wrong, wrong dream and at such a time, when poor Mrs. Turner . . .'

She lay awake until the morning brought her cousin to Pemberley.

He was waiting in the saloon, and stood as she entered. He looked just the same as ever. She could hardly believe it.

"Henry, you are home from Belgium," she said, offering her hand to him.

Still she stared. He was absolutely unchanged. He was Henry

Fitzwilliam, her cousin, her guardian, her dear, dear friend. He meant a good deal, certainly, but he was nothing more than that.

"I believe you have fallen in love, Cousin," he teased. "You used not to be so distant." He kissed her cheek. Darcy looked at his sister in surprise, as she stood there.

"Georgiana, in your sister's absence, have you no duty to perform?"

"Of course. Forgive me. Pray, will you not sit down, Cousin?" She rang the bell, and ordered tea. She came back, sat with them by the window and looked out onto the lake. Henry was replying to Darcy's questions about the battle.

"I resigned my commission as soon as I decently could."

"We are very proud, Cousin. When do you receive your medal?"

"I did nothing for my men that they would not have done for me. Their loyalty is more that any man could ask."

"I doubt not that you have earned it."

"It is not enough for our aunt. She demands to know why I am not Brigadier-General Fitzwilliam, ret." They both laughed, but the girl remained silent.

Henry shrugged and glanced at Georgiana. Seeing her lost in thought, he said quietly, "I lost a quarter of my men, Darcy, in two days. The officers were brought back to England, but the men—buried in a field. I have written to their families; I cannot leave them to wait, endlessly, for a loved one who simply never returns."

"I understand. One of my tenants has asked me to inquire after his son."

Georgiana turned her head quickly. "What? Do you mean Bentridge? Has his son neither sent a message nor returned? The army does not inform the families of the fallen? I had no idea of this."

"Do not alarm yourself, Georgiana. I imagine they rely upon the officers to do so," said her brother.

"Indeed you must not worry. I am culpable for indulging in this gloomy talk in your presence!" said Henry. "I shall turn to a more cheerful theme. I had hoped to be able to present Colonel Kentley to you, but he will be obliged to remain in Paris these many months."

"Colonel Kentley?" said Darcy.

"Yes, his promotion is most timely."

"I do not recall the name. Have we met?"

"No, but I confess I am surprised you have not heard of him. I did not imagine there was any secrecy in the matter."

"In what matter, Henry?" urged Georgiana. "Why are you being so mysterious?"

"Come, come! You will have to tell us now."

"My good friend Kentley is engaged to marry Miss Bingley."

Georgiana flushed scarlet. Darcy gave a sigh of relief.

"Of course," said Georgiana, in a tone of brittle graciousness. "Naturally, we knew she was engaged to be married and we were so delighted."

"We have not seen Miss Bingley since she returned from Brussels, and have received no further communication from the Hursts, so . . ." muttered Darcy.

Henry looked from one to the other, and smiled.

"Tell me," he said. "Did you mistake the identity of Miss Bingley's intended?"

Georgiana burst out, "It was told me by Mrs. Hurst, and you did not contradict it in your letters, so we supposed it to be true."

"Did I not mention it?"

"I hope you were not disappointed, Henry."

"I was delighted to hear of Kentley's success. Others may have misunderstood how matters were between us. However, I hazarded a guess at the true direction of Miss Bingley's inclinations."

Georgiana felt an inexpressible calm.

"It is no brilliant match for Miss Bingley," said Darcy.

"Indeed, Kentley has done well. Yet, do you know what he said to me? 'I am a madman, yet what a splendid creature she is.'" Darcy laughed, but Georgiana was strangely silent.

"Kentley is of a very respectable family. His promotion is most opportune, for they will not be wealthy. They will live with his mother and older brother for several years at least. He hopes to purchase a small estate at some time, if his wife can be persuaded to part with her fortune. It is tied up in her name for life. He does not see himself being in a position to resign his commission for many years."

"Caroline will want an estate," declared Georgiana.

"Will she? Of course you know her so much better than I," said Henry. "Now you must tell me of the wonders of Deepdene. Father was most gratified at the news you had gone there."

"We were not there above three days," muttered Darcy.

"I was surprised to hear of your being seen passing through Derby yesterday, for I imagined you would stay much longer with the marchioness. Where is Mrs. Darcy? Taking an early walk, I imagine."

"She is at Kympton, Cousin. I am afraid we were in receipt of some worrying news that brought us home early from Deepdene."

"Her absence should have been my first concern. Now I understand why you both seem so out of spirits. Tell me what has happened."

"Mrs. Turner is gravely ill. It is feared she will not be with us much longer."

"Mrs. Darcy will be most grieved if her sister passes. Even you, Darcy, I imagine must have some considerable affection for her, after having her at Pemberley so much."

"I have some urgent business," mumbled Darcy. "Will you excuse me for half an hour?"

"Of course," said Henry. "Let us walk down to the lake, Georgiana."

They stood at the lake's edge, looking out at the grey expanse of the water. Georgiana broke the silence.

"Fitzwilliam and I are all alone just now. We stopped at Kympton for an hour, but Mrs. Turner was not well enough to receive us. My brother felt we would be relieving Mr. Turner of a burden by going home." She turned and put her hand on his arm. "Oh, Henry, I fear this will be her final illness. She has seemed so happy since her marriage. How unfair life can be."

"Her death would go hard with Mr. Turner, certainly. For myself, there was a time when I would rather have had a few months of happiness, than none."

"Dear Henry, are you very unhappy still?"

He turned to her.

"Sweetest girl, no. I am long recovered from what seems now a foolish infatuation."

She smiled and turned to look over the cold ripples of water.

"Georgiana—" He took her hand. "I cannot tell you what your affection and kindness meant to me in those first months after your brother's marriage. Truly, I think God could not give a man a greater gift than your love."

He smiled at her with infinite tenderness. She looked back at him, smiling, but feeling a nervousness too much like fear. Had she not always loved him, better than all the world? Yet she would do anything to put him off. Still he held her hand, enclosed in both of his, as though he would never let it go. If he asked her, she would accept—naturally, she would. She could not deny him anything.

He went on. "I have learned from you a lesson more precious than gold. Do not look so modest, Georgiana. You do not hold yourself in a fraction of the esteem that others do." She blushed to the roots of her hair, but said nothing.

"Dearest Georgiana, you have taught me how much more important is a true and steadfast love than all the wit, beauty and wealth in the world. I would seek a partner whom I love with all my heart and soul, and who values that love. This is what I wish for you and for me."

She trembled from head to foot.

"What have you to say, dear?"

She looked at him, full of the most unaccountable feeling.

She thought of the heroine of her favorite novel, who was unable to say nay to her lover when he wished them both to drown themselves in a lake. Georgiana could no longer admire her willingness to embrace that watery death. Still, she must answer Henry, and tried to think of the words.

In the silence, he turned and looked out over the lake.

"I wonder where they are, Georgiana."

"Who, Henry?"

"Why, these perfect loves awaiting us. I imagine that we have not met them yet. I am sure I have not met the lady. Until I do, you are the queen of my heart, my child and my dearest friend."

She began to laugh and laugh and could not stop.

He blushed. "You must think me a complete idiot."

"No, Henry, not you. Not you."

CHAPTER 35

KITTY DRIFTED INTO SLEEP, barely waking when she coughed.

At midnight, she awoke.

"Lizzy," she whispered.

"Dearest Kitty."

"It was always my secret desire to be like you, Lizzy—" Then came the noisy battle for the indrawn breath. "Am I not a foolish girl?"

Elizabeth felt an exquisite tenderness then, tenderness like a bruise.

"I always loved you, Kitty, though I scarcely told you so," she whispered.

Kitty smiled. "Do you wuv me, Wizzie?" she gasped. There was a horrible rasping sound from her throat. Elizabeth looked at her in consternation, not unmingled with fear. "You cannot . . . have forgotten?" Kitty said.

Only then Elizabeth realized Kitty was laughing at the family joke of a three-year-old Kitty trailing after the sister she adored. Now her eyes, enormous in her thin face, asked for the familiar response.

"Oh, very well then, I love you," said Elizabeth, in a poor imitation of the snapped response of old. "How I have wasted my opportunities to love!" she thought.

Kitty smiled again and her eyes closed.

Her struggle for breath continued through the night. The physician dozed off at times, but Elizabeth was beyond fatigue. Edward sat in dumb wakefulness on the other side of the bed.

Towards morning Kitty's eyes flew open. Elizabeth searched frantically for understanding in their vacancy. Kitty seemingly struggled to see clearly the face before her.

"Edward," she whispered.

"I am here, darling Kitty," he said.

"Edward, I made you promise . . ."

"I will always hold your memory sacred."

"No, Edward." She looked at him in a moment of clearest focus.

"I release you." He saw, in the girl's eyes, a glimpse of the woman he would never know.

He sank to his knees, clutching her hands. "Do not leave me, Kitty, I beg you."

She put one thin hand upon his face.

"Thank you, Edward." His lips framed the question, but he could not speak.

"You, only you . . . made me feel . . . of significance . . . in the world."

Elizabeth covered her eyes with her hand.

Kitty slept. The silences between gasping breaths seemed interminable.

Her eyes opened once more. Elizabeth dared not look at Edward, for her sister seemed to stare into another realm. Kitty closed her eyes. There was a sound from her throat, then silence.

Elizabeth and Edward sat there for a long time in the silence, until Wilkins came and led Elizabeth away, undressed her and unpinned her hair. She put her hands over her ears at the horrible sound of Edward's cry. She lay on the bed, thinking she might never sleep again, and fell asleep at once.

Before dawn she awoke and waited for Wilkins. She was numb with weariness, but knew she could sleep no more. She breakfasted with Edward, who seemed not to have slept at all. Elizabeth found her throat so tight that she could not eat. She took a few sips of tea.

"I hate to leave you, Edward."

"Truly, do not concern yourself on that account. Mother is here and I expect the Bingleys this afternoon. I have had a letter from Rushly."

"There is none better than my sister to assist you. Has Mr. Darcy sent a carriage for me?"

"Your coachman says he left Pemberley at first light. The horses will be rested sufficiently to leave before luncheon, if you wish."

"Goodbye for now." For the first and last time, she kissed her brother-in-law's cheek.

Wilkins sat with her in the carriage, longing to be of assistance, but her mistress seemed unaware of her existence.

Elizabeth had not wept since her first knowledge of her sister's illness. She looked from the window at field and farmhouse, sweep and fell. Nowhere could she see the familiar. "Everything is become strange," she thought. They reached the gates of her home. "No. I am the stranger," she thought. "Pemberley will never again be so dear to me. This is not truly my home as I am no longer loved and honored by its master."

From the top of the hill, where the drive curved down to the house, she could see right across the lake. On the far side, she made out the distant figures of Georgiana and her cousin. They looked up, and waved. She raised her hand and turned away her head.

She climbed the steps and went in. Mrs. Reynolds came to meet her. Elizabeth barely took in her words of condolence.

"The master is with the steward, madam. Shall I send for him?"

Unhearing, Elizabeth passed her and mounted the stairs to her dressing room. As she went up, the window shades were silently lowered, one by one.

Once in her nightgown, she said, "Leave my clothes just as they are, Wilkins. You need rest yourself."

Alone, she opened the door of her bedroom. In the light coming in at the edges of the curtains, the cold emptiness of the room was revealed, and the undisturbed cover of the bed. She gave a little cry. He was not there, of course. There would be no comfort in the cold silk of those sheets. She went across to the door to his room. He would have slept there, she knew. She would lie in his bed with the scent of him in the sheets. She decided that, if the door were locked, she would give up hope. She reached out, her hand shook, the knob turned, and the door swung open.

She heard his footsteps cross the room behind her.

"You wish me to go." She turned, leaned against the door frame for an instant, took a step towards her own bed and was falling.

She sighed as his arms caught her. She leaned against him.

"Why did you labor so to steal my heart, only to reject me?" she whispered. "I have loved you from my soul . . . and you . . . "

She moaned as he lifted her into his arms. She felt the warmth of him, of his shoulder against her cheek.

He said, "My beautiful Elizabeth, why did you not tell me?"

She wanted to say, "I did, I did tell you," but it would not have been true. Always she had let him believe that she loved him less than she did.

"I was afraid."

"I am too dull a man for you to fear the loss of my affection. There are no bounds to my love for you."

She kissed him, looking at him most tenderly, and said, "It is true that you are very dull."

He lowered her onto the bed. "I believe I have earned some little flattery, one compliment, perhaps, after two years and a half of devotion."

"I may think of something, by and by."

She laughed and her eyes filled with tears. In his arms she wept, for relief, for happiness and for grief.

CHAPTER 36

THROUGH THE FOLLOWING DAYS, side by side with the pain of Kitty's death, there was a new kind of happiness growing between Darcy and Elizabeth.

Although doted upon, even spoiled, as a child, Darcy nevertheless believed—in his heart—that his worthiness lay in his position in life and in his ability to emulate the father whom everyone had so much admired. Now a wonderful notion had entered his head that Elizabeth loved him, and deeply, for the man that he was, rather than in spite of it.

It was some days before she could ask, "Why were you so cold towards me at Deepdene?"

He mumbled a few disjointed sentences, while she looked at him with growing incredulity.

"I cannot believe it," she said. "You were jealous? And of Peregrine Whittaker, of all men? You must have known I disliked him."

"You disliked me at one time."

"So it followed that every man I disliked, I should finish by falling in love with? In any case, I did not dislike you when I first knew you. I hated you and that is a much more promising passion."

"Do you deny that you gave me cause?"

"Certainly I did not do so intentionally. I have never sought his company."

"No, but he took every opportunity to speak to you, and you did nothing to discourage him. You were laughing at me together that last evening." She blushed. "You said something about me. What was it?"

"That . . . you never converse with toads. That is hard to believe, I know. It was a rather silly conversation. Forgive me, dearest, but I was hurt and angry. You rebuffed me in front of him."

"You rebuffed me the night before when I wanted desperately. I believed I knew how to approach you, so that you could not help but show me if your heart were still mine."

"You seemed to have withdrawn your love and approval of me, yet still . . . I was there for your use."

"Good God! Elizabeth, my own! You felt that?" He bent his head over her hands and kissed them tenderly. "All I wanted was proof of your love."

"Fitzwilliam, how could you think I would dishonor you?"

"I did not imagine you would behave dishonorably, but I could not bear the notion that you might prefer another man, in your heart."

"You would never have doubted the depth of my feelings for you had I been more candid."

A quiet little interval passed. Then she said, "I do hope you noted my attempt to mollify you. I thought it very dutiful of me to apologize when my behavior had been so exemplary."

"I did not perhaps receive your apology very graciously."

"You were generosity itself," she said. Skillfully mimicking Darcy's chilly tone at the time, she said, "You have done nothing to justify complaint."

There was that instant reaction of pained hauteur with which he had always met anything like derision. He felt her shaking with repressed laughter as she kissed him.

He began to laugh.

Elizabeth received a kindly letter of condolence from Lord Bradford. He humbly begged to be allowed to pay his respects in person, as he would be passing through Lambton on a particular day. Georgiana had as good a grasp of arithmetic as any young lady and knew it would be six weeks to the day since his walk in the Deepdene pleasure gardens with her.

It may be safely assumed that she arranged for her sister and brother to be unfortunately prevented from joining them in another walk. The water was glistening blue in the sun. This time she gave not a single thought to jumping into the lake; she only thought of jumping over a canal.

Lady Catherine, perhaps, had experienced enough of the loneliness of being always right. She thought, more often than she liked, of the kiss she had denied her daughter when they parted at Rosings. She received a letter from Darcy that quite scotched the plan she had formed of bringing Georgiana to live with her. However, the news it contained of Georgiana's engagement was highly gratifying to her family pride. Yet what pleasure could she have gained from the connection if she were not on speaking terms with that branch of her family? She reflected that it was, after all, the third epistle Darcy had sent her since their estrangement. While it lacked a tone of humility and apology she would have liked, Lady Catherine de Bourgh did something she never did. She compromised.

From Lady Catherine de Bourgh to Mr. Darcy

My dear Nephew,

Pray convey my condolences to your lady on the sad passing of her sister, Mrs. Turner. May she bear this loss in Christian spirit, with the assistance of Our Lord. May she comfort herself with the hope of her deceased relative's ultimate ascension into heaven, to be reunited with others of her particular station.

I thank you for your early information of Georgiana's engagement. Naturally I will keep this information confidential until Mrs. Darcy is out of mourning for her sister.

Fitzwilliam, this marriage will make some amends to me for your own reprehensible conduct two years ago.

Indeed, God, in His wisdom, compensated my daughter with a marriage more brilliant, one may say more suitable, than that which had been foreseen.

It is my expectation that Georgiana, when elevated to the title of marchioness, will remember her origins and pay appropriate respect to those relatives who were born superior to her in station.

I was affronted that you omitted an invitation to Pemberley from your letter. This oversight will be rectified shortly.

Lady Catherine de Bourgh

"Wonderful!" cried Elizabeth. "Pray do not look long in the mouth, my love. I know you are fond of her, really."

"I have no inclination for her society if she does not treat my wife with respect," he muttered.

"Think what gratification I shall feel on teaching her to do so," she said, and laughed at his expression of alarm.

"A jest, my dearest," she said, but he did not know whether to quite believe her.

"Well, she is my mother's sister, and I take comfort in the fact that she is acknowledging you at last, albeit with so little grace. She has had many trials with the younger branches of the family."

"Next year, sometime, you will represent the youngest branch no more," said Elizabeth.

"Can you mean, Elizabeth, that I am to be a parent?"

"You must own me to be obliging."

"Indeed, I do."

EPILOGUE

Pemberley
Spring, 1826

THE CHESTNUTS SPREAD THEIR FAMILIAR shade across the grass, the ducks and swans swam in circles on the lake, and the scent of the flowers drifted deliciously on the breeze.

Mr. Bennet looked around him. What gratification Mrs. Bennet would have enjoyed at this scene! Three years had gone by since his lady's nerves finally succumbed to life's assaults. He sighed.

"What is it, Papa?" Mary leaned over him. "You are thinking of Mama, I know. Find comfort, as I do, in knowing that she is in heaven and looking down upon us now, blessing us."

He groaned, "Oh, God."

"Did you say that you are cold, dear Papa? See how your blanket has slipped from your knee. You will take a chill." She tucked the blanket around his legs. Lydia laughed aloud.

"Lydia!" said Jane, gently. She turned to her father, "Mama died with such pride in her family and joy in her grandchildren."

"Lord, the fuss she made when your Henry was born, Lizzy," cried Lydia. "Such an achievement—for all her praise, one might have thought you had produced a giraffe!"

Her husband gave a great snort of laughter, and wiped his big purple nose. Darcy frowned, but Lydia was not afraid of him.

George Wickham had always believed that his brother-in-law ought to support him, and finally he'd had his wish. Darcy had paid all the expenses of the discreet home for the well-heeled insane in Belgium where Wickham spent his last days. After a few years of remission, the final stage of syphilis had addled his brain so fast that he had little time to repent his past or fear his future.

Lydia had proved a more prudent matron than maiden, never relenting in her refusal to risk further infection. She always did fall on her feet. At five and twenty, she was a buxom, attractive widow and retired to a watering place to live on Wickham's half-pension and her annuity, augmented for her by her relations. There she met a middle-aged widower who suited her very well. He was scarcely over mourning his second wife, a well-bred young woman, when some less elegant quality in Lydia caught his eye. On their engagement, he fastened a diamond necklace around Lydia's plump white neck and stole a kiss beneath her ear.

"Oh, you are a devil, Houlter!" she smirked.

He beamed fondly on her now, and his chest puffed out at the sight of the swelling beneath her sash.

Mr. Bennet rolled his eyes. His gaze wandered to his eldest daughter. Dear Jane, at the height of her beauty, with a lovely full figure, was holding the youngest of her five children in her lap.

Jane and Bingley had proved her father wrong in his prediction that they would never be able to make decisions. Good natured and accommodating as they were, they came to all sorts of conclusions about what to have for dinner and which carriage to take out for a drive. Even in more important matters, Darcy let Bingley run his own life, so long as he obtained approval before taking action.

Jane never seemed to notice this, marvelling only to see her father give way under the domineering care of his maiden daughter.

"If only Mary had enjoyed the happiness of marriage," she thought.

However, Mary was reasonably content with her lot. It had been a blow when Mr. Brown had married a young lady with five thousand pounds and dimples, but when Mary thought back, she recalled faults in his character that would have made difficult that total submission she felt was called for in a wife. She had yet to see a man worthy of that from herself.

In Hertfordshire she reigned supreme as the only daughter remaining with the district's foremost gentleman of means. Only lately had she cause to reflect on other possibilities when one of Uncle Phillips's clerks had paid considerable attention to her at her aunt's recent dance party. Would he raise his sights to such a height as to pursue her? Could she stoop to consider him, if he did?

Mr. Bennet looked at Elizabeth and smiled. She must have travelled on a rocky road at times, learning when to give in graciously and over which matters to assert herself. For Darcy, past forty now, was as wilful as ever, was strong and clever, and was her husband. Yet her self-respect and, yes, her pride, had won Darcy's respect and her father could not have hoped for a better marriage for her.

"Only Kitty is missing," mused Mr. Bennet. "In life she seemed to lack substance to fill even the limited role allotted to her; yet in death she left a gap that no-one could fill." He sighed.

"Here are Mr. and Mrs. Turner arriving," said Darcy, going across the grass to greet them.

For a time, Turner's friends had feared he would never get over Kitty's death. Then, two years later, officiating at Emily Edgeley's wedding to a young curate, he encountered Anna again. She had felt tears pricking her eyelids at the sight of the premature lines etched in his face. Anna had never allowed herself to ask too much of life. She never expected to take the place of the pretty, light-hearted girl to whom he had attached himself with such devotion. Nevertheless, by the time he again heard Anna play, Edward was falling in love once more. He only broke through all her careful reserve when he knelt on her father's worn carpet to ask her to be his wife. Elizabeth had welcomed the opportunity to know her better, and came to highly value her friendship. Now Anna was received as a regular guest at Pemberley.

Mr. Bennet's grandchildren romped on the grass at a distance, under the eyes of a small army of governesses, tutors and nannies. One of the boys ran to plant himself in front of the old man.

"I have beaten them all, Grandpapa, even George and John, and they are twelve years old! I am the strongest and the cleverest."

"You are plainly the most conceited," said Darcy.

"Am I, sir? Am I, Mother? Is it conceited of me to be proud of my achievements?"

Elizabeth smiled. "If you believe those achievements place you above others, Henry, you are indeed conceited."

"Pride cometh before destruction, and an haughty spirit before a fall," intoned Mary. Henry stared.

"None shall say I am haughty or proud when I am a man," he declared. "I mean to be just like my papa."

Elizabeth could not resist a little sideways glance at her husband, and he had the grace to faintly blush. There were strange grimaces on the faces of the others and a smothered snort from Lydia. Darcy felt a quick surge of indignation.

The rumble of wheels presaged the arrival of an enormous barouche.

As Darcy and Elizabeth escorted a grand old lady across the lawn, the children assembled in order of rank.

"Well, Henry Darcy," she said. "It is your birthday."

"Yes, Lady Catherine. I am ten years old."

"Do not expect congratulations from me, my boy. I consider it no especial achievement to reach such a puny age. Here is your sister, also much grown. Catherine!" The little girl's dark curls bobbed as she curtsied to her great-aunt. Darcy had been happy enough to name his daughter for Elizabeth's sister, with the proviso that she not be addressed as "Kitty" for he loathed pet names. As the indomitable old lady sat receiving the reverences of each person in turn, little Catherine pressed up to her grandfather's side, with the confidence of a favorite, and whispered, "Aunt Mary is very wise, Grandpapa." Her great dark eyes sparkled. "Many could learn a lesson of humility from her."

"Hush, child!" he said, but could not resist a chuckle.

At that moment, Anne, Countess Reerdon, emerged from the house, leaning on the earl's arm. She went to Lady Catherine and kissed her most graciously.

"Lady Reerdon!" said Elizabeth. I hope you have benefited from your rest."

"I thank you," said Anne faintly. "I feel a little better."

"Her headache is much improved, I think," said Reerdon. "However, she is still very weary from the journey. No, Freddie! Be gentle with Mama, she is not well. I have taken the liberty of sending to London for her ladyship's doctor, ma'am."

"It is not a liberty in the least. Dr. Wells will always be made comfortable here, my lord."

"Humph! I hope I shall not be expected to share a table with a physician," said Lady Catherine. "Nowadays one never knows what to expect. Why, only last February, I had a barrister not three persons down from me at the Goddards' table."

"Oh, really, Mama!" snapped Anne. "Sir Egbert is received everywhere. He is the Solicitor-General."

"He is in receipt of a salary!" roared Lady Catherine, her lip turned up.

"I suppose not all clever fellows can be born rich," said Reerdon.

"Indeed," agreed the countess. "And I hardly think my doctor can be rated as an ordinary physician."

"Oh, Papa, look who is come!" Little Catherine began to run across the lawn.

Elizabeth and Darcy walked over to where a carriage was drawing up in front of the house. The footman opened the emblazoned door and respectfully handed out a tall, graceful figure, all in black.

Her hosts bowed.

"Marchioness," said Darcy. "You do us honor. Welcome, your Ladyship."

"Oh, Fitzwilliam, pray don't!" she cried, lifting her heavy black veil.

The marquess emerged from the carriage. He greeted his hosts, then turned to his wife.

"Georgiana, dear. Try to accustom yourself to it." (It was their first excursion since the old marquess finally passed away at the age of two-and-eighty.)

Georgiana did accustom herself to her position. She had always been silent in company, yet now her each word was treated as a special favor. It was disconcerting to have her formidable aunt give way to her but the compensation was that Lady Catherine never scolded her again.

Anne and Georgiana had elevated themselves beyond the excesses of Lady Catherine's influence. Her Ladyship had some compensation in Henry's wife. She had frowned in displeasure when she first saw the dark curls and expressive eyes of Henry Fitzwilliam's betrothed; he always was a fool for that type. They were left behind at Rosings to await the birth of their second child. Mrs. Fitzwilliam's high spirits had proved easier to quell than those of a certain other lady.

Lady Catherine bent her severe gaze upon Elizabeth. The evident happiness of that marriage was galling. Why had Darcy not got the whip hand at once? Above twelve years married, and his wife was still always the first in his thoughts, the first to whom he turned to share laughter, the first to consider in everything. It was outrageous, when the woman ought to have been meekly thanking him, every day, for the honor and benefits he had conferred upon her.

What benefit had her nephew obtained from the union? None that her ladyship could perceive.

Yet he had benefited immeasurably. Darcy was learning a lesson of faith in himself. Demanding of others, he was even more demanding of himself. Confusing talents and performance with human essence, he had feared losing Elizabeth's love to someone who embodied everything that he was not. She had no need for such a man. She had already all the resources for laughter and diversion within herself. She needed him, his strength and uprightness and the utter steadfastness of his affection. She could only fully love and learn to express that love when she had learned trust, which childhood experience had denied her.

One day, when looking back on their various misunderstandings, Darcy had quietly said, "It is as Bolingbroke wrote, 'Truth lies in a little and certain compass, but error is immense.'"

"How very learned you are. How shall I catch you up?"

"You cannot, and that is as it should be."

A little frown had appeared between her eyes. He continued, "Otherwise I should find it impossible to guide you."

"I see," said Elizabeth and laughed at all the adventures and misadventures to come.

Helen Halstead was born in Adelaide, South Australia, in 1950, and works as a teacher. She has been a fan of Jane Austen's ironic humor and exquisite prose from the age of thirteen.

In 2004, Helen self-published *A Private Performance* in Australia to acclaim for the book's evocation of Austen's world.

In *Pride & Prejudice*, Jane Austen
brought together one of the most beloved literary couples
of all time—Elizabeth Bennet and Fitzwilliam Darcy.
Now, *Mr. Darcy Presents His Bride* continues the story of
these passion-filled newlyweds as they enter London's
glamorous high society.

This page-turning novel finds Elizabeth and Mr. Darcy
entangled in the frivolity and ferocity of social intrigues.
Although Elizabeth makes a powerful friend in the
Marchioness of Englebury, the rivalry and jealousy among
her ladyship's prestigious clique threatens to destroy
the success of her new marriage.

Written in the style of Jane Austen, full of humor and
sardonic wit, *Mr. Darcy Presents His Bride* brings Regency
society vividly to life and continues the romantic, sometimes tragic, stories of other popular *Pride & Prejudice*
characters including Georgiana Darcy and Kitty Bennet.

ISBN10: 1-56975-588-4
ISBN13: 978-1-56975-588-4

51495

9 781569 755884

Ulysses
Press

$14.95

Distributed by
Publishers Group West